DESERVING REESE

The Refuge, Book 3

SUSAN STOKER

CHAPTER ONE

Gus "Spike" Fowler frowned in irritation as he adjusted his large body in the too-small airplane seat and tried to calm his dark thoughts. Ever since he'd gotten a call from Bubba, a former Army teammate, asking if he'd heard from Woody, another member of their unit, Spike had harbored a bad feeling in his gut.

Spike missed his teammates, but not the shit they'd done as Delta Force Operatives. They'd put their lives on the line more times than anyone could count and it had been a relief to put all of that behind him and join Brick and the men at The Refuge.

But when Bubba called, telling him that Woody had gone down to Colombia after hearing from a woman who'd been a translator for them on a mission—and hadn't been heard from since—the hair on the back of Spike's neck had stood up. That feeling of trepidation still plagued him.

And it only got worse when he'd learned that Woody's younger sister, Reese, was thinking of heading down to South America to find her brother.

Spike had always admired the relationship between the

two siblings, even if he didn't completely understand it. He wasn't close to his own family. He hadn't seen them in years, and the last time he'd gone home for the holidays, he'd regretted it. His parents didn't know why he was "hiding out" in the backwoods of New Mexico, and he and his sister had absolutely nothing in common and therefore little to talk about.

Jack Woodall and his sister were extremely close, however. She was two years younger than Woody, who was overly protective of her. During down time on missions, he'd entertained their team with stories about Reese, and the pride in his voice when he'd talked about how great she was doing after she'd graduated college was easy to hear. For her part, Reese had constantly emailed her brother when they were out of the country, and when possible, she'd travel to wherever he was stationed to welcome him home from missions.

When he moved to Kansas City, Missouri, after getting out of the Army, Reese followed.

Spike envied the bond Woody and Reese shared. He'd also met her a few times, and had definitely been impressed by the woman personally. She was tall; only a couple inches shorter than his five-eleven. Her blonde hair was usually up in a messy bun and she always had a smile on her face. Her curvy body definitely made her stand out. She was friendly and bubbly and passionate about her work...and he had a feeling she likely brought the latter to the bedroom, as well.

She was gorgeous, inside and out. But Spike had never given any indication that he was attracted to the woman—nor had his teammates—out of respect for both her and Woody. Not that Woody would have minded if one of his friends dated his sister; it was more that their jobs had been so uncertain. As Deltas, they were deployed more than they were home, and they all knew any kind of serious relationship would be extremely challenging, both for them and their significant others.

Besides...when they were on missions, the team *talked*. About the women they'd dated, sexual conquests, the things they'd done, the things they *wanted* to do. Given everything they'd revealed to each other during long nights in the trenches, it would be extremely awkward to date *any* teammate's sister.

Still, he'd thought about Reese a few times in the years since he'd gotten out of the Army. Wondered if she was still living in Kansas City near her brother. If she'd gotten married, had any kids.

Apparently, the answers were yes, no, and no. After talking with Bubba, Spike learned that she was still single, still in Missouri, still very close to her brother.

Which was why he was currently on his way there. To meet with Reese, find out what he could about where Woody had been headed, and any other information she had, before reassuring her that her brother was most likely just fine and enjoying spending time with Isabella, the translator he'd apparently never been able to forget.

But deep down, Spike was worried. It wasn't like Woody to go off the radar like he had. And that he'd not kept in contact with his sister just made Spike's concern worse.

"Stop worrying," Tiny said from the seat next to him.

Looking over at his friend and co-owner of The Refuge, Spike sighed. "I can't help it. And for the hundredth time, you didn't need to come with me."

Tiny shrugged. "I did. Tonka and Brick weren't going to leave their women, and we've had a lot of the same special forces training. If something *is* wrong, we can work together to find your friend and get him home safely."

Spike couldn't deny that having Tiny by his side would be welcome if he had to head down to Colombia. While Tiny had been a SEAL, and he was Delta, he wasn't wrong that they'd had similar training.

"Tell me more about Woody, the translator he went down to see, and the sister," Tiny ordered.

"Woody's a few years younger than I am, but he was a damn good Delta. Always ready to do whatever it took to get the mission done. Sometimes he was impulsive, but we could usually rein him in."

"So you aren't surprised that he headed down to Colombia when he heard the translator might be in trouble," Tiny remarked.

Spike shook his head. "No, but it's not because of his impulsive nature. He and Isabella had a connection from the start. We all saw it. But they both did their best to keep things professional. The mission we were on down there wasn't especially dangerous. We were working with the National Army—specifically, their special forces branch, AFEAU—on a joint mission. Isabella was assigned to our group to translate when necessary. When we left the country, they exchanged information. As far as I knew before now, that was the extent of it.

"But now, Bubba tells me that they've been keeping in constant contact since then. Said Woody's been studying Spanish, and he and Isabella always planned on meeting back up at some point. I guess when he heard she needed help, he didn't hesitate to head down there."

"Help with what?" Tiny asked.

"I'm not sure. Bubba didn't know either, and apparently Woody didn't tell Reese exactly what was wrong. Just that Isabella asked for his help on getting her and her brother out of the country," Spike said.

"That doesn't sound good," Tiny said with a shake of his head. "How old is her brother?"

Spike frowned as he tried to remember. "I'm not sure, but I think eighteen or nineteen now."

"So not a kid."

"No, definitely not a kid. He was a young teenager when we were in the country, but I don't remember Isabella saying much about him, other than she was raising him after their parents died."

"So if she was translating for your team while you were in Colombia, she has to have some pretty high connections. The AFEAU is very secretive. Could she have gotten on the bad side of their government?" Tiny asked, keeping his tone low so no one would overhear. Not that it was likely. The seats around them were empty, since the plane wasn't packed, which was a relief.

"Anything's possible. I'm more concerned about the fact that Woody hasn't contacted Reese. There's no way—and I mean *no way*—he'd purposely worry his sister. They're extremely close."

"Yeah, that's definitely not a good sign," Tiny agreed.

They fell silent as they continued to make their way toward their destination. Until eventually Tiny asked, "So, what's the plan?"

Spike shrugged. "Talk to Reese. Find out what Woody told her, if anything. Determine if she's overreacting, maybe ask Tex to see if he can find the translator's address and, if need be, head to Colombia to see for ourselves that Woody's all right."

He wasn't surprised when Tiny simply nodded. "Does Reese know we're coming?" he asked.

Spike sighed. "No. I got her number from Bubba, but she didn't answer when I called. She knows me, though. We've met a few times."

"She's probably gonna think you're there to bring her bad news," Tiny warned.

Spike frowned. Shit. He hadn't thought about that. The last thing he wanted to do was cause her any angst. It simply felt...*wrong* that someone with her sunny personality should ever feel even a moment of fear. "In that case, the first thing out of my mouth will be reassurance that we aren't there for a death notification," he decided.

The two friends quieted once more, and Spike couldn't help but let his mind wander back to Woody. Where was he? Was he in trouble, or was he simply enjoying time with the woman he'd gotten to know over the years? Spike couldn't decide and figured it could be either option. He didn't think Woody would be inconsiderate enough to worry his sister, but if he and Isabella were making up for lost time after being apart for years, it was possible the rest of the world just dropped away...or he didn't feel the need to talk to his sister about his love life.

But given his bond with Reese, Spike's gut insisted that wasn't the case.

The plane ride seemed to be taking forever. And the longer they were in the air, the more stressed Spike became. The more scenarios went through his brain about why Woody wasn't communicating with Reese and his friends.

By the time they landed, Spike felt jittery and off-kilter. It had been a long time since he'd felt nerves like this, and he didn't like it.

When he first became a Delta Operative and started going on missions, he was even-keeled and nothing much rattled him. But with each mission, and given the death and destruction that came with the majority of them, he'd slowly changed. His steady nerves began to fray and with each assignment, all he could think of more and more was all the ways things could go wrong.

He was assured by two different therapists that what he was feeling was normal...but it didn't feel normal to constantly picture his teammates blown to hell, or wonder how it would feel to step on an IED. When he couldn't shake the negative thoughts, and when his body literally began to break down on him before missions—shaking, vomiting, unable to concentrate—Spike knew it was time to get out.

He hated to quit. He hadn't been raised to be a quitter, but the last thing he wanted was his mental state affecting the lives of his teammates. When he finally sat down with them to explain, he was surprised to learn they were *all* dealing with some of the same things. They weren't experiencing the physical symptoms, but the reality of being a Delta and constantly being deployed and putting their lives on the line had taken a toll on the entire team.

They'd all gotten out of the Army around the same time, and while Spike didn't keep in touch with his former teammates regularly, when he *did* reach out, he was happy to hear how well they were doing.

Spike took a deep breath. He needed to keep his shit together. For Woody. He needed to make sure Reese saw nothing in him to be concerned about. That she'd trust him to figure out what happened to her brother.

This wasn't a Delta mission. He could do this. He didn't have a choice.

CHAPTER TWO

"She's not here," Bubba said unnecessarily.

Spike's former teammate had picked up him and Tiny from the airport, and they'd gone straight to Reese's apartment. Except she hadn't answered the door. Nor was she answering her phone.

Spike had a bad feeling about the situation. It was one thing for her brother to be missing, but the fact that Reese also couldn't be reached wasn't sitting well with him.

Bubba started making some calls to people he knew in town, trying to figure out if Reese was at work. They'd already talked to a neighbor, who didn't recall seeing her lately. Spike knew in his gut that they weren't going to find her in Kansas City.

One thing Woody had always mock-complained about was how stubborn his sister could be. How she was impulsive and acted without thinking, especially if she was concerned about someone else. Spike suspected that Reese had gotten tired of sitting around, worrying about her brother. That she'd made the decision to head down to Colombia to find out for herself if he was all right.

He took his own cell out of his pocket and dialed Tex's number.

Tex was a former SEAL and a computer genius who'd always told the owners of The Refuge that if they ever needed anything—*anything*—to not hesitate to reach out for assistance. He was a huge reason why The Refuge even existed at all...he'd helped Brick, the former SEAL who'd originally conceived of the place, connect with all the men who had eventually become his co-owners.

"What's wrong?" Tex immediately asked in the slight southern accent he'd never lost, even though he hadn't lived in Texas for years.

As quickly as he could, Spike explained where he was and why, then said, "We can't find Reese, Woody's sister. Her car's not at her apartment, she's not answering her phone, and a neighbor said he hasn't seen her in a few days."

"You think she went to Colombia," Tex said.

"I hope like hell I'm wrong, but yeah," Spike agreed "Okay, hang on..."

Spike resisted the urge to tap his foot as he heard Tex's fingers clicking on a keyboard. Absently, he realized the hand holding his phone to his ear was shaking...and his heart rate was higher than normal. He *hated* his body's physical reactions to danger.

Still, his current anxiety gave him pause. He hadn't felt like this when Jasna, the daughter of a Refuge therapist, had been missing and they'd all frantically searched for her. And his heart rate hadn't gone above a hundred when they'd found out a sexual deviant was prowling The Refuge property, attempting to kidnap Brick's woman, Alaska.

He'd thought he'd finally worked through the shit in his head and gotten past all this. It was extremely disheartening to realize he hadn't. That his body was still letting him down when he needed to be at his strongest. He was particularly confused as to why he was feeling this way *now*, when he'd handled the recent harrowing events with Alaska and Jasna just fine.

But he didn't have time to wonder long before Tex was speaking.

"All right, it looks like she left four days ago. Took a red-eye flight from Kansas City to Dallas, then to Colombia, arriving late the next morning. I'm texting the address of the hotel where she's booked."

Spike was relieved Reese wasn't lying dead in a morgue somewhere in Kansas City, but less than happy to hear his suspicions had been correct. "Any idea where Isabella lives?"

"I've got an address for the translator, but it's several years old," Tex said. "I'm sending that too."

"Thanks." Spike took a deep breath. "No other movement on Reese? No return flights booked? Can you track her cell?"

"No, no, and no," Tex said, dashing Spike's hope for a quick resolution to the situation.

"Shit," he swore.

"I've booked you and Tiny a flight," Tex said. "It leaves in three hours. I'll continue to do what I can from here to help, but I'm thinking getting your boots on the ground down there and going to her hotel to find Reese, or talking to the employees to see what you can find out, will get you a lot further than anything I can do remotely."

That's what Spike was thinking too. "Right."

"Keep your phone on," Tex said firmly. "I'll make sure international rates are active and I expect you to check in with me frequently. I can also track you if you leave it on.

If I don't hear from you regularly, or if you go dark, I'm gonna send in the troops."

Spike felt a wave of relief go through him. More often than not on missions, he and his team had been on their own. If the shit hit the fan, there was no expectation of any assistance coming because much of what they did was top secret. They went into countries they weren't supposed to be in, like North Korea, Iran, Russia, and China, and the US couldn't risk an international incident if they got caught.

So knowing Tex had his back was a huge weight off his shoulders, though in no way a surprise. Tex's mission in life seemed to be helping as many people as he could, in any way possible. He was known in literally every military circle, no matter how covert. He was like Kevin Bacon, connected to damn near every single person in the country in some way.

"Spike?" Tex asked. "You hear me?"

"I hear you," Spike told him. "And thanks."

"Why do people always want to thank me?" Tex grumbled. "I'll send any new intel I get. Be safe."

Then the older man clicked off the connection. Spike took a deep breath and turned to Tiny. "Looks like we're headed to South America."

He didn't seem surprised or even too concerned. He simply nodded, then asked, "What'd Tex say?"

"Reese flew to Colombia," he informed his friends. "I've got the address of the hotel she booked and the last-known address for Isabella. But that's about it."

"Damn!" Bubba exclaimed, pocketing his phone. "What do you need me to do?"

"If you hear from Woody, or anything about what's going on, let me know," Spike said.

"That's a given. You need any gear?"

Shit. He should've brought some of his own stuff. It was just another thing that proved Spike wasn't thinking at the level he should've been. "Yeah, that'd be great," he told his friend. "Our flight leaves in three hours," he warned. "So we need to be quick."

Bubba merely nodded and led the way down the stairs toward the parking lot.

"You think this is gonna go bad?" Tiny asked as they followed the former Delta.

"Let's just say I don't have a warm and fuzzy feeling," Spike told him.

Tiny nodded yet again, as if Spike had confirmed his own feelings about the situation.

Three hours later, after borrowing gear from Bubba and boarding the plane to Colombia, Spike opened his phone and clicked on the file Tex had sent. He scrolled past pages of text, stopping on a picture of Reese Woodall. If anything, she'd gotten even prettier since he'd last seen her.

She still had her long blonde hair and blue eyes, but she had even more curves than before. And Spike approved. Her body was fucking *gorgeous*. He'd always been a sucker for a well-built woman. He had nothing against skinny chicks, but in his opinion, there was nothing better than being able to dig his fingers into a woman's fleshy ass as she bounced on his cock...seeing her tits shimmy and shake as she moved.

He liked a little extra meat on a woman's bones, and between looks, personality, and smarts, Reese was literally the epitome of everything he wanted in a partner.

Reading the profile Tex had put together made a streak of pride course through Spike. He already knew Reese was smart, but she'd been moving up the ranks of her engineering firm and taking on increasingly difficult projects. She also spent her spare time volunteering at an animal shelter, a women's center, and at a Boys and Girls Club. Tex had even dug up a video clip of her giving a speech at a fundraising event. She was funny, engaging, and her smile lit up the entire stage.

Of course, no one was perfect. Spike recalled Woody constantly bitching about how his sister didn't care enough about her own safety. How she didn't think twice about walking to her car in the dark after a volunteer shift at a homeless shelter in a not-so-great part of town. Of how she refused to admit when she was wrong. How she loved designer handbags so much, her collection was reaching ridiculous proportions.

Spike couldn't speak to most of that, but considering he was on a flight to Colombia at that very moment, it was clear Reese's disregard for her own safety was still alive and well.

He was almost embarrassed by how many times he'd watched that video clip. It was a good thing Tiny was seated a few rows ahead of him and couldn't question his sudden interest in Woody's sister.

But the more his admiration for the woman grew, the more worried he became. Where was she? Had she found her brother? Had someone hurt either her or Woody? He had too many questions and not nearly enough answers.

The quick trip to Missouri to reassure himself, and Reese, that his old friend was fine and not in any danger had morphed into something that felt far more urgent. In Spike's mind, this was no longer a trip to find Woody—it was to make sure Reese was all right. That she hadn't gotten in over her head.

He didn't know why he was so worried about a woman he barely knew...but he was. He had the oddest feeling that if anything happened to Reese, he'd miss out on something huge.

It wasn't normal, this attraction and concern for a woman he hadn't spoken to in years. But his shaking hands, nausea, and pounding heart told him that if he didn't find her and get her back to the States safely, he'd regret it for the rest of his life.

Taking a deep breath, Spike tried to control his body's fight-or-flight response. He needed to get control of his emotions so he could be at the top of his game when they landed. Reese was relying on him. As was Woody. Maybe even Isabella and her brother too.

But something was wrong. Spike knew that as well as he knew his name. He and Tiny were going to find out what it was...and do anything necessary to get everyone home.

* * *

Reese questioned what the hell she was doing for the hundredth time. What had possessed her to come down to Colombia on her own?

Her brother, that's what—or rather, *who*. When he'd been in the Army, going on countless missions, she'd worried about him constantly. At the time, it hadn't been unusual to not hear from him for weeks.

But this was different.

Woody wasn't in the Army anymore. And he had promised, *promised*, to keep in touch. He'd said he was going down to Colombia to meet up with Isabella, the woman he'd been in love with forever, and bring her back to Missouri.

The first day she didn't hear from him, Reese hadn't been too concerned. But when another day went by, then a third, and he hadn't responded to her texts or voice mails, she knew in her gut that something was terribly wrong.

She'd even called Bubba, one of Woody's old team-mates who lived in Kansas City, and he hadn't heard from her brother either. He'd done his best to reassure her that Woody was probably fine, that he was perfectly capable of taking care of himself, and Isabella and her brother too, but Reese wasn't so sure. The longer he went without contacting her, the more she thought about her brother being tortured or thrown into a dark cell somewhere.

It wasn't rational. There was no reason for anyone to kidnap her brother. But she couldn't stop thinking about it anyway. And really, how much did reason factor into kidnapping? She had no idea what she could do if anything bad had happened, but she felt a deep-seated need to be in the same country as Woody regardless.

So she'd impulsively bought a ticket and flown to Colombia. Stupidly, she hadn't told anyone where she was going. She'd sent an email to her boss saying she needed to take a week off work, and since she rarely took sick days or vacation time, her request was immediately approved.

Even worse, she'd left her phone in the bathroom in the Dallas airport, and didn't realize until she was back in the air. Reese swore sometimes if she didn't have bad luck, she'd have no luck at all.

She'd checked into her hotel in Bogotá and then taken a taxi to the address Woody had given her for Isabella, but no one was home. She tried to talk to the neighbors, but they either didn't speak English or didn't answer the door when Reese knocked. She'd called dozens of the nicer hotels in the city, attempting to discover if Woody had booked a room somewhere. Again, her zero grasp of Spanish made it a less-than fruitful effort.

She was now at a loss as to what to do next. She had no clue how else she might go about tracking down her brother. It was frustrating as hell, but Reese couldn't bring herself to go back to Missouri. Woody was somewhere in this country, and she wouldn't leave until she found him.

However, that would have to wait temporarily. Her second day in the city, she'd eaten something that hadn't agreed with her—and she'd been stuck inside her hotel room for the last day and a half, alternating between puking her guts out and pooping. She was scared to go too far from the bathroom.

It was embarrassing and disgusting. She'd flown all the way to South America to find her missing brother, only to be brought to her knees by a stupid hot dog she'd bought on the street.

Okay, it wasn't exactly a hot dog...but it had kind of looked like one.

Her stomach growled as Reese lay on the double bed in her small hotel room, staring at the ceiling. She was finally hungry again, but she didn't want to risk eating anything just yet and exacerbating her stomach issues. She was pretty sure whatever irritant she'd ingested had worked its way through her system by now, thank goodness. But better safe than sorry. Or...sorrier. And it wasn't as if she was wasting away.

Reese was well aware that she was overweight. She'd tried various ways of working out, but had honestly hated all of them. She'd attempted walking, riding a stationary bike, jogging (which had been a joke), swimming, Pilates, water aerobics...even yoga. She'd ended up quitting each one. And that was a problem for someone who loved food so much.

Since she needed to lose some weight, maybe this stomach bug was a good thing.

She sighed, thinking about the *real* cause of her love affair with food...she ate when she was lonely and unhappy. And with every year that passed, and each unsuccessful date, she was eating more and more.

She'd tried dating co-workers, with disastrous results. Had gone the online dating route, and that was even worse. She hadn't stooped so low that she'd asked Woody to set her up with any of his friends...but she was seriously considering it.

The problem was, Reese had no idea where to find a man who was genuinely looking for more than sex. Even the older men she'd dated had no desire to be in a long-term relationship. Her few female friends had been lucky enough to meet their husbands in college. But Reese was beginning to think she'd be single forever.

Which sucked. She considered herself a good person. She donated to charity, volunteered her time to help others, had a good-paying job, a decent head on her shoulders...and even with the extra weight, she didn't think she was horrible to look at. But time and time again, men didn't bother to contact her after a first date.

She was ashamed to admit that she'd even put aside her lifelong reservations and had indulged in a couple one-night stands, in the hopes that sexual chemistry might spark some deeper feelings for either her or her date. She'd only succeeded in making herself feel cheap, so she'd stopped that fairly quickly.

Besides, taking her clothes off in front of a virtual

stranger wasn't exactly her idea of a good time. They always said the right words, claimed to find her sexy, but she could see the disappointment—sometimes even disgust—in their eyes and body language.

Reese sighed when her stomach growled again. She needed to go find something to eat. This time, she'd be smarter about it and only get packaged food. Nothing from the street vendors, no matter how good it smelled. And no ice in her drink—that was one of the first things Woody had hammered into her head from all his travels overseas.

She sat up, determined to find something to munch on, even if it was only a candy bar from the small store downstairs in the hotel. Then she'd figure out where to go next in her search for her brother.

She didn't even get off the bed before there was a knock at her door.

Reese froze, staring at the wooden door across the room. She had no idea who would be on the other side. It wasn't as if she knew anyone in Colombia. For a heartbeat, she wondered if Isabella or Woody had gotten word that she was here and looking for them, and had come to tell her that they were fine and she could go home.

She instantly sagged at the thought. If it was Woody, he would've called out to her immediately. Let her know it was him.

She stood, and as quietly as she could, tiptoed to the door. She had every intention of pretending she wasn't there, but she still wanted to see who was knocking.

Reese leaned into the door, holding her breath, and peered out through the security peephole.

All she could see was a green eyeball blinking back at her.

Gasping, she stumbled backward and stared at the closed door.

"Reese? I know you're there. I saw the light change as you looked through the peephole. Open the door. We need to talk."

The man's voice was deep and sexy, like the narrators of some of her favorite audio books. She shivered, even while frantically trying to figure out what to do.

"Reese? You know me. It's Gus Fowler. I'm a friend of your brother's. We were on the same Delta team."

Blinking in confusion, Reese stood stock still. *Gus?*

She *did* know him—she'd had a crush on the man forever.

She could still remember the first time she saw him. She'd gone to welcome her brother home from one of his missions and had met all his teammates. But the only one who really made a lasting impression was Gus...who her brother and his friends called Spike. He hadn't talked or smiled much, but she'd felt his gaze on her throughout the evening.

They'd all gone out for dinner, and Gus had ended up sitting on one side of her, with Woody on the other. She'd been so self-conscious around him, she'd ended up ordering a salad. It was ridiculous; she tried hard not to bow to public opinion, ordering a salad at a restaurant when she really wanted a burger...but he'd made her feel off-kilter.

When he'd offered her a French fry, she hadn't been able to resist. The next thing she knew, he'd cut his huge steak in half and split his fries with her. Afterward, she'd been utterly embarrassed that she'd eaten half his meal. When Woody teased her about it, Gus had told him to shut the hell up and leave her alone.

He had a strong chin, high cheekbones, and the greenest eyes she'd ever seen. The last time she'd seen him, his hair was receding a bit, but that wasn't a turnoff. How could it be when he was the most masculine man she'd ever met in her life? And when he'd taken off his coat, revealing tattoos covering his right arm from shoulder to wrist, she'd nearly melted right then and there.

But the last thing Reese would ever consider was dating one of her brother's former Army teammates. They were...intense. Bossy. And physically perfect in every sense that she could see. She'd never measure up, and she didn't even want to try.

But that didn't mean she hadn't thought about Gus over the years. She was too chicken to ask Woody about him, but he'd once mentioned in passing that he and six other men had joined together to open some kind of resort for men and women suffering from PTSD. She'd never tell Woody that she'd immediately looked up The Refuge and checked out the website.

From what she could tell, Gus and his new friends were doing very well for themselves, and she was proud of him for helping others battle their demons.

"Reese?"

Shit. She'd been standing there staring off into space, and the man she was thinking about was on the other side of the door.

"What are you doing here?" she blurted, then mentally kicked herself. She should've stayed quiet. He would've left eventually. Maybe.

"Bubba called. Said you hadn't heard from Woody. I went to Kansas City to talk to you, but you'd up and left already. Open the door."

Reese blinked. He'd gone to Kansas City? That was the

last thing she'd expected him to say. Without thought, she moved toward the door, unlocked and opened it.

She stared at the man standing in front of her.

Good Lord, the years had been good to him. Dammit.

Why was that? Why did men seem to age gracefully, while women...okay, *she*, only got wider and more wrinkles?

He smiled at her but made no move to step inside her room.

And that smile...

Reese felt a tingle between her legs and did her best to ignore it. This man wasn't for her. No, if anything, seeing him after all these years made it even more obvious how far out of her league he really was. And she needed to concentrate on finding Woody.

"This is Tiny, a friend of mine. Can we come in?"

For the first time, Reese noticed the man standing behind Gus. And she had a feeling her mouth was hanging open, but she couldn't help herself. Gus was good-looking, but the man at his side was...beautiful. With his dark hair and piercing hazel eyes, he reminded her of a famous actor, but she couldn't place which one at the moment.

Then she realized she recognized him from a picture on The Refuge's website. She'd stared at it often enough to know that he was one of the seven owners of the retreat.

"Um...yeah. Come in," she stuttered and stepped back.

Gus and the other man came inside and shut the door behind them. They didn't move away from the door, as if they wanted to give her space, not make her feel uncomfortable in any way. Reese appreciated it. She felt discombobulated. She trusted Gus. He was her brother's friend. But it was weird that he was *here*.

"Seriously, Gus, what are you *doing* here?" she asked as she backed into the room and sat on the end of the bed.

21

Gus's lips twitched. "Oh, you know, we decided Bogotá might be a great place to vacation."

Reese's brows furrowed, then she snorted. "You're kidding. Right?"

"Yeah, Reese, I'm kidding. We heard you came down here to find Woody, and we wanted to help."

"Help?" she asked skeptically. "Not drag me home?"

"Would you go if I asked you to?" he inquired with a small tilt of his head.

"No," Reese said firmly.

"Right, so we came to help you find your brother so we can *all* go home."

Her respect for the man rose exponentially. The fastest way to piss her off and make her dig in her heels was to tell her she couldn't do something. She supposed Gus probably knew that, since it was one of Woody's greatest complaints about her. She had no doubt he wasn't thrilled she was here, but at least he wasn't immediately talking down to her and telling her she was an idiot for coming.

"What have you found out? You've been here a while now."

Reese felt her face heat and hated that she was blushing. "Yeah, um, well...I went to Isabella's address the first day and she wasn't there. And I couldn't get anyone to talk to me. Well, anyone who spoke English, that is," she said, hoping that information would be enough to distract Gus from asking what she'd been doing since then. But of course, she didn't have that kind of luck.

"And then? What about the last two days? Where have you been looking?"

Reese looked down at her hands. She shouldn't be embarrassed. Her body was just doing what bodies did when they were in foreign countries and were fed questionable meat products from an even more questionable vendor on the street.

"I've been here."

She peeked up at Gus and Tiny, and saw both men watching her intently.

"Here?" Gus asked. "In the hotel room? Are you all right?"

Reese sighed. She was going to have to tell them why she'd been in the room and not out looking for Woody. "I ate something that didn't agree with me. But I'm okay now. Good. Fine."

"Montezuma's revenge," Tiny muttered sympathetically.

Instead of letting her gloss over the fact that she'd been pooping her guts out for the last two days, Gus walked over and sat beside her on the bed. "That's tough. Ice?"

Reese did *not* want to talk about this. But if he could be cool about it, so could she. She shook her head. "No. Woody told me never to get ice when I was in a foreign country. I was hungry and frustrated when I returned from Isabella's place. There was a guy selling some hot dog things on the street, and I couldn't resist."

Gus winced.

"Yeah, I know," Reese said with a shake of her head. "It was stupid."

"Not necessarily. There are plenty of street vendors that are safe."

"When's the last time you had a mystery meat hot dog from a street vendor?" she asked.

Gus's lips twitched again. "Um...never."

"Right," Reese said with a roll of her eyes. "Anyway, I've been here because, well, you know." She gestured toward the small bathroom. "But I'm better now. What's the plan on finding Woody?"

"We haven't eaten," Gus said, ignoring her question. "We came straight here from the airport. How about we go downstairs to the restaurant and grab something? We can talk about our next steps while we eat."

Reese opened her mouth to say she wasn't hungry, but her stupid stomach chose that moment to growl. Loudly.

"Right, that answers that. You're probably dehydrated too. Tiny, you want to head down and get us a table? Reese and I will be right there."

His friend smiled and nodded before turning toward the door. Reese couldn't help but wonder why Gus wanted to speak to her in private.

As soon as the door shut, he turned to her and reached for her hand. Oddly, she wasn't mad about it. If he'd been anyone else, she would've pulled her hand away and asked where he got off touching her without permission. That was her usual reaction to anyone who acted overly familiar. But...this was Gus. She knew him. Kind of. More importantly, he was there because of his concern for her brother.

And she could secretly admit that having this man touch her was anything but offensive.

When he ran his index finger over the pulse point on her wrist, goose bumps broke out on her arms. She prayed he didn't notice as she did her best to control her reaction.

"Are you really okay?" he asked quietly. "I've been there. We were on a mission to Venezuela and I stupidly accepted a drink from a local we were trying to impress. Spent the next two days wishing I was dead. I couldn't go more than ten feet from a toilet. The guys were sympathetic, but they also gave me so much shit...no pun intended."

Reese was too distracted by his grin to respond.

"Anyway, it took a while for me to feel normal again. Don't be embarrassed about this. Seriously."

Okay. *Not* embarrassed. Not a chance in hell of that happening. "Okay," she said as breezily as she could, trying to act like a woman unashamed of discussing diarrhea issues after eating food in a foreign country. *Yeah. Right.*

"We're gonna find Woody," Gus told her next.

Reese was well aware he hadn't let go of her hand, but she wasn't going to be the one to interrupt this...moment... or whatever it was they were having. "Of course we are," she said as confidently as she could.

Gus smiled. A full-blown smile this time. Not just a twitching of his lips or self-deprecating grin. Then he sobered. "Will you trust me and Tiny to find him and bring him back to Missouri?"

"Yes. But if you're asking me to leave while you do that, the answer is no."

He sighed. "I had to try."

"You knew I'd say no?" she couldn't help but ask.

"Yeah. From everything Woody has said about you, I had a feeling you would insist on being in the thick of things."

It felt both good and weird to get confirmation her brother had talked about her to his teammates. To this man. "I'm not stupid. I know I don't have the skills you or my brother have. But I'm not helpless either. Sometimes people are more comfortable talking to a woman than a man. And no offense, but you *are* a little intimidating. Maybe I can be an asset to you and Tiny."

She appreciated that Gus didn't immediately dismiss her words. "Maybe. Let's get something to eat, make sure you're properly hydrated, and we can plan our next steps. I hope it won't offend you if Tiny and I head back to Isabella's and do our own knocking on doors."

"Not at all. Maybe she came back in the last two days. She and Woody could've been off on some sort of vacation or something and now they've returned." She didn't really believe that, but she could hope.

Gus didn't dismiss her thought, but he didn't agree with her either. Reese had to admit that he was being very diplomatic, and she appreciated it. "Hopefully we can get some more information after being there...or my friend back in the States who's doing what he can on his end will get back with me. Come on. Let's go get some grub."

He stood, still holding her hand and using it to tug her to her feet. Reese didn't protest as he led them toward the door.

To be honest, she was relieved Gus was here. Not only because she felt safe with him—which was a weird thing, since she hadn't spent that much time in his presence; since he'd been a Delta with her brother, she cut herself some slack for being so trusting, so fast—but also because she had no idea what to do next to try to find Woody.

She was out of ideas, and since she didn't speak Spanish, her options were limited. Having Gus and his friend here was a blessing. Her hope increased that they would be able to find Woody, and Isabella, and they'd all be okay.

CHAPTER THREE

Spike did his best not to stare at Reese. She was even prettier than the picture Tex had provided. Maybe it was that she was older and seemed to have more confidence in herself. Maybe it was the way she'd blushed so adorably while trying to sidestep around what she'd been doing for the last two days. Whatever it was, Spike had to keep reminding himself that he was here to find Woody...not seduce the man's sister.

Besides, Reese lived in Missouri, and he was in New Mexico. Even if they hit it off, there weren't too many engineering jobs he was aware of near The Refuge.

Although...Los Alamos National Laboratory *was* just down the road. It was one of the largest science and technology institutions in the world. The employees conducted research on national security, space exploration, nuclear fusion, renewable energy, medicine, nanotechnology, and probably a lot more things he had no clue about. Spike knew from talking to Woody that Reese was one of the top engineers in her field. He suspected a place like Los Alamos would jump at the chance to recruit her.

Mentally shaking his head, he concentrated on the here and now. They had to find Woody and get home before he could even start to think about anything else... namely, seeing if the intense spark he and Reese seemed to have could go anywhere. He didn't miss the way she'd stared at him when she opened the door to her room. The way her shoulders relaxed when he took her hand. Nor the goose bumps that rose on her arms when he brushed his finger along her wrist, trying to reassure her.

They'd ordered lunch, and Spike couldn't help but remember another time and place when he'd shared his steak and fries with her. Today she played it smart, considering the state of her stomach, and ordered soup and rolls.

"Right, so, Woody came down to visit with Isabella. What do we know about her?" Tiny asked.

Glad for his friend's question—Spike was having a hard time taking his attention away from Reese—he took out his phone and pulled up the information Tex had sent. "She's twenty-eight and has worked for the Colombian government for about a decade," he said.

"She was young when she started," Tiny observed.

Spike nodded in agreement. "I thought so too. But when we met her, she was extremely professional and competent, even though she was still pretty young at the time. She was raising her brother on her own, and her job allowed her to make fairly decent money in order to do so."

"Woody said Angelo, her brother, was struggling. It was one of the reasons he said he was coming down here," Reese added.

"Struggling how?" Tiny asked.

Reese shrugged. "I don't know. Woody didn't tell me

28

much. Just that he was finally going to get off his ass and do what he should've done years ago. I think he always felt as if he was too old for her...not that eight years is much of an age difference at all. But she also loved her job as a translator. Woody didn't want to take her away from that. And even though his interest in her has only grown, and they talked and emailed constantly, I think he wanted to let her grow up a bit more too...be sure of what she wanted."

Spike sighed. "Something had to have happened though. She had to have told him something big to make him suddenly come down here on a whim."

"I don't think it was a whim," Reese said solemnly. "I have a feeling he'd been thinking about it for a long time. Whatever she told him probably just gave him the final nudge he needed. Personally, I'm glad he finally did something about his attraction to her. He hasn't dated at all since getting out of the Army, and it was more than obvious it was because of Isabella."

"But?" Tiny asked.

Reese looked at him with her brows furrowed. "But what?"

"I can hear a note of reticence in your tone."

She sighed. "It's not that I didn't want him to be with Isabella. But she's here, and he's in Missouri. And there's no way she's going to leave her brother if he doesn't want to come to the States. Not after practically raising him single-handedly. I know it's terribly selfish, but I really don't want Woody to move here. I...I'd miss him too much."

Once again, Spike was in awe of Reese's relationship with her brother. He might not understand it, but he

29

respected it. And it was a two-way street. Woody always said the most important person in his life was his sister. That if she ever needed *anything*, he'd bend over backward to provide it.

Then there was the promise he'd extracted from Spike...

His mind went back to that particularly harrowing mission. They were pinned down by enemy forces, bullets flying all around them...and Woody had turned to Spike and made him swear that if anything happened to him, Spike would take care of Reese. Make sure she was all right. Of course, Spike had promised without question.

Before Woody had turned his attention back to surviving the firefight, Spike could've *sworn* he'd heard his friend mutter something under his breath about how much easier it would be to look after Reese if Spike married her.

He didn't get a chance to ask Woody to repeat himself, and neither had brought it up after they'd arrived safely back in the States.

Being next to Reese now, and seeing firsthand her love for Woody, her stubbornness, her bravery in coming to Colombia when she wasn't even sure where to start looking...Spike suddenly thought that if he fulfilled such a huge request for *anyone*, it would probably be for this woman, who knew more about sacrifice than most.

He'd loved others in the past. At least, he *thought* he had. But now he wasn't so sure. Not after seeing the lengths Reese was willing to go to find her brother. He wasn't close to his own sister. Sure, he'd try to find her if she was missing...but he silently admitted that might have more to do with familial obligation, rather than a deep sibling bond.

He was a little jealous of Woody and Reese's relationship, if he was being honest.

Spike made a mental vow right then and there to do whatever it took to make sure brother and sister were reunited.

"I get that," Tiny was saying. "I felt that way about my brother."

Spike looked at his friend in surprise. He'd never heard him mention a sibling before.

"He died," Tiny said flatly, addressing Spike's obvious curiosity. "He was a Marine. I was on a mission at the time, and didn't find out until I got home. By then, it was too late for me to say my goodbyes. To this day, I can't help but wonder if he knew I wasn't there. And the real shitter is, he was completely alone. Our dad's in prison, and our mom died a few years before he did. I would've done anything for him...but when it really mattered, I let him down."

Reese leaned over and grabbed his hand across the table. "You didn't let him down," she said almost fiercely.

Spike was startled by the vehemence in her tone, and it was obvious Tiny felt the same way, because he stared at her with wide eyes.

"If he was aware at all, I'm certain your brother knew you would've been there if you could. He was in the military. That means he understood that you were on a mission and couldn't come running back home whenever you wished. I wasn't in the service, and I still knew that if I'd been hurt while Woody was away, his priorities had to remain with his team and his mission. I would've known deep down in my heart that he was off saving the world, and that's a far more important and useful task than sitting in a hospital, holding my hand and feeling helpless. And..."

I'm going to go a step further and say your brother was probably *glad* you weren't there."

"Glad?" Tiny choked out.

"Not because he didn't love you, or because he was mad at you or anything. But because he would've wanted you to remember him at his strongest. Not languishing in a hospital bed," Reese said gently.

While Tiny digested her words, Spike couldn't help but place his hand on Reese's thigh under the table. He wanted her to know he appreciated what she was doing. Needed to be connected to her in that moment.

She glanced at him briefly, then turned her attention back to Tiny.

"Yeah," he said on a sigh, after a long pause. Then he squeezed her hand before pushing his chair back. "I'm gonna use the restroom. I'll be right back."

Spike watched his friend walk away, knowing he needed some privacy while he regained his composure. "Thank you," he told Reese softly.

She turned to him and put her hand on top of his, still resting on her leg. "For as long as I can remember, I've looked up to Woody. He's always been larger than life to me. I was scared every minute he was on a mission...and I know he went on more than I even knew about. But I was always proud of him."

"He's proud of you too. I can't tell you how many times he told us all about your academic prowess."

Reese rolled her eyes. "Just what a girl wants to be known for."

Spike tightened his grip on her thigh. "Gotta say, I'd much rather be with a smart woman, than with someone who's pretty but has nothing between her ears."

When she just rolled her eyes harder, it was obvious she thought he was blowing smoke up her ass, and Spike wanted to make sure she knew he was dead serious. "When I was in college, a friend dated a woman who complained that the Pittsburgh Steelers was a derogatory name for a football team...because people who stole things couldn't help themselves."

Reese's lips twitched.

"Another one of his dates wanted to know why non-alcoholic drinks were called virgin."

She grinned slightly.

"And yet another wanted to know why the starving people of the world didn't just go to the nearest Walmart and buy some ramen since it was really cheap."

Reese burst out laughing. "Okay, okay, I believe you," she said when she had control over herself.

"And when a woman has both smarts *and* looks?" Spike continued. "She's completely irresistible."

They stared at each other for a long moment, Spike making sure his meaning was clear, before Reese blushed and looked down at the empty bowl in front of her.

Kicking himself for making her uncomfortable, and knowing his first priority had to be finding Woody, Spike squeezed her leg once more before slipping his hand out from under hers and picking up his napkin to wipe his mouth.

Deciding it was a good time to change the subject, he said, "So when we're done here, we'll head over to Isabella's. See if we can learn anything else from any neighbors, and then go from there. If you want to stay here and rest up, since you've already been there, we'll come back to get you before going anywhere else."

"Nope."

"No? No what?" Spike asked.

"You aren't leaving me behind. Wherever *you* go, *I* go. You're not gonna run off and do your top-secret Army stuff without me."

Spike couldn't help but grin. "Top-secret Army stuff?" he asked with a small chuckle.

"Yeah, whatever it is you guys do. You'll ditch me in a heartbeat, and I'm not having it."

"First of all, we aren't going to be knocking down doors and holding people at gunpoint to get answers. I think your imagination is running amok. We're going to do the same thing you did...try to communicate with people to see if they've seen Woody or Isabella recently. Secondly, we aren't going to ditch you."

She looked at him skeptically.

"We aren't. We respect your need to find your brother. You wouldn't have come all the way down here if you weren't concerned and you didn't have his best interests at heart."

Spike held up a hand when she opened her mouth to speak, continuing before she could interrupt. "With that said, if shit goes sideways...I'll stash you somewhere safe so fast, your head will spin. Woody would kill me himself if even one hair on your head gets hurt. So, I'm okay with you going with us while we're searching for information, but if I think things are getting dangerous—in *any* way—you're out."

"That's not cool," she said with a frown.

"When's the last time you shot a gun?" he asked.

Reese pressed her lips together.

"That's what I thought. What about running from

someone who's determined to get his hands on you to do harm?"

"That's not fair," she protested.

"Of course it's not. Dealing with bad guys and assholes is *never* about fair. I need you to be safe and healthy when we find Woody. If you aren't, he's going to lose his mind. And if Isabella is hurt, he'll have to divide his loyalty between the two of you, which could make him reckless enough to do something stupid, which in turn could hurt any or all of us."

"Now you're just being mean," Reese pouted.

"I'm being realistic. Woody's going to freak out as it is when he finds out you're here. While Colombia isn't dangerous like an active war zone would be, there's still plenty of corruption and people involved with the drug world who won't think twice about taking a pretty American for their own nefarious intentions. I've already promised to keep you in the loop. All I'm asking is that if the shit hits the fan, you let Tiny and me take care of things, and you stay in whatever safe place we put you."

She stared at him for a long moment, and Spike held his breath. He wished he could stash her in her hotel room and make her stay there until he found her brother, but after everything Woody had said over the years about his sister, Spike knew without a doubt that wasn't even an option.

"All right."

He waited for her to say more. When she didn't, he asked, "All right? You'll do what Tiny and I say, and you'll be cool if we tell you to stay behind because things are too dangerous?"

Reese sighed. "Yes. Look, I'm not stupid, Gus. I have no idea what I'd do if someone pointed a gun in my face.

I'm really good at calculus or using elementary quantum mechanics to solve an equation that equals one, such as in the derivation of the Stefan-Boltzmann law, but running isn't my thing. Nor is getting out of handcuffs that are chained to a wall behind my back while a drug lord films my last words to send to my brother to try to extort thirty million dollars from him."

It was Spike's turn to burst out laughing. "Right," he said, staring at her for a long moment.

"What?" she asked a little belligerently.

"I like you," he blurted.

She looked surprised, then confused, then skeptical. "You don't know me."

"Your favorite show when you were little was reruns of *Wonder Woman* with Lynda Carter. You like cherry yogurt, but not berry. You're a morning person. You've read a gazillion books in your life because you prefer books over TV or movies, and you've given over ten thousand dollars to charity in the last three years," Spike said without missing a beat.

Reese's mouth fell open. "What...how...holy crap!"

Spike smiled. "I know you," he said unnecessarily. "Woody's got a big mouth. But there are still a hundred other things I *want* to know about you but don't."

He waited...knowing she wasn't going to be able to let his statement go. That was something else he knew about this woman. Her curiosity was extreme. It's what made her such a good engineer.

"Like?"

"What you like to do on a first date. If you sleep with a top sheet or not. What your all-time favorite book is. What you prefer to eat for dessert. If you'd ever consider dating a former military man who sometimes struggles to live a normal life after everything he's seen."

He hadn't meant to blurt out that last part. But after a long pause, she shrugged and said, "What's normal, anyway?" Then added, "And there's literally no point to a top sheet. I don't even understand what it's for."

Spike grinned.

"We good to go here?" Tiny asked as he sat in his chair.

He jerked in surprise. Shit, his friend had totally gotten the drop on him, which wasn't like Spike at all. Normally, he was aware of everyone at all times. Living through as many ambushes as he had would do that to a person.

"We're good," Reese said. "*You* good?"

"I'm good," Tiny said with a small smile. "And how many times are we going to say good?"

"I'd say a good many more times," Spike said.

The giggle that came from Reese felt like a warm blanket. He liked seeing her happy.

"Right. I'll go pay and we can get going," Tiny said with another small smile—this one aimed at Spike. And it was more like a smirk.

"Just put it on the room," Reese told him as he stood.

"Not happening," Tiny retorted as he headed for the hostess stand.

She turned to Spike and groused, "You guys are just like Woody."

"Yup," Spike agreed. "Come on, let's go see what we can find out about your brother and Isabella." He held his hand out to her...and something extremely satisfying flashed through him when she took hold and let him help her stand.

This woman was so far out of Spike's league, he had no idea what her words meant earlier. Or who Stefan-Boltzmann was, or what the hell his law had to do with math. Didn't matter. The more time he spent with her, the more he wanted to know.

But first...they needed to find Woody. Then he'd worry about the fact that he was more attracted to Reese Woodall than he'd been to any woman in a very long time.

CHAPTER FOUR

Reese was having a hard time keeping her mind on the task at hand. All she could do was stare at Gus's ass as he walked up the stairs to Isabella's apartment in front of her. Not only was the man built like a brick house, he was funny. And considerate. And when he'd put his hand on her leg as she was comforting Tiny, it had taken all of her strength not to lean into him.

It was also refreshing that he didn't seem to be turned off by her intelligence. So many other men in her past had claimed that her knowledge didn't bother them, only to turn around and say or do something that belied their words.

But now wasn't the time or place to get giddy and girly about a man like Gus paying such close attention to her.

Looking around, Reese shivered. This neighborhood wasn't the best, but it wasn't the worst either. She just had a bad feeling that she was being watched. She'd felt the same way when she was here before, but it seemed worse now. She was grateful for both Tiny and Gus's presence. They made her feel much safer.

She wasn't thrilled with Gus telling her she'd have to stay at the hotel if things got intense, but she also didn't want to be a liability. The truth of the matter was, Tiny, Gus, and Woody were all trained to be badasses when the shit hit the fan. Tiny may have been a Navy SEAL, but she figured he was just as capable as her brother and Gus.

But she, on the other hand, was hopeless. Just as she'd told Gus, when Woody had tried to teach her how to get out of handcuffs, she'd failed miserably. It was just after he'd gotten out of the Army, and he'd been determined to teach her some advanced self-defense moves.

She hadn't been able to get out of his hold when he'd grabbed her, no matter how hard she tried or how many tricks he'd shown her. The zip-ties had bruised her wrists, and she hadn't been able to get out of those either. In the end, after hours of practice, he'd simply told her she'd better not get into any situation where she needed to physically defend herself, or she'd be screwed.

She was pissed at the time, but he was right. She was much better at using her brain to get out of situations than brute strength. So if Gus and Tiny thought they might be getting into some sort of dangerous situation, she was more than okay with staying behind while they did the physical stuff.

Not that it made her happy thinking about Woody being in danger, but she knew her limitations.

"Stay close," Gus said softly as they neared Isabella's door. It was obvious he felt the tension in the air. Reese wondered if he felt the eyes on them as well, and figured he likely did.

He knocked on the door, and no one answered. Same as Reese had experienced a few days ago. But in contrast to her visit, Tiny took something out of his pocket, stepped close to the doorknob, and popped it open within seconds.

"What...how?" she stuttered as Gus put his arm around her waist and ushered her inside the apartment.

"Stay here," he ordered, before he and Tiny stalked through the apartment. That was the only word she could find to describe how they were moving. Neither had a weapon, but it was obvious they were being very cautious and could probably disarm anyone they came across.

She looked around while the guys were gone. The place was small and tidy. But not sterile. It looked lived in...cozy. There were a few pictures scattered here and there. A pair of shoes on the floor, probably where someone had kicked them off when they'd arrived home. A small TV sat on a table against the wall and there were a few DVDs stacked haphazardly to the side. A rumpled blanket sat on an old light brown couch. The kitchen had some old appliances on the counters, but there were no dirty dishes in the rack next to the sink.

All-in-all, Reese got the impression that the people who lived here weren't rich, but they'd made a comfortable home with what they had.

Gus and Tiny returned to the living area.

"Are they here?" Reese asked reluctantly. Because if they were, it wasn't good.

"No, the place is empty," Tiny answered.

"Breathe, Reese," Gus said, stepping into her personal space. They were almost eye-to-eye, and she did her best to relax her muscles. "They aren't here. We're going to search the rooms more thoroughly and see if we can find anything that will lead us to where they might've gotten off to."

Taking a deep breath, Reese nodded.

"We probably don't have a lot of time," Tiny observed. "It's highly likely we were seen coming in here."

"You felt the eyes too?" Gus asked.

"Oh yeah."

"So did I. More so than the last time I was here," Reese told them.

Gus nodded. "Something's up. I don't know what, but there's an edginess in the air. As if the residents are scared and waiting for something to happen."

"So let's get searching and get the hell out of here," Tiny suggested.

"Reese, you take the kitchen and living room, and Tiny and I will search the bedrooms," Gus decided.

For a moment, she was surprised he was letting her help, but then she straightened her shoulders. Why *couldn't* she help? She was here, and she knew her brother better than anyone.

Gus gave her a look, and for a second, it seemed he wanted to say something else, but he simply nodded at her and headed back down the hallway leading to the bedrooms.

Ten short minutes later, Reese was already frustrated. Both rooms were small so her search was quick, and she hadn't found anything that would be any use in figuring out where Woody and Isabella might have gone. All she'd discovered was spoiled food in the small fridge and a disconcertingly empty pantry. She'd been under the impression that Isabella was doing all right for herself. She had a good job with the government and, from what Woody had already told her, was making decent money for the area.

But looking at the food in the kitchen and even the sparse furniture in the living room, it seemed that wasn't the case. She heard Tiny and Gus talking down the hall as she gave one more look around the room.

And something caught her eye.

Walking over to the corner of the living area, she bent down and picked up the broken watch on the floor. It was Woody's. She'd bet everything she owned on that. Their dad had bought it for him when he'd first become a Delta Force operative, and her brother had worn it every day, saying it reminded him of family.

He'd been here—and something had to have happened for him to leave it behind.

Examining it closer, Reese saw that the band had been broken. The pin that held it to the watch face had popped out. On the surface, it didn't mean much...but she was still worried.

She turned to call out for Gus when she saw both him and Tiny exiting the hall looking extremely concerned.

"We're going," Gus told her abruptly, holding out his hand.

Without thought, Reese headed for him and let him wrap his arm around her waist as he turned her toward the door.

"What'd you find?" she asked.

"Trouble," Tiny muttered.

"What is that?" Gus asked, not answering her question but nodding to her hand.

Reese held it up. "It's—"

"Woody's watch," Gus finished for her.

"It was sitting on the floor against the wall. He never takes it off. I make fun of him all the time because he's got a perfect white circle of skin under it, where the face is against his wrist."

"Yeah," Gus said absently as he pocketed the watch.

Tiny looked out the peephole of the door and frowned. "We've got company," he informed them.

"Shit. How close?" Gus asked.

"Coming up the stairs. We have to go out the back."

Out the back? Wait, they were on the second floor. There *was* no back.

Reese looked between the two men, but didn't have time to voice any of her questions before Gus was turning her around and ushering her down the hall.

They entered the master bedroom and Tiny immediately went to the window. He cautiously peered out of the blinds and nodded. "Clear."

While Tiny was opening the ridiculously small window, Gus put his hands on her shoulders. "We've got to go out this way."

Reese wanted to say "duh" but refrained as he kept speaking.

"We found some concerning things in Angelo's room. I'm guessing whoever was watching us arrive made a call and let someone know we were here."

"Someone we don't want to talk to," Reese deduced.

"Exactly. But we found an address, so once we get you back go the hotel, Tiny and I are gonna go check it out."

Her first instinct was to protest, to beg to go with them, but she'd promised. So Reese simply nodded.

"Thank you," Gus said fervently, and despite the circumstances, Reese couldn't help but feel a little thrill inside that she'd pleased him.

"It's gonna be a tight fit."

Reese turned at Tiny's words, checking out the window set high in the wall. "Tight fit? There's no way you guys will fit through there." Hell, it was going to be iffy on whether *she* would fit. She was much...rounder...than Tiny

44

or Gus. They had more muscles than her though, and broad shoulders.

Then something else occurred to her. "Um, please tell me there's a fire escape out there."

"Nope. But there's a beautiful gutter that might as well be a ladder. I'll go first, then you'll come out after me and I'll help you with your descent. Spike'll go last, protecting us from above."

"Wait, protecting us? From what?" Reese asked, just as a loud thump sounded from the front of the apartment.

"Shit. We're going," Tiny said as he grabbed the sill and jumped up, managing to swing his legs out the window like some sort of circus acrobat. His head disappeared in seconds.

"I'm not sure about this, Gus," Reese said, but he didn't give her time to think about what they had to do. He simply leaned over and picked her up like he was Rhett Butler and she was Scarlett O'Hara from *Gone with the Wind*.

Utterly shocked—no one in her entire life had *ever* carried her like this—Reese wrapped her arm around Gus's neck as he stuck her legs out the window.

"Turn and face the building when you get out there. Use your feet against the gutter to slow your descent."

"OhmyGodOhmyGodOhmyGod," Reese muttered as she clung to the windowsill. She was about to tell Gus there was no way she could do this when she heard a loud bang from inside the apartment. Whoever was at the front door had obviously broken it down, and if she didn't get her shit together, there was a huge chance Gus would be hurt...or worse. He didn't have a gun and it was likely whoever had kicked in the door *did*.

Moving faster than she thought possible, Reese turned

so she was facing the building and forced herself to loosen her death grip on the windowsill. She felt Tiny's hand on her calf and it gave her the courage to grab hold of the gutter and slowly let her body slide downward.

She didn't dare look up *or* down, so she felt more than saw Gus above her. Letting out a sigh of relief that he was out of the apartment, she continued her descent. It wasn't too far to the ground, since they were only on the second floor.

She heard a shout above her head—and that was all she needed to move faster. Loosening her hold, she slid down the gutter like her life depended on it. And when she heard more loud, angry shouting in Spanish, she thought it just might.

Before her feet touched the ground, Tiny was grabbing her around the waist and pushing her in front of him, away from the building. "Go!" he said urgently.

"Gus!" she protested.

"I'm here."

Reese had never felt so relieved to hear someone's voice before. Then it was *his* hand on her back, urging her to run.

She had so many questions...what did they find in Angelo's room, who were the men who'd broken into the apartment, where were they going, where was Woody...but now wasn't the time.

When a loud crack of gunfire echoed around them, Gus urged her to run faster.

Reese wasn't a runner. She hadn't lied about that. But at the moment, she felt as if she could give any Olympic champion a literal run for their money. There was something about someone *shooting* at her that gave her the needed motivation to move her ass.

She, Tiny, and Gus ran around buildings, across streets, and even across a wooded park. But Gus wouldn't let her slow down, and now that they were out of immediate danger—she hadn't heard any more gunshots behind her—she realized she was breathing like the out-of-shape, overweight thirty-four-year-old that she was, whose only exercise consisted of walking to and from her car a few times per day.

"Just a little farther," Gus told her, sounding disgustingly *not* breathless at all.

Saving her breath, Reese nodded. The last thing she wanted was to slow these men down. If something happened to them, she'd never forgive herself. They were here because of her. Because she'd come down here looking for her brother on her own.

She should've asked for help. Instead, she thought she'd waltz down to Colombia and find him within hours. For a smart woman, she'd been incredibly stupid. Her brother's friends were special forces. She *so* should've called one of them.

But it was too late now. She'd made her bed and now she had to lie in it. She ignored the stitch in her side and how the soup she'd eaten earlier was threatening to come up. She needed to deal with whatever was happening as best she could and not be a liability.

But that was easier said than done. Especially when it felt as if she couldn't get any oxygen into her lungs.

"We'll stop here for a moment," Gus said, and Reese had never been so glad to hear six words in all her life. She leaned against the side of the building they'd stopped next to and bent over, doing her best to catch her breath while Tiny and Gus talked above her.

"What now?" Tiny asked. "We could circle back around to get our rental car."

"I'm thinking they've probably already clocked it."

"Yeah. And if they're who we think they are, they'll already know who *we* are—and why we're here."

Reese straightened. "Who are they?" she asked as evenly as she could. She saw Tiny and Gus share a look. "Please don't lie to me," she pleaded. "I'm guessing since we went out a freaking window and people were shooting at us, they aren't exactly the neighborhood welcome party."

Gus stepped into her personal space and Reese looked up at him. "Best we can tell without knowing for certain, they're cartel."

Reese forced herself not to react outwardly. She wanted to be tough and strong. But inside she was freaking the fuck out. "Like, a drug cartel?" she asked.

Gus's lips twitched, but then he got serious. "Yeah."

Reese swallowed hard. "Okay. Now what?"

Gus stared at her for a long moment with a look she couldn't interpret.

"What?"

"You aren't freaking out?" Gus asked.

"Would it help if I did?"

"No."

"If it makes you feel better, I'll freak out later. Once we find Woody and Isabella and her brother and get the hell out of here."

"Right. So...I'm guessing they'll know who we are, and since we rented a room in the same hotel where you've been staying, it's not going to take them long to figure out that we're with the same woman who visited the apartment a couple days ago."

"So it's not safe to go back there right now."

"Exactly," Gus said.

"Then what's the plan?"

"I'm thinking we go and get Woody and the others," Tiny said from next to them.

Reese jerked. She'd almost forgotten he was there. With Gus so close to her, and watching her so carefully, she'd only been aware of him.

Tiny held up a slip of paper.

"What's that?"

"It was inside a box with the drugs we found in Angelo's room."

"He had drugs in his room?" Reese asked.

"Yeah," Tiny said grimly.

"That can't be good," she said, which felt like a total understatement.

"Where is it?" Gus asked his friend.

Tiny nodded at the cell phone he'd been using to look up the address. "In the woods outside Bogotá."

"How far outside?" Gus asked.

"About thirty miles east of the city."

Reese's belly rolled.

"Shit. We need transportation," Gus said.

"And I'm thinking maybe a call to Tex to find out what we're walking into would be good too," Tiny said.

"Although we don't want to give them much time to prepare for our arrival," Gus countered. "So it wouldn't be smart to wait until tomorrow."

Reese's head swiveled back and forth as the men discussed their next steps.

"Where are we gonna get a car?" Tiny asked.

Gus pressed his lips together in thought.

"What about that one?" Reese blurted as she pointed

toward a beat-up old pickup truck parked in an alley across the street.

Both men's heads swiveled toward her.

She pushed down her embarrassment at what she was about to admit. "I mean, I'm sure you guys can do it too... but those older models are fairly easy to hotwire. We could leave some money or something in its place."

"You know how to hotwire a car?" Tiny asked incredulously.

She shrugged and nodded.

"Marry me," he joked.

Reese grinned.

Gus frowned. "I don't know."

"How else are we gonna get there?" Tiny asked. "You were right, we need to get out there and see what's up before anyone has time to regroup. You know as well as I do that those guys at the apartment aren't going to be content to just let us walk away. They're going to want to know why we were there and what we want. And it's likely the drugs are connected to Woody's disappearance."

"You think the brother is dealing?" Gus asked.

"No clue. But around here, being part of the cartel is considered a good safety net. And having someone like Isabella to translate for them would be a boon."

"How do you think Woody's involved?" she asked.

"Bad timing?" Tiny said with a shrug. "I don't know. But we don't have any other leads at the moment. If we get to this address and there's nothing there, or Woody and the others aren't anywhere to be seen, we can come back to Bogotá and keep looking."

Gus looked down at Reese, then back at his friend.

"If you leave me at the hotel, those men could come and grab me," she said. "Try to get information out of me about you two." She wasn't trying to be dramatic or manipulative. She was genuinely worried about being on her own now. "If you weren't with me, there's no way I could've gotten out of that apartment. I'm safer with you two than on my own. I promise I'll leave the shooting and lurking about to you two. I'll stay where you put me—but please let me come with you."

Gus looked at his friend.

"It's up to you," Tiny said.

Gus sighed and looked back at her. "If something happens to you, Woody will never forgive me," he said.

"Nothing's going to happen to me when I'm with you." Reese wasn't a fortune teller. She had no idea what would happen in the future, but one thing she *did* know, without a single doubt, was that she believed her words one hundred percent.

"All right. But if I tell you to do something, you do it. Immediately. Without question. Understand?"

Reese quickly nodded.

"I'm going to regret this," Gus said more to himself than to her, but he looked both ways up and down the street. There wasn't anyone around.

"Come on. Let's do this. You can show off your hotwiring skills," he told her.

"And you'll leave some money in place of the car?" she asked as the three of them quickly walked across the street and ducked into the alley.

"You've got a soft heart," Gus murmured, turning away from the truck to make sure no one approached.

Reese shrugged as she leaned into the driver's side to get to work on the truck.

"Not saying that's a bad thing, just an observation," Gus said. "And yes, I'll leave some pesos. It won't be enough to cover the cost of the truck, but if this thing even runs I'd be surprised."

In seconds, Reese had the engine started, and Gus stared at her with admiration. "That was fast."

"I'm that good," she couldn't help but brag.

Gus and Tiny chuckled.

"Scoot into the middle," Tiny said. "I'm driving."

Reese wanted to protest, but she'd promised Gus she would do what they asked without questioning them. So she moved to the center of the seat and soon she was sandwiched between the two huge men. Tiny backed out of the alley and Reese held her breath until they were well away from where they'd stolen the truck.

"Call Tex," Tiny ordered. "See what he can find out about where we're going. The more info we have, the better off we'll be."

Reese stayed quiet as they headed east out of the city. She had no idea what they were driving into, but she prayed it would lead to Woody.

CHAPTER FIVE

Spike didn't like this. Not at all.

Having Reese with him changed everything. He hadn't thought much about putting himself in danger when he was on the teams. He did what he had to do and that was that. But seeing the fear, and determination, in Reese's eyes as he basically threw her out the window wasn't something he wanted to repeat.

She'd been so damn brave, and he was as proud of her as he could be. But that didn't mean he wanted her to continue on the search for her brother with him and Tiny. He would much prefer to stash her somewhere safe. But that was the problem. He had no idea where "safe" was at the moment.

Even as he worried about what they'd find when they got to the address they'd lucked out with in Angelo's room, Spike realized that his hands weren't shaking. He wasn't nauseous.

He wasn't sure why. He was in as much danger, or more, as he'd been any other time he'd had a physical reaction. The only difference was that it wasn't just his life at risk, or Tiny's, but Reese's as well. If anything, his body should be reacting *more* now. Instead, it was as if his mind realized the importance of keeping his shit together to make sure Reese was safe.

Whatever the reason, he was relieved that outwardly, at least, he appeared calm, even if he was still worried about the entire situation.

Spike glanced at Reese and immediately wanted to take her into his arms. She was sitting ramrod straight between him and Tiny in the old truck. Her eyes were wide and she was clenching her hands together in her lap. She looked distressed, and Spike hated that.

He'd spoken with Tex and he'd given them as much of a head's up about where they were headed as he could by looking at satellite pictures. There was a house in the middle of the jungle. It wasn't a mansion, but it also wasn't a rundown shack, like most of the houses in a nearby village. And considering that they'd found what looked like several thousand dollars' worth of drugs in Angelo Hernandez's room, it was highly likely they were headed to a stash house of some sort.

At this point, Spike could only speculate, but he and Tiny had a short conversation and agreed that it was likely Angelo had gotten in over his head in regard to the drugs, probably owed the cartel money—and they'd come to collect. Perhaps they'd already known about Isabella's bilingual ability and decided she'd be an asset to their organization. Or maybe they took the sister to make sure Angelo did what they wanted.

Or maybe they took her for more despicable reasons.

But taking Woody wasn't a good sign. He would've fought back, definitely. Kidnapping an American citizen could be a gold mine…if a ransom was paid. But Reese hadn't received any kind of demand.

Spike's head hurt, thinking about what may have happened to his friend. And there was a chance the three weren't at the address at all. For all they knew, Woody and Isabella could be holed up in some romantic love nest, while Angelo was hanging with friends.

But Spike didn't believe that. Neither did Tiny nor Reese, for that matter.

Glancing once more at the woman beside him, he thought of the way she'd so easily hotwired the truck they were currently riding in. The way she'd insisted on him leaving some money for the owner. She was constantly surprising him.

Most surprising of all…Spike found that he felt more alive right now than he had in years. And it wasn't because of adrenaline or because his life was in danger.

His hand moved without thought, reaching over and covering Reese's fidgeting hands in her lap. Touching her was becoming a necessity, not simply a way to try to keep her calm.

"So…cars, huh?" he asked, wanting to take her mind off of what they might find at the end of their journey.

She shrugged. "Woody was always tinkering on some sort of engine when we were growing up, and since I adored him and wanted to do everything he did, I learned as much as I could about cars."

"I can just picture you toddling around behind him," Spike said with a small smile.

"Annoying him, you mean," Reese said. "Did he tell you about the time I followed him and his date to the drive-in?"

Tiny chuckled from behind the wheel, but Spike didn't take his gaze from Reese. "No."

"Well, he was in the tenth grade and had just gotten his driver's license. I hated the girl he was dating. She was a total bitch, and even though I was only two years younger than she was, she treated me as if I was five. She also acted one way in front of Woody and another behind his back. She pretended to be the nicest person in the world when he was around, and when he wasn't, she was picking fights with other girls and bullying them until they cried. I tried to warn my brother, but he wouldn't listen. I was just his annoying little sister, after all."

"What'd you do?" Spike asked.

Reese grinned, and Spike couldn't help but think she was absolutely adorable.

"First, I told my parents that I was going upstairs to study for a test I had the next week. Then I snuck out and went to the drive-in on my dirt bike. I shimmied under the fence and found Woody's truck. They were sitting in the back, making out, of course. I knew how much his date hated bugs and creepy-crawly things, so...I'd brought along a few spiders I'd caught around the house and let them loose in the truck through a cracked front window, while they were too busy kissing to notice me. And by a few, I mean around fifty of the suckers."

Tiny burst out laughing at her audacity.

Reese grinned wider. "She completely flipped out. And when Woody ran to grab paper towels at the concession stand to wipe up the mess her drink made when it spilled, she was standing next to the truck, and I was hiding under it. I grabbed her ankle—and then she *really* lost her mind. By the time Woody got back, she was babbling about a killer lurking at the drive-in. When Woody didn't find anyone near the truck, she decided the place was haunted and she'd been grabbed by a ghost!

"It was hilarious. Juvenile, yes...but I was, in fact, a juvenile at the time. And trust me, the girl deserved it. When Woody came home, I was back in my room, studying innocently. He broke up with her about a week later because he couldn't stand her constantly bringing up what happened and insisting a ghost had tried to snatch her. It wasn't until we were both in college that I confessed what I'd done."

"Was he mad?" Tiny asked, a huge smile on his face.

"Nope. He said he knew she was a bitch all along but since he was a teenage boy, and she was known for putting out, he didn't care at the time," Reese said with a chuckle.

Spike could easily picture a mischievous young Reese, torturing her brother's girlfriend.

The grin on her face faded and she looked over at him. "Do you think he's okay?"

And just like that, the mood in the truck shifted from amusing thanks to her funny story, to something more ominous.

"Yes," he told her without hesitation.

"You can't know that."

"I can and I do. Your brother and I have been through a lot together. A *lot*. And you know I can't give you any details, but suffice it to say, Woody's ability to get himself, and those around him, out of the middle of a shit storm is legendary. And we might not even find him, Isabella, or Angelo at the address we're headed to," Spike said.

"You don't believe that," she said without any question in her tone. "Otherwise we wouldn't be wasting our time." She gave him a look. "I realize that you and Tiny might know more than you're telling me. You might have found something else back in that apartment that you're keeping close to your chest. And honestly, I don't care. All I want is to find Woody and make sure he's safe."

Spike's esteem for the woman next to him rose.

"Are we gonna talk about the plan when we get there or what?" she asked next.

Spike met Tiny's gaze over her head for a moment, before his friend turned his attention back to the road.

"The plan is for us to park this piece of crap somewhere safe and out of the way, then do some recon. You'll stay with the truck while we go in, hopefully find Woody, and get the hell out of there."

Reese rolled her eyes. "Right, because it'll be that easy," she said sarcastically.

Spike shrugged. "Sometimes it is."

She pressed her lips together and stared out the front windshield.

Spike didn't like that she'd dismissed him so easily. "I'm not lying or trying to downplay what's going on. You know as well as I do that messing with the cartel is bad news. But seriously, sometimes not overthinking or overengineering things is the best way to approach a problem."

Reese looked at him again. She reluctantly nodded.

"I was on this mission once," Tiny piped up, "and the objective was to go into a house full of insurgents, identify a specific HVT—high-value target—and bring him back to base to be interrogated. We spent twelve hours devising a very complicated plan to not only get into the house, but how to figure out which of the men was our guy when we did—and get him out without killing anyone else, which would've started an international incident and possibly a firefight we wouldn't win since we'd be outnumbered ten to one.

"In the end, our team leader said, 'fuck it,' walked up to the damn door, knocked, asked to speak to the HVT, and he *actually* came to the door, as easy as you please. After a few words, he agreed to come with us to the base to have a chat with our commander. It was unbelievable, but it worked."

"So you're saying if we knock on the door and ask for Woody, they'll bring him out?" Reese asked with a look on her face that clearly stated she thought Tiny was completely nuts.

He chuckled. "No. All I'm saying is that we could sit here and go through a million scenarios, but without knowing the layout of the house, how many people are there, what the area around it looks like, and a hundred other little details, any plan we make will be fucked before we even start."

"I don't like winging things," Reese mumbled.

Spike couldn't exactly disagree with her. He wasn't thrilled with all the unknowns at the moment, but Tiny was right. They couldn't plan anything without having intel. He was still holding Reese's hand, and he tightened his fingers around hers. "We're gonna find him." As far as reassurances went, it fell a little short, but to his relief, Reese sighed and nodded.

"Okay, you guys are the professionals here, I'll let you do your thing. But please don't count me out. I can help," she said.

Spike didn't dismiss her words, because there was a chance they really might need her to help in some way. The odds weren't looking good. With only two of them, even if they were highly trained special forces operatives, if things went sideways, they were definitely fucked.

"We hear you, Reese," Spike said after a long moment.

"And trust me, when the time comes, if we need you, we won't have any problem asking for your help."

He had no clue what kind of help that might be. The very last thing he'd *ever* do was put her in danger intentionally. She wasn't coming into the house with them, Spike was adamant of that. But he wasn't going to dismiss the idea that she could do something to assist. After all, while he or Tiny could've hotwired the truck, she'd done it a hell of a lot faster than Spike could've managed.

He didn't let go of Reese's hand for the remainder of the drive, and he was relieved she didn't seem to be disturbed by how tightly he was holding onto her. Maybe because her grip was just as tight.

By the time they neared their coordinates, Spike was more than ready for action. Sitting around was never his favorite thing, and being in the truck for so long with no clue what they were driving into was seriously making him jittery.

Tiny pulled down a dirt road, although calling it a road was being generous. There were just two deep ruts where other vehicles had traveled before them. The truck being green and brown with plenty of rust worked in their favor, as it served as natural camouflage in the trees and bushes.

A couple minutes later, Tiny pulled off the trail, moving the truck as far into the woods as he could—which wasn't very far at all.

"We're about half a mile from the house. I need you to stay here, but not in the truck. If someone comes by and sees it and decides to investigate, it would be better if you weren't in it," Spike told her. "No matter what happens, *please* stay here. If we come back with Woody and you aren't here, it won't be good."

Reese nodded as she stared at him with wide eyes.

"I don't have a weapon to leave with you, so your best bet at this point is to stay hidden. Do not let anyone see you. Understand?"

She nodded again.

Spike stared at her for a long moment. Then he looked over at Tiny. "Can I have a minute?"

He and Tiny hadn't been on any missions together, but just like at the hotel, the other man immediately understood that Spike wanted some time alone with Reese. He quickly nodded. "I'll see what kind of foliage I can find to try to hide the truck better." Then he climbed out of the vehicle without waiting for a response.

As soon as the door closed, Spike turned so he was more fully facing Reese and put a hand on her cheek. It was an intimate gesture, but he couldn't stop himself. "If Woody's here, I'm gonna find him."

"Okay," she said softly.

"But you need to understand something. If we get back to this truck and you aren't here, I'm gonna be..." His voice trailed off. So many words came to mind, but he wasn't sure which to use. Pissed. Worried. Frantic. Upset. Devastated.

It made no sense. The connection he felt with this woman. Yes, he'd already felt as if he knew her a bit after hearing Woody talk about her for years. But it had been a long time since he'd seen her in person. Despite that, something deep within him had known from the second she'd opened that hotel door that Reese was different from anyone he'd ever dated. And he wanted—no, *needed* a chance to get to know her better.

If she got hurt, or worse, he instinctively knew he'd lose his chance at what Brick and Tonka had found. Knew that as well as he knew his own name.

But if he tried to explain it to her, she'd probably freak out.

"I promise not to do anything stupid," she told him, staring at him with her gorgeous blue eyes. "While I'd do anything to get Woody out of here safe and sound, I don't want you and Tiny to sacrifice yourselves to make that happen. If you get to that house and it's too dangerous to get inside...don't do it."

Spike's mind went back to one of the many missions that had stuck inside his brain, making him feel unfit to be around normal society after he'd finally called it quits with the Army. They'd been in some country...hell, he couldn't even remember which one now, but there had been shelling all around them and endless gunfire. His ears rang with the constant barrage of noise, and all he could smell was gunpowder and smoke from the fires caused by the RPGs exploding in the buildings.

A woman had appeared out of nowhere. She was crying and hysterical. She spoke broken English and she'd run right up to Spike and grabbed his arm. He'd been seconds away from using his elbow to break the bones in her face, having run into women used as decoys more than once on missions, when she'd begged him to rescue her husband. Apparently, he'd gotten trapped under some rubble in a nearby house.

It wasn't so much that she'd been desperate enough to approach him and his team of deadly looking soldiers...but her words that had stuck with Spike after all these years.

Military coming. You soldier. You die to save husband! He better than you.

It was stupid to put any weight to her words. It shouldn't have mattered that the woman thought his life was worth less than her husband's, simply because he was a soldier. The woman had been desperate and scared out of her mind. But Spike couldn't help thinking that she was right. He was in *their* country, killing people...and for what? To this day, he didn't know.

So Reese telling him that she didn't want him to sacrifice himself for her brother, who she'd known her entire life and loved enough to come to a foreign country to try to find him on her own, meant a lot.

No, it meant everything.

Her words soothed some of the hurt he'd held onto for years.

"No one is sacrificing themselves," he told her gruffly. "We're *all* getting out of here."

Reese pressed her lips together, then took a deep breath. "I don't...I want...*Shoot.*"

"What? You can tell me anything."

"I've had a crush on you forever," she blurted. "I know it's stupid and stereotypical...kid sister likes her older brother's friend...but there it is. I just wanted you to know that I'm in awe of you. And proud of what you and your Delta team did for our country. I think you're amazing and I've looked up The Refuge online and it's awesome. And no matter what happens...I'll never forget that you came down here looking for Woody."

Her words sent warmth cascading through Spike. He and Tiny needed to get going. The longer they were here, the greater the chance of discovery and the higher the possibility that whoever had chased them out of Isabella and Angelo's apartment would show up and let everyone know what had happened. But he couldn't tear himself away from this woman just yet.

"I didn't come down here for Woody," he admitted.

Her brows furrowed in confusion. "You didn't?"

"No. I came here for *you*."

He watched as a blush bloomed in her cheeks and she licked her lips. "Oh."

Spike couldn't help but smile. "That's all you're gonna say?"

Reese nodded. "I think so."

"All right. And for the record...I think you're pretty awesome too. And when this is done, and we're back in the States safe and sound...I'd like to explore whatever this is that's happening between us."

"Really?"

He hated how surprised she sounded. This woman should never question her appeal. Ever. "Really."

"I'd like that."

Spike nodded. There was more he wanted to say. But he could see Tiny waiting not so patiently outside the truck. "I need to get going."

Reese gave him a worried smile, then brought her hand up to where his rested on her cheek. She covered it, turned her head, kissed his palm, then dropped her hand.

He could feel her lips on his skin as if the kiss had branded him. "Be safe," he choked out of a tight throat before blindly reaching for the door handle. He needed to go, *now*, before he changed his mind about going at all.

Spike didn't look back at the truck after he shut the door. He couldn't. Knowing Reese had a crush on him made him want to let out a jubilant whoop like a goddamn kid. He was more determined than ever to get back to her —with her brother in tow. She'd agreed to see him when they were safe, and even though the logistics of that were going to be tough, he wasn't going to let the opportunity pass.

"You ready?" Tiny asked when he approached.

"Yes."

"She okay?"

"Yup. Let's do this."

Tiny nodded and the men headed off through the trees toward their target. They had no idea what they'd find when they got there, but Spike hoped it would be Woody, Isabella, and Angelo—alive and unharmed.

CHAPTER SIX

"What the hell?" Tiny said as he and Spike lay under some bushes near the house.

Spike frowned. He'd been thinking the same thing. They'd expected to find armed guards, people milling around, a busy trap house. But instead, it seemed as if they were looking at an abandoned structure. As far as they could see, no one was there.

"Is it a trap?" Spike asked.

"No clue. But I'm thinking this will be our best chance to get in, see if Woody's there, and get the hell out," Tiny said.

The hair on the back of Spike's neck was standing straight up. Something wasn't right, but they didn't have the time or manpower to wait.

Moving quickly and efficiently, the two men went from the cover of the trees, to behind an old car, to the back of the house. There was no fence around the place, as the trees of the jungle served as a natural barrier. Tiny already had his lock-picking tool out and ready. The man never went anywhere without it.

"Ready?" he asked.

Spike nodded and his vision narrowed as he focused on the task at hand. Get in, take out any resistance, hopefully find Woody, get the hell out. Neither of the men had a weapon, but he hoped they'd find some in the house.

Moving as if they'd worked together their whole life, Tiny and Spike made their way to the back door. Tiny had the door open in seconds, and they quietly stepped down a hall.

The house was large. Large kitchen, which was empty. Open-concept living area, again deserted. There were cups and plates and some trash strewn about the space, indicating that someone had been there—several someones—fairly recently.

The two men continued to move through the house on silent feet. The first floor was empty, so they made their way up the stairs to the second floor. It only took five minutes to clear. They found several guns in one of the rooms, but with every door they opened without finding humans on the other side, Spike's worry increased. It was looking as if the address they'd found in Angelo's room was a dead end.

The last door they opened on the second floor was another bedroom—and it had a spiral staircase tucked into the corner, leading down. It was an odd place for stairs.

Even odder that they hadn't seen spiral stairs anywhere on the first floor, leading up to this room.

Spike looked at Tiny and gave him a nod, his heart rate speeding up. This was it. It had to be. There was no reason for a staircase to be here. It spiraled downward into the darkness, and Spike knew without a doubt that they were about to find something. Hopefully, it would be Woody, Isabella, and Angelo.

He held the gun he'd pilfered from one of the bedrooms tightly as he took point and slowly descended the stairs. As he went down, Spike heard voices. They were low, masculine, and he prayed he wasn't about to come face-to-face with an entire roomful of cartel members who would be more than happy to shoot trespassers.

When he and Tiny reached the bottom of the stairs, they immediately knew they were in an underground bunker or basement of some sort. There was just enough light to see their immediate surroundings. There was a small open space at the bottom of the stairs, with a hall that led to the right and left.

To the right, in the direction the light was coming from, the hallway led to a room they couldn't see, and they heard voices speaking in Spanish around a corner created by the entranceway. Spike assumed there was another way to get in and out of the basement around that corner.

In the hallway to the left, there were two doors. Tiny silently went to the first and put his ear against it.

He turned to Spike and gave him a thumb's up before he went to work on the lock. Spike wasn't sure what the gesture meant. Did it mean he hadn't heard anything, or that he had?

More tense than he'd been in a long while, and wishing he had on the bulletproof vest he'd worn while on Delta missions, Spike held his breath as Tiny popped the lock. He carefully opened the door, gesturing for Spike to precede him inside.

Spike heard a small noise the second he stepped over the threshold—and instinctively turned toward it and lifted an arm to protect his face.

Which was a good thing, because less than a second

later, someone struck him, hard. The room was dark. There were no windows to aid him as Spike fought whoever had attacked.

Tiny fumbled with his phone and clicked on the flashlight. The bright light pierced the dark, and Spike flinched as his eyes attempted to adjust even as he continued to protect himself.

"Delta," Tiny said in a low whisper. Then he repeated it. "Delta!"

And just like that, the person attacking Spike stilled.

When he caught sight of his former teammate, Spike breathed out a sigh of relief. "Woody," he said, his tone barely a whisper as he locked eyes with his friend.

They were both breathing hard from their brief hand-to-hand combat. Glancing around the space, Spike spotted Isabella in a corner of the room, out of harm's way. Woody had obviously planned to fight whoever came into the room, and he'd done a hell of a good job.

He studied his friend carefully. He had a black eye and a cut on his forehead, but otherwise he seemed to be moving without any trouble, which was a huge relief.

"Holy shit, is that you, Spike?" Woody asked, the disbelief easy to hear in his voice. "How the hell are you here?" Even as he spoke, he turned to Isabella and held out his arm. She stepped toward him without hesitation, settling against his side as his arm went around her shoulders.

"Bubba called," Spike told him. "Your sister decided to come to Colombia to find you when you didn't answer her calls. I thought it would be a good idea to make sure she didn't get herself into any trouble, so here I am. Woody, this is Tiny, he's a former SEAL who works with me in

New Mexico. Not Delta, but I figured he'd be better than nothing."

Special Ops teams had an ongoing friendly rivalry, and Spike knew Tiny wouldn't be offended by his words.

But Woody didn't seem to even hear that part. "*Reese* is here? Fuck! Shit! *Damn it.* The girl doesn't have any sense. Why the hell would she come down here?"

While Spike had some of the same feelings, now definitely wasn't the time to get into that. They needed to get the hell out of there.

"I'm assuming this is Isabella Hernandez? Where's Angelo? Is he here?" Tiny threw the questions at Woody in rapid succession.

"*Sí*, I am Isabella. And we are not sure where Angelo is."

"He was taken with you?" Tiny asked.

"Yes," Woody said. "They knocked me around a bit, then dragged us all to a car and hauled us off. No one said much, wouldn't answer our questions. And when we got here, they separated us."

Spike shared a look with Tiny. They needed to check the other room. They'd gotten lucky with this one, maybe they'd find the kid behind the second door.

"All right, here's the plan. There's an unknown number of men in a room at the other end of the hallway, but the staircase that leads up to the second floor is out of their sight line. You two head up and through the house. Go east through the woods. Reese is waiting with a truck about half a mile away. We'll check the other room for Angelo and be right on your heels."

"I'm not leaving without my brother," Isabella insisted.

Spike couldn't help but think of Reese. He shook his

head. Two women, both stubborn as hell and loyal as the day is long.

"You go. I'll make sure he gets out," Woody told Isabella.

"No!" she said, shaking her head. "We've been over this. He's all I have. I can't lose him!"

"And you won't. I said I'd get him out," Woody told her firmly. Then he sighed when Isabella straightened her spine, giving him a look. "Okay, but you stick right by my side. Got it?"

Isabella nodded immediately.

Spike would've grinned at the look of frustration on his friend's face, but they needed to get moving. He reached into the waistband of his pants and handed Woody one of the two guns he'd taken while clearing the bedrooms.

Woody palmed the weapon, nodding at him in thanks.

Tiny clicked off the light and they all paused to let their eyes adjust to the darkness once more. Several minutes went by while Tiny listened at the door. The conversation of the men didn't wane. They didn't seem to have any clue at the opposite end of the hall.

"All right, headed out. Don't make any noise whatsoever," Tiny said. His warning was more for Isabella's benefit than anyone else's.

Tiny slowly opened the door and motioned for the others to follow. They filed out and Spike made note that both Woody and Isabella seemed to be walking without any difficultly.

Tiny went to the second door and tried the knob.

To no one's surprise, it was locked. He made quick work of picking the lock to get inside and they entered cautiously.

There was no need for a flashlight...because there was a

small lamp in the room, along with a pallet on the floor. It was more than Woody and Isabella had been afforded in their prison.

When the man inside stood, Spike tensed. This was no boy. It was obviously Angelo, because Isabella went straight to him and hugged him hard, but he wasn't what Spike had expected. He was huge. Tall, muscular, sporting almost a full beard.

He and Isabella spoke in Spanish. Spike frowned. Though their conversation was whispered, it was obvious they were arguing about something.

"We need to go," Tiny said, quietly but firmly.

Angelo glanced at him, then back at his sister when she said something. The young man nodded. He looked completely scared, and Spike couldn't blame him. They'd been lucky as hell so far that no one had heard all their noise. The chance of all of them getting up the stairs, through the house, and back to the truck without being discovered was slim to none, but Spike would rather take his chances out in the jungle than inside this bunker or the house itself, where they could be trapped.

Tiny took point and led Isabella and Angelo up the stairs, followed closely by Woody and then Spike. With every light tap on the metal stairs, Spike expected one of the men around the corner to hear them and come running with guns drawn, but that didn't happen. They made it up the stairs, and down to the first floor, then tiptoed through the still eerily empty house toward the back door. They all paused and looked around carefully before slipping outside to the cover of the random car, then into the jungle.

Just when Spike thought they'd basically won the hostage lottery and gotten out unscathed, a shout rang out from a large truck that pulled up along the side of the house.

To his dismay, men piled out of the canvas-covered back. There had to be at least a dozen, and they all looked pissed way the hell off.

Shots rang out as their group of five ran deeper into the trees.

They'd been so close. *So damn close!* Spike honestly wasn't sure how they were going to outrun the men giving chase, who seemed a little too trigger happy for his peace of mind.

As he wove in and out of the trees and prayed none of the bullets flying through the air managed to find him or anyone else in the group, he had a moment to be thankful Reese wasn't with them. He was concerned about Isabella and the others, but not like he would've been if *Reese* was out here, trying to avoid being shot.

They weren't even attempting to be quiet anymore, there was no need, and instead ran as fast as they could through the trees to make it back to where Reese should be waiting with the truck. Spike prayed no one had spotted their getaway vehicle.

If they had...they were screwed.

* * *

Reese forced herself to stay calm. She was hunkered down in the jungle behind some trees and foliage about forty feet from the truck. She wished she had some bug spray, because she was getting eaten alive by the insects around her. They were probably putting out some sort of pheromone to their bloodsucking buddies that there was fresh meat available for feasting.

She was also sweating in places she hated to sweat, both from anxiety and the humid jungle. There was nothing remotely attractive about boob sweat. Or butt crack sweat. And Reese had a feeling when she eventually stood back up, she'd have wet spots on her clothes in very embarrassing places.

But no matter how uncomfortable she got, she refused to move from her hiding place.

Especially now.

She had no idea how long she'd been hiding when a large military-style truck rumbled down the path. She held her breath and prayed it would keep going, but of course it didn't. It stopped several yards from their stolen truck, still easily visible despite being parked in the woods off the rutted trail. Two men got out—one from each side of the cab—and a third lifted the canvas flap in the back to peer out.

From her vantage point, seeing the many pairs of eyes looking out of the back of the truck almost gave Reese a heart attack. If they all got out and started searching the area, she'd most definitely be found. She tried to make herself even smaller and cursed the extra pounds on her frame.

The two men from the cab approached the old piece-of-shit truck, which had run remarkably smoothly, and peered inside. They had a short conversation...

Then, to her amazement, they hurried back to their vehicle and climbed inside.

She breathed out a huge sigh of relief. That had been way too close.

But when the truck left, it did so in a rush—as if the driver somehow knew the old pickup was a sign that something was happening at the house he was obviously headed for.

Biting her lip, Reese debated what to do. She certainly couldn't exactly follow them. And she wouldn't break her promise to Gus by following where he and Tiny had disappeared into the jungle.

If the more than dozen men who'd just passed went to the house and caught Gus and Tiny inside, there would be nothing she could do but go back to Bogotá and try to find help. She could call Bubba or go to the US Embassy, but by the time anyone else got out here, it would probably be too late.

No. If she was going to do something to help, it wasn't going to be driving back to the city.

Moving slowly, and doing her best to listen over the beating of her heart in her ears, Reese headed back to the truck. She needed to be ready to leave at a moment's notice. Somehow she knew without a doubt that when Gus and Tiny returned—hopefully with her brother, Isabella, and Angelo in tow—she needed to be ready to go. Right that second.

She made it back to the truck without anyone leaping out from behind a tree yelling "gotcha!" It was ridiculous to think about the boogeyman jumping out of nowhere in the middle of the jungle, but she was so far outside her comfort zone right now, she was hardly rational.

The engine would make noise when she started it, but she needed to get the truck turned around and ready to get the hell out of there. With sweat pouring down her face and into her eyes, Reese grabbed the wires under the steering column and started the engine. It sounded way too loud to her ears, but she ignored it and put the truck in reverse. She backed out and pointed the nose of the truck back the way they'd come.

She was sitting there, trembling, worried, and wondering what to do next, when she saw movement to her right.

Her eyes widened when she saw Tiny running full tilt toward her. Followed closely by a woman, a man she didn't recognize, then Woody and Gus.

Relief hit her so hard, she sagged in her seat.

But the relief was short-lived, because Tiny was yelling at her to move over, to let him drive. Woody practically threw whom Reese assumed was Isabella into the front seat and then climbed into the bed of the truck with the unknown man.

Tiny was standing at the door on the driver's side and frantically gesturing for her to slide over.

"Get in!" Woody yelled from the back. "Let her drive!"

"I don't think—"

But whatever Tiny was going to say was cut short when more shouts sounded from the trees to their right. Then something pinged off the metal of the truck, making Reese flinch.

Gus slammed the passenger door behind him after he'd jumped inside next to Isabella and yelled, "Go, go go!"

Waiting a split second to make sure Tiny made it inside the bed of the truck, Reese slammed her foot down on the gas pedal and the truck lurched forward. The back tires spun, sending the truck careering drunkenly as the tires attempted to get traction, then they shot forward.

She spared a glance behind her and saw all three men in the back were ducked down low as three *other* men stood in the middle of the dirt road, shouting at her in

Spanish as they fired their weapons in an attempt to make her stop.

But she wasn't stopping. No freaking way.

Gus was holding onto the dashboard with one hand, half turned in the seat to stare out the back window. "Shit, they're comin' after us!" he yelled. "Go faster, Reese. Get us the hell out of here!"

Glancing back once more, she saw the same military truck barreling down the crappy trail. She didn't need Gus to tell her to put the pedal to the metal. Even though she was already going too fast for the road conditions, she pressed a little harder on the gas. Her eyes narrowed and she focused solely on the road ahead of her. She could do this.

Had pretty much *trained* for this exact moment.

There was a small opening in the back window of the truck, letting Gus talk to Woody and Tiny. "Pull over and let me drive!" Tiny yelled.

But Reese wasn't stopping. No way.

"She's good!" Woody yelled back.

"She's not trained for this!" Tiny protested.

"The hell she's not! She's got this. I fucking promise."

Her brother's faith in her felt good, and while Reese was fairly confident in her abilities, she hadn't ever been in a situation where her driving skills were a matter of life or death. The bullets those men were firing from the truck weren't blanks. If one of them got off a lucky shot and took out a tire, they were all fucked.

Isabella bent over almost in half, covering her head and praying under her breath.

"You're doing good, Reese," Gus said in an almost normal tone of voice.

Adrenaline coursed through her veins—and suddenly,

Reese felt like she had years ago, while participating in the Grand Prix race at her university. Though she felt the need to explain why her brother was confident she could get them away from the assholes chasing them. If for no other reason than to assure Gus.

"I was one of the very few women drivers in the annual go-cart race at my university," she said, loud enough to be heard over the noise of the wind whooshing through the cab. "There was a lot of trash talking from the male drivers. Purdue University takes their Grand Prix seriously. It's a huge deal. My engineering club decided to enter. Hold on!" she yelled suddenly.

Reese swerved around a huge rut in the road that would've sent them airborne if she'd hit it dead-on. She spared a glance behind her to make sure all three of the guys in the back were still there, sighing in relief when they were. Turning her attention back to the road, she continued her story.

"I was picked to be the driver for our club and in the end, placed third...much to the amazement of the other drivers. Our car wasn't the flashiest, wasn't the most expensive or even the fastest, but I was the best driver on that track." She wasn't bragging. Okay, that was a lie. She was bragging a little. The memory of how surprised everyone had been that a woman placed, especially one who wasn't a member of the popular fraternities and sororities that usually dominated the race, was a fond one. She liked doing things no one expected of her...and succeeding.

But this wasn't a go-cart, and she wasn't a college kid participating in a fun, harmless race.

Reese used everything she'd ever learned about cars and racing—and her determination not to let her brother get kidnapped again—to pull away from their pursuers.

She didn't care that they were being bounced around like pieces of popcorn in a microwave, all she cared about was getting away.

"In case I forget to tell you later, you're fucking amazing. We're almost back to the main road. Take a left," Gus said calmly.

It was a good thing he knew where they were, because Reese might be a good driver, but she had a shit sense of direction. She didn't remember which way she was supposed to go and probably would've gone right instead of left.

She made the turn, barely keeping the truck from sliding off the side of the road into a ditch, and floored it when they were once again on asphalt.

Seconds later, a loud whoop sounded from the bed of the truck, and Reese looked in the rearview mirror fearfully.

"They didn't manage the turn! They're in the ditch! Good job, Reesie!"

Reese hated that nickname. "I've told you a million times not to call me that!" she shouted back at her brother in irritation.

She heard him laugh uproariously.

Her heart was still pounding ten minutes later when they pulled onto the highway that would take them back to Bogotá. She felt jittery and a little weak, but figured it was the drop from the adrenaline rush she'd experienced.

"You're okay," Gus said from her right. "Take a deep breath. Good. Now another."

Having him there to talk her down was a relief. She concentrated on the cadence of his voice rather than reviewing what just happened in her mind. "Is Woody all right? Isabella, are you okay?" she asked.

"I'm okay," the woman replied softly.

Reese barely heard her over the rushing of the wind through the broken window behind their heads. She hated that the three guys were in the bed of the truck, because it was anything but safe, but there wasn't much choice since the pickup didn't have a backseat.

"For the record...anytime you want to drive, I have no problem with that. I don't think anyone could've gotten us out of there in one piece like you did," Gus told her.

His praise felt good. Really good. She'd wanted to hold her own, and show this man that she wasn't helpless. Until now, she'd been a liability, and they all knew it. She might not know how to shoot, or be in shape enough to run a mile, but she'd been able to get them away from the bad guys because of her experience. She figured that tipped the scales in her favor, at least a little bit.

"Where are we going?" she asked, forcing herself to concentrate on what was to come. She might've gotten them away from the cartel guys, but there was no telling what would happen now.

Instead of answering, Gus turned to the woman sitting between them. "Isabella, you and your brother have a choice. Do you want to come with us? Or stay?"

She looked at him. "I want to stay with Woody."

Gus nodded, then turned to yell out the back window. "Woody?"

"Yeah?"

"Are Isabella and her brother staying with you?"

"Hell yes!"

"Spike, we have an issue," Tiny called out.

"What?"

"Woody was hit."

Reese's blood ran cold, and she instinctively took her

foot off the gas at the same time Isabella gasped and turned, trying to look out the back window.

"I'm fine!" Woody called out. "I told him not to say anything!"

"How bad?" Gus yelled.

"Not great," Tiny said. At the same time Woody yelled, "A scratch!"

"Head toward the airport," Gus told Reese firmly.

Reese took her eyes off the road long enough to shoot him a quizzical look. "Shouldn't we go to a hospital?"

"I'd rather get the hell out of here. We have no idea what kind of connections those guys have, and if they're with the cartel, I'm guessing it's a lot. Going to a hospital will bring too much attention to us. There's no way we could hide an American with a gunshot wound."

"But Tiny said he wasn't good," Reese protested.

"Woody's a tough son of a bitch. And Tiny didn't say he was critical. We'll get him help as soon as we can."

Reese wanted to keep protesting, but she didn't exactly want to go through another shootout. Or be on any drug cartel's radar.

"Anything you're going to regret leaving behind with your luggage?" Gus asked. "We can't exactly go back to the hotel to get it."

Reese thought about it for a moment, then shook her head. "No."

"Good."

"But I don't have my passport. It's in the little safe in the hotel room," she said with a frown.

"Tex'll take care of it."

"Seriously? He can do that?" Reese asked.

"The man can do just about anything," Gus said without a hint of concern in his voice.

"What about Woody? And Isabella and Angelo? I'm guessing they don't have their passports either. Or you and Tiny, for that matter."

"We have ours," Gus told her. "I've got a secret pocket sewn into the leg of my pants. As does Tiny. We've learned it's better to be prepared for anything."

"Oh. I wish I'd thought about something like that," Reese said a little wistfully.

"It's not an issue." Then he turned to Isabella. "I'm sorry, but it's too dangerous to go back to your apartment."

"I know," she said sadly. Then shrugged. "But stuff doesn't matter. My brother and I are safe, that's the most important thing."

Gus nodded in agreement.

Reese's mind was going a million miles an hour. She wasn't sure how they were all going to get out of the country without passports, but if Gus said his friend would take care of it, she'd believe him. She was just so damn relieved that they'd been able to find Woody, and Isabella and her brother, and that they would hopefully be getting home soon.

As it turned out, they made one stop on the way to the airport, and that was so Tiny could run inside a touristy tchotchke shop to purchase a shirt for Woody that wasn't covered in blood.

Reese took the opportunity to hug her brother hard. She never wanted to let go, and she got a little emotional when she was finally able to touch him and see for herself that he was all right. The bullet wasn't imbedded in his shoulder, thank goodness, but he was still bleeding. Like the badass he was, however, Woody insisted he'd be all right until they could get to the US.

When they all got back into the truck, Tiny insisted on

driving, which left Gus in the back with Angelo and Woody.

At the airport, Tiny went to an airline counter to speak to a representative. Reese was fully expecting them to be kicked out since they had no tickets, no luggage, and four of them had no passports.

To her utter shock, they were quickly escorted through security to a gate where a plane was already parked and half filled with passengers. They were seated in two rows toward the back of the plane, with Reese in a window seat next to Gus, and Tiny next to him on the aisle. Her brother, Isabella, and Angelo were in the row in front of them.

The teenager had been quiet, not saying much, although he and Isabella had a long conversation in Spanish before going through security. Reese had no idea what it was about, as she didn't speak Spanish, but it seemed to be pretty intense. Both Isabella and her brother looked scared. Reese figured maybe they were worried about being stopped by airport security.

Woody had looked concerned about them both, but he was also as white as a sheet, so he probably didn't feel up to pressing Isabella for details.

"I can't believe we walked into the airport twenty minutes ago and now we're on a flight to Dallas," she said.

"Told you Tex was good."

"You weren't wrong. Although it's a good thing we're not sitting next to strangers because I have to smell awful."

To her surprise, Gus leaned over, nuzzling the back of her ear with his nose and causing a cascade of tingles throughout her body. He sniffed long and loud before sitting back and smiling. "Nope, you smell fine."

Reese chuckled. "Right, so says the man who probably smells as bad as me. For the record...I'm not a fan of hot-as-hell jungles with bugs the size of my head who like to suck blood."

"Noted," he told her with a small grin. Then his hand rose and he rubbed his thumb over an itchy spot on her neck. "You do have a few bites. I'm sorry we took so long."

She rolled her eyes. "I wasn't passive-aggressively bitching about the time it took you to infiltrate a house, free not only my brother and his girlfriend, but also her huge brother who looks like he could be thirty instead of eighteen, *and* get out of there in one piece."

"Good to know," he said. "And *you* should know..." He started, but didn't finish his thought.

"Yeah?"

Gus sighed. "The tickets Tex bought are all to Santa Fe."

Reese blinked.

"I guess he assumed you would all be coming to The Refuge. And for the record, I think it's a good idea. Woody needs some medical attention, and there's no place in the world better for healing than our mountains. But if you really want to go back to Kansas City, I'll see about switching your ticket when we get to Dallas."

Reese wasn't sure what to say. The part of her who'd had a crush on Gus forever was jumping up and down with excitement, but the practical part was screaming that it was a bad idea to spend more time with this man who, with every passing minute, she was falling for harder and harder.

"What's Woody doing?" she asked.

"Tiny spoke with him before we boarded, and he has

no problem going to New Mexico. It's probably a good idea for him to lay low for a while, just in case."

"Wait—what? You think the cartel will come after him?"

"I don't know."

"Shit."

"He'll be safe at The Refuge. As will Isabella and her brother. The cartel doesn't know anything about Tiny or me, so there will be no way for them to trace anyone to us. They probably *do* know where Woody lives, and if they decide to come after him, that'll be the first place they look," Gus told her.

Reese glanced out the window, deep in thought as the plane headed toward the runway. She felt Gus's hand on her arm and turned to face him once more.

"I swear you'll all be safe there. And I *did* say that I wanted to see where things between us could go when we got back to the States. The way I see it, you can make sure your brother heals properly, he can have some time with Isabella to figure out what their next steps will be, and you and I can get to know each other better."

"Is there even room for all of us? From what I've read online, you guys are always booked up," she said, stalling as she tried to figure out what she should do.

"You been reading up on us?"

Reese felt her cheeks get hot, and she shrugged. "Well, I told you I'd visited the website. Any self-respecting girl with a crush and mild stalker tendencies would do the same thing." She did her best to make light of her sponta-neous admission, when inside, she was freaking out more than a little bit.

Tiny joined the conversation and said, "Your brother, Isabella, and Angelo can take my cabin. It's got two rooms.

I'm sure I can room with one of the others for a while, they won't mind."

"And I've got two rooms too," Gus said before Reese could ask her next question. "You can stay with me."

She narrowed her eyes mock suspiciously.

He chuckled, but then got serious. "You're safe with me," he promised.

"I know," she said without thought. And she did. If she'd learned anything over the last...day? Jeez, had it really been just hours since he and Tiny had knocked on her hotel door?

As if he had the same thought, Gus asked, "How's your tummy holding up? We'll ask the flight attendant for some extra water when she comes around. You have to still be dehydrated after...you know...and having your blood sucked out in the jungle."

Lord, thank goodness he hadn't said the word diarrhea. She was embarrassed enough as it was. "You need some too."

"Hell, we all need a long drink and a good meal," Tiny said with a small smile on his face. His eyes were closed and his head was resting against the back of his seat, but it was a good reminder that she and Gus weren't exactly alone and had no privacy.

The pilot came on and announced that they were about to take off. Minutes later, as the plane rose in the air, Reese let out a long, relieved sigh. She was suddenly exhausted. The day was finally taking a toll on her and it was all she could do to keep her eyes open. Her muscles were sore from being clenched in terror and she did feel a little off after not eating for basically two days, then running around like she was some sort of GI Jane.

"Sleep," Gus ordered as he put an arm around her shoulders and pulled her against him.

Reese went gladly. She shifted in her seat to try to get a little more comfortable, and Gus pulled back just long enough to raise the armrest between them before settling her against him once more.

She sighed and closed her eyes.

"Think about it. I promise you'll love The Refuge. Alaska and Henley will be thrilled to meet you. And you'll love Melba and Scarlet Pimpernickel and all the other animals."

Reese smiled. She'd seen pictures of the cow and calf on the website...and she felt a little tendril of excitement run through her. "If Woody goes, I will too," she mumbled sleepily.

Gus's arm tightened around her for a moment before relaxing. "Good."

There were logistics Reese needed to straighten out. So many. Like letting her boss know what was going on, buying clothes, paying her bills remotely, replacing her credit cards and cell phone, getting a new ID, and probably a hundred other things...but for now, she was done. Mentally and physically.

She let herself relax. She was safe, her brother was safe...and she was in the arms of the man she'd had a crush on forever, who she'd honestly never expected to see again. She'd worry about the future later.

CHAPTER SEVEN

"Didn't you just leave, like, yesterday?" Brick asked when Spike entered the lodge at The Refuge with Tiny, Woody, Isabella, Angelo, and Reese.

"And why am I not surprised that you returned with four extra people?" Stone said with a laugh.

Spike would've felt bad, but he knew his friends were joking. The first thing Brick had done when he saw them enter was go to the kitchen and ask Luna and Robert to make a bunch of extra food for breakfast.

They'd landed in Dallas for their layover with no issues, but then had to deal with some red tape in order for Isabella and Angelo to enter the country. But Tex came through again, and after some negotiating and a few emails back and forth, they were granted asylum and allowed to continue to their next flight to Santa Fe.

The sun had just come up, and even though Spike was exhausted, he was also wired. Thrilled that Reese and her brother had agreed to come to The Refuge. Isabella and Reese had wanted Woody to promise he'd go to the hospital the second they reached Santa Fe, but like Spike expected, he'd refused, saying a gunshot wound would cause more questions than he was comfortable answering. He didn't want to do anything that might bring attention to himself, or to Isabella and her brother.

So Spike and Tiny had done their best to clean and patch him up at the airport in Dallas. He'd been lucky. While his arm would be damn sore for a while, the bullet had gone straight through and hadn't hit any vital blood vessels or arteries. Woody had always been a tough son of a bitch, and this proved that little had changed since they'd left the teams.

And his sister was equally tough. She was the reason they were all standing here now, in fact. If it hadn't been for her having the truck ready to go, and her incredible driving ability, they'd all either be dead or back in that bunker, being held hostage.

They were escorted to one of the largest conference rooms in the lodge, and Reese and Isabella were now on the other side of the room being fussed over by Alaska and Henley. They were sitting at a table, and Jasna, Henley's daughter, was going back and forth from the kitchen, bringing water, plates and silverware, and some fresh-squeezed orange juice. Robert and Luna would soon bring in breakfast, so everyone could eat before they headed to their cabins for some much-needed down time.

Angelo was sitting to the side of the room by himself, with his arms crossed, looking uncertain. Spike hated not being able to communicate with the kid—because he had a lot of questions. Questions only Angelo could answer. Nothing about what they'd all just been through made much sense, and Spike had a feeling Angelo would be able to fill in a lot of the holes.

"Want to give us a rundown of what happened?" Brick

asked once the women were occupied. It wasn't that they were purposely trying to talk without the others overhearing, but they were used to keeping what they did on the down-low. Not to mention, they didn't want to upset Isabella and Reese by rehashing the close call they'd had.

"Woody? You want to start?" Spike asked.

His former teammate nodded. "As you know by now, I went down to Colombia because Bella called me in a panic. She said she thought the apartment was being watched, and she was scared, both for herself and Angelo. She'd been hearing rumors at work that certain people weren't happy about her assignments with the government. She feared either being kidnapped herself, or someone using her brother to force her to give up information about some of the clients she'd translated for in the past." He ran a hand through his hair in agitation. "I'd basically do anything for her. I've loved her forever, but we both made excuse after excuse as to why we wouldn't work. That didn't keep us from calling and communicating on a regular basis.

"Anyway, I told Reesie where I was going and caught the next flight out. I went straight to Isabella's apartment. I didn't see people lurking around, didn't get the sense that anyone was watching. I stupidly figured she was overreacting. But clearly my instincts have dulled since leaving the military." He shook his head. "I had one perfect day and night with Bella before the shit hit the fan."

Woody sighed. "The men who took us...they basically just walked right into the apartment. They knocked me around a little bit, but it wasn't necessary. I wouldn't have risked Isabella's safety by doing anything stupid. We did what they asked without protest. They took all three of us to that house where you found us. Locked Bella and me in one room, and put Angelo in the other."

"What did they want you for?" Pipe asked.

"I have no idea," Woody said with a shake of his head. "That's the weirdest part. They didn't demand anything."

"We found drugs in Angelo's room," Spike said quietly. "A *lot*. It's how we found you guys. There was an address with the drugs."

Woody's eyes widened. "*What?* No. Angelo isn't into that. Isabella's warned him for years about staying away from the cartel recruiters."

"I'm just telling you what we found," Spike told him.

"Fuck!" Woody said, a dark scowl on his face.

"Woody?"

They all turned and saw Isabella standing near them, looking extremely nervous. Their plan to keep her out of the conversation had obviously failed.

"It's okay," Woody assured her without hesitation, grabbing her hand.

"I talked to Angelo at the airport in Bogotá. About what happened. He...he said he was recruited by the cartel," she confirmed, her voice shaking. "He swears he told them that he was not interested—until they threatened me. He was forced to courier drugs, but he did not do so, was trying to figure out a way to stop. He said he hid the drugs in our apartment instead of delivering them to the person he was supposed to...and that is why the cartel came to the apartment and took us."

Everyone frowned. Spike resisted glaring over at the young man sitting against the wall. He understood being between a rock and a hard place...but his actions had ultimately gotten his sister and Woody kidnapped. And the outcome could've been so much worse.

"What happened when you got to that house?" Tiny asked Woody.

Woody sighed. "Not much. The only time we saw anyone was when they opened the door to bring us food and water...which wasn't very often. I was still trying to figure out what I should do when you two showed up," he finished, gesturing to Spike and Tiny.

"That doesn't make much sense," Owl said. "When Stone and I were taken captive, we were immediately interrogated and tortured. I mean, it wasn't as if they really wanted any information, they just wanted to make us suffer. Get it on film so they could brag that they'd captured two American helicopter pilots."

Spike hating hearing about Owl and Stone's captivity. They'd gone through hell after their chopper was shot down while on a mission. They'd been extremely lucky to be rescued, and they both knew it. Their story had been plastered all over the news channels. The entire nation had seen clips of them being tortured by their enemy.

"That's what I thought," Woody said. "I kept waiting for them to come in, separate Bella and I...and frankly, kill me. I would've been just another casualty of the war on drugs. But instead, they did nothing. Just left us alone."

"Maybe they were using you guys to threaten Angelo some more. Using you as leverage."

Woody sighed. "That does seem likely."

"Does anyone else think our escape seemed a little too easy?" Tiny asked.

Spike had a feeling if Reese heard that question, she'd strongly disagree, but he'd been thinking the same thing. Why was the house empty? And they'd been able to get all three captives out of that bunker without anyone noticing. They'd been as quiet as possible, but had they been so quiet that *none* of the men around the corner had heard them? He didn't think so. If it hadn't been for that truck full of men, they would've gotten off without anyone noticing...which seemed impossible.

"It's like they *let* us go," Woody agreed.

"Why would they do that when they made the effort to pick you up and lock you away in the first place?" Tonka asked.

"I don't know that either," Woody said with a frown.

"I've been thinking the same thing as Tiny," Spike said. "Which was another reason I invited you all to stay here for a while. If the cartel had some nefarious reason to let you go without too much trouble, they won't be able to track you here."

"Do we think having Angelo here is going to be an issue?" Tiny asked.

"No!" It was Isabella who answered. "He knows what he did was wrong. And he was relieved to be rescued. He's glad to be away from all of those people. There is no way he would do anything that might cause me harm yet again."

"I don't like the idea of bringing trouble to your doorstep," Woody said.

Spike stared at his friend. "If you thought I was just going to drop you off back in Kansas City without a second thought, you don't know me as well as I thought you did."

"It's just that, this place...hell, Spike, it's called The *Refuge*. How much of a fucking refuge is it gonna be if drug cartel members come looking for us?" Woody asked.

"If something happens, it won't be the first time trouble has found us here, and it probably won't be the last," Brick said firmly. He proceeded to give Woody a brief rundown of Alaska's recent troubles, then about what happened to Jasna. He continued by saying, "And while the people who come here are looking for tranquility, none of them are naïve. They know bad things happen to good people no matter where they might be. They know that better than the average person, in fact. We're seeing more and more guests who have been victims of random violence. Or an incident at their workplace where someone went off the deep end.

"While this *is* a refuge, it's also a place where almost everyone who comes here is ready and willing to do what's necessary to keep others safe. We've seen it firsthand. Besides, this place is much more defendable than an apartment in...Kansas City, was it?"

Woody nodded.

"Right. We're in the middle of nowhere, we've put up more cameras, and we know this land like the back of our hands. If someone does manage to sneak up on us, they'll find out we aren't a bunch of hicks hiding out in the backwoods. But all that is a moot point, because like Spike said, the people who kidnapped you don't know about this place. You can stay here as long as you want, for free."

"Oh, hell no, I'm paying," Woody said.

"No, you aren't," Pipe argued. "You're a member of Spike's team, and teammates stay for free. As do the people they're here with. Meaning Isabella, Angelo, *and* Reese."

"I can't...that's...*shit*, Spike. Tell them that's just not right."

But Spike simply smiled. "Welcome to The Refuge, brother."

Everyone slapped Woody on the back as they wandered back to what they were doing before the group had arrived. Tiny said he was going to make sure his cabin was ready for Woody, Isabella, and Angelo, and to pack to stay with Pipe. Brick headed over to Alaska, still sitting with the other women. Isabella went over to tell Angelo what was going on, Tonka left to go to the barn, and Pipe went to check on Robert and help bring food into the room. Lastly, Owl and Stone left to round up the guests who were going on a hike in half an hour.

That left Spike and Woody.

"How are you really feeling? That arm has to hurt like hell," Spike said.

"It's fine. We need to talk about something else right now," Woody said, sounding serious.

"What? Is anything wrong?"

"No. Maybe...I've seen how my sister looks at you," he said bluntly. "And don't think I didn't notice *your* interest when I told stories about Reesie in the past."

Spike blinked in surprise. "I'm not sure what you want me to say here," he admitted.

"I want you to tell me you're going to treat her right. Be the man she deserves. She's a damn good woman, Spike. Smart, hardworking, loyal. Hell, the second I didn't contact her when I said I would, she risked everything to come to fucking Colombia to find me. She could've called Bubba or any of my other friends, but she probably didn't even think about doing that. She did what she felt was right. You couldn't possibly do any better than her."

"I've only been around her for twenty-four hours or so," he reminded him.

"Yeah, and you about lost your mind when we were being shot at and you thought she was going to get hurt. You practically shoved me out of the way to get to the cab of that truck so you could be with her. You stayed right by her side at the airport, made sure you got the seat next to her on the plane.

"Don't bullshit me, Spike—you like her. And I'm telling you I'm completely all right with that. If you were to become my brother for real, I'd be fucking thrilled. I'm *also* telling you that you're not good enough for her. But I'd say that about literally anyone she ended up with. So all I'm really saying is...don't hurt her. If you do, I'm gonna be pissed."

"I'm not going to hurt her," Spike said between clenched teeth.

Woody's voice gentled. "She hasn't had a lot of luck with dating. And I can't believe I'm standing here talking about my sister's love life, but I adore her enough to make sure you know that men have treated her like shit because she doesn't fit into society's mold of what a woman should look like. And it infuriates me."

"There's nothing fucking wrong with the way she looks," Spike growled.

Woody stared at him for a long moment. Then he smiled. "I'm gonna be the best uncle ever."

"What?" Spike blurted in confusion. One second his friend was acting all tough and protective over his sister, and the next he was...*What?* Spike wasn't sure.

"She'll be good for you," Woody said. "She'll keep you on your toes. And it helps that Los Alamos has that lab here. She'll need something to keep her mind stimulated. And before you tell me that it's a tough job market and there's no guarantee she'll get hired here...you're wrong. They'd jump at the chance to bring her on board. She's that good at what she does."

Spike's mind was spinning. "So you're...what? Already marrying us off? And with that uncle comment, expecting us to have kids? I thought you'd wanna smash my face, thinking about me having sex with your sister."

Woody shrugged with a grin. "I like confounding people. Reese isn't a kid, man. If she was sixteen, I'd be holding a shotgun to your balls, warning you not to touch her. But she's not. And she'll be an awesome mom. And wife. And I know you, Spike. You're one of my best friends, even if we've barely spoken in the last five years. She can't do better than you."

"Again, I've only been around her for a *day*, Woody. I don't think you should be imagining nephews and nieces just yet."

Woody got serious. "As I said when I started this conversation, I've seen the way she looks at you, and how you look at *her*. I spent way too much time fucking around when it came to Isabella, and I could've lost her. So I'm telling you—don't wait. Don't second-guess things. When you know, you know.

"And look, all I'm doing is giving you permission. If things don't work out, they don't work out...but don't hold back because she's my sister, or because you think relation-ships are supposed to work a certain way. She'll treat you like gold. You'll never have a woman love you so fiercely."

Longing hit Spike hard. He'd dated a fair number of women, but he'd never felt an instant connection like he did with Reese. "Noted," he told Woody with a small nod.

"Good. Now, my arm hurts like a son of a bitch, I'm starving, and I'm exhausted beyond belief. Hell, I don't even know what time it is, since I lost my damn watch. I'm gonna go sit and eat breakfast with Isabella and my sister."

Spike blinked, then smiled as he reached into his pocket. He'd forgotten all about the watch Reese had found in Isabella's apartment. With everything that had happened since then, it completely slipped his mind. He pulled out the watch and held it out to his friend. "You mean *this* watch?"

Spike grinned at the incredulous look that crossed Woody's face. "What the hell? Where'd you find that?"

"At Isabella's place."

"I didn't think I'd ever see it again. It was a gift from my dad. Thanks, man."

"Don't thank me. Reese found it. And you putting it back on to cover that creepy white patch on your wrist is thanks enough," Spike joked.

"Whatever." Woody got serious then, speaking low again. "I heard what you said about the drugs in Angelo's room, Spike. I'm not ignoring it. And I know what Isabella said, about her brother being forced...but I'm not thrilled that his actions got us all kidnapped. We had a lucky escape—and I'm going to make sure all his ties to those assholes are well and truly cut. After we get some rest, I'll talk to the kid and see if I can break through that hard outer shell of his, ask what the hell he was thinking getting involved with the cartel in the first place, despite their threats."

Woody yawned deeply, clearly exhausted. "I'm also gonna take your friend up on his generous offer to let us stay in his cabin. But take note," he added, waving a finger as he stood. "We aren't going to sit around on our asses. Put us to work. I'm serious. If we're going to stay here until things calm down and we're sure no cartel members are gonna show up at my place in Kansas City, then I need to contribute. Isabella will feel the same way."

"There's always stuff to do around here," Spike assured him.

Woody gave him a look. "Thank you," he said softly. "Seriously. If anything had happened to Isabella or Reesie...I'm not sure I ever would've forgiven myself."

Spike stood and took a step forward, briefly hugging his friend. He'd learned since his time in the Army that showing emotion wasn't such a bad thing.

Woody hugged him back with his good arm, then turned and headed for the table across the room. As soon as he sat, Reese stood and came over to Spike. Her brow was furrowed and she looked extremely concerned about something.

"What's wrong?" he asked immediately.

"That was my question for you. Is Woody all right? What's going on?"

"He's fine, and nothing's going on. He's just grateful for a place to stay for a while until things calm down."

"Oh...are you sure?"

"I'm sure," he said firmly. As Reese's shoulders relaxed, he noticed how tired she looked, as if a strong breeze could knock her over. "I've got food at my cabin," he blurted.

She frowned. "Okaaaay?"

Spike mentally slapped his forehead. "What I mean is, we could go there now, you could shower while I make something to eat, then you could get some shut-eye."

She stared at him for a long moment. "I'm tired," she admitted. "But there're a million things I need to do."

"They can wait," Spike said firmly.

"You don't even know what they are," she protested.

"Shopping, phone calls, work, credit cards..." he guessed. "They can all wait. I've got shampoo and soap, T-shirts and sweats you can wear to bed. I can talk to Alaska and Henley about taking you shopping—trust me, they'll love that—and you told me on the plane that your boss wasn't expecting you back for another few days. You can take a few hours to nap, Reese."

"Well, when you put it that way," she said with a small smile, "I wouldn't mind a break from everyone. Not that I don't love my brother, and I'm enjoying getting to know Isabella and the others, but I'm used to spending a lot of time by myself and could use some alone time to recharge."

Taking the hint, Spike said, "I'll leave you to it once I let you into my cabin."

"Oh! I didn't mean you. You can stay. I mean, that is...if you want. Shoot! I'm not trying to kick you out of your own house. I'm guessing you're just as tired as me. You said you didn't get much sleep on the plane, and I was using you as a pillow on both flights. And, I have to admit, I'm not much of a cook. You might be risking me burning your cabin down if you leave me to my own devises in your kitchen."

Spike grinned. "Yeah? It's a good thing that I'm a decent cook then, isn't it?"

"Uh-huh," she said with a shy smile.

"You want to say goodbye to your brother before we head out?" he asked.

"Will Robert be upset if I don't stay?" she asked, her brow wrinkling in concern.

Warmth settled in Spike's belly. He loved how considerate she was. He'd been around more than his fair share of selfish people in his life, and they'd always turned his stomach with how oblivious they were to other people's feelings. "Not at all. You'll have plenty of chances to eat his food and tell him how delicious it is."

Without another word, Reese turned and headed back

to the table. Spike followed along behind her. She waved at everyone. "I apologize for bugging out on you guys, but I'm dead on my feet. Spike had an offer I couldn't refuse... a hot shower, food I don't have to make, and a bed."

Alaska's brow shot up, and Henley chuckled.

Reese blushed bright red. "Er...I don't think that came out right."

"Go!" Alaska said with a huge smile. "We'll catch up later."

"Do you think you could point me in the direction of some good shops where Isabella and I can get some clothes and stuff, after I wake up?" Reese asked.

"Of course," Henley said with a smile. "I'd love to show you around and take you to all the best places in town."

"And there's a British shop that sells the most delicious chocolates," Alaska piped in.

Reese smiled. "Awesome."

"Thank you so much," Isabella said softly from next to Henley.

"Just come back up to the lodge later, whenever you're ready. I'll probably be at the front desk doing some admin stuff," Alaska told her.

"I will, thanks."

"It's good to have you here," Henley added. "You and Isabella and Angelo."

"Thanks. It's good to be here. I'll talk to you guys later. Woody, if your arm starts hurting, let someone take you to an emergency clinic in town. If you won't go to the hospital, you should at least see a doctor to get it checked out."

"Yes, Mom," Woody told her with a roll of his eyes.

"And speaking of Mom, you should probably call her and Dad and let them know where we are," Reese told him. "I haven't had my phone for five days, so I don't know if they've called. But they have no idea you even went on a spontaneous trip to South America—and they *definitely* don't know that I followed you down there. You'll need to do some fancy talking to explain how the hell Isabella and her brother ended up here in the States."

"Thanks for not telling them," Woody said. "They would've been so worried."

"As if I wasn't?" Reese asked with a roll of her eyes.

"You're the best sister anyone could ask for," Woody said with a grin.

"I know I am," she responded.

They smiled at each other.

"I'll make things right with Mom and Dad," Woody assured her.

"And I will make sure he goes to the doctor," Isabella said.

Reese grinned at her. "Good. He can be stubborn."

Isabella looked at Woody and smiled at him lovingly. "I know."

"Come on, you're about to crash," Spike said, putting a hand on Reese's arm to steady her. He had a feeling she hadn't even realized she was swaying on her feet.

She waved again at the table in general, then turned and said, "*Hasta luego*, Angelo."

The teenager just looked up briefly.

As they walked toward the door, Reese said, "I know that you guys found drugs in his room, and it's likely that they were all kidnapped *because of* those drugs, but I still feel kind of bad for him. I'm glad he's away from all of that, and safe, but it has to suck to not understand what everyone around you is saying. I know because it's how I felt when I was in Colombia."

There she went, being considerate again.

"Yeah," Spike said, not sure her concern wasn't misplaced, but not wanting to talk about the kid right now. He wasn't immediately willing to just believe Angelo's version of his involvement with the cartel, and would stay on his toes around the kid, but Reese was probably right about not understanding English. It would be hard for anyone new to the States.

As he walked with Reese toward his cabin, he pointed out different parts of The Refuge. The guest cabins, the trail that led to Table Rock, where the other owner cabins were located, the barn. He quickly opened his door when they got to his place, and he studied her reaction as she entered. His place wasn't huge—none of the owner cabins were—but he'd made it his home. He had landscape paintings on the walls, blankets on the back of the couch and the easy chair, a flat-screen TV and, of course, lots of books.

He'd always been a reader, and while he'd switched to ebooks due to ease and his lack of space, he still loved the feel of an actual book in his hand.

Spike held his breath as he waited to see what Reese thought of his home.

"It's cozy," she told him with a smile.

Spike winced. "Cozy-good, or cozy meaning not enough space and you're being polite?"

She chuckled. "Cozy-good," she reassured him. "While I'm not sure I'd ever want to live in one of those tiny houses, I also don't need or want a ten thousand square foot home."

"You didn't even look twice at the kitchen," he observed.

"I told you that I can't cook. I mean, it looks nice, but

I'm more impressed by your bookshelf than your stainless-steel appliances."

God, could this woman get any better? "Let me show you where you can shower and sleep," he said in a low voice, gesturing toward the hallway off the main living area.

He could've put her in the guest room, which had a small bathroom next door, but without hesitation he brought her straight to his modest master suite instead. When he entered, he couldn't help but look over at the bed. The covers were mussed, as he hadn't made the bed before flying to Kansas City. Now all he could picture was Reese lying there, her blonde hair on his pillow, a smile on her face as she used a finger to beckon him closer.

His fingers itched to trace every inch of her body, find out what made her moan and squirm, and which places she liked to be touched best.

Forcing his attention away from his bed, and cutting off his inappropriate, lustful thoughts, Spike headed to his closet. He didn't have a dresser, had instead built shelves and a few drawers on one side of his walk-in closet. All his T-shirts and jeans were stacked neatly on the shelves, with his socks and underwear in the drawers.

Without conscious thought, he began mentally reorganizing the space to accommodate Reese's clothes.

Shit, he was doing it again—picturing her permanently in his space when it was completely premature.

He grabbed a navy-blue T-shirt and a pair of gray sweats and exited the closet. Reese was standing where he'd left her, looking around with interest. He wondered what she was thinking, but decided it was better he didn't know.

"They'll be big, but Alaska and Henley will get you

sorted later. I'll wash the clothes you've got on while you're sleeping."

"You don't have to do that. I can do it when I get up."

Spike shook his head. "It's not a big deal, hon. I'll throw your stuff in with mine." The endearment popped out without effort, and he waited for her to call him on it. But she merely smiled.

"Okay. Thanks."

"You're welcome. Now, what do you want to eat before you crash? Eggs? Pancakes? Hamburgers?"

"For breakfast?" she asked with a small laugh.

"I think our internal clocks are messed up enough at the moment that it doesn't matter what we eat. Whatever sounds good, I'll make."

"In that case...maybe pancakes and a salad? I'm craving the carbs, but I always try to balance what I'm eating with some veggies or fruit of some sort," she said a little self-consciously.

"Sounds perfect. Take your time, there's plenty of hot water."

She nodded, and Spike forced himself to hand the clothes to her and leave the room, when he *really* wanted to take her in his arms and hold her like he'd done on the plane.

"One day, man," he muttered as he returned to the kitchen. He had to keep reminding himself to take it easy. But the more time he spent with her, the more he *wanted* to spend. That was unfamiliar territory. He'd enjoyed spending time with previous girlfriends well enough...but he'd never felt this desperate *need* to be with them every second. Reese was completely different.

Taking a deep breath, he headed for his fridge. He knew he had everything necessary to make her what she wanted, because he hadn't been gone that long and he'd been to the store right before he left for Kansas City.

For the first time ever, Spike had a guest in his cabin that would be spending the night. He heard the water turn on, and it made him smile. It was nice not to be alone. Even better because it was Reese there with him.

CHAPTER EIGHT

Reese lay in Gus's bed and stared up at the ceiling. The shower felt wonderful, but she liked smelling like him when she was done even better. She'd used his shampoo and soap, which were slightly scented like men's cologne. She didn't mind in the least. Then he'd fed her a stack of pancakes, and she would've been embarrassed by how fast she scarfed them if he hadn't eaten just as quickly. Even the salad seemed to taste better than anything she'd ever made for herself.

After they were done eating, she'd tried to do the dishes, but he'd pushed her down the hall back to his bedroom and ordered her to sleep. It was cute how embarrassed he'd gotten when he realized he hadn't changed his sheets. He'd started to do just that, but Reese stopped him, saying she was so tired she didn't mind.

In reality, she wanted to be surrounded by his scent.

He'd reluctantly agreed and left her in his room, closing the door almost all the way, but leaving it open a crack so he could hear her if she needed anything. It was extremely sweet, and if she hadn't been crushing hard on the man already, she certainly would be now.

Turning onto her side, Reese inhaled deeply. His pillow smelled most like him, and she closed her eyes and felt herself relaxing even more. She usually didn't sleep well away from home. She'd tossed and turned in the motel in Bogotá, jerking at every unfamiliar sound. But with Gus's scent in her nose, she instinctively knew she was safe.

If someone had told her a week ago that she'd be here now, sleeping in the bed of the man she had a huge crush on, she would've rolled her eyes and told them to get real. But here she was. Gus had told her that he wanted to explore what was happening between them, but she couldn't help wondering if his feelings toward her were situational. She was his teammate's sister, and they had known each other for quite a while. It was possible that he was simply feeling protective and worried because of the situation, and now that they were back in the States and she was safe, he'd realize he wasn't attracted to her in *that way* after all.

Deciding that right now, when her belly was full and she was two seconds away from crashing, wasn't the time to think about Gus's thoughts about her, Reese did her best to quiet her mind and sleep.

When she woke up later, she looked at the clock on the table next to the bed and was surprised it was so late. She hadn't meant to sleep so long. It was dinnertime, and any chance she had to go shopping today had slipped by. Worried about what Alaska and Henley might think, she sat up...

And groaned.

In all the craziness of the last day, she hadn't realized how sore she would be from all her running and window-escaping and jungle-crouching. Every muscle in her body hurt. She'd been more physically active while in Colombia than she had in a very long time. She wanted to lie back down and not move, but instead, she stood slowly and shuffled toward the door. She was still half asleep, but she needed to see Gus. Make sure everything was still all right.

She walked into the living area and inhaled. Something smelled absolutely delicious. Not as good as Gus's pillow, but it came in a close second.

"You're up," he said, moving toward her from the kitchen.

Reese simply stared at him. He'd put on a pair of gray sweats, much like the ones she was wearing, and she couldn't tear her gaze away from his crotch. All the memes on the Internet about men wearing gray sweats were true. She hadn't thought much about it before this moment.

She swallowed hard. Gus was big...all over. She could see his thigh muscles under the gray cotton, but more than that, she could see the outline of his cock. Her nipples tightened involuntarily and all she could think of was how perfectly beautiful this man was.

Then she thought about the fact his sweats and T-shirt weren't actually all that big on her. They were close to the same height, and weight, and she was embarrassed at how well she filled out his clothes.

"Eyes, Reese," Gus ordered.

She jerked in surprise and whipped her gaze up to his.

"As much as I love your eyes on my body, I don't like the look that crossed your face just now. What were you thinking?"

"Um...that those memes about gray sweatpants weren't wrong," she blurted, then wrinkled her nose in embarrassment as she looked anywhere but at him. She was always a little out of it when she first woke up.

"Uh-huh. It's pretty clear you like what you see, and I'm thrilled. But *after* that part. What put that look of discomfort on your face? Do you not want to stay here anymore? I promise you're safe with me, but if you want me to figure out other sleeping arrangements, I will."

"No! It's not that. I just...you thought your clothes would be big on me, and they aren't," she told him honestly as she tugged on the bottom of the T-shirt. "Most guys want girls to be slender and petite. They *like* when their clothes swim on a woman."

"I'm not most guys. And while I haven't thought much about what I look like in my sweats, I have to say, I like them on you *much* better."

She looked at him skeptically.

"I love your curves, Reese. I love that I can see every dip and valley while you're in my clothes. It's sexy as hell."

She looked down at herself and saw her nipples pushing against the fabric of his shirt. Her thighs were definitely defined in the sweatpants, and she could just imagine how her ass was stretching the material.

"I tried losing a bunch of weight a few years ago," she told him. "And I did lose a bit. But I felt like crap. It sucked all the joy out of my day when I had to count every single calorie that went into my mouth. I'm always tired after work, and having to go for a jog or to the gym always made me dread going home. I decided that while I wanted to be healthy, I wanted joy back in my life even more. I'm usually okay with who I am and my size, even if sometimes societal pressure gets to me. But generally, I eat what I want in moderation, work out when I can—but don't beat myself up when I don't—and try to love myself for who I am."

"Being healthy is good, but accepting yourself is better," Gus said. He'd taken a step toward her, and they were standing extremely close now. "And from where I'm standing, I wouldn't change a single thing about you. To be crystal clear, I'm not turned off by your size. I have to confess, I checked on you a few times while you were napping, and the sight of you in my bed..." He exhaled heavily. "Let's just say that I liked it...a lot. And as I said, you filling out my clothes is sexy as fuck."

He placed a hand on the side of her neck and pulled her even closer. Her breasts brushed against his chest, and Reese raised her hands and put them on his sides as she studied him.

"You asked if everything was all right after I talked to your brother," he said.

Reese licked her lips nervously and nodded.

"He was basically telling me how awesome you are. And that he approves if I want to court you."

"He said that? *Court* me?" Reese asked in disbelief.

"Well, not in those exact words."

"Thank God. Because if he'd said the word, 'court,' I seriously would've hauled his ass down to the doctor myself because something is seriously wrong," Reese joked.

Gus grinned. "But I'll tell you something—even if he'd told me that you were off-limits, I would've told *him* to fuck off."

Reese's heart began to beat faster. "Yeah?"

"Yeah. What I want to know is how *you* feel about being courted by me. I'd like to go out with you. Get to know you better. I'm attracted to you, Reese, but if this is weird for you, if you don't want anything other than friendship, I'll accept that."

Was this real? Was this actually happening? "No!" she blurted. "I mean...it's not weird. I'd like to get to know you too."

His smile grew. "Good. And as far as I'm concerned, you can wear my sweats and tees anytime you want. But not in public. Only here."

She frowned. "Why?"

"Because if the other guys saw you like this, looking all sexy, sleepy, and rumpled, I'd have to kill them."

A shiver went through Reese. A good one.

Gus's eyes darkened, and his thumb caressed her jawline. "Can I kiss you?"

Reese licked her lips again. "Yes," she whispered, holding her breath as his head lowered.

His lips brushed hers once, twice. Before he took a deep breath and pulled her into his embrace.

The kiss had been so short, so chaste. She wanted more. But she didn't want to push her luck. She could hardly believe she was standing here at all, in Gus's arms, wearing his clothes, and he'd said he wanted to go out with her. She'd take what she could get, as long as she could get it.

"Are you hungry?" he asked as he pulled back but didn't let go.

Reese couldn't help but grin. "Starved," she told him as she looked at his chest.

He laughed, and Reese felt the rumble move through her since they were plastered together.

"For food," he clarified. "I made cauliflower mac and cheese. It doesn't have any pasta in it, but small cauliflower florets. I promise while it doesn't taste like pasta, it's still delicious."

"It sounds awesome," she told him honestly.

He breathed out a sigh of relief. "Thank goodness. I was afraid you were going to tell me you hated cauliflower."

"Nope. I mean, I don't want to eat it at every meal, I love me some bread and carbs, but as I said earlier, I'm okay with eating healthy, just not counting every calorie that goes into my mouth."

"Well, I'll tell you right now that I'm not sure how healthy it is. I used a shit-ton of cheese," Gus said with a grin.

"Cheese makes everything better," Reese told him.

He stared at her for a long moment.

"What?" she asked.

"You're more awake now," he observed.

She shrugged. "I'm always a little out of it when I wake up. I sleep hard."

"It's cute. You need coffee in the mornings?"

"Need? No. Want? Yes."

"Black?"

Reese wrinkled her nose. "Um, no. Cream or milk, sugar, and some sort of flavoring."

"So you don't need coffee, you need a cup of flavored sugar masquerading as coffee," he teased.

Reese wasn't offended. "Pretty much."

"It's gonna be fun to grocery shop with you," Gus said. "Learn what you like and what you don't, and what your go-to foods are."

"You're weird," she said, needing to break this intimate bubble they were in. Thinking about shopping with him, filling one cart, laughing and joking about snacks and deciding what to make for dinners, was too much right now. She'd yearned for exactly that in the past. Not necessarily with this man, just with someone in general. She wanted to love and be loved. And thus far in her life, she hadn't even come close.

As if he could feel her discomfort and need for a bit of distance, Gus dropped his hand from the side of her neck. He stepped back and took her hand. "Come on. It's almost ready."

"Can I help with anything?" she asked as they walked toward the kitchen. Her neck tingled where he'd been touching her.

"You could get our drinks."

He requested a glass of ice water, and she got busy finding the glasses while he served up the ooiest, gooiest plates of cheese and cauliflower that Reese had ever seen. She grabbed some paper towels and forks while she was at it, and before long they were both seated at his small round table.

"Oh my God, Gus, this is the best thing I've ever eaten," Reese said after taking her first bite.

"I'm glad you like it."

"Like it? I'm gonna marry it and roll around in bed with it!" Reese exclaimed, then immediately closed her eyes and put her forehead in her hand in embarrassment. "Sorry, forget I said that."

Gus chuckled. "Forget it? Never. I can't get that image out of my mind now."

Right. Now she wanted to die.

But Gus being Gus, he didn't let her wallow in her embarrassment. "The best thing I've ever eaten was when I was in Texas. I was visiting some friends of mine who were also Delta. They took me to the Texas State Fair, and

I had no idea what I was about to experience. When they heard I'd never been to a state fair before, and had never eaten any deep fried food—I mean, deep fried *fair* food—they insisted I try just about everything. Peanut butter banana cheeseburgers, bacon, pecan pie, cheesecake, and of course, Oreos. But the best thing I tried, and I still dream about it today, is the deep fried peanut butter and jelly sandwich. I would swear to God I'd died and gone to heaven. I ate two of those things—and paid for it. My stomach hurt for the next three days, but it was totally worth it."

Reese giggled, and Gus returned her smile.

"If I could've, I would've kidnapped that guy who made it and brought him to my house and forced him to make me one every day. So I get it." Gus nodded at the plate in front of her. "There's going to be plenty of leftovers for tomorrow too."

"Oh, the man's bringing out the big guns," Reese teased.

"Absolutely."

They bantered back and forth for the rest of the meal, and this time Gus let Reese help him clean up when they were done. Using Gus's phone, she made a quick call to Alaska to figure out a time to go shopping the next day. She said she'd get with Henley, since her schedule was more fixed, and they'd set it up.

The rest of the night went by smoothly. Reese felt at ease with Gus. Didn't feel as if she had to watch every word that came out of her mouth, like she had around other men she'd dated. It was a little uncomfortable at the end of the night when she went to *his* room to sleep, but once again, Gus didn't make her feel weird about it. He simply did what he needed to do in his bathroom, then left her to it.

As she lay down in his bed for the second time, contentment spread through her. Reese had no idea what the next few weeks would hold. She needed to talk to her boss and figure out if she was going to be allowed to take an extended leave of absence. She enjoyed her job, but knew there were several companies in the Kansas City area that would bend over backward to hire her. So if she had to quit and find a new job, it wouldn't be the end of the world. She'd miss her co-workers, but she wasn't exactly friends with them either. They saw each other at work, and that was that.

And if she was being honest, having a break from her job would be welcome. She'd been getting bored and needed a new challenge. Maybe this was an opportunity to make a change.

Everyone at The Refuge had been so friendly and welcoming so far, and she'd fallen in love with the place on sight. Of course, she'd already read a lot about it online, but seeing it in person was completely different. And knowing her brother was safe, and was finally with the woman he'd loved forever, made her feel good inside too.

Turning, she inhaled Gus's scent deeply into her lungs. Yeah, it was almost scary how well things had turned out. She'd gone to Colombia not knowing what was going to happen, and now here she was. In Gus's bed. Of course, he wasn't there with her, but she couldn't help hoping that one day he just might join her.

Not caring that some people would tell her she was being naïve about what Gus might want from her, Reese fell asleep with a smile on her face and an anticipation about the future she hadn't felt in a very long time.

CHAPTER NINE

Spike watched Reese from across the room. She seemed... happy. Which, to be honest, was somewhat of a surprise to him. She had a lot on her plate right now. A lot to be worried and stressed out about. But she was remarkably unflappable.

Their second day in New Mexico, Woody had arranged to have her SUV, along with his vehicle, sent from Kansas City to The Refuge. They'd arrived two days later, and she was thrilled to be able to drive herself around again...not that she went many places. She'd gone shopping with Alaska and Henley and had gotten a new cell phone. A couple days later, she returned to town and picked up groceries to replenish his fridge and pantry, much to his annoyance, because he wasn't a fan of her spending her own money on food that they were both eating.

Especially when she was currently without a job.

He'd come in from helping Tonka expand the corral one evening to find that she'd talked with her boss, and because she wasn't sure how much longer she'd be gone, he'd had to regrettably let her go.

Reese hadn't seemed upset. Had merely shrugged and told him that she'd expected as much, since she couldn't expect her boss to just hold her job without any idea when she'd return. She assured him that she had money saved up and she'd be fine without a job for a while, and she was looking forward to relaxing.

Although, he hadn't really seen her relaxing much in the last week. She'd been up at the lodge every day helping Robert and Luna in the kitchen...not cooking, but shuttling food out to the guests and making sure everyone had whatever they needed.

She'd also helped Carly, Jess, and Ryan with the laundry when she ran out of other things to do. Spike wanted to protest, tell her that she wasn't here to work, but since she seemed happy to stay busy, he didn't want to upset her unnecessarily.

She spent time with Isabella as well, getting to know her. It was obvious her and Woody's relationship was moving along quickly, and Reese admitted to Spike one night that she was loving the thought of having a sister-in-law.

Jasna's school year had started shortly before his trip to Kansas City, so Reese had taken to spending part of her afternoons down at the barn with the animals, helping Tonka until Jasna arrived. All-in-all, she'd jumped in with both feet to get to know everyone, and she had no problem pitching in to help wherever she could.

There were a few days when Spike hadn't even seen her until dinnertime, when she reappeared at his cabin. She spoke a million miles an hour as they ate, telling him all about her days and what she'd seen and done.

She was bubbly and friendly, and the more time Spike

spent around her, the more he knew he'd never want her to leave.

This morning, after he'd made her a coffee that wasn't really a coffee, and while they were eating breakfast, he brought up something he'd been thinking about for the last two days.

"I thought, if you didn't already have a hundred things planned for the day, that I'd take you to see one of my favorite places at The Refuge."

Reese looked up at him with twinkling eyes. "Yes!"

He grinned. "You don't want to know where it is or how we're getting there?"

"Nope. If it's your favorite place, I know it's going to be magnificent."

"And if I said it involved rock climbing gear, would you still be as excited?" he joked.

"Yup. Although I've never done anything like that, so you'd have to teach me how to do it. Wait—am I too heavy for the equipment or anything?"

She didn't look stressed out when she asked, merely curious, but Spike still didn't like hearing it. "First, I'll teach you whatever you want to learn. Second, you aren't too heavy for *anything*." He was scowling by the time he finished speaking.

Reese reached over and put her hand on his arm to soothe him. "I wasn't being self-deprecating. Not really. There are a lot of things I can't do because of my size. Or things that wouldn't be smart. And being strapped up and hanging by a rope or pulley system or whatever's used in rock climbing sounds as if it might have weight limits. I was just making sure, because there's nothing worse than getting excited about doing something, only to find out I can't."

"There's nothing wrong with your size," Spike growled. "And do you really think I'd suggest something if I thought you wouldn't be able to do it? No way in hell." He answered his own question without giving her time to comment.

"You really don't care that I'm big...do you?" she asked with a tilt of her head.

"You aren't big," he countered. "You're perfect. And no. You're literally one of the nicest people I've ever met. Since you've been here, you've volunteered to help just about everyone. I think if there was a vote, I'd be kicked out and you'd be chosen to take my spot as co-owner of this place with the other guys. I've even seen you trying to talk to Angelo with that translation app on your phone. He hasn't exactly been Mr. Congeniality since he's gotten here, but that doesn't seem to faze you at all. You just keep on smiling and doing whatever you can to make him feel more comfortable and welcome."

"He's in a foreign country, doesn't speak the language, and he's a teenager," Reese said, as if that explained Angelo's standoffishness. "And from what you said, he had a hell of a decision to make...either sell drugs to keep his sister safe, or refuse and possibly get her killed. It was a crappy situation to be in, and I feel bad for him. Besides, it looks like Woody and Isabella are falling hard and fast, and if they get married, he'll be related to me, basically. I want him to know I care and I'm here if he needs anything."

There. That. Her soft heart was something Spike both admired and worried about because it could get her hurt in the future.

"He's not exactly a kid," he felt obligated to mention. "He's old enough to put on his big-boy pants and put in a little bit of effort. I'm not saying I think he should be digging holes for the new fence by the barn, but there are various opportunities here for him if he tried just a little bit. New Mexico has a large Spanish-speaking population, he could easily find a job in Los Alamos if he wanted to."

"It's only been a week," Reese said gently. "He was ripped away from everything he knew, without any of his possessions. We need to cut him some slack."

Spike was in awe of Reese once more. She was generous to a fault. Kind. Understanding. But where Angelo was concerned...he wasn't sure it was warranted. Yes, it had only been a week since they'd arrived from Colombia, but Isabella was flourishing. Loving every minute of her time here at The Refuge. Her brother, not so much. He didn't think it was solely because Isabella spoke English, and her brother didn't. Though he admitted that was obviously to Isabella's benefit.

"We have no idea what people are going through when we see them," Reese said with a small shrug. "They might look put together and fine on the outside, but behind closed doors, they could be falling apart. Their home life might be a mess, and they're just putting on a happy face in public. It's not a chore for me to treat people with kindness. Besides, it makes me feel good to help others and work hard."

"And that's why I'm so drawn to you," Spike admitted.

She smiled shyly at him.

He wanted to push their plates away, stand her up, push her back onto the table and have his wicked way with her right then and there. But he also didn't want to freak her out. He had no problem giving up his bed. Imagining her there, on his sheets, under his blankets, using his pillow...it ignited something primal in him. When she'd told him she felt bad for taking his room while he used the spare, Spike refused to even think about switching. He wanted her right where she was.

Thinking about her in his shower, using his towels to dry her naked body, walking around his room, using his things, kept him in a constant state of arousal. He'd never act on it unless he was sure she felt the same way, but he liked knowing she was in his space.

He had a feeling she liked it too. She hadn't said anything, but she was still using his body wash, though she'd had opportunities to pick up her own. She smelled like him, which he liked a hell of a lot. Even sitting next to her right this moment, with her smelling like him, Spike felt proud. It was ridiculous really, but he hoped that it was maybe a sign that she would be open to entering into a more-than-friendship relationship sooner than later.

"So...what are we doing today?" she asked after tucking a lock of hair behind her ear. "What do I need to wear? Will it take all day? I told Jasna I'd be here when she got home from school so I could hear all about her day. Seventh grade isn't the easiest, you know. At least her friend, Sharyn, the girl she met from the camps they attended last summer, is in her classes."

Spike grinned. He wasn't surprised she wanted to greet Jasna when she got home from school. She'd bonded with the girl and had listened to her go on and on about the animals she'd spent all summer with, without showing any hint of impatience. "Hiking pants, T-shirt, boots," he told her. "The place is about three miles from here, but it's not a hard hike."

Reese rolled her eyes. "So says the man who's in shape and looks like he could walk the Appalachian Trail without stopping."

Spike smiled, but quickly got serious. "I wouldn't

suggest it if I didn't think you could do it, Reese. Trust me."

She met his gaze head on. "I do."

Fuck. This woman. Spike curled his fingers into fists and held onto his control with everything he had. He wanted her. Every inch. Last night, he'd masturbated after they'd gone to bed. Her giggles reverberated in his head, her smile the only thing he could see when he closed his eyes every night. He'd taken his cock in his fist and exploded after an embarrassingly short amount of time stroking himself, but his release wasn't nearly as satisfying as he'd hoped.

"I'll clean up, you go on and get ready," he said after a long pause.

"Are you all right?" Reese asked gently. "You seem...off."

There she went being all sweet and kind again. "I'm good," he told her. "How could I not be when I get to spend the day with you?"

Her cheeks turned a pretty pink at his compliment.

"I feel as if I have to steal you away from everyone else to get some one-on-one time with you," he teased.

Reese rolled her eyes. "Whatever," she said. "You've had more important things to do than babysit me." She stood up, but Spike's hand shot out and grabbed her forearm, stopping her in her tracks.

"That's not true. You need a ride somewhere, I'll gladly take you. If you're hungry, I'll make you something. You get nervous about what happened in Colombia, I'm happy to talk it through with you. You're more than a guest, Reese. You're more than just my buddy's sister. We've mostly tiptoed around our attraction to each other, but I'm not sure you realize that you've got me wrapped around your little finger. You say the word, and I'll bend over backward for you."

"Gus," she whispered.

Spike wanted to kiss her more than he wanted almost anything in his life. But he held himself back. He wouldn't push himself on this woman, even though it was the most difficult thing he'd ever done to not pull her against him and show her with more than words how much she was starting to mean to him. How much he needed her goodness and sunny disposition in his life.

"Go change so I can show you one of the many reasons I fell in love with this place," he said gently.

Reese nodded, and he dropped his hand from her arm. She looked down at him for a long moment, before turning and heading toward his bedroom.

Spike had actually stood and taken a step after her before realizing what he was doing. The vision he had in his head of backing her into his room and onto his bed before falling down on top of her had almost overridden his common sense.

Taking a deep breath, he forced himself to pick up their empty breakfast plates and take them into the kitchen. He was already dressed and ready to go, but wanted to pack a small bag of snacks and water for their hike.

After a few minutes, he'd gotten control of himself once more. Spike hadn't realized how difficult it would be to have Reese living with him while keeping things mostly platonic. Hell, it had only been a week, and he was more attracted to her than anyone he'd ever dated before.

Every word Woody had said about his sister was true. She was everything he'd ever wanted in a woman, and he didn't want to do anything that might scare her off or make her wary to be around him. Spike vowed to be a perfect gentleman, so she'd have no cause to regret her decision to stay in his cabin.

"Is this okay?" she asked, making Spike jump. He couldn't remember the last time someone had snuck up on him...and Reese wasn't even sneaking. He'd been so lost in his head that he simply hadn't heard her. Turning, he ran his eyes up and down her body.

She had on a pair of khaki hiking pants she'd bought a few days ago when she'd been shopping with Henley, Alaska, Jasna, and Isabella. The boots on her feet weren't new. They'd been included in the boxes that had been shipped from Kansas City with her Ford Escape. She wore a pale green T-shirt that somehow brought out the blue in her eyes. It had a picture of a sloth hanging from a branch and the words, "Life is good, Take it slow" beneath.

He smiled. "You're perfect," he said, letting some of the desire coursing through his veins shine through in his words because he literally couldn't help it.

He wasn't surprised when Reese rolled her eyes. "Hardly. But thank you. I don't think I'll get cold, but I have a jacket I was planning on tying around my waist, just in case."

Spike wasn't expecting rain, but he approved of her thinking ahead. "I'll shove it in my pack, so you don't have to worry about it," he said as he walked toward her, unable to stay away.

"That bag on the floor? It's huge!" she said with a laugh. "What else do you have in there?"

"I'd tell you, but then I'd have to kill you," he deadpanned.

Reese giggled, and Spike wrapped an arm around her

waist and pulled her into him. So much for being a gentleman. That lasted a whole three minutes.

She let out an adorable *oof* as she collided with him, but her smile didn't dim.

"I want to kiss you," Spike said in a voice that sounded nothing like his usual calm tone.

Several seconds went by before she said, "Well? What are you waiting for?"

"Your permission," he said seriously.

"Anytime you want to kiss me, you can," she said breathlessly. "Okay, maybe not in front of Woody for a while. I mean, I talked to him, and he's cool with us, but he's still my brother and making out in front of him would be weird. Oh, and maybe not in front of Jasna. She's cool, but it's even weirder to make out in front of a kid. Come to think of it, it might—"

Spike couldn't wait for her to finish talking. She'd given him carte blanche to kiss her, and he wasn't waiting another second to do just that. He cupped her neck, pressing his other hand firmly against her back as he tilted his head and leaned in.

He felt her fingers in his hair—then he couldn't think about anything other than how her lips felt under his. How soft she felt against him. The hand at her back pressed harder, sliding around her, wanting to feel every inch.

Their tongues twined together, and he could taste the mint from the toothpaste she'd obviously used after changing. His fingers tingled, as did his toes. His erection pressed against her belly, and it was all he could do not to grind against her.

He'd kissed her before, but it had been a chaste touching of lips, nothing more. This was...overwhelming.

Exciting. He could taste the promise of a future in this kiss. And when she moaned deep in her throat and dug her fingernails into his scalp, Spike clutched her to him harder as he made love to her mouth.

He had no idea how long they'd been kissing before she lifted her lips from his. But she didn't pull back. Instead, she buried her face into the side of his neck and clung to him just as hard as he clung to her.

To his surprise, Spike found that he was breathing hard. Practically panting. His cock throbbed and he was two seconds from coming right then and there in his pants. That hadn't ever happened to him. He enjoyed kissing, but it was always a means to an end. A precursor to the good stuff.

With Reese, kissing *was* the good stuff.

Her breaths wafted over his skin, making goose bumps break out on his arms. His hands shifted, the one at her neck sliding to her back, while the one at her waist inched down to her ass, and he couldn't stop himself from kneading the generous globe for a moment before gripping her tightly and holding her in place against his throbbing dick.

"Holy crap," she murmured against his neck.

Spike smiled, relieved he wasn't the only one feeling this. He licked his lips, tasting her there, and said, "Yeah."

He felt her head lifting, and he looked at her. Spike couldn't stop his gaze from going to her chest. He could see her nipples through her bra and T-shirt, and a giddy mix of relief and pride went through him. She was obviously just as turned on as he was, and it made something inside him relax a fraction. He'd known she liked him, but seeing the proof that she was just as affected by their chemistry made him less desperate somehow.

He vowed to enjoy the anticipation and excitement of their new relationship.

Reluctantly letting go of her ass, Spike brought his hand up to her face and brushed his fingers against the rosy pink of her cheek. Her lips were a little swollen, and he loved the feel of her fingernails against his scalp and arm, where she'd grabbed him to hold on while they were kissing.

"I'm not going to kiss you in front of Woody. He's not opposed to our relationship, but you *are* his little sister."

"So we're in a relationship?" she asked shyly.

"Yes," Spike answered definitively.

"And..."

"What? You can ask me anything. Tell me anything."

"I know. It's just that this is so soon. But I haven't felt this way about a guy before. You already know I had a crush on you before, but now...are we...can you...I want to be exclusive," she finished quickly.

Spike framed her face and fixed his gaze on hers. "As you can see, there isn't exactly a slew of women out here to date," he said.

"But there's lots of guests," she interrupted before he could go on. "And I've seen how some of them look at you and the other guys. I'm guessing plenty would be happy to have a vacation fling."

"My friends and I have never, and *will* never, mix business with pleasure," he said sternly. "That's the best way to fuck up a good thing. I'm not going to sleep with any of the guests—and hell yes, we're exclusive. I don't want anyone else but you, Reese. You're all I can think about."

She smiled shyly at him as she grabbed hold of his wrists. "I'm having a hard time wrapping my head around this," she admitted. "I mean, I know I'm a good person and I deserve to be loved the way I've always wanted, and to have a man of my own. But this has been...sudden. And you have no idea how many times I've dreamed of being right here. Of hearing you say the things you're saying to me right now. But I'm also a realist. I know what I look like, and it wasn't as if we've even seen each other since you got out of the Army."

"You look like heaven. Like home. Like someone who enjoys life to the fullest. Who laughs a lot, and who's passionate about the smallest thing. And while I can't say I had a crush, I've thought about you *a lot*. Always asked Woody about you when we were on the teams. You intrigued me from the moment we met, but since I figured there wasn't a chance you'd want an old, tattooed recluse like me..." He shrugged.

She smiled. "You aren't old. And you aren't a recluse. Did you really ask Woody about me?"

"Yup."

Her smile widened. "So we're doing this."

"If by *this*, you mean dating, kissing, continuing to getting to know each other, eating together, watching movies, and hopefully one day very soon, making love... yes," Spike said.

She swallowed hard. "Okay."

"Okay?" he verified.

She nodded.

He tilted her face up to his and lowered his head once more. He kissed her again. This time the kiss was less passionate and more...loving. Their tongues swirled together lazily as they learned the taste and feel of each other. It was Spike who broke it off. He was on the edge, and if he was going to show her his favorite place at The

Refuge, he needed to stop touching and kissing her and get going.

"You ready?" he asked.

"Can I make a coffee to go?" she asked.

Spike had a feeling she didn't know her thumb was brushing back and forth on the inside of his wrist. She was so sensual. When they did finally make love, she was going to blow his mind, of that he had no doubt.

"I already made one for you."

"You did?" she asked in surprise.

That was another thing. She was always so shocked when he did something nice for her. As if no one had ever taken care of her before. Well, that part of her life was a thing of the past. He'd bend over backward to make sure he spoiled her.

"Yup. I've also got water for later...you know, to wash that sugar from your so-called coffee out of your system."

She laughed and playfully swatted his arm. "Whatever."

He liked this. Yes, he liked the kissing and making out, but he liked the good-natured banter between them as well.

"Come on," he said, grabbing her hand and towing her toward the kitchen. It was only a few steps and there was no need to hold her hand, but he liked touching her. Liked having her near him. He handed her the travel cup of coffee and watched as she took a sip.

"It's perfect," she said with a smile.

Another pang of longing went through Spike. He shoved away the unexpected feeling of vulnerability by saying, "Of course it is."

This woman was his kryptonite. Now he understood why some people did stupid things in the name of love.

He jerked in surprise at the sudden thought, and

covered it by dropping Reese's hand and reaching for his backpack. He folded her jacket and stuffed it inside as he considered the idea.

Love? Did he *love* Reese? He wasn't sure. It hadn't been long at all since they'd reconnected. Did he respect her? Yes. Admire her? Definitely yes. Was he in awe of her? Absolutely.

But love?

Maybe.

In the past, that might have freaked him out, especially so soon. But now, as he held open the front door for her, smiling when she thanked him and walked outside, he was simply...content.

There was a time in Spike's life when he thought he'd never be able to truly relax. The things he'd done and seen ran through his head like a never-ending movie, day after day, year after year. The horrors of his past were always there, lurking in the background, ready to spring forward and mess up a perfectly good day. He'd resigned himself to always being tense. To being on alert.

But being around Reese dulled those thoughts. Hearing her laugh put him at ease. Her pleasure in the smallest things was a joy to witness. And kissing her? Getting lost in all that was Reese?

It was everything.

If he could love *anyone*, it would be this woman. But for now, he was going to enjoy spending time with her. Showing her why he loved this part of New Mexico. Yes, they'd agreed to date exclusively, but eventually the real world would intrude and she'd go back to Kansas City. They'd both have hard decisions to make when that happened, but until that time, Spike was going to do everything in his power to live in the here and now. And to enjoy the hell out of having Reese around.

"Well, you coming? Or are we going to stand outside your cabin all day staring at the trees around us?" she sassed.

"I'm coming," Spike said with a smile, as he locked the cabin door and turned her way.

"Why do you lock the door? Are you afraid of the guests stealing something?" she asked with a tilt of her head.

"Not really. It's a habit. But no place is a hundred precent safe."

"Good point," Reese said with a nod.

Spike pocketed his keys. "Ready?"

"Ready," she said with a huge smile. "Lead the way."

"How about we go together?" Spike asked, holding out his hand.

If possible, her smile got bigger. "Sounds good to me."

She put her hand in his. Spike noticed how his hand seemed to engulf hers, which he liked for some odd reason. She wasn't a small woman, but to him, she seemed delicate and so damn feminine. The softness to all his hard edges.

They walked hand-in-hand toward the trees. There was no official trail to where they were going, but Spike didn't need one. He went to the place they were headed when he needed some peace and quiet. When he wanted to recharge and get away from the demons in his head. He couldn't wait to show it to Reese.

CHAPTER TEN

Reese couldn't stop smiling.

She probably looked like an idiot, but she didn't care.

Her lips were still tingling from their earlier kisses. She hadn't lied, it was hard to believe Gus was interested in *her*. He was that guy every girl dreamed about taking one look at her and falling madly in love. The prince from *Cinderella*. The cute billionaire stranger who sat next to you on a plane and took you home to his mansion and declared his everlasting love.

Okay, those examples might be a stretch, as Gus didn't have a drop of royalty in his blood and as far as she knew, he wasn't a billionaire.

But she felt giddy inside that he was here with her, holding her hand, kissing her as if he'd never get enough, and generally being attentive and protective. She liked it. A lot. She was an independent woman, had always been that way. She didn't need a man, but she couldn't deny that she *wanted* one.

Her panties were still damp from the way he'd held her tightly against him as they'd kissed. She'd felt his cock—

his *huge* cock—against her belly, and all she'd wanted to do was rip his clothes off right then and there and go down on her knees and taste him.

But she could be patient. Maybe. It had been a long time since she'd had sex, and she'd never had it with someone she wanted as badly as she wanted Gus. He'd hinted that sex would be in their future—making love, he'd called it...swoon—but she had a feeling he'd try to be a gentleman and go slowly when it came to intimacy.

Reese didn't want slow. She'd wanted Gus for what seemed like forever. And she couldn't help but think that maybe his attraction toward her might fade quickly. That he'd decide he didn't want an overweight thirty-something engineer, and would rather have a skinny, bubbly twenty-year-old.

Shaking her head, Reese tried not to think about that. She'd accepted long ago that she was who she was and vowed not to change for any man. But...making sure Gus knew she was all for the physical intimacy that came with dating was definitely on her agenda. She didn't want to wait some random period of time that society deemed acceptable before making love. She was ready now.

Peeking through her lashes at Gus, she smiled. He was made to be out here in the wilderness. He looked more relaxed and his strides were confident. She loved the sight of the tattoos on his arm, and how they flexed with his muscles as he shifted the pack on his back.

"What's that look for?" he asked with a small grin.

Reese shrugged. "I'm just happy."

"You're always happy," he returned.

She frowned. "That's not true."

Gus raised a brow.

"I wasn't happy when I couldn't get a hold of Woody. I

wasn't happy I had to go down to South America to try to find him when I had no idea where to start, other than Isabella's address. I wasn't happy when I got sick and had to stay in my hotel room instead of looking for them. I wasn't happy when I was alone with the truck and you and Tiny went to that house, putting yourselves in danger. I wasn't happy when we were being shot at and chased by gun-wielding drug cartel goons. I'm not happy when Angelo won't talk to me. I'm not happy when—"

"Okay, okay," Gus said with a laugh. "You're happy most of time then. When you aren't fiercely worried about your loved ones. Or your friends."

Reese thought about that and gave him a small nod. "It's better for my peace of mind to focus on the good parts of life more than the bad."

"Which makes you different from about eighty percent of the world."

"That's not true," she protested.

"It is. When you go on social media, most of the posts are about the shit happening in people's lives. They're complaining about one thing or another. I've seen your posts...you talk about the flowers you saw in the park. About how thrilled you are for a co-worker who got a raise. The present you bought for a friend's son for his birthday."

"I get upset," she protested. "I get worried and mad just like everyone else."

"I know, but you don't dwell on it. I think it's wonderful. And people like being around you because of it."

"You included?" she couldn't help but ask.

"Me especially. But that doesn't mean that you can't be sad or angry around me. I don't want you to think I expect you to always be upbeat and chipper. In fact, I *need* you to be comfortable enough with me to let me see any darker parts of you, as well as the happy ones."

"I'm not used to letting people in," she admitted.

"You can trust me with your real feelings," Gus told her as he squeezed her hand. "Lord knows I've got enough nasty shit swirling around in my head that nothing you do or say will faze me."

"Was it bad?" she blurted.

"It?"

"The missions. Being a Delta. Always being in danger, sent into unsafe places and asked to be Superman."

"Not always. But a lot of the time, yes. It's why I finally called it quits."

"You didn't quit," Reese said fiercely. She stopped walking, forcing Gus to stop along with her.

He huffed out a breath. "I did."

"No, you had enough. Any sane person would. There's only so much a person's psyche can take. I admire you for knowing when the time was right."

"Have you been talking to Henley?"

"About you specifically? No. About some of the horrible things our military guests have seen and done? Yes. I'm proud of you, my brother, and the rest of your team and what you all did. But I'm relieved that you're not doing it anymore. I hated every second of when you guys were deployed. I dreaded getting *that* call, *that* visit, that would inform me someone had died. It's selfish, I know that, but I was so damn thrilled when I heard you were getting out. Woody too."

"It's not selfish," Gus said gently.

"It is, but I don't even care. You're here and safe. Woody's safe...well, he would be if he didn't head off into Drug Cartel Land to rescue his girlfriend and her brother.

"I guess what I'm trying to say is that if I can trust you with my feelings, you can trust me with yours. I don't expect you to tell me any details that'll make Uncle Sam come after you and lock you away for years and years. But if you need space, you've got it. If you need to talk, I'm here to listen. If you need to come out here into the woods and just be silent, we can do that too."

Reese let out a small surprised noise when Gus yanked her against him. But she recovered instantly and wrapped her arms around him when he hugged her tightly.

"I'm not used to talking about the shit in my head, but if it becomes too much...I'll let you know."

Reese melted against him. She could hear birds over-head, the wind rustling the leaves in the trees, and the beat of Gus's heart. If she could spend the rest of her life right here, in his arms, with the peacefulness of the world surrounding them, she would.

He pulled back, kissed her lightly, then grabbed her hand. "Come on, we've still got a mile or so to go."

"How do you know where the heck we are and where we're going?" she asked when they started walking again.

He shrugged. "I just do."

"My sense of direction sucks," she informed him. "I can drive the hell out of anything with wheels. Cars, trucks, go-carts, motorcycles. But knowing which way to go is a bit trickier for me."

Gus laughed.

"Before cars were made with GPS in them, I was always hopelessly getting lost."

"Close your eyes," Gus said.

Reese immediately did as he asked without a second thought.

He stopped and spun them in a few circles. "Now, open your eyes and tell me which way we were just heading."

Reese laughed as she looked around her. All the trees looked the same. And she couldn't see any kind of trail where they'd just walked either. "I have no idea."

"Seriously. Take a breath and look around. Look for clues. Where did we just come from?"

"Seriously yourself, Gus. I really have no idea. Every leaf and branch looks the same. I don't know."

He frowned. "That isn't good," he said, more to himself than to her. "The Refuge is at the edge of thousands of acres of woods. I need to teach you how to use a compass and how to track a little bit."

"You can try," she said without conviction. "But Woody's attempted more than once to teach me some of that stuff. I'm hopeless."

"You aren't hopeless," he said without thought.

Warmth spread throughout Reese. It was such a small thing, yet she couldn't help but love how he stood up for her. "Okay, smart guy. Your turn. Close your eyes so I can spin you, and you can tell *me* which way we come from."

He shut his eyes with a small smile and let her spin him around. When he opened his eyes, it took about two seconds for him to get his bearings and point to the left. "That's where we walked. I can see the scuffs in the dirt. And that way is north," he pointed in front of them, "and that way is Los Alamos." He pointed in a different direction.

"No one likes a smart aleck," Reese said.

"You do," he countered.

He had her there. "Whatever," she muttered.

Gus laughed and grabbed her behind the head and

leaned in to give her another kiss. She had to admit, she liked how free he was with his kisses. No, she loved it.

"Are you hungry? Do you need a snack? Maybe some water?"

"No, I'm good."

"All right. We'll have a picnic when we get there. Come on, it's not too much farther."

"Okay, great human compass, lead the way."

"One day I'm gonna make you lead us out to the spot I'm going to show you," he said as they started walking again.

"Is that a threat?" she asked with a smile.

"Nope. Not at all. I just really want you to be able to find your way around here. The thought of you being lost in the forest makes me feel physically sick."

She squeezed his hand once more. "Don't worry. I like hiking and being out in nature, but I have no intention of ever wandering around on my own. I'll stick to established paths or with you."

"But I could get hurt. And you might have to go back to The Refuge to get help."

Reese shook her head. "Nope. Not happening. And we need to stop talking about you being hurt."

"Okay. But you'll humor me and try to learn about navigating, right?"

Reese sighed. "Of course. But don't get your hopes up. I'm really not good at directions. Just ask Woody. He'll tell you."

Gus squeezed her hand and they continued on their way.

"So...I haven't asked...and if you don't want to tell me, it's okay. But how did you get your nickname?" Reese asked.

Gus smiled. "You know most of us get our nicknames from basic training, right?"

"Yup. Except for Woody. He's been Woody his entire life. His friends in elementary school started calling him that because of his last name, and it stuck. Everyone calls him that, even our parents."

"Right. Well, when I was in basic, one of the DI's—drill instructors—decided to do something different for PT one morning. He brought us to the sand pits and set up a net. We played volleyball for two hours straight. And trust me, that shit is just as hard as doing pushups and sit-ups. Anyway, they put me in front and time after time, I spiked the ball, earning our team points. And points were very important because whoever lost each game had to run laps, do jumping jacks, and other physical shit." He shrugged. "After a while, everyone started calling me Spike because of how good I was at spiking the volleyball."

Reese stopped walking again and stared at him in disbelief.

"What? What's wrong?"

"*That's* the story behind your nickname?"

"Yeah, why?"

"It's not what I expected," Reese said with a small chuckle.

It was Gus's turn to laugh now. "What did you expect? Killer? Bubbles? Flat?"

"Flat?" she asked.

"Flatulence."

"Oh, Lord, no. Please tell me that isn't a real name someone was given."

"Of course it is. So is Bubbles. You can see why I was all right with Spike."

"Yeah. But I like calling you Gus."

"I like it too," he said with a small smile.

He was looking at her with such intensity and tender-ness, it was all Reese could do not to yank him against her and force him to his back on the ground right then and there. "I just...it felt weird to call you Spike when I wasn't a part of your team. When Woody first told me about his teammates, I decided there was no way I could call anyone by their nickname."

"You can call me whatever you want," Gus told her. "Now, come on, if we stand out here in the forest all day, we'll never get there."

They walked in a comfortable silence for another ten minutes. Then Gus said quietly, "We're getting close. I'm going to need you to stay here while I go ahead and check things out to make sure everything's safe."

"Safe?" Reese asked.

"Trust me."

She nodded.

"Do. Not. Move. Understand? Especially now that I know how easily you get turned around. Please stay right here and don't move an inch. Okay?"

"Of course. I'm not going to go wandering around on my own," she told him a little defensively.

"I know you aren't. But if something spooks you and you start running, you could end up a lot farther away than you think. And there are some steep spots not too far from here. I don't want you tumbling down a ravine or anything and getting hurt."

"Will something spook me?" she asked curiously.

"I'm guessing you aren't terribly familiar with the woods, so it's possible a critter could run by and scare you."

"As long as it's not a bear, I'll be good," Reese said.

"What doesn't kill you makes you stronger...except for bears...bears will kill you."

Gus smirked and shook his head a little, but said, "Right. I'm not going to be gone long." Once again, he kissed her briefly before turning and heading away.

Reese leaned against a tree and smiled. She could really get used to being Gus's girlfriend. He made her feel special. And those kisses...

"Ready?"

His voice made her jump. It didn't feel as if he'd been gone more than a minute, but obviously she'd been daydreaming for longer than she'd thought. "Jeez," she said, putting a hand on her chest, hoping to calm her frantically beating heart. "You scared me."

"Sorry."

"Everything's okay?"

"Yup." Instead of taking her hand, he wrapped an arm around her waist. "Close your eyes," he requested. "I want to lead you there and don't want you to see it until I'm ready."

"You won't let me fall?" she asked.

"Never."

His response was so fervent, Reese didn't think twice about shutting her eyes and leaning into him.

He kept her against his side as he walked her forward. It was a little disconcerting, but she trusted Gus to keep her safe and not let her walk into a tree or trip over her feet.

She felt a slight temperature change as he walked them forward, and the smell in the air changed as well. She no longer felt the slight breeze against her skin, yet she was cooler somehow, and it was all she could do to keep her eyes shut until he told her she could open them.

"Okay, you can look now."

Reese opened her eyes eagerly—and had to blink a few times to adjust to what she was seeing. She'd expected to be standing at some kind of vista, like Sitting Rock or Table Rock. But instead she was...in a cave.

But it wasn't just any cave. There were drawings all over the walls.

"Holy crap, Gus!"

"It's amazing, isn't it?" he said reverently.

"They're petroglyphs, right?" she asked.

"Yeah. Anywhere from three hundred to twenty-five hundred years old. I mean, I'm not an expert, so I have no clue, but I've seen the ones down near Albuquerque at the Petroglyph National Park and these seem to be similar. There are also some called the La Cieneguilla Petroglyphs west of Santa Fe that look like this too."

"How'd you find this place?" she asked, still whispering.

"I got lucky," Gus said. "I was out hiking one day, while we were still building The Refuge. All the pounding from the cabins being built was getting to me, and I headed off into the woods. It started raining, hard, and I stumbled upon this cave and was glad for a place to get out of the rain. To my amazement, when I looked around, I saw all this indigenous rock art. I spent hours in here, examining as many of them as I could, imagining who might've put them here and why."

Reese took a step away from Gus and walked up to one of the walls. She didn't touch the precious drawing, but put her hand above one of them on the wall. "It's amazing to think that humans were here, right where we're standing, creating these works of art. I wonder what their lives were like. What their dreams were..."

She turned to look at more drawings. There were

human figures, hunters, suns, some sort of animal playing what looked like a recorder, intricate triangles, a badger-like creature with five large claws on its foot, and even smiley faces. Everywhere she looked, there were different drawings. "Do they tell a story?" she asked.

She couldn't look away from the wall of the cave even as Gus stepped close and wrapped his arms around her from behind. He rested his chin on her shoulder as he looked at the wall with her.

"I'm sure they do," he said. "I don't know what they are, but I've made up many in my head, over the years that I've been here. That one, for instance," he said, pointing toward a stick figure holding something long and pointy. "That's the male of the house, out hunting." He continued to point out different pictures near the first. "And that's the sheep he's hunting. He brings it home to his woman, who's in front of a fire. They have a feast, and when the sun goes down, they make love, which produces that baby...there."

Reese smiled. Her Gus was a romantic. He wasn't exactly "hers," per se, but in this moment, in this cave, she felt like he was. The paintings on the walls could literally mean anything. She wasn't even sure what many of the drawings were. But if Gus wanted to think the squiggles near the hunter was a fire, she wasn't going to contradict him.

She turned in his embrace and locked her hands behind the small of his back. "Thank you for showing this to me."

"You're welcome. You want to eat?"

"Sure."

He twined his fingers with hers and stepped farther into the cave. It was darker back here, but she should've known Gus would be prepared. He leaned over and picked up a flashlight he must've used earlier to make sure the cave was empty of critters and walked them to the wall on one side, where thousands of pine needles were neatly piled on the ground.

As if he could feel her question, he said, "I told you, I come here a lot. And the ground is hard." He shrugged. "Figured I might as well be comfortable while I'm here."

Gus helped her sit before settling down next to her. To Reese's surprise, the pine needles were surprisingly comfortable. He pulled his backpack over and dug inside for the baggies of food he'd packed. As they nibbled on almonds and trail mix, Reese couldn't tear her gaze from the walls around them. It was like being in a different world.

The troubles of the twenty-first century seemed so far away as she sat there thinking about the people who'd carved the drawings into this cave. Who probably used it for shelter once upon a time.

"Wait," she said after a moment. "Have you told anyone about this place? Historians? Archaeologists? Anyone?"

Gus looked a little sheepish. "No. I'd planned on it, but then I thought about how many people would be tromping around out here. Ruining this little piece of paradise. Eventually, I will. But I figured these drawings have been here for this long, waiting a few more years won't hurt anything."

Reese leaned against him and sighed. "I agree."

"When I'm here, all my troubles seem to fall away," he admitted softly. "The people I've killed, the explosions, the burning buildings from RPGs, the traumatized kids and women, the kidnapped soldiers and civilians I've helped rescue...they disappear. All I can think of is who the people might've been who were here before me. What were they thinking? Were they drawing pictures to entertain their kids? Were they leaving a diary of sorts? Were they bragging about their hunting skills? Recording their history? I just don't know. But it fascinates me."

"It's amazing," Reese agreed.

He looked at her. "You aren't disappointed I didn't bring you to a beautiful vista?"

She chuckled. "No. I'm scared of heights."

Gus looked surprised. "You are?"

"Yup."

"But you climbed down that gutter like a pro," he said.

Reese shrugged. "Did I have a choice?"

"Well, not really."

"Exactly. You were inside the apartment, and I knew whoever was after us had just broken in. If I didn't move, you would've gotten hurt. So I did what I had to do. That doesn't mean I liked it. I didn't."

"You surprise me every day," Gus said quietly. "In a good way."

Before she could respond that she was just doing what she had to do in the moment, Gus leaned toward her and gently pushed her backward until she was lying on the pine needles.

"I'm thinking there was more going on in this cave than people drawing on the walls," he said with a small smile, hovering over her.

"Yeah? Hmmm...like eating?"

"That too," he said before lowering his head.

Reese was more than happy to meet him partway. She lifted her head, and then they were kissing. And somehow it felt different lying down.

Several minutes went by, and when Gus lifted his head

to look down at her, they were both breathing hard. Reese's hand was brushing up and down his biceps as he propped himself over her, and she liked the look in his eyes a hell of a lot.

"We aren't making love for the first time in a cave," he said firmly.

"I don't know...the temperature isn't bad, it's private, and like you said...I bet there was lots of this kind of thing going on back in the day," Reese teased. The truth was, she was more than ready to tear Gus's clothes off, as well as her own, and let him have his way with her.

"The first time I have you, it'll be in my bed, where I've imagined us together since that first nap you took there."

Her belly clenched with desire as she stared up at him.

"I'm gonna taste every inch of your body, get my mouth between your legs and feast. After we make love, we'll shower together...then I'll go down on you again. Then I'll hold you all night long and thank my lucky stars that you let me anywhere near your delectable body."

Reese's mouth was dry as dust. She wanted that. So very badly. "When do I get a chance to go down on *you?*" she managed to ask.

Gus's eyes closed, and he took a deep breath before looking at her again. "You want that? To suck my cock?"

"Yes," she said breathlessly.

"Then you'll get it. Me."

Reese looked past Gus up at the ceiling of the cave. She hadn't noticed before, but there were even drawings up there. She met Gus's gaze again...and almost melted at the mix of lust and tenderness she saw. "Someday, you'll bring me back here and make love with me?" she asked.

"Anything you want, you'll get," he said solemnly. "I

can't think of a better way to honor those who came before than to take you here. Where hundreds and thousands of years ago, men and women did the same thing."

Reese lifted her head and kissed him softly, trying to show him without words how much she liked and appreciated him.

"But..." he said, sitting up and pulling her with him. "If I don't get you out from under me, all my good intentions will be shot to hell. I brought you something though..."

He turned to rifle through his pack, and Reese took the opportunity to admire him some more. Some people might be turned off by his tattoos. Or think his hairline wasn't masculine enough. Or not like the veins in his arms, or his hard muscles. They might be insulted by his protectiveness. But not Reese. She liked everything about this man. And she was still pinching herself that he seemed to like her back.

He turned back to her with something in his hand. And when Reese looked down, she chuckled. He was holding a baggie with three chocolate chip cookies inside.

"Tell me those are Robert's cookies," she pleaded.

"They're Robert's cookies," Gus said obediently.

"Gimme!" Reese teased.

With a smile, Gus opened the bag and held one out to her. She took a huge bite and closed her eyes in bliss. "I have no idea what he does to make these so good, but I'm convinced he puts some sort of illegal drug inside to keep us addicted."

Gus laughed. "I wouldn't doubt it." He finished his and held out the last cookie to her.

"We could split it," she suggested.

"And risk getting shanked by you?" Gus said, deadpan. "No way, it's all yours."

Reese wasn't offended. He'd heard her talk about how much she loved Robert's chocolate chip cookies more than once over the last week. She had a feeling she'd gone overboard in her enthusiastic praise, but she wasn't an idiot. If Gus was offering it to her, she was going to take it.

"Remind me of this later so I can thank you properly," she told him suggestively.

He licked his lips and said, "Oh, I will."

After she'd finished the cookie and taken a long drink of water to wash it down, he leaned in and kissed her again. It wasn't a short kiss. They were upright this time, but the lust between them sparked to life just as hot and fast as when she was on her back.

"You taste like chocolate," he murmured after a while, his thumb brushing her cheekbone.

Reese might've been embarrassed by that, but at the moment, she was feeling too mellow. And too turned on. If Gus had suggested they throw caution to the wind and go at it right then and there, she would've agreed wholeheartedly. But she couldn't deny that the thought of him taking her in his bed, where she'd dreamed about him doing just that for the last week, was more appealing.

Gus took a deep breath and moved away, lying on his back and putting his hands under his head. "I love it here," he said after a moment.

"Thank you for sharing it with me," Reese told him, lying next to him. They remained like that for a while, side-by-side. Neither speaking, just absorbing the history of the place. After several minutes, still without a word, Gus reached for her hand. They held hands as they stared up at the roof of the cave.

Reese couldn't remember ever being happier.

Eventually, they had to leave. Gus packed up their

trash and made sure they left not a trace of themselves behind before hugging her tightly, then leading the way back toward The Refuge.

Things had changed between them in that cave, and while Reese wasn't dumb enough to think that sexual chemistry and lust meant they'd get married and live happily ever after, she couldn't help but feel optimistic about their future.

She hadn't brought up moving to the area, and he hadn't either. But she hoped that was where they were headed. At the moment, living in his cabin was a temporary arrangement until Woody was completely healed and Gus's friend said it would be safe to go back to Kansas City.

But, not for the first time, Reese was considering not leaving. She had no problem finding an apartment in Los Alamos, because she didn't want to put Gus in an awkward position, but she hoped he'd want to continue to date her if that happened.

She'd be lonely if she moved out, but she also didn't want to outstay her welcome. Gus was used to being alone, just as she was. But if, after they dated a while and she was working in town, he wanted her to move in with him at The Refuge, she wouldn't refuse.

Blushing at the thoughts running through her head, Reese tried to think about something else. About how Jasna was doing in school. What topic she might use to try to engage Angelo the next time she saw him. How Woody's arm was doing. Anything to dampen the increasingly needy feeling she had about the man currently holding her hand and leading her through the woods.

As if he could read her mind, Gus tightened his fingers and turned his head to smile at her.

Yes, it was safe to say Reese's crush was quickly blossoming into more as she got to know the man behind the piercing green eyes and quiet demeaner.

Smiling, she decided to go with the flow. Whatever happened would happen, and thinking too hard about it wouldn't change a damn thing. She'd enjoy being with him while she could and go from there.

CHAPTER ELEVEN

"Can we talk?"

Spike stiffened. He'd been dreading this. But honestly, he'd been expecting Woody to want to have a chat with him before now.

Ever since he and Reese had gotten back from the cave, he hadn't been able to keep his hands off her. Every chance he got, he was touching her. Putting his hand on the small of her back when they walked, holding her hand, sitting next to her at meals at the lodge with a hand on her knee...he wasn't surprised her brother wanted to have a word. Sure, he'd said he was all right with them dating, but thinking about it and seeing the proof right in front of his face were two completely different things.

"Sure," Spike said as breezily as he could.

"You want to take a walk?" Woody asked.

Spike nodded. "Table Rock?" he asked. It wasn't a difficult walk and if his old friend was going to tell him he'd changed his mind and didn't want him dating Reese, he'd definitely need the calm that the land could bring.

The two men walked leisurely toward the trail that led

to the overlook. There was a large flat rock there, hence the name Table Rock.

"How's your arm doing?" Spike asked.

"It's good. We already would've been out of your hair except Tex says there's been some action on the dark web about me, and Kansas City was mentioned. I'm not about to put Isabella or her brother in danger again."

"You think it's the cartel?"

Woody shrugged. "I'm not sure who else it would be."

"Why do they care so much? I mean, no offense, but you aren't exactly an HVT for them, and I can't imagine Isabella is either," Spike said.

"I agree."

Spike considered not saying what he was thinking, but this was his friend. They'd saved each other's lives more than once and they'd always been honest with each other while on the teams. It had been two weeks since they'd returned from Colombia...and it was time. "What about Angelo?"

Woody was silent for a moment, then he sighed. "Yeah, I've been thinking about that too. I know he told Isabella he was forced to work for the cartel...but what if he wasn't?"

Even though he was the one who'd brought up the possibility that Angelo could be the reason for the intel on the dark web, Spike felt compelled to say, "He was locked in a room just like you and Isabella. If he was actively working with them, wouldn't he have been with the other men down in that basement, involved in whatever plans they were making?"

Woody nodded. "I desperately want to agree with you, but I'm just not sure right now. He's been pretty moody since arriving in the States."

"Maybe he's feeling guilty about everything that happened," Spike suggested.

"Maybe," Woody agreed, but it was clear he wasn't completely buying that excuse for Isabella's brother.

It was frustrating as hell not to have any answers, but it had to be even worse for Woody. "I guess the big question now is, are you, Isabella, our guests and staff, and Angelo in any danger of the cartel coming here to finish whatever it was they were trying to do in the first place?"

"No." Woody's answer was immediate and heartfelt.

"You can't know that," Spike said carefully.

"I *do* know that," Woody countered. They'd reached Table Rock and he turned to face Spike. "Look, I know what I said when we first got here. I had many of the same concerns as you're voicing right now. I realize Angelo hasn't exactly been friendly, but at a minimum, I'll never believe he'd do *anything* that would put Isabella in danger, no matter what he was doing with the cartel. Yes, getting involved in the drug trade at all puts them both in danger. I can't know for sure if Angelo fully realized the consequences. What I *do* know is, those two have been through hell. It's been the two of them against the world since he was a kid. I'm not saying he's an angel, because he's not, but there's no way he'd tell a bunch of cartel members where she is so they could come here and harm her."

Spike wasn't so sure, but he respected his friend's difficult situation.

"And if it comes to it...I'll take Isabella and Angelo away from here."

"That's not what I'm suggesting," Spike said firmly. "We're more than able to protect everyone. We've learned a lot since that asshole came after Alaska and the thing with Jasna. As I told you before, we've got cameras on the road and placed strategically along the property line. If anyone steps into our forest, we'll know about it."

"This place is awesome," Woody said.

Spike wasn't thrilled with the change in topic, but he allowed it. He was still confused about what exactly had happened in Colombia. From Woody being kidnapped along with Isabella and Angelo, to the drugs, to finding the three of them unguarded in the house, to their almost too-easy escape, to not having any answers about *anything*, even two weeks later. It was frustrating, but he was more than happy that no one had been seriously hurt. And the connection he'd made with Reese was a dream come true.

"Yeah, it is," Spike belatedly responded.

"I appreciate you and your friends letting us stay for a while."

"Of course. When we started this place, we discussed it and decided that if any of our old teammates needed it, they were welcome here free of charge," Spike told him.

"It's needed," Woody said quietly, as he stared out over the trees in the distance. The view from Table Rock was amazing on a normal day. But today, with the weather in the low seventies, with autumn quickly approaching, it was especially beautiful. "This place, I mean. The things we saw and did...they can get overwhelming."

Spike nodded.

The wind blew around them as if attempting to chase away the bad thoughts swirling in their brains.

Then Woody cleared his throat and turned to Spike. "So, the reason I wanted to speak to you is twofold. I told you a second ago that if it came down to the safety of you and everyone who lives and works here, that I'd leave with Isabella and Angelo..."

"Yeah?" Spike prompted when his friend paused.

"I'm going to take her back to Kansas City, once Tex tells me the interest online has died down." He held up his hand when Spike started to protest. "You've been more than generous. And I want to go home. More importantly, I want to take Isabella home. To *my* home. The Refuge is awesome, but it's not mine."

"I understand," Spike said.

"I'm gonna give Tex a few more weeks because the last thing I want to do is put Isabella in danger, but we can't stay here forever. I think the faster we get to Kansas City, the more comfortable Angelo will be. He can find his feet. No offense, but there isn't a lot for him to do here. There aren't people his own age that he can meet and jobs are pretty scarce."

"I'm sure if we asked around we might find him something temporary for the next month," Spike suggested.

"I'll have Isabella talk to him about that. But I really brought you out here to ask about something else. And I need you to be honest."

Spike tensed. "Of course."

"How much of a disruption would it be if Isabella and I got married at The Refuge?"

Spike stared at his friend for a beat, speechless, before grinning widely. "Not at all!" he exclaimed.

Woody rolled his eyes. "You're such a guy. There are a million details that go into a wedding. I'm guessing Alaska, Henley, and your employees might think it's a disruption."

Spike shrugged. "I'm sure you're right, but if you think anyone will mind regardless, you're crazy. And to be honest, we've had a few guests inquire about the same thing, but we haven't felt comfortable saying yes as it wasn't something we'd even thought about. If you don't mind it being a low-key thing, since The Refuge *is* a place for people to relax and I'm not sure a huge party would be appropriate, I'm sure it'll be okay."

"All right, but you need to talk to your friends. Make sure it's not an issue. I mean, we could always go to the courthouse when we get home, but I wanted to give Isabella something to remember. She's worked her ass off for so long, I'd love to pamper her and make her feel special on our wedding day."

"I'm happy for you, Woody," Spike said sincerely.

"It's fast..." his friend said, his words trailing off.

Spike laughed. "Fast? Are you serious? You and Isabella hit it off years ago when we first met her. We all knew you two were meant to be."

"All right, I'll give you that, but we've only been *together*-together for a few weeks," Woody protested.

"You love her?" Spike asked.

"So much it scares the shit out of me."

"She love you?"

"Yes," Woody said without any hesitation.

"Then who cares what everyone else thinks."

"You're right."

"I know," Spike said with a smirk.

"Should we talk about you and my sister now?" Woody asked with a gleam in his eye.

"I'm thinking *no*," he retorted.

Woody got serious. "She seems...settled."

"What does that mean?"

"Don't get all protective on me. I'm just saying you guys are good for each other," Woody clarified. "She's probably gonna want to go back to Kansas City when I do," he warned.

Spike stiffened.

"I expect you'll convince her otherwise."

"I'm going to try," he said slowly.

"She's already quit her job. She loves it here, everyone can tell. She's gotten close to Alaska, Henley, and Jasna. And even to your other employees. There's a sparkle in her eye that I haven't seen in a long time."

"You're really all right with us being together?" Spike asked.

"Hell yes. If I can't trust my sister with one of the people I'd trust to have my back when we're surrounded by insurgents and minutes from running out of ammo, who the hell *can* I trust with her? You gonna hurt her?"

"No."

"You gonna beat on her? Control who her friends are? Keep her a prisoner in your cabin?"

"What the fuck? No. Where's this coming from?" Spike asked, getting pissed.

"Then why would I be upset that you and her are together?" Woody asked, not alarmed in the least by his friend's anger.

Spike did his best to calm himself. Woody wasn't warning him away from Reese. Was doing the opposite, in fact. But he didn't like to think of *anyone* doing that shit to her. She was an independent woman, and the thought of anyone stifling her, or trying to control her in any way, made him physically sick.

"I've never met anyone like her," Spike said after a moment. "She could do so much better than me, and I know it. I don't deserve her, but I'm going to do every-thing in my power to be the kind of man *she* deserves. I don't know what will happen in the future, but I'd never hurt her, Woody. I give you my word as a Delta that she's safe with me."

"I didn't doubt it for a moment," Woody said seriously.

"And you underestimate yourself. You two were meant for each other. Just make her happy, and I'll be content."

"I'll do my best."

The two men stared at each other for a long moment before Woody said, "You ever think this is where we'd end up?"

"Honestly? No," Spike said.

"She loves you," Woody said quietly.

Spike didn't have to ask who he was talking about.

"I can see it in her eyes. Don't fuck this up, Spike. I mean it. You won't find a better woman than Reese."

"I know," he said simply. And he did. "Thank you."

"For what?" Woody said.

"For not being a dick about me and Reese. For trusting me with her. For being an awesome brother. For saving my life so many times. For being a damn good friend."

"You can thank me by marrying my sister and giving me lots of nieces and nephews."

"That again?" Spike asked, rolling his eyes.

"Hey, we aren't getting any younger. And I want my kids to have cousins to play with," Woody said with a smile.

Spike had always seen his Delta team as his family. And now his friends here at The Refuge. But the thought of having children of his own, of holidays together, of driving to Kansas City to visit the cousins...he wanted that. More than he ever thought he would.

"Yeah," he agreed.

Woody slapped him on the back, then groaned. "Fuck, I forgot my arm," he bitched.

Spike rolled his eyes. "How about we get back so I can ask the others about the wedding thing, and you can tell

Isabella to get with Alaska and Henley so we can get the ball rolling."

Woody didn't even hesitate, heading for the trail without another word.

Spike would've laughed at his friend's eagerness to get back to Isabella, but he was feeling the same way about Reese. It hadn't been that long since he'd seen her, but he couldn't wait to see how her day was going. They'd made out that morning on the couch after breakfast, and it was all he'd been able to do to stand up and start his day. The time was coming when neither of them would be able to control themselves any longer. He wanted that with every fiber of his being, but he was also enjoying the build-up. The anticipation.

And he couldn't wait to see Reese's reaction to finding out her brother was getting married. She was going to be ecstatic.

* * *

Angelo stared down at the ridiculous game he was playing on his phone, bored out of his skull. He was relieved his sister had gotten him a replacement cell phone, but he hated it here. Hated being in the middle of nowhere. Hated not being able to understand what anyone around him was saying. Hated feeling like he was stupid.

Hated the United States.

He'd lied to his sister. Something he'd had to do more frequently in recent months. Convinced her he was glad to get away from the cartel. Told her he'd been forced into selling drugs. But neither of those things were true. Not at all.

He wanted to *be* someone. Wanted the respect and

power the cartel members had. And he knew she wouldn't like it. Would be so disappointed in him.

He loved Isabella, but he needed to be his own man.

Back in South America, he was becoming someone important. He had a valuable job and felt as if he belonged. Here in the States, he was less than nothing.

His sister had told him countless times over the years how bad the cartel was. That he needed to stay away from anyone involved with them at all costs. But she didn't understand. She worked her ass off for pennies. The cartel had *big* money. Lots of it. They could've already moved out of their shitty apartment and into a house more beautiful than they ever dreamed if he'd begun to work for them years ago.

But he was eighteen now. Not a kid anymore. Isabella couldn't tell him what to do or who to be. It was past time he manned up and did what he needed to do to secure his future. Time to take care of his sister for once, now that he was a man.

He'd made the first steps toward doing just that. Then he'd fucked up. He hadn't done it on purpose, but he'd screwed up all the same.

He'd picked up the drugs he was supposed to deliver without incident—then mixed up the delivery date for the drop. He'd missed it. He'd fully intended to explain the accident to his contact, Pablo, but the man had been *pissed*. He'd come to the apartment with others, snatching up Angelo without letting him say a word.

But they'd grabbed Isabella and her American boyfriend as well, threatened to kill her if Woody did anything out of line.

Angelo had been scared, but the men Pablo had delivered them to promised to let them all go...eventually. They were making a point, one Angelo got loud and clear. If he fucked up ever again, Isabella would pay the price.

Then the Americans had come and ruined everything! He'd wanted to protest. Tell Isabella that he had everything under control, but she didn't give him the chance. In order to keep his sister safe, he'd gone with them willingly when they'd left the drug house.

One thing had led to another, and he'd quickly found himself on a plane to America. The "rescue" escalated so fast, it made his head spin.

He never wanted to leave Colombia.

He wanted to stay and become somebody.

He'd never have the respect and power here in the States that he could have back in Bogotá. He needed to get home. And his sister had given him the means to do just that. He just had to be patient. Which sucked.

It wasn't easy to figure out how to get in touch with any of his contacts back in Colombia. It wasn't as if he'd memorized their numbers. Why would he? He could just click on the fictitious names he'd programmed into his contacts list on his cell phone.

The phone that was still back in Bogotá.

He'd checked social media, sending various messages with a few members, but so far no one had gotten back to him. Angelo suspected they were once again trying to teach him a lesson. Making sure he knew that he was low on their totem pole of power. He understood that, but he hated waiting.

In the meantime, he'd been in the US for a week, and he'd come to realize that he'd have to at least pretend he liked being here in this desolate place. Isabella had sought him out after breakfast yesterday morning, saying she was worried about him, and claiming that Woody was too. To appease his sister, he'd make an effort to be friendlier. He didn't want to. Didn't want to be anyone's pity project, and even without understanding English, he knew that everyone felt sorry for him. But making them suspicious would be far worse.

Woody wasn't stupid. Neither were his friends. If he continued to be standoffish and moody, they'd begin to wonder if he was hiding something. Perhaps figure out he'd lied about wanting to leave South America, about being forced to work for the cartel. And if they figured that out, he'd never get back home. And he might be cut off from his sister altogether, which he didn't want.

"*Hola!*" a cheerful voice said from nearby.

Angelo internally groaned. It was Reese. From what his sister had told him, she was the very reason he was here and not at home, building his new life. She was Woody's sister, and she'd gone down to Colombia to find him.

Stupid woman. She didn't even speak Spanish. How the hell did she think she was going to find her brother?

She was the reason the other guys had come and eventually "rescued" him.

It was all so fucking dumb! If only everyone had minded their own damn business, his sister and Woody would've been released. They'd have gone to the US, leaving him in Colombia to build his empire.

Reese approached the porch of the cabin where Angelo was staying with his sister, fumbling with her phone, and Angelo braced himself. She was using that ridiculous app to try to talk to him. He wished everyone would just leave him alone. If it wasn't Reese, it was that brat, Jasna. Trying to lure him to the barn to see cows. As if he wanted to be around a bunch of smelly farm animals.

He sighed. He'd just decided he needed to be friendlier. Needed to play their game so that no one suspected how badly he wanted to leave.

"How are you? Robert is having tamales for lunch. Want you to come and eat?"

The app was always mixing words up. Yes, Angelo could understand what Reese was asking, but he didn't want to be around anyone. Didn't want to have slow, stilted conversation through an app.

Apparently he paused a little too long before answering, because Reese said something else into her phone, then the robotic voice of the app translated. "I'm sorry you aren't happy here. Are you excited about getting your sister married?"

Angelo looked up at that, frowning as he asked, "*Qué?*" He waited impatiently as Reese spoke into her phone once more before the app translated her words.

"Oh, you don't know? I am so sorry, I'm sure sister of yours was going to tell you soon. I feel bad about telling to you. They will be ceremony here at The Refuge in week two."

Angelo was stunned. The woman was right. Of course Isabella would tell him about marrying Woody. Might have tried to tell him already...if he hadn't been avoiding her because he didn't enjoy lying to his sister.

He smiled at Reese, although he had a feeling it was a sickly attempt.

The look on his face seemed to surprise Reese nonetheless, but she recovered quickly and returned his grin. "You want to eat?"

Angelo nodded and said, "Give me a minute."

The app translated his words and she smiled even bigger as she nodded several times.

Turning, Angelo went into the cabin, shutting the door behind him. He took a deep breath. Then another.

He wasn't unhappy about the news, really. Isabella needed someone to look after her. A man to take on her burdens. At least until Angelo could do so himself. But marrying Woody meant that she'd stay *here*. In the US. And she'd want him to stay too.

That wasn't an option. Angelo would do whatever was necessary to get home.

Looking out the window, he saw Reese waiting for him patiently. Before going up to the lodge, he wanted to try once more to get in touch with his contacts back home. They'd eventually help him, he had no doubt about that. Things might be intense for a while when he returned. He needed to atone for fucking up the drop, and for allowing his sister and the American to escape. But he'd do whatever grunt work they deemed appropriate in order to get back in the cartel's good graces.

He quickly typed out another message on social media. Once again reassuring the cartel that he was sorry about screwing up the delivery and he was doing everything in his power to get back home.

Staring off into space, willing Pablo to reply, Angelo resolved to do anything necessary to climb the ranks of the organization as quickly as possible. He was going to be respected. *Feared*. People would one day talk about him in hushed tones, would never dare to defy him.

His future was in Bogotá. Not in the States. Not being a minority in a country that looked down on anyone who didn't have white skin and spoke perfect English. His sister might be all right with being a second-class citizen, but not Angelo.

He was going home. As soon as he could figure out how.

And with that, he took a deep breath and turned back to the front door. He'd go to lunch with the annoying American to assuage suspicion, to stay under the radar. So when the time came, he'd be able to leave without anyone suspecting anything.

Stepping outside, he gave Reese a polite nod, silently following behind her as they made their way up to the main lodge.

CHAPTER TWELVE

"This is so cool!" Alaska said with a huge smile.

Reese had to agree, and not just because it was her brother's wedding they were planning. She was in Los Alamos having a late lunch with Isabella, Alaska, Henley, Jess, Ryan, and Luna. They'd had to wait until after Henley's group session with a few of the guests, and after Jess and Ryan were finished with the housekeeping tasks for the day.

They'd all met at Rose Chocolatier in Los Alamos, an amazing chocolate shop that made specialty cakes and goodies for events. They were tasting several different kinds of cakes to decide which to serve at Woody and Isabella's ceremony.

The Refuge definitely had wedding fever. Over the last week, everyone had gotten into the spirit of the occasion, and since it was the first wedding at the venue, they wanted to do it right. Hudson, the landscaper, was working overtime to make a wedding arch for the ceremony, and Robert and Luna had spent hours with the happy couple deciding what food to serve at the reception.

Woody had managed to find an officiant from town willing to come out to marry them, and the paperwork had already been filed. Their parents were ecstatic; they'd heard all about Isabella over the years, and they'd already bought their plane tickets and made reservations at a hotel in town. Woody and Isabella being married would allow her to stay in the US legally, and Tex had taken over making sure everything was smooth on that front.

The ceremony wasn't going to be huge. Any guests booked at The Refuge on the wedding day would be invited, as well as all the employees, along with Reese and Woody's mom and dad. But it wasn't the size of the event that mattered, it was the joy of the occasion that had Reese all excited.

Her brother was getting married.

It was almost too hard to believe. For years, he'd been adamant about not wanting to date. And she knew it was because he was in love with Isabella. She was so happy things had finally worked out for them both.

She grinned, and Henley asked, "What's funny?"

"I was just thinking about my brother. It's so hard to believe he's getting *married*."

"Why?"

"No offense," Reese said, looking at Isabella. "But he's a dork."

Everyone chuckled.

"I mean, I read romance. I see the covers on the ones that feature a Navy SEAL or some other kind of badass military hero...and I just have to laugh. Because Woody doesn't look anything like that. He's not all huge and muscular, he's not almost seven feet tall, and he thinks grunting is an acceptable way of communicating."

The girls all giggled again.

"You want to know what I see when I look at your brother?" Isabella asked.

"Um...not if you're going to even hint at something sexual," Reese told her with a wrinkle of her nose.

Isabella smiled and shook her head. "No. When I first met him years ago, I was immediately drawn to him because of his observation skills. I know that doesn't sound very romantic at all, but he was always on alert. His gaze never stopped scanning the area around him."

"That sounds kind of paranoid," Luna observed.

But Reese understood what Isabella meant. She'd seen it in her brother, Gus, and the rest of their Delta team when she was around them. But Woody seemed to have it in spades. She didn't know what happened to make him so hyper-alert. Probably didn't want to know.

"It is and it isn't," Isabella told Luna. "We were walking from one building to another for a meeting, and I wasn't watching where I was going because I was translating for a government official who was with us. I stumbled, but before I hit the ground, Woody was there. He'd seen the uneven walkway and was moving toward me even before I started to fall.

"That's just one example. When we talked on the phone, he always seemed to know when I was having a bad day, I guess by the tone of my voice. He makes me laugh, makes me feel safe, and when we video chatted, I was always the center of his attention. I thought after a year or two he'd get tired of me. But he never did."

"He was always talking about you," Reese told her soon-to-be sister-in-law. "Every time we got together, he'd have some story to tell about something you did. He bragged about you all the time and is so proud of all you've accomplished."

Isabella blushed and smoothed a lock of dark hair behind her ear. "I am proud of him too. I don't need a romance book hero. Why would I when I have Woody? When we were in that room, I was so scared. But Woody was calm and focused. He kept telling me that he'd get me out of there. That no matter what, he'd keep me safe. I don't know what would've happened if those men tried to hurt us, or tried to take me away from him, but I have no doubt that he would've done everything in his power to keep that from happening."

Reese's eyes welled up with tears. She couldn't imagine how scared Isabella must have been, but knowing that her brother had remained calm and so sure that they'd be okay made her love him all the more.

"Okay, now I'm crying," Alaska said as she wiped her cheeks.

"Right? I need to find me someone like Woody," Luna said.

"I love my husband, but I'm thinking if we found ourselves kidnapped by a drug cartel, Eric wouldn't be nearly as competent," Jess said with a chuckle.

Everyone laughed, lightening the mood.

"Well, thank goodness you won't have to worry about that," Henley said. "None of us will. We're here, The Refuge is safe, and we're going to celebrate with a wedding in less than two weeks!"

"What did you guys think of number three?" Alaska asked, pointing to the piece of cake on the right side of their plates. They were tasting three different cakes at a time, and they were all numbered to keep them straight.

As everyone discussed their favorite samples, Reese looked over at Ryan. She didn't know the other woman very well, but she was always friendly and willing to help with anything that needed to be done around the lodge. She was quiet, kept to herself, but, much like the owners of The Refuge, always seemed to be very aware of everything going on around her.

"You okay?" she asked quietly as the others debated if they liked the chocolate swirl or the red velvet cake better.

Ryan looked at her and smiled. "Of course. Why wouldn't I be?"

"Well, I can be forgiven for being mushy since it's my brother who's getting married. Isabella's enthusiasm is obvious, Alaska and Henley are insanely happy with their men, Jess is married to a man she adores, and Luna is too busy with college to seriously think about settling down. So...that leaves you."

Ryan shrugged. "I'm good."

"You're single, right?"

"Oh, yeah. Totally single," she said fervently.

"You're pretty," Reese told her. "I mean, *really* pretty. And there are a lot of good looking guys at The Refuge. You ever thought about getting together with one of them?"

"No," Ryan said almost too quickly.

Reese managed to hide her smile. She wondered which of the guys had caught her eye. "Why not?" she asked.

Ryan shrugged. "I'm not going to be here forever. I took this job to get away from...well, let's just say I needed a break from life. And where better to do that than in the middle of nowhere?"

Reese frowned. She didn't like the note of...trepidation...she heard in the woman's voice.

"Although," Ryan went on, "it's actually been kind of exciting so far. I don't mean that in a bad way, but I was expecting to come here and be bored out of my mind. But it's been anything *but* boring."

Ryan turned to face Reese, and the intense look in her brown eyes pinned her in place. "You're lucky to have Woody," she said. "He loves you so much, it's easy to see. You guys have a great relationship. Even when you're sniping at each other, you can tell neither of you are seriously upset. I don't get along with my brother, like, *at all*, so seeing the two of you is...nice."

Reese reached out and put her hand over Ryan's where she was holding her fork with a grip so tight, her knuckles were white. "I know we just met, but you can talk to me, Ryan. If something's wrong, I can help. Or I can talk to Woody or Gus and they—"

Ryan interrupted her by laughing. It was a forced sound. Almost painfully so. "Oh, no, I'm good. Promise." Then she leaned forward and asked, "Do you think the others—or the owners of the chocolate shop—would rebel if I suggested that we try a vanilla or strawberry cake?" She smiled, but the emotion didn't reach her eyes.

Reese wanted to call her bluff and encourage the woman to talk to her, but if she didn't want to share whatever was troubling her, Reese suspected no amount of pushing would make her open up. So she let the subject drop...but she vowed to keep her eye on Ryan. "I was thinking maybe a pound cake," she said.

For a moment, she saw relief in Ryan's gaze, before she wiped all emotion from her expression except for the fake smile. She turned to the others. "Reese and I vote for trying something that *isn't* chocolate."

Everyone began to talk at once, and the owner of the bakery, who was standing nearby, stepped forward and offered to bring out a marble cake with both vanilla and chocolate mixed together.

The rest of the tasting went without a hitch, and by the time they were all ready to leave, Isabella had chosen a dark chocolate cake with chocolate frosting, and ice cream with every slice served to break up the richness.

Everyone split up at that point. Henley was going to the school to pick up Jasna, Alaska and Luna were headed back to The Refuge, Jess and Ryan were going to their own homes in town, and Reese was taking Isabella to the grocery store before they too headed back to The Refuge.

"How are you acclimating to life here in the States?" Reese asked as they drove toward the store.

"I love it here," Isabella said with a huge grin. "It's weird not being in a city though."

Reese smiled at her. "Yeah, this isn't exactly Bogotá, is it?"

"No. But I like it."

"Kansas City isn't nearly as crowded as Bogotá was, but it's got a lot more going on than Los Alamos," Reese told her. Then she went on to tell her about some of her favorite restaurants and things to do in the city. She got serious as she pulled into a parking spot and turned off her engine. "Do you think you can be happy there?" she asked.

Isabella turned to her and nodded. "I can be happy anywhere Woody is."

Reese loved hearing that. "I know he's already working some of his connections to see if he can find you a good job—and of course he can do his accounting work from anywhere—and there are more and more Spanish-speaking people in the US, so I have no doubt you'll be able to find something you love that pays well."

"I hope so," Isabella said. "But even if I don't find

something, that's okay too. Because Woody and I want to start a family together as soon as we can."

Reese's eyes lit up. "Seriously?"

Isabella nodded a little shyly. "Yes. I've always wanted a baby, but raising Angelo was hard by myself and I didn't want to do that again. Do not get me wrong, I love him, but it was extremely difficult. Especially in Bogotá."

Reese wanted to do a little jig at hearing she might become an aunt sooner rather than later, but she refrained. "How's he doing? Angelo, that is. I was really happy he came up to the lodge for lunch with me the other day, but he seems...stressed. Or maybe sad."

Isabella sighed. "He does not like it here. I was hoping he would be as relieved as I was to get away from the city. To leave the constant worry and fear behind. But instead, he seems lost."

"It can't be easy for him to be uprooted from everything he knew."

"It is not. But what he knew was mostly poverty, gangs, and struggle," Isabella said. "He's being...I am not sure what the word is...ingrateful?"

"Ungrateful?" Reese asked.

"Yes. That is the word. He should be happy he no longer has to worry about money for dinner. And that he's safe from being forced to work for the cartel anymore. Instead, he is moping. When I told him he should study English, he agreed, but he hasn't actually started any lessons yet." Isabella bit her lip in worry and sighed. "I do not know where the sweet little brother I raised has gone. It's like I do not even know him."

"He's still a teenager," Reese soothed. "I mean, I don't have kids, but from everything I've heard from friends, they get like this. I know he's basically an adult, but he's been uprooted and taken away from everything he knows. I think the longer he's here, the more he'll settle. And being in Kansas City will be good for him. It'll be a little bit more familiar since it's very busy, a faster pace. There isn't a lot to do around here, so I can understand why he'd be out of sorts."

"I hope you are right. I worry about him. But at the same time, he *is* an adult. I've spoiled him, given him everything I could simply because I didn't have the same things when I was a child."

Reese wasn't sure what else to say. She wanted to help both Isabella and Angelo, but wasn't sure how to go about doing so.

Isabella took a deep breath. "Enough of that. Thank you for coming with me today and for everything you are doing to help with my wedding. I am so happy to be marrying Woody. I would not care if we went to the court-house and had a simple ceremony, but he is insisting on giving me a wedding."

"I'm thinking Woody wants the ceremony as much as, or more than, you do," Reese told her. "Don't tell him I said this, but when he was little, he used to pore over our parents' wedding album. He was obsessed with Mom's big poofy dress, and I think—no, I *know* he wants to have the same memories."

The two women shared a smile.

"My badass special forces brother can be a sappy fool sometimes," Reese teased.

"I love him," Isabella said seriously. "He is so good to me. I don't know that I would've gotten through the last few years without his support. Being with him is a dream come true. I never expected him to come down to

Colombia when I told him I was scared, and yet he did. I will do everything in my power to make him happy."

"You don't have to *do* anything for him to be happy, just being with you does that," Reese said.

Isabella smiled shyly. She looked over at the grocery store, then back at Reese. "You and Spike seem happy together."

"He's amazing," Reese said, not reticent at all to talk about Gus. "I've never been with a man who's so...attentive."

"Maybe it is the special forces part of them," Isabella suggested. "They have seen so many bad things, they go out of their way to protect and look after us because they know the evil that is in the world."

Reese thought she probably had a good point. "But are they with us because of who we are, or because they're clinging to something good in an otherwise evil world?" she blurted. She probably never would've asked that question to anyone other than her brother's woman.

Isabella remained quiet for a moment, which Reese appreciated. She wasn't immediately answering with what Reese longed to hear. She was honestly thinking about the question.

"I believe with all my heart that Woody is with me because of the connection we have. There is no reason for him to have waited for me. We had a long-distance relationship of sorts for years. At any time, he could have said it was too hard. Given up. Found another woman to protect and treat like she is the most important person in his world. But he did not. He kept emailing, calling, and video chatting with me. When I was sad, he cheered me up. When I was angry, he listened to my complaints. When I was lonely, he was there to keep me company.

"I do not believe Woody, or your Spike, would date a woman simply to be with someone. While I love your brother, he is not the most patient man in many ways. The fact that he waited for me proves that he is with me because he loves me. Not because he wants to forget the bad things he has seen and done."

Reese nodded and closed her eyes in order to keep her tears from falling. She wanted to believe Gus was with her for the same reasons. But they didn't have the history Isabella and Woody did. Yes, they'd known each other for years, ever since he and her brother were on the same Delta Force team, but they hadn't been *together* until recently.

When she felt Isabella's hand on her arm, Reese opened her eyes.

"Spike looks at you like Woody looks at me. His eyes follow you when you are in the same room but not together. You are sleeping in his cabin. He could have found another arrangement for you, but he did not. He is not thinking about the evil in his past when he is with you. He is with you because of who you are, Reese. And why would he not? You have been kind to me and my brother, you are generous, beautiful, smart, and you make him laugh. What else could he want?"

Reese smiled. "You're good for my ego," she said softly.

"I am not...what is the phrase...putting butter on you. I am serious."

Chuckling, Reese said, "Buttering you up is the phrase you're looking for."

Isabella blushed. "I know English, but there are many sayings that make no sense, which I am still learning how to use."

"Your English is amazing. I've never understood why

people who have learned English as a second language are so hard on themselves. English is a seriously hard language, and anyone who speaks it when it's not their native tongue has my utmost respect."

"See? You are kind," Isabella said. "Not everyone thinks the way you do. They are impatient and get irritated when they hear anyone with a non-American accent. I think Spike is not stupid. He has seen the amazing woman you are. I believe he is surprised that you are still single. He's not wasting time in making you his."

Reese loved hearing that. So damn much. "I want to make him mine too."

"Sex," Isabella said. Her cheeks reddened, but she kept speaking. "It is the way to the heart."

Reese laughed. "I still don't want to talk about you and my brother having sex, but...really?"

"Yes. Men, they like it. A lot. And they can more easily express their emotions during intimacy. I had the same fears about Woody, about being with him. And now we are getting married and planning a family."

"Because you had sex?" Reese asked skeptically.

"Because we have very *good* sex," Isabella said with a small, secret smile.

"So you're saying I should put my reservations about moving too fast aside and jump Gus?"

Isabella frowned. "Jump on him? No, that could get you or him hurt."

Reese giggled. "Another English phrase. Jump him means have sex with him."

"Ah, then yes, you and Spike should jump. He wants to. It is obvious."

"Yeah?" Reese asked.

"Yes. You have a cabin to yourselves. You should invite

him to your bed. It is more difficult with Angelo in the same cabin as Woody and me, but we still have found a way to have time for ourselves."

"Okay, we're talking about you and my brother having sex, we need to stop this conversation right now," Reese said with a small chuckle. But she couldn't stop thinking about Isabella's perspective. Did she think it would be as easy as a little sex to make Gus love her? No. But...she had a good point. Men often let their guards down during intimacy, when they otherwise might keep their emotions in check.

The two women shared a smile just as both their phones started dinging.

Pulling hers out from her pocket, Reese saw a message from Gus.

GUS

> Are you all right? Alaska and Luna returned from your outing, said you and Isabella were going to the store. Just wanted to check and make sure all is good.

Looking over at Isabella, she saw the other woman smiling as she read the text she'd received. She looked up. "It is Woody. He is worried and wanted to check on me."

"Same with Gus."

"I told you," Isabella said a little smugly. "If he did not care, he would not be texting to check on you."

"How about we assure our guys that we're okay, go

inside, get the stuff on our lists, and get back to The Refuge?" Reese asked.

"Yes."

Reese's fingers flew over the screen as she responded to Gus.

REESE

> We're good. Just having some girl talk. Some soon-to-be-sister talk before shopping. I'll be home soon.

She hit send, then what she'd written sank in.

Home. She'd said she'd be *home* soon. She worried for a moment that she was overstepping. Gus's cabin wasn't her home. But it had sure felt that way over the last couple of weeks. Being there with Gus felt more like a home than the apartment she'd lived in for years in Kansas City. She couldn't decide if that was sad or exciting.

GUS

> Will you pick up some heavy cream? It's in the cooler next to the milk and creamer. I found a recipe for bacon ranch chicken that I think you'll love and I want to try it out.

She couldn't stop smiling. The fact that Gus thought about her when he saw a recipe and wanted to go to the trouble of making it for her made Reese feel really special. And that he had to tell her where to find what he wanted in the store was kind of funny. But he obviously knew she'd have no idea where the heck to find heavy cream, because it wasn't as if she'd ever bought it before. She hadn't lied about not being a good cook.

REESE

Of course. Anything else you want or
need?

GUS

Nope. Just you getting home safe and
sound.

There it was again. That word. Home. But this time
he'd said it, not her. Once more, her thoughts returned to
what Isabella had suggested. About sex. She and Gus had
both been holding back. And all of a sudden, she had no
idea why they were both waiting. They wanted each other,
that was obvious. From the way Gus was always touching
and kissing her, he'd made that very clear.

She quickly texted back before she could talk herself
out of it.

REESE

It feels as if it's been days since I've seen
you rather than just hours. I want you,
Gus. I don't want to wait anymore.

She nervously waited as the three dots danced across
her screen, letting her know he was typing a reply.

GUS

You want me, you've got me. Drive safe.

Looking over at Isabella, Reese saw she was smiling as she
texted with Woody. She was still grinning when she put
her phone in her purse. "Shall we get this done so we can
get back to our men and reassure them that we can leave
their sides for a few hours without incident?"

Reese didn't know what she and Woody had spoken about in their texts, but by the pink in her friend's cheeks, she had a good idea. "Absolutely," she said as she turned and reached for the door handle.

The shopping trip didn't take long, as both women were eager to get back to The Refuge. Butterflies swam in Reese's belly. Was she really going to do this? Have sex with Gus Fowler? Get naked with him, let him see her body without a stitch of clothing?

Yes.

Hell *yes*, she was. And she couldn't wait.

* * *

"She good?" Woody asked Spike after looking up from his phone.

"Yeah," he replied. They'd talked to Alaska and Luna when they're returned from Los Alamos, and when Isabella and Reese hadn't arrived shortly after the other women, they'd both gotten concerned.

After texting to make sure they were all right, Spike was even more impatient than he'd been a few minutes ago. He had no idea what Reese and Isabella had talked about, but if it had given her the courage to come right out and tell him she didn't want to wait to be with him, he was grateful.

Then he promptly began to second-guess himself. What if she wasn't talking about sex? What if she was talking about waiting for something else? He racked his brain, trying to think of anything else she might be insinuating, but he came up blank.

Now that he was thinking about sex with Reese, he couldn't stop. He wanted to get his hands on her. Wanted to feel her curves against him. Needed to taste her, feel her around his cock, hear her moan as he took her.

He was having a hard time keeping his erection at bay, and the last thing he wanted was for Woody to see him getting turned on.

"I'm leaving in less than two weeks," Woody reminded Spike.

"I know."

"Have you talked to Reese about staying yet? I heard her talking to Angelo yesterday, using that app she found that translates her words. She was telling him how much he was going to like Missouri, and all the places she wanted to show him."

Spike tensed.

"I looked on Los Alamos National Laboratory's website at the jobs they currently have open. There's an Accelerator Operator position available. It's in their Engineering, Operations, and Physics department. It's not exactly in her wheelhouse, but I have no doubt she'd be able to not only convince them to hire her, but excel at it as well."

"You've checked out jobs for her?" Spike asked incredulously.

"Of course I have. She quit her job back home, which tells me all I need to know about how serious her feelings are for you. Get your head out of your ass, Spike. My sister could get a job anywhere she wanted, but she'd be an asset to our country right here in Los Alamos. You want her to stay, don't you?"

Spike didn't even have to think about the answer to that question. "Yes."

"Then give her a reason," Woody said, quietly but intensely. "I'm going to hate not having her down the road from me, so to speak, but if I made a relationship with Isabella work and she was thousands of miles away in a foreign country, I can remain close to my sister if she stays here in New Mexico. Especially when I know one of my best friends is looking out for her, along with his six former military badass friends."

Eagerness and anticipation swam through Spike's veins. He'd been dreading Reese saying she was leaving basically from the moment they'd arrived back at The Refuge. He'd frankly been surprised she'd stayed as long as she had. There really wasn't a good reason. Her brother had healed remarkably quickly. Chatter online had died down in the last week, indicating the cartel in Colombia may have given up the idea of coming after Isabella or her brother. Even if Woody stayed for a bit longer...it was probably safe for Reese to get back to her life in Missouri.

But she was still here. He wanted to believe it was because she was as reluctant to leave Spike as he was for her to go.

And now she'd come right out and told him a few minutes ago that she wanted him.

Spike was officially done being noble. Or patient. Or whatever the hell he was doing. He'd never wanted a woman the way he wanted Reese. He had her brother's approval, not that he needed it, but he was glad to have it anyway. There were jobs open at the National Laboratory that she would excel at, and she seemed happy and content here at The Refuge.

If he was going to have everything he'd ever wanted, as Brick and even the prickly Tonka had managed to find, he needed to get his thumb out of his ass and go for it.

The worst thing that could happen was that he and Reese would sleep together and realize they weren't actually compatible in that sense after all—which Spike had a feeling was *not* going to happen. But on the other hand, maybe they'd have amazing, mind-blowing sex that would bring them closer together. It could spur Reese into looking for a job here and moving to The Refuge permanently.

Even if there was only a ten percent chance of that happening, Spike would take those odds.

Woody clapped his friend on the shoulder and smirked. "I see it's finally sinking in."

"What is?" Spike asked.

"That my sister could have any man in the world. She's a hell of a catch, and frankly I'm disappointed with my gender because no one has snapped her up already. But I'm thinking now it's because she was waiting. For you."

The hair on the back of Spike's neck rose. He liked that. A hell of a lot.

"I think I'm gonna skip dinner at the lodge tonight," he said.

Woody grinned. "Yeah?"

"Yeah. I want to cook for Reese. You still want to hike the perimeter of the property tomorrow? You feel up to it?" Spike asked.

"Yes to both questions. But not too early. I like to let Isabella sleep in since she hasn't been able to truly relax in the last ten years or so of her life."

"Maybe we can grab lunch, then go?" Spike asked.

"Sounds like a plan. And, Spike?"

"Yeah?"

"I'll email Reese the link to the site with the available jobs at the lab in the morning."

Spike understood his friend's warning. He needed to have a serious talk with Reese about wanting her to stay before she received that email. He would've been irritated at Woody's interference in his life, and his sister's, but he couldn't dredge up the energy to be pissed. Not when Reese staying was what he wanted more than he wanted to breathe.

He nodded at his friend, then turned and headed for his cabin. He hadn't lied, he *had* found a chicken recipe he wanted to make for Reese...but now all he could think about was having her under him, over him, in the shower, on her knees, and everything in between. He was officially obsessed, and he didn't give a damn.

* * *

Angelo grinned. *Finally*, something was going right. He'd finally gotten a message back. He'd either groveled enough, or somehow made it clear that he'd left South America against his will. And that he was still very loyal to the cartel and would do whatever it took to get back there to start working again. And this time he wouldn't screw up. He'd learned his lesson.

And he'd done it. Pablo had reached out.

PABLO

Where are you?

ANGELO

Fucking America.

PABLO

Where?

ANGELO

New Mexico. I want to come home, but I have no money.

PABLO

Is your sister with you? And the American?

ANGELO

Yes. They're getting married. I want nothing to do with that. I just want to come home and work for the cartel. There's nothing for me here in the US.

PABLO

Why should we take you back? You fucked up.

ANGELO

I know, and as I said in my messages, I will do whatever it takes to make it up to you. I am loyal to the cartel. I swear it.

PABLO

It won't be easy.

ANGELO

I can do it.

PABLO

I am not so sure. You will have to prove your loyalty. Saying the words does not make it true.

ANGELO

What do I need to do?

PABLO

How do we know this isn't a trap? That you aren't now working with the American to bring trouble to our door?

ANGELO

I'm not! I swear!

ANGELO

Pablo? Are you still there? I don't even like my sister's boyfriend. I hate his friends. I just want to come home. Here, I am nothing but a stupid foreigner. Back home, I'm respected.

PABLO

Fine. I will wire you money for a bus ticket. You can take it to Mexico and an associate will pick you up.

ANGELO

Thank you!!! So much.

PABLO

I need an address.

ANGELO

I'm at a place called The Refuge. It's literally in the middle of nowhere. But they have cameras. And I don't think I should get mail here. It would be weird if I got a letter from Colombia. They are paranoid. My sister says the reason we haven't already left is because they are worried the cartel is looking for them. I asked why the cartel would care about someone as unimportant as her or her fiancé. She looked at me like I was dumb.

PABLO

I'm not sending you a letter. I meant, I need the address of the place where I can send money. Wire, like send it electronically.

ANGELO

Right, sorry. I'm sure there's a place like that in the town near here, Los Alamos. I'll get back with you.

PABLO

Tell anyone we've talked, and you're dead.

ANGELO

I won't! I promise. I just want to get out of here.

PABLO

You do this, and you'll belong to the cartel. We don't give money to just anyone, and we don't go out of our way to rescue members who've screwed us.

ANGELO

I know, and I'm ready to pledge my loyalty to you and to the cartel.

PABLO

We'll see how loyal you are. Get me that address.

ANGELO

I will.

For the first time in weeks, Angelo was excited. He was going home! He'd tried to be a little more receptive to the people here, but inside it was killing him to smile, to pretend he was happy, that nothing was wrong.

As a car approached the cabin, he glanced up to see Isabella. Returning from town with Reese...the cause of all his troubles in the first place.

Angelo scowled. He didn't like the woman, but he understood her loyalty to her brother. Angelo loved his sister more than anything...but he wasn't a kid anymore. She had to see that. Had to know he was ready to be his own man. She didn't approve of the cartel, but she'd never actually given them a chance. Couldn't understand how much *better* their lives would have been if he'd started working for the cartel years ago. They would've had money. A lot of it. They could've moved to a bigger house, she could've quit her job working for foreigners and lived an easy life.

But instead, they'd been going without. Scrimping and saving and they still never had enough.

He didn't want to leave her behind...but once he was back home and making good money, he'd reach out to Isabella. Tell her how much he missed her. If given the chance, he knew he could care for his sister better than the American. He'd have more money than Woody could ever dream of making. Maybe he could convince her to return to Colombia.

Isabella had taken care of him when their parents died, going without for years so that Angelo could have more. He wanted to return that loyalty, be the provider for once, but his sister was so stubborn! She wouldn't listen to him.

Angelo sighed, some of his excitement dimming. He knew it wouldn't be as easy as asking Isabella to come home. But he also knew that one day, she'd be sorry for her choices. When the American got tired of her and dumped her, when she was alone and broke and had no one, she'd reach out to him. And Angelo would happily welcome her back. He'd prove to her that all her ideas about the cartel were wrong. That they were savvy businessmen who were providing a product that was very much in demand.

Why was it wrong to make money? It wasn't. If the cartel didn't distribute the drugs, someone else would. And someone else would make all the money that Angelo wanted his share of, desperately.

It was only a matter of time before he was back where he belonged. Where he could *be* someone. But first, he had to find a place in Los Alamos that transferred money. He could make some calls, but it wouldn't be easy since he'd have to find a place that spoke Spanish. Then he needed to find a ride into town to retrieve the cash. He couldn't drive himself, and he couldn't ask his sister or Woody. They'd ask too many questions.

He'd figure it out. His friend Pablo was going out on a limb to bring him home, and Angelo wouldn't let him down. He'd do whatever he had to, including smiling and laughing to convince everyone that he wasn't planning on leaving here as soon as possible to go back to South America and the cartel.

CHAPTER THIRTEEN

Spike was having a hard time controlling himself. But even though he might be desperate for Reese, he wasn't going to act like a neanderthal. When she'd arrived home from her shopping trip, she seemed...shy. As much as Spike wanted to drag her to his room and finally, *finally*, join her in his bed, he forced himself to greet her with a long, slow kiss, then turned his attention back to the dinner he'd begun cooking.

The cabin smelled delicious, like bacon. The meal he'd made could in no way be called healthy, even though it included baked chicken. The heavy cream, bacon, and cream of mushroom soup made sure of that.

It was obviously the right call not to jump her bones the second she walked in the door, because Spike could see her relaxing as the evening went on. Besides, he wanted to talk to her about her future first. Specifically, finding a job in Los Alamos. And since Woody would be emailing her a link to the job he'd found at the laboratory in the morning, he wanted to be very clear where he stood before she received it.

They sat down to eat, and Reese leaned in and put her nose over the steam rising from her plate, inhaling deeply. "This smells so good," she told him with a smile.

"It totally does," he agreed as he picked up his spoon. He'd cut the chicken into bite-size pieces, and it had ended up more like a creamy soup than chicken with sauce over it, but he didn't mind. He took a taste, and Reese did the same thing.

She closed her eyes as she chewed, moaning deep in her throat.

And just like that, Spike's cock hardened. Reese had no idea how sexy she was. It was taking every ounce of his discipline not to leap across the table and say to hell with the food.

"I assume it's good?" he asked with a grin.

"Good? Gus, this is *amazing*."

Spike didn't know what it was about her insistence on calling him "Gus" that affected him so much. Maybe it was because it separated him from his military persona. It wasn't that he wasn't proud of what he'd done, but there were times when all the shit in his head was just too overwhelming. The use of his name reminded him that he was someone *before* the military, and he was still that person after. Or at least, he could be.

And he liked that Reese, herself, was mostly separate from that part of his life.

They made small talk as they ate, but there was an undercurrent of sexual tension. Reese kept sneaking looks at him under her lashes, and when she licked her lips, it was all Spike could do to stay in his seat.

When he was finished with his meal, Spike pushed his plate aside and rested his elbows on the table and leaned in, keeping his gaze fixed on Reese. He hadn't thought much about his small kitchen table. It was round, and pretty much only big enough for two people. He was across from Reese, but they were as close as if they were sitting side-by-side at the huge table up at the lodge.

She took the last bite of her meal, then looked over at him. Spike reached out a hand and she took it without hesitation.

"I was talking to Woody today," he started...then lost his train of thought as Reese ran her thumb over the top of his hand. Her fingers were soft and warm, and he had a sudden vision of his cock in her fist as she caressed him.

"Yeah?" she asked with a raised brow.

Spike cleared his throat and forced himself to concentrate. The faster he got through this conversation, the faster he could get Reese to his bed. "We were talking about him going back to Kansas City after the wedding."

"Yeah, he's mostly healed up, and since we haven't heard anything from your friend Tex about the cartel still looking for him, he thinks it's safe to go home. I know he wants to get Isabella settled, and see about finding Angelo a job to keep him busy. It's obvious he's still struggling hard to acclimate, but he seems to be making more of an effort lately."

"Yeah, I've noticed that too," Spike said. He didn't completely trust the kid, but he *was* trying harder to fit in. It made Spike soften toward him a little bit.

Then he took a deep breath and stopped beating around the bush.

"I want you to stay," he blurted, continuing before she could say a word. "I know you've lived in Kansas City for a long time, but I don't want you to go. I've gotten used to you being here, and I already can't imagine waking up without you. Woody looked into jobs at the Los Alamos

National Laboratory and he thinks there are a few you'd love. He's going to send you a link tomorrow, but I didn't want you to get it and wonder where I stood about you staying. I'm all for it. One hundred percent. I'd move to Missouri to be with you, but I'm not sure how that would work with ownership here at The Refuge."

Reese squeezed his hand, and Spike shut up. He was rambling anyway. He practically held his breath to see what she thought.

"I've already looked at the lab's website," she admitted with a self-conscious shrug. "My boss back in Missouri said he'd give me a glowing recommendation...and I've been working on my resume."

"You have?"

She nodded.

"So you want to stay?" Spike asked, needing to hear the words from her mouth.

"Yes."

Spike stood so fast, his chair teetered on two legs and would've crashed to the floor if he hadn't grabbed it at the last minute with his free hand. He didn't let go of Reese's as he stepped around the table and pulled her to her feet. "The dishes can wait. I can't," he declared.

He heard her giggle, but more importantly, she didn't protest when he started toward the hallway, practically dragging her behind him.

Before he'd made it two feet into the hallway, though, his phone rang in his pocket. He was going to ignore it, but he didn't get a lot of calls. When he did, they were usually important.

He stopped walking and took a deep breath before looking behind him at Reese. "I have to get that."

She nodded.

Without letting go of her hand, Spike reached into his pocket and pulled out his cell. He saw Brick's name on the display.

"What's up?" he asked in lieu of a greeting.

"I'm sorry to interrupt you, but we have a situation. One of the guests had a flashback and took off into the woods in a panic."

"Shit," Spike swore.

"Owl, Pipe, and Tiny went after him, but a few of the other guests are unsettled now. They're worried, talking about heading out into the woods to help look for him. I really need you up at the lodge, helping to keep everyone calm."

"I'm on my way," he said without hesitation.

"Thanks. I appreciate it."

"No thanks necessary. See you in a minute or so," Spike told his friend before clicking off the connection. He took a deep breath. Then another, before turning to Reese.

"What's wrong?"

"There's an issue with one of the guests, and I need to go up to the lodge."

She frowned. "Are they okay? What can I do to help? I can go with you."

Spike didn't really want her around any potentially volatile guests. It wasn't that he didn't trust the men and women who were there right now, but anyone could be a risk if their PTSD got the better of them.

He tried to remember what the stories were behind the men and women currently booked at The Refuge. Three combat veterans, one woman who'd been robbed and raped in an alley, another who'd had the shit beaten out of her by her husband, a guy who'd been carjacked... And he couldn't remember the stories of the others. He didn't know what the history was of the man who'd run into the woods, but the last thing he wanted was Reese in danger.

"They'll be okay, and I'd prefer you stay here. You can package up the leftovers and put our dinner dishes away. Then relax. Hopefully, I won't be too long."

"Okay," she agreed immediately.

Spike closed his eyes in gratitude that she was being so amenable.

As if she could read his mind, she said, "I would never want to be in the way. You and your friends know much more about this kind of situation than I ever will."

"You aren't in the way," he protested as he stared down at her. "I'm just frustrated that we were interrupted."

Reese smiled and stepped into him. Spike's arm immediately went around her waist and pulled her closer, until she was plastered against him from her hips to her tits. His cock twitched, but he ignored it.

"There's no rush. I'm not going anywhere. Tonight, tomorrow...after my brother's wedding."

Fuck, this woman. "I wouldn't be upset to come home and find you naked in my bed," Spike blurted.

She grinned seductively, but didn't agree or disagree. She merely leaned in and kissed him. Spike forced himself to end the kiss before it got out of hand. Brick and the others were expecting him, and he couldn't let them down.

"I have to go," he said reluctantly.

Reese nodded and tried to step out of his embrace, but Spike tightened his arms around her, not letting her escape just yet.

"This isn't exactly the most exciting place to live," he said, feeling the need to warn her. "I don't want you to decide to stay then regret it."

"I won't regret it," she insisted. "While I enjoyed living near a big city, I've loved being here just as much. People in town already know me. They smile and wave when I drive by. The cashier in the store today even asked how I was acclimating, and when Isabella and I were talking about visiting the thrift store in town, she told me the best days to go because she knew when they put out new stuff. I love that she made me feel like a local. But beyond all of that...you're here."

Damn, with every word out of her mouth, Spike wanted to stay even more. He settled for kissing her hard, then physically setting her away from him. "I'll be back as soon as I can."

"Okay."

He forced himself to back away, not wanting to take his gaze from her for even a second. Then, knowing if he didn't leave now, he wouldn't leave at all, Spike spun and headed for the door. "Lock this behind me," he ordered. He had no idea where the guest was who'd run off into the woods, but he didn't want to chance him circling back and maybe thinking Reese was an enemy and coming into the cabin to hurt her.

"I will," she said without protest.

Taking one last look at her, Spike opened the door and left.

* * *

Eight long hours later, Spike let himself back into his cabin. He was tired. Bone-deep tired. He hadn't expected to get back this late. It was three in the morning, and the guests were finally all safe and sound in their cabins. The man who'd run off into the woods had thought he was being chased by terrorists intent on recapturing and torturing him. Spike had joined the search for him in the woods, and it had taken hours to finally track him down. Then it had taken another hour to *talk* him down, to convince him that he wasn't in danger.

The guests had been spooked and didn't want to go back to their own cabins until the man was found. Spike couldn't blame them. No one wanted to come face-to-face with a man who'd temporarily lost his grip on the here and now.

Henley had come up to the lodge to talk to the man, and was still there. Tonka was staying right by her side to make sure she was safe.

It had been an exhausting night for everyone, and Spike was more than glad that everything had turned out all right and no one had gotten hurt.

After locking the door, he looked over and saw that Reese had left a light on in the living area for him. He stood there staring at the simple gesture for a long moment. This was the first time in his life that he'd come home, from a mission or otherwise, and someone cared enough about him to make sure he wouldn't trip over his own feet when he arrived.

He was starving, but he needed to see Reese more than he needed to put something in his belly. He turned and headed for the bedroom. He pushed the door open quietly and saw that she'd not only left a light on in the living room, but the en suite light was on too. He could easily see Reese in his bed, under his comforter. She was on her side, clutching one of his pillows in her arms.

He wanted to slip under the covers with her, pull her into his embrace, and finish what they hadn't even had a chance to start earlier. But it was late—or early, whatever —and he didn't want to disturb her obviously deep sleep.

Sighing heavily, Spike closed the door, leaving it open a crack, then turned to head to the smaller bathroom in the hallway. The shower wasn't nearly as nice as the one in his room, but he didn't want to risk waking Reese. He needed to get the stink of the night off him, then get some sleep. There would be plenty of opportunities to make love with Reese. He wanted the moment to be right. Wanted to take his time. Make sure she knew how much he respected and admired her. He wanted them both to be wide awake for their first time.

Thoughts of Reese in his head, Spike showered in minutes and was asleep and dreaming, almost before his head hit the pillow on the full-size bed in his guest room.

CHAPTER FOURTEEN

Reese's hands were under Gus's shirt, and she pushed it up and over his head. Two days had passed since the PTSD incident...when they'd been steps away from his bedroom before he'd been called away to work.

Two days since she'd woken up alone, disappointed and worried that he might've changed his mind about being with her. But when she'd seen his dirty clothes on the floor of the guest bathroom, and how exhausted he still looked lying in bed, she'd realized that he must've gotten home extremely late. She'd managed to stay up until midnight, but had fallen asleep waiting for him to return.

He'd been apologetic upon waking, but she'd shut him up with a kiss. He hadn't been able to stay with her that morning because he'd promised to check in on the guest who'd had the PTSD episode, and the last day and a half had been spent making sure the man and all the other guests were really okay.

Since Gus had been so busy, Reese spent some time filling out an application for the National Laboratory, helping with more of the wedding prep, and attempting to talk with Angelo. She'd also hung out with Isabella and assisted with random chores around The Refuge, including spending some time with the guests herself, along with Alaska. Making sure everyone had what they needed, joining them in various activities to take their minds off the PTSD incident.

This was the first time neither she nor Gus were needed since the other night, and Reese was more than ready to pick up where they'd left off. In fact, they were even standing in the hallway.

She got Gus's shirt over his head and without hesitation, leaned down and licked one of his nipples.

"Damn, woman!" he exclaimed. One of his hands went to the back of her head, encouraging her. The other went to the waist of her leggings and burrowed under, palming one of the globes of her ass with his large, warm hand. He squeezed the flesh tightly when she closed her lips around his nipple and sucked, hard.

His back arched, and Reese smiled as she continued doing her best to drive him crazy. She felt a little feral. She'd been fantasizing about Gus for longer than she could remember, and now that this was actually happening, she was almost desperate.

She let go of his nipple with a pop and grinned as she looked up at him. His hand was still down her pants, and he jerked her closer, grinding his erection against her belly. "I want you," he said, his chest heaving as he did his best to control his lust.

"It's a good thing, because I want you too," she reassured him.

He was reaching for the hem of her shirt when someone knocked at the door of the cabin.

They both froze.

"Ignore it," Gus ordered as he began to lift her shirt.

But whoever it was, they knocked again, harder this time.

"I can't believe this," Gus muttered as he lowered her shirt and rested his forehead against hers.

Reese couldn't either. But if someone was there, they obviously needed something.

"Reese? Are you in there? I'm worried about Scarlet Pimpernickel," Jasna called out from the front of the cabin. "Tonka's in town and she's mooing pathetically and I can't find anyone else to help!"

Reese wasn't sure that was true. There were always people around, and the guys never left the property all at the same time, not when guests were in residence.

"Shit. You want me to go with you?" Gus asked.

Reese sighed. "No. I'm sure it's nothing. She's just a little paranoid. I'll go with her to the barn, make sure everything's okay, then come back."

"Okay." Gus sighed. "I might as well start something for dinner. Unless you want to eat at the lodge?"

Reese bit her lip and looked up at him from beneath her lashes. "It's Taco Tuesday," she said with longing.

Gus chuckled. "Right. The lodge it is."

"It's not that I don't want to be alone with you, but whatever Robert and Luna do to the meat is outstanding. And their queso is to die for."

"You don't have to convince me," he said.

"*After*, though, I'm all for coming back here and ignoring any and all phone calls and knocks on the door," she reassured him.

Gus's hand tightened on her ass and he kissed her once more, hard and fast. "Go with Jas before she has a coronary. She loves that calf more than anything."

Reese put her hand on Gus's cheek, sighing when he pulled his hand out of her leggings. She loved how he touched her. With control and passion. And a little bit of the same desperation she felt.

He turned her and gave her a little push. "Go, before I change my mind," he joked.

Straightening her shirt, Reese gave him a small smile before heading to the door.

* * *

They didn't get to enjoy Taco Tuesday together at the lodge, after all. Once Jasna was assured the calf was fine, Reese was intercepted by Alaska. The two women, along with Henley and Isabella, had gone to Los Alamos for dinner, meeting Ryan at a Mexican restaurant in town. Alaska had suggested it as a sort of mini-bachelorette party for Isabella. Woody and Spike had dropped them off, and when they'd returned two hours later to bring the women back to The Refuge, had found them completely hammered from the restaurant's very strong margaritas.

Apparently, someone also had the great idea to do a few shots after the drinks, and those had pushed them over the edge from tipsy to drunk.

"They're completely shitfaced," Tonka said with a laugh when he saw the women in the lodge after they'd returned.

He wasn't wrong.

Alcohol wasn't allowed on The Refuge property. The last thing anyone needed was the guests trying to use it as a way of deadening whatever it was that was causing their PTSD.

"Henley's been working her ass off," Tonka continued. "She deserves to cut loose a little."

"I'm not sure what we would've done without her here the other night," Brick agreed.

"She was amazing," Stone added. "She was able to calm our guest better than any of us had."

The guest in question had left that morning, and his regular psychiatrist had already called and talked with Henley about what had happened, and how she could best help him in their upcoming sessions.

"Alaska and Reese were pretty awesome too," Tiny added. "They spent a lot of time with the other guests yesterday, making sure they were calm and happy."

"Don't forget about Isabella hanging with Jasna so Henley could take extra counseling appointments. That was a huge help," Owl threw in.

Spike agreed with his friends, and he was grateful everyone had worked as a team to keep what could've been a volatile situation under control. Though he had to secretly admit to also being a little frustrated. Tonight was supposed to be his and Reese's night. But he wouldn't make love with her when she was three sheets to the wind, especially not for the first time.

Still, he had to admit she was adorable. All of the women were. They were sitting in the lodge, laughing and joking with each other.

"I'm thinking it's about time we shut this down," Brick said dryly when Alaska almost fell out of her chair, and the other women laughed so hard they were crying.

As if they'd all just been waiting for someone to call it a night, Tonka, Woody, and Spike moved at the same time. They headed for their women, saying their good nights to the other guys as they did.

Spike approached Reese and couldn't keep the smile off his face as she tilted her head back to look up at him from her seat. "Hi!" she said happily.

"Hey," he returned, putting a hand on her shoulder to steady her.

Reese continued to smile up at him. "You're beautiful," she slurred.

"Time for us to go home," he told her, still grinning.

"Home," she mused and closed her eyes. "Your cabin is home."

Her words hit Spike hard. Had he ever truly felt as if he had a home? He'd had places to sleep between missions, apartments that were nothing more than a place to store his stuff. Even after moving into the cabin here on the property, he wasn't sure he truly saw it as a home. It was where he slept, and convenient to where he worked, but a home? Not really.

But since Reese had arrived, it felt more and more like the place where he belonged. Where he looked forward to going to at the end of the day, simply because she'd be there. And while she hadn't moved in officially, she'd gotten a few boxes of her things from Missouri that her neighbor had boxed up and stowed in her car before its transport. Having her clothes, shoes, and even a few knickknacks around the cabin had solidified her presence. It made Spike grin every time he saw her things mixed in with his.

"Can you walk?" he asked gruffly, trying to hide his pleasure at her thinking about the cabin as home.

"Pbsshaw," she muttered before standing—and promptly swaying to the side. If Spike hadn't been there to hold her up, she would've fallen on her face for sure. "Of course I can walk!" she insisted, even as she grabbed

Spike's arm with a death grip. "Tonight was awesome," she told him. Then she turned to the other women who were similarly holding onto their men. "Tonight was awesome!" she proclaimed again.

"Awesome!"

"Super-duper awesome!"

"*Muy bien!*"

"Remember, we're gonna all meet in the morning and have breakfast together," Henley said excitedly.

The men all chuckled. It was more than obvious none of them would be in shape to get up early, let alone want to eat.

"See you in the morning!" Alaska said with a wave as Brick led her to the door.

"*Mañana!*" Isabella offered with a huge grin. It was cute how she reverted to Spanish when she was drunk. Woody put his arm around her and guided her out of the room, following Brick and Alaska.

"We're gonna go down and check out the aminals!" Henley said as she gazed at Tonka adoringly.

"Is that code for sex?" Reese asked bluntly.

Henley attempted to wink, but in reality, she just closed both her eyes hard, then opened them again. "Shh-hhh. Yes! We don't wanna wake Jasna. And Stone's in our cabin babysitting, although she'd die if we called it that, and we don't want to interrumpt him."

Spike fought his smile at the way Henley kept mispronouncing words. And she wasn't exactly using her inside voice.

"We aren't having sex in the barn," Tonka told her firmly.

Henley pouted. "Why not? Reese is gonna have sex

with Spike, and I'm sure everyone else is too. Why can't we?"

"I'm *so* having sex," Reese piped in, nodding like a bobble head. "We keep gettin' interrupted and I want Gus's dick in me. So we're gonna go *do it*. You two should too. Ha...two should too..." She dissolved into giggles.

Spike rolled his eyes.

"We're going to the barn because you're so loud right now," Tonka told her.

"And to have sex," Henley insisted.

"Sure, yeah," he said, clearly placating her.

"Have fun with the sex," Reese called out, the alcohol completely loosening her tongue.

"Come on, sweetheart. Let's get you home," Spike said as he leaned over and picked her up, one arm under her knees and the other behind her back.

To his surprise, Reese stopped talking and stared at him with wide eyes as he followed behind Tonka and Henley.

"What? What are you thinking, beautiful?" he asked when they were finally outside and on their way to his cabin.

"You're carrying me."

Spike nodded. "I am," he agreed.

"*No one* carries me. I'm too big. Plus-size. Heavy. Fat."

"You aren't fat," Spike growled, pissed off that she'd use that word to describe herself. "Curvy, yes. If you want to say plus-size, you can use that too—but don't ever call yourself fat again."

"Gus..." she whispered.

He looked down at her and saw tears in her eyes. "Do *not* cry," he ordered.

Her arms had come up around his neck, and she turned

her face so it was buried in his chest as he carried her. "No one's ever carried me like this before. I didn't even think it was possible! I just...I love you, Gus! So much."

Spike stopped in the middle of the path to his cabin. He looked down at the woman in his arms, and it felt as if his entire world spun on its axis right then and there. It wasn't as if he thought he and Reese were dating casually. He wouldn't enjoy her being in his space so much if they were. And he wouldn't be so impatient for her to get a job to definitively tie herself to the area. But her coming right out and saying those words felt life-altering.

Except...she was drunk. Shitfaced. Completely blotto.

He began walking again.

She didn't say anything else, but he could feel her hot breaths through his shirt, and each one made his cock twitch in his jeans.

When he arrived at his cabin, he said, "I need to put you down so I can unlock the door."

She merely mumbled against him.

"Reese?"

"Hmmmm?"

"Hold onto me," he ordered instead of explaining further.

"I am," she said.

Spike slowly lowered her legs to the ground and wrapped his arm around her waist when she collapsed against him, giving him most of her weight. He managed to unlock the front door and shuffle them both inside.

"Good, we're home. Can we have sex now?" she slurred.

Spike didn't answer, instead picking her up again, loving the mewing sound that left her lips as she snuggled into him once more. He carried her down the hall to his room and put her down on his bed. He turned on the small lamp on the nightstand and sat on the mattress beside her hip.

He leaned over her and brushed her hair away from her face with his free hand.

Reese closed her eyes and leaned her head into his touch.

"Sleep, sweetheart," he said gently.

"Are we having sex?" she asked sleepily.

"Eventually. But not tonight."

She pouted and her eyes opened. "But I want to."

"I do too, but I want you conscious when we make love."

Reese sighed. "I drank too much," she said sadly.

"You do that a lot?" he asked.

She shook her head. "Don't like bars. Don't trust guys there. But tonight, with my new friends...and with you...I felt safe."

Spike liked that answer. A lot. "Good. Because you *are* safe when you're with me. And here on The Refuge."

"This is the most amazing place ever," she told him. "I'm so proud of you. You could've sent that guest off to the hospital but instead you took care of him. Made him feel safe too. Didn't make him feel embarrassed."

"It wasn't his fault. And there's no way we would've sent him to the clinic in Los Alamos."

"I know. Because you're awesome," Reese said. "Did I thank you for coming to find Woody?"

"Yes."

"Thank you."

Spike grinned. Fuck, she was so damn cute.

"Gus?"

"Yeah, babe?"

"I want you but I'm afraid."

"Of what? Me?" Spike asked, appalled at the thought.

"Of you seeing me."

He relaxed. "You have absolutely nothing to be afraid of."

"I have rolls," she admitted.

"And I have scars," he said with a shrug. "I got this tattoo sleeve to cover some of them."

Her eyes lit up as she ran her hand up and down the arm in question, which he was using to prop himself up next to her. "I like it."

"I'm glad. What else?"

Reese frowned.

"What else do you want to tell me while your inhibitions are down? Give it all to me, so I don't accidentally trigger any of your insecurities later." Spike figured he might as well find out what he could while she was drunk. Maybe it wasn't fair or ethical, but he didn't care. He'd do whatever it took to make this woman his.

"Nothing." She didn't look him in the eyes when she said it.

"Come on, Reese. Talk to me."

"I've never had anyone go down on me before," she blurted. "I've never sucked a man's dick. I want to, but I don't want to do it wrong or choke. Peppers give me gas. I've masturbated in your bed but I was afraid you'd hear me so I buried my face in your pillow when I came. Years ago, I bought a romance book after I met you for the first time and crossed out the names and changed them to Gus and Reese. I've read that one dozens of times. I used to bug Woody all the time about you, asked him a million questions. I love math, even though it's not cool. I was totally not popular in high school, and I had a crush on one of the football players, then I learned he was making fun of me with his friends and it hurt a lot. I've never slept with a guy...*slept* with them, like stayed the night. My first time hurt but the guy didn't care, he just kept thrusting in and out. I want kids—at least three. I was scared to death to go to Colombia, but I had to because Woody was missing and he's the only person who's ever loved me and didn't want to change me. And I'm so happy here that I'm afraid it's a dream and I'll wake up and it'll all be gone."

Spike stared down at Reese, his heart in his throat. When he'd encouraged her to talk to him, he hadn't expected all that. It was one very long spiel. And he felt unworthy of such heartfelt confessions.

He leaned down and kissed her gently. "It's not a dream. When you wake up in the morning, I'll be here."

"Okay. Good," Reese said and her eyes closed.

"You feel sick?" Spike asked her.

"Uh-uh."

"Are you sure?"

"Yeah. Tired."

"Okay, sweetheart. Sleep."

"Will you stay?"

Spike didn't answer right away. Could he even sleep next to her and control himself?

Yeah. He could. "I'm staying."

She smiled. "Good."

Spike stared down at her for a long time after she fell asleep. She might not be comfortable in her clothes, but it wouldn't be the end of the world for her to sleep in them. He eventually roused himself enough to stand. He removed his shoes and socks, and Reese's as well—because who wanted to sleep with socks on?—and covered her with the comforter. Then he headed to the bathroom to get ready for bed.

When he reentered the room, he changed into a pair of flannel sleep pants he never wore, but for some reason still had in his drawer, then climbed under the covers and scooted up against Reese. She'd rolled onto her side, and he plastered himself to her back, wrapping an arm around her waist.

She mumbled something under her breath and pushed her ass back against him. Instead of getting turned on, Spike felt...content. This was the first time he'd slept in his own bed since Reese had arrived, and he loved how the sheets smelled like her.

A sudden vision of them lying together, just like this, when they were old and gray sprang into his mind.

He fell asleep with a smile on his face. The world might be conspiring against them when it came to making love, but in many ways, holding her like this while she slept was even better.

CHAPTER FIFTEEN

Reese drove into Los Alamos with Angelo in her passenger seat, glancing over at him occasionally. Of course, he didn't turn to look at her, simply sat there with a slight frown on his face as he stared out the front window.

Unbelievably, she and Gus *still* hadn't made love. It felt as if the universe was conspiring against them. One night, Jasna had needed help with her math homework, and Tonka and Henley were about to go crazy and asked if she could help. By the time she got back to the cabin, Gus had fallen asleep on the couch, exhausted after helping Hudson with landscaping all day.

Another evening, Gus had helped Tonka with an emergency rescue of a couple sheep a hoarder in town had been keeping in her basement.

Then, to her embarrassment, Reese had gotten her period. And while she knew plenty of people had sex during that time of the month, she didn't want to have to worry about bleeding all over his sheets their first time.

Gus had been great, telling her not to worry about it.

He'd kissed her deeply and said he understood and that he'd wait.

The morning after she and the other women had gotten drunk had been both wonderful and awful. She wasn't hung over—she never was after she drank—but when she recalled all the things she'd told Gus, she wanted to die. But he hadn't brought up any of that stuff, and it wasn't as if Reese was going to.

She even remembered telling him that she loved him. And while it was a little mortifying that she'd done so, and he hadn't responded in kind, she understood. Things had moved really quickly between them, and while she knew her own heart, she wasn't surprised he might need some more time. Or maybe he thought it was just the alcohol talking. Then there was her huge word vomit shortly thereafter. It was possible she'd freaked him out by her emotional outburst.

Waking up in his arms had been a dream come true, literally. She'd dreamed about him all night, his scent lingering in her nose. It wasn't until she woke up that she realized why. She'd turned in the night and had her nose buried in the crook of his neck. Her arm was around his chest and one of her legs had hitched up over his thigh. She was holding onto him as if he would disappear any second.

She'd tried to slink out of bed and regroup, but he'd grabbed the arm across his chest and tightened his hold around her shoulders. "Stay," he'd mumbled, and Reese had immediately stilled, not really wanting to move anyway. Being held by him when they were both half asleep was so nice. Intimate.

Eventually, they'd gotten up and didn't talk much about the previous night. But ever since then, he'd slept in the master bedroom with her. Even though they still hadn't had sex, they kissed...a lot. And he'd actually taken off her shirt—and started sucking on her nipples—before she'd been called to help Jasna.

The anticipation and lust simmering between them had reached ridiculous proportions, and Reese had no doubt when they eventually made love without interruption, it would be the most amazing thing she'd ever experienced.

Until then, she loved spending time with him, no matter what they were doing. She didn't *need* sex to love Gus, she already did, but when it finally happened, it would solidify her feelings permanently. She knew that like she knew her name.

This morning, Isabella had called and asked if she minded driving Angelo into Los Alamos later in the afternoon for his final tuxedo fitting. She was trying to tie up some loose ends for her wedding and had gone into town hours earlier, but was meeting them at the shop. From there, Woody would pick them up and drive them back to The Refuge.

When she'd gone to the cabin, Angelo had stared at her for a beat, then took a deep breath and smiled. Though it wasn't so much a smile as it was a grimace. Still, Reese was hugely relieved he was at least trying to acclimate. It had been almost a month since his arrival in New Mexico, and while he did come up to the lodge to eat a few times a week, Reese wasn't exactly sure what he did with the rest of his time.

She'd continue to cut him some slack though. She'd never been in his position, and if she found herself living, say, down in Colombia, with a bunch of people she didn't know, in the middle of the mountains, and didn't speak the language and had no idea what people around her were saying, she supposed she would probably be reticent around others as well.

It was in her nature to make the best of things. Foreign languages weren't her forte, but she'd been trying to learn. At least basic words. When Angelo did come up to the lodge, he didn't socialize much. He'd downloaded the translation app on his phone, but he didn't use it often, opting to play games on his phone or scroll through social media instead.

Since Reese was driving, she couldn't use the translator app at the moment. So the atmosphere in the car was a little awkward and silent, and Reese hated it. She was relieved to pull into the small parking lot outside the tuxedo rental shop. She forced a smile on her face and turned to Angelo. "We're here!" she said unnecessarily.

Angelo nodded and offered a slight wave as he got out and headed for the store.

Wishing there was a way to communicate better with him, Reese got out and followed. She'd say hi to Isabella then head over to the office where she had her first interview for a position at the National Laboratory. She'd been a little surprised they'd contacted her so quickly after receiving her application, but Gus said he wasn't shocked in the least. She was living in the area and had the credentials to back up her expertise.

Angelo and Isabella were talking in rapid-fire Spanish, but when she walked toward them, they stopped. Angelo gave her a look she couldn't interpret, then turned and headed for a changing area.

"I'm sorry I interrupted," Reese told Isabella.

"It is fine," Isabella said. "He's struggling, but I'm glad he's at least trying. He had friends back in Colombia. He was popular and was always out with someone in the evenings. I worried about him then, just as I do now. But in a different way."

Reese stepped forward and hugged her friend. It felt as if she'd known Isabella for years...and she kind of had. She'd talked to her on the phone a couple of times at Woody's apartment, and she'd heard so many stories about her and Angelo from her brother that it was as if they were already friends by the time they actually met. "He'll come around," she told her. "How can he not with an awesome sister like you?"

Isabella took a deep breath and nodded. "Thank you for bringing him here. Are you nervous about your interview?"

Reese shrugged. "Not really. I mean, I want the job, but I'm also there to interview *them*. If I've learned anything over the years, it's that interviews are for both sides...I want to make sure it'll be a good fit for me as much as they want to make sure I'll be what they need."

"That is a good way of looking at it," Isabella said.

"Enough about me, are *you* excited? You're getting married in three days!" Reese said excitedly.

Isabella chuckled nervously. "I am scared to death."

"About what?"

"That I will say or do the wrong thing."

Reese smiled. "No one is going to be taking notes or judging you. Especially not Woody. He's waited for this day since the moment he met you."

Isabella blushed. "Me too," she said softly.

"I'm happy we'll be sisters for real," Reese told her. "I've always wanted a sister."

Isabella beamed.

The moment was broken when Angelo said something from across the room.

Isabella turned her head and replied. Then she looked back at Reese. "I need to go. Tell me all about your interview later?"

"Of course."

Reese hugged the other woman once more then called out a goodbye to Angelo, but she didn't hear him respond.

After she pulled into the parking lot of the office building where her interview was taking place, she put her keychain into her purse and pulled out her phone. She sent a quick text to Gus.

REESE

I'm here. Heading inside. Wish me luck.

GUS

You don't need any. You've got this. Call me when you're done and on your way home.

REESE

I will.

Her fingers itched to finish her text with "I love you," but she refrained and hit send. Then she silenced her phone, put it in her purse, and took a deep breath before opening her door and striding toward the building.

* * *

An hour and a half later, feeling extremely relieved and happy, Reese pushed open the cabin door. "Gus?" she called out.

He was in front of her in seconds. "So it went well?" he asked as he took her purse from her and placed it on the kitchen counter.

Reese nodded. "Yes. They offered me the job right after the interview was over! It's more money than I was making in Missouri too. The offer is contingent on me passing a background check, but I'm not worried about that in the least." She knew she had a huge, goofy smile on her face.

She quickly sobered a bit. "This is your last chance to change your mind about me moving here," she warned. "Once I take a job, I'm here. I don't back out on my responsibilities so if you're feeling the least bit weirded out about us, or about me living and working in Los Alamos, now's the time to say something before I officially accept the job."

She wasn't sure what she expected Gus to say or do—but it wasn't to grab hold of her hand and drag her down the hall.

"Gus?" she asked nervously.

He didn't speak until they were in the bedroom, standing by the bed. "You expecting any calls?"

"What? No."

"Your period's done, right? I saw your pills in your bag in the bathroom, you've started a new pack."

Reese blushed a bit. She wasn't used to talking about such personal things with a guy. But she nodded.

"I'm not letting another minute go by without having you," he said in a low, gruff tone. "Nothing, and I mean *nothing*, is going to stop me. I'm not changing my mind about you, Reese. And you aren't going to be living in Los Alamos. You can work there, but you'll be living here at The Refuge. With me."

As if realizing how bossy and insane he sounded, he sheepishly added, "If you want."

Reese smiled and threw her arms around his neck. "I want," she assured him.

Then Gus lowered his head and kissed her. It was deeper and more passionate than the kisses they'd shared to date, as if he'd been purposely reining in his lust until he knew they could finish what they started.

Nothing was holding them back now.

Reese's hands moved over Gus as she tore at his clothes. He did the same with her until they were in nothing but their underwear.

"Bed," Gus practically growled.

Reese's nipples hardened at hearing the impatience and dominance in his voice.

She stepped backward and her legs hit the mattress. She sat, then quickly scooted fully onto the bed. Her breath caught as Gus hooked his thumbs into his boxer briefs and shoved them down his long legs.

His cock was hard, the head almost purple. It bobbed as he took one step toward her. Reese swallowed. He was... beautiful. Men generally weren't described that way, she knew, but there was no other word for it. The muscles in his arms rippled as he crawled up the bed, settling between her legs. His tattoos seemed even more masculine against the golden tan of his skin. She could see the veins in his opposite arm. She didn't know where to look, where to touch first.

"Look at me," Gus ordered, and Reese's eyes immediately went to his.

"I feel as if I've been marking time until you came into my life," he told her. "Everything I've done, everything I've seen, it's all led me here. To you."

Tears immediately welled in Reese's eyes.

"No crying," he said sternly with a soft smile.

"I can't help it," she whispered. "I...this...I'm having a hard time truly believing this is my life. That I'm here. That *you're* here. With me."

Gus's gaze dropped from hers and he moved, scooting forward on his knees, pushing her legs farther apart. She still had on her bra and panties, but she'd never felt more naked. He brushed his fingers along her cheek. Then his palm flattened on her upper chest, slowly moving downward, passing over her breastbone, down her belly—which she sucked in—over to her hip and down one of her thighs. Everywhere he touched, goose bumps rose on her flesh.

"Gus," she whispered, overwhelmed with emotions and feelings.

"You're mine," he said on a growl. "I'm going to do everything in my power to deserve you. To make you proud to call me yours. To make you happy."

"You already do," she told him.

"You're so beautiful," he said reverently.

For the first time in her life, Reese *felt* beautiful.

Gus settled over her, resting an elbow on the mattress by her shoulder until his warm, naked skin covered her like a blanket. He ran his fingers up and down her arm lazily, as if they had all the time in the world.

"You feel as if you were made to be mine," he whispered. "You're so soft against my hardness, but I have no worries that you're going to break or I'm going to hurt you when I take you the way I've dreamed."

Reese felt herself dampen at his words. Her nipples hardened in the cups of her bra, and suddenly she resented the scraps of fabric keeping her from feeling all of Gus against her body. She squeezed his biceps and purposely dug her blunt nails into his skin.

His cock twitched against her.

"As much as I love your sweet words," Reese said, "if you don't hurry up and fuck me, someone's going to interrupt us and we're going to have to postpone this...*again*."

Gus chuckled, and feeling his laughter against her skin was a new experience. Intimate.

"Sweetheart, as I said earlier, nothing is going to keep me from getting my cock deep inside your hot, wet body. The world could literally explode and I still wouldn't stop. Dying while being buried inside you would be a fantastic way to go. You're moving in. Here. With me."

He paused, and Reese realized he was actually asking her a question while phrasing it as a command. She'd already told him she'd live here, but she'd say it as many times as he needed.

"I am," she agreed.

"You're going to marry me."

She raised a brow at that. She didn't mind his bossy tendencies, but this was one thing she wasn't willing to bend on. "If you ask me properly...maybe," she said snarkily.

He grinned. "And you're going to have babies with me," he said, without addressing the proposal thing.

"Yes," she breathed.

"You're going to be such an asset at your new job. They're going to wonder how the hell they ever got along without you. You already fit in perfectly around here, and everyone already loves you. We got here fast, but it's so right, Reese. Please tell me you feel it too."

"I feel it too," she said without hesitation. "Gus?"

"Yeah, sweetheart?"

"Please stop torturing me. I've dreamed about you making love to me for years. I want you. Need you. Stop talking."

In response, Gus lowered his head. He took control of their kiss, and Reese was more than happy to let him.

As he kissed her, Gus shifted his legs and his hand pushed at her panties. She helped as best she could without losing his mouth. Eventually, she kicked the underwear off and happily spread her legs as he returned between them. His cock felt hot against her belly, and she moaned when he lifted his head.

"Arch your back," he ordered.

Reese did so, and one of his hands moved under her back and he deftly released the clasp of her bra. Within seconds, she was nude beneath him. He lifted slightly and stared down at her naked body. For a moment, she felt self-conscious. Her belly wasn't flat, her thighs touched when she walked; without her bra, her boobs were saggy. But then Gus groaned. It was a guttural sound, coming from deep within his chest.

He bent and wrapped his lips around one of her nipples, making Reese gasp in surprise. She arched into his touch and closed her eyes as ecstasy swam through her veins. His other hand went between her legs, and Reese spread them even wider for him.

She was already wet, and would've been embarrassed about that, but Gus didn't give her any time to think. His thumb found her clit, and she jerked. He lifted his head from her nipple to murmur, "Easy, Reese."

She stared into his eyes for a moment as his thumb swirled around her hardening bundle of nerves. His hand seemed to engulf her entire pussy, and for once in her life, she felt almost petite.

His fingers moved to play in the moisture seeping from between her legs. Then he eased a finger inside her body. Reese moaned.

"Gus, please," she cried.

"Not yet," he said, almost to himself as he eased a second finger inside her.

Reese tried to thrust up against him, but his body gave her little room to maneuver. He'd put his weight back on his elbow, and he was looking down at his hand between her legs as he continued to caress her.

"Is this what you did when you were here in my bed alone?" he asked as he used his thumb on her clit and put his pinky and ring fingers deep inside her body. It was as if he was holding onto her in the kinkiest, most sensual way possible, and Reese loved how...*controlled* she felt.

"Yes," she moaned.

"What did you think about as you were touching yourself, making yourself come?"

"You," Reese admitted without any embarrassment whatsoever. "I buried my nose in your pillow so all I could smell was you and imagined it was your hand touching me."

"Fuck," Gus said, and she felt his cock throbbing against her thigh.

"Did *you* masturbate?" she got up the nerve to ask.

"Of course I did. In the shower, in the guest bed, every chance I got," he admitted.

Reese's belly tightened. She looked down and licked her lips. She could picture him stroking himself in her head. See the come spurting out of the tip of his cock and covering his hand and belly.

"You like that," he said. Once again, it wasn't a question.

"And you like thinking about me getting off in your bed."

"Hell yeah, I do," he said without hesitation. "Although I'd like it better in person. Come for me, Reese. I need you nice and wet so I can take you the way I've dreamed. I don't want to hurt you, you're so tiny, and I'm so big."

She blinked. Had anyone in her entire life ever described her as tiny?

No. The answer was definitely no.

She felt him adjust, and then Gus was straightening to his knees. She spread her legs, not feeling the least bit of embarrassment as she did so.

Gus took his cock in one hand as he continued to rub against her clit with the other. Even though she'd masturbated that morning in the shower, she felt her passion quickly rising once again. It felt more intense now. Maybe because Gus was in charge of her pleasure. He wasn't easing off as her orgasm approached.

"Gus," she murmured as she spread her legs farther apart. She grabbed hold of his wrist without interrupting the hand on her clit, and the other grabbed his biceps. She could feel his arm flexing under her hand as he stroked himself.

"That's it. You're creaming all over my hand. My sheets. I'm gonna smell you for hours after this, and I'm not going to want to wash it away. Come for me, sweetheart. Let me see it. Get yourself ready for your man."

Her man. Yes. He was *hers*, and she'd do whatever she had to do to keep him.

Her legs began to tremble and her chest felt tight. "Gus...I'm...holy crap..." Reese couldn't think straight. She'd never felt this primed before. As if she was on the verge of exploding from the inside out. No orgasm she'd given herself had ever felt so powerful. It was an almost scary sensation. She began to panic slightly.

But then Gus was there. He leaned over until his face was directly above hers as his fingers continued their determined assault on her clit.

"I've got you. Let go, Reese. I'll catch you."

And that was all it took for her to drop all her inhibitions and let the orgasm wash over her. She shook and trembled in his arms as she went over the edge. She couldn't think. Couldn't see. Couldn't hear. All she could do was feel. She'd never experienced anything like this before in her life, and she never wanted it to end.

"So beautiful," was the first thing Reese heard when she finally began to come down from her orgasmic high. "So fucking beautiful. And mine. All mine."

She wanted to roll her eyes at his ego, but she *was* his.

"You with me?" Gus asked as he stared down at her. His hand was lazily caressing her pussy, keeping her on edge but not overstimulating her sensitive clit.

"Yeah," she whispered.

"I know you're on the pill, and I'm safe. I haven't been with anyone in a very long time, and I've been tested since the last time I had sex, even though I wore a condom."

Reese frowned. "Stop talking about other women," she bitched.

Gus grinned. "Sorry. I'm trying to ask if I can take you bare. It's okay if you say no, I've got a box of condoms in the drawer next to the bed. But I'd never do anything to hurt you or put you in danger."

"I'm good too," she told him.

"Yes, you are. And I had no doubts," he told her. "Make your choice, Reese. Now. Condom or no condom?"

"I trust you," she said reverently.

Seconds after the last word was out of her mouth, she felt the tip of Gus's cock against her folds. She arched her back and widened her legs as far as they'd go, feeling the stretch in her inner thighs.

He didn't go slow. He didn't ease his way into her. He pushed in to the hilt in one swift motion. Reese swore she could feel him at the tip of her cervix. His entrance didn't hurt, exactly, but she hadn't had anyone inside her in a long time, and a slight twinge of discomfort made her flinch.

She felt his pubic hair tickle her skin and his balls lay heavily against her ass. To her surprise, one of his hands went under her and spread her ass cheeks apart even while he lifted her. Amazingly, she felt him go even deeper.

Her belly clenched and she let out a small whimper as her inner muscles desperately tightened around his cock.

"It's okay. You're okay. Breathe, Reese. I'm not going to move until you're ready. But you feel so good. You have no idea! I'm sorry I hurt you. I couldn't wait. The second I felt you close around me, I had to have more. I'm gonna stay right here until you say I can move."

His words soothed her. She felt as if her pussy was on fire, but the longer they lay there, the better he felt. She took a deep breath, then another. Then opened her eyes and stared up into Gus's green gaze, which was locked on her face.

His jaw was ticking as he ground his teeth together, his brow drawn low, and it looked as if he was in pain. But he was running a hand through her hair gently and reverently. She'd never seen anything as beautiful in her life. Her Gus was a man full of contradictions. Hard and unbending one minute, tender and loving the next.

She loved every part of him. And he was hers.

* * *

It took everything in Spike not to move once he was inside Reese's body. All the training he'd had, all the discipline he'd learned in the Army. Every ounce of his willpower to give her time to adjust to his size. He was an asshole for not going slower. For not giving her a chance to get used to him in increments as he entered her.

But nothing felt as good as being inside her. Nothing. He could feel every throb of her heartbeat from inside her, and every time her muscles twitched, he felt them ripple along his sensitive bare cock.

The truth was that he'd never made love without a condom. He was fully prepared to put one on with her too. He was an asshole for not having that discussion before the heat of the moment. But when she'd come on his fingers, he'd been too desperate to get inside her.

He'd waited forever to be right where he was. His whole life. The second he entered her, Spike knew this was it for him. *She* was it. He'd never make love to another woman again. She was all he wanted. All he needed. And he'd do whatever it took to make sure she was happy and content. He wouldn't give her a reason to leave him. Whatever it took to keep her loving him, he'd do it.

His teeth were clenched so hard, he could hardly speak. But he absolutely refused to move until Reese was ready. He'd hurt her, and he could've killed himself for that. But it was too late to redo things. All he could do was stay still and let her body adjust to him.

Reese attempted to shift under him. "Gus?"

Fuck, he loved the sound of his name on her lips. "Yeah?" he managed to croak out.

"I'm okay. You can move."

Just those few words made his cock twitch deep inside her. "Are you sure?" he asked.

"Yes. I need you to move. Please!"

He might like the sound of her begging some other time, but right now, he hated it. He didn't want her to have to plead for anything. He reluctantly took his hand off her ass, palming the mattress. The movement pushed his cock a little deeper inside her.

They both moaned.

Spike froze. Shit, had he hurt her?

"*Move*, Gus. I mean it! Now!"

His lips twitched. He could feel the marks of where her fingernails had dug into his skin and he contemplated going to a tattoo shop and having them immortalized, but the thought flitted away when she reached down to where they were connected and fondled his balls.

With a groan, he pulled out slowly, feeling her fingers dancing along his shaft, before he pushed back into her body.

"I can't believe you fit," she said in awe.

"We were made for each other," he groaned as he pumped into her once more.

Her hand came back up and took hold of his arm as Spike made love to her slowly and tenderly. It was taking all his restraint not to fuck her hard. His balls were pulled up to his body, ready to release, but he didn't want this to be over so quickly.

"Faster, Gus," she ordered.

He ignored her. The feel of her silky body felt too good to rush this.

"*Gus,*" she whined.

"If I go any faster, I'm gonna come," he said honestly.

"So? Isn't that the point?" she asked breathlessly.

"Not this first time. I'm memorizing the feel of you. The sight of you under me. The sight of my cock disappearing into your juicy cunt. I can see your juices coating me and it's the most erotic thing I've ever witnessed. I love hearing your moans and hearing your pleas. Your tits bouncing on your chest make me want to latch on and never let go. Your hair on my pillow is a fucking dream come true. Let me have this. Please, Reese!"

Spike didn't care how pathetic he sounded. He'd beg until he was blue in the face.

But his Reese didn't make him. She simply gave him a shy smile.

Seeing her acquiescence to his needs made a spurt of precome shoot from his cock. Spike felt it and groaned, reaching between them to grab the base of his dick to keep from coming right then and there.

Reese giggled, and he felt the reverberations go up his cock and straight to his heart. He'd thought he was in control of their lovemaking, but right then and there, he realized he wasn't in charge of shit. She was. She had his heart in her hand, and he never wanted her to give it back.

Pushing inside her once more, Spike sat up. He rested his ass on his heels and pulled her into his lap. He couldn't move much in this position, could barely thrust, which was probably a good thing. He wasn't inside her as deep as he had been, but he had a clear view of where they were connected. Of how her pussy lips stretched around his shaft and how wet she was. More importantly, her clit was within easy reach, for both of them.

"Touch yourself," he ordered.

"What?" she asked breathlessly.

"Show me how you masturbate while thinking about me."

He felt her clench around his cock.

"I...I can't," she protested.

"Yes, you can. Do it, Reese. Please. I want to feel you come around my dick. Show me what you like."

"I like when *you* touch me," she protested.

"Then I'll touch you while you touch yourself," he said easily, bringing his hands up and covering her ample tits. He felt her nipples harden under his palms even though he hadn't even directly stimulated them.

"Oh, shit! Okay. But I expect you to reciprocate."

"You want to watch me stroke my cock?" he asked, purposely being crude.

"Yes."

"Only if I get to come all over your tits," he told her.

She smiled up at him. "Deal."

His dick jolted inside her once more, as if it had a mind of its own and had heard what she'd said and thoroughly agreed.

"Now, Reese. I need you to come on me."

She moved one of her hands down her body until she was touching her clit. Her hips bucked as she began to rub herself.

It was one of the most carnal and erotic things Spike had ever had the pleasure of seeing. Reese squirming in his grasp while he felt every twitch of her inner muscles. The world literally could've come to an end right then and there, and he wouldn't have noticed. His entire focus and attention was on the beautiful sight of Reese's fingers working her clit. Her knuckles rhythmically brushed against his belly as she pleasured herself.

"I'm close," she gasped after a very short period of time. But she didn't need to tell him, he knew. He could tell by the way she was strangling his dick. By the way her hips attempted to thrust upward, with little luck because of how he was holding her. By the way her legs widened around him and a pink flush formed on her upper chest.

Keeping his gaze glued to her pussy, Spike pinched her nipples hard.

That did it. Her hand dropped away from her clit and she came with a shout.

Spike's fingers continued where she'd left off and he forced her orgasm to continue. He would never get enough of the feel of her coming around him. He made a vow right then and there to do this every time they made love. Have her come before him, while he was buried deep inside her body. He'd never felt anything like it.

While she was still coming, he scooted her ass off his lap and back onto the mattress. Then he fucked her. She was even tighter than before, her muscles clenching hard as she came, but she was wetter too, allowing him to thrust fast, brutally, in and out of her channel without hurting her.

His balls drew up even tighter, and Spike mourned the fact that his first time making love with her was almost over. But he couldn't hold back anymore.

Pushing himself into her as deep as he could, he loosened his iron control and came.

It felt as if he'd never stop. His cock twitched for what seemed like an eternity as he poured his seed into her. He came so much, and so hard, he could feel their combined juices coating his balls as he kept his groin flush against hers. Even when he was done, and no longer hard, Spike refused to pull back. There was no need. He could stay buried inside her for as long as he wanted since there was no condom to deal with. He liked that.

No, he fucking loved it.

"Holy crap," Reese muttered under him. "I think you killed me."

"But what a way to go, huh?" he asked, feeling off-kilter himself.

"Are you going to move?"

"Nope."

"I can't breathe all that well."

That got him moving. But Spike still didn't pull out. He simply rolled, holding her ass to keep her in place until she was on top of him.

"Mmmmm," she murmured, snuggling into him and burying her nose in the crook of his neck.

Spike's arms tightened around her, and he sighed in contentment.

"That was..."

"Stupendous. Earth-shattering. Amazing. Fantabulous. Fucking *awesome*," Spike finished for her.

She chuckled, and once again Spike felt it from the inside out. Unfortunately, her muscles tightening to laugh squeezed his now limp cock out of her body.

"Shoot," she said with a frown.

Now that his cock had been evicted, Spike rolled until Reese was under him again. He framed her face with his hands and kissed her. Long, slow, and deep, showing her without words how much their lovemaking meant to him.

When he was done, he pulled back and began to inch down her body.

"Gus? What are you doing?"

"I wanna see."

"See what?"

"Your cunt filled with my come. And I want to make sure I didn't hurt you."

"You didn't. Gus, seriously, get back up here," she said, trying to physically pull him back up her body, but he refused to budge.

He lay between her legs and spread them so he could see her pussy. The sight that greeted his gaze made the caveman inside him stand up and beat his chest. Her cunt was swollen and a little red. But it was his semen, slowly leaking out of her channel, that had him utterly enthralled.

Reese flopped her head back down on the bed as if resigned.

Using a finger, Spike ran it up her folds, catching their juices before easing his finger inside her body.

She moaned a little. "Sore," she said softly.

Spike was sorry for that, but he didn't regret what they'd done for a second. It was hard to believe something so small could accommodate his cock. Intellectually, he knew that women's bodies were born to stretch. Hell, they had to in order to give birth. But seeing her tiny opening like this, up close and personal, had him in awe of Mother Nature.

After a moment, Reese said his name again. This time he looked up at her face and saw her cheeks were pink with what had to be embarrassment. He wanted to tell her she had nothing to be uncomfortable about, that he was going to know her body better than she knew it herself after a while, but instead, he simply moved back up her body until she was once more lying in his arms.

She sighed.

"I hope that was a happy sigh," he said.

"It was," she agreed.

They lay there, arms and legs entwined, for several long minutes...before Spike's phone began to ring on the nightstand where he'd put it earlier.

"No. Just no," he muttered.

Reese giggled against him.

He ignored the phone. Until it started ringing again.

"For fuck's sake!" he exclaimed, rolling over to grab it. "*What?*"

"Sorry to interrupt. It's Tex."

"What's wrong?"

"Maybe nothing. I just spoke to Woody, thought you'd want to know what I've been able to find out, as well. There's been some movement with the cartel, but nothing about Kansas City or The Refuge."

"What do you mean by 'movement'?" Spike asked, the remnants of his warm and fuzzy feelings from moments ago fading.

"It sounds like they're sending some guys to the Mexican border."

"I don't understand," Spike said. "Does that mean they're going to cross illegally to try to find Isabella or Woody?"

"Not necessarily. They frequently send people across. Both to get their members *into* the country—so they can intimidate and threaten those who work for them in the States—and back *out* of the country. All illegally, of course."

"So what are you saying?" Spike asked, wishing he was still lying there enjoying the aftermath of making love with Reese.

"I'm saying I think their current movement likely has

nothing to do with any of you. After Woody and Isabella get married this weekend, they can go home to Missouri, and you and Reese can make plans for your own futures there in New Mexico."

"Wait—how'd you know she was staying?" Spike asked.

Tex chuckled. "I have my ways. And tell her good job on negotiating that salary during her interview...they probably would've gone ten thousand higher, but she was smart not to settle for their first offer."

"You are a spooky son of a bitch," Spike told him with a shake of his head.

"You know, I'm still waiting for someone to name their firstborn after me. I think Tex has a nice ring to it, don't you?"

Spike burst out laughing. "No."

Tex chuckled. "It was worth a try. Happy for you, Spike."

Warmth spread through him. He looked down to see Reese's eyes glued on his face as her fingers absently ran over the various scars he had on his chest from an explosion he'd been caught in, when shrapnel had torn him up.

"Thanks," he said softly. "Any word on the person who saved Jas?" he asked.

He heard Tex sigh in frustration. "No. But I'm gonna figure out who it was eventually—and how he managed to send that untraceable text to Tonka, letting him know which bunker Jasna was in."

Spike had no doubt the incredibly talented computer genius would do just that.

"Have a good time at the wedding. I'll be in touch," Tex said, then disconnected without another word.

Spike clicked off the phone and threw it back onto the table before settling down with Reese in his arms.

"Everything okay?" she asked.

"Yeah. That was Tex."

"I gathered."

He proceeded to tell her what Tex had said, and she sighed happily. "I'm so relieved. The thought of someone coming after Woody or Isabella here in the States is literally my worst nightmare come true. I've always been afraid someone from one of your missions would come after you when you came home. I know it's irrational, but I couldn't help it."

It wasn't as irrational as she might think. The US had enemies all over the world, and none of them were happy when special forces came in and fucked up their plans. But after being out for five years, Spike had finally stopped looking over his shoulder all the time, though he was still cautious.

He was just about ready to start round two—he definitely wanted to go down on Reese, and he'd promised to show her how he'd touched himself while thinking about her—when *her* phone rang from somewhere in her clothes on the floor.

"You've got to be fucking kidding me!" Spike bitched.

Reese giggled.

"I swear it's a conspiracy. Keep Spike and Reese from making love," he complained.

"Hey, we managed to sneak it in this time," she said as she reached across him, leaning over the side of the bed to grab her phone from the floor.

The position put her ass right in Spike's view, and he couldn't resist touching her. Between her legs, she was still wet as fuck, and he could still see his come dripping out of her pussy.

Reese squealed when he dipped his finger back inside

her body, but she didn't immediately sit back or smack his hand away.

Having her bent over like this gave Spike other ideas. Carnal ones. He wanted to take her while she was on her hands and knees. Wanted to pull out and come all over her ass and rub it into her skin. Mark her as his.

After a long moment, she eventually sat back up, and Spike had to drop his hand.

"You're sex crazed," Reese said with a shake of her head, but he saw the excitement in her expression before she looked down at her phone.

He devoured her naked body with his gaze as she sat on the bed and checked her voice mail, and it was all Spike could do not to push her backward, rip the phone away, and do all the things he'd fantasized about during the last month.

"Shoot. That was Isabella. She wants to ask me some questions about the ceremony," Reese told him, biting her bottom lip. "She sounds nervous. The last thing I want is her freaking out and deciding she isn't ready to marry my brother."

"Then you should go," Spike forced himself to say.

"I know," Reese said with a sigh. "Gus?"

"Yeah?"

"I...this...You're a dream come true. *My* dream come true. I loved everything we did. All of it. Every second. And I can't wait to do it again."

"I'm not going a week and a half again, Reese. No matter *who* needs my help. Even if I come home at three a.m. again, I'm crawling in bed and waking you up to make love."

She smiled. "Okay."

Just that one word made Spike's cock sit up and take

notice. It wanted to be back inside Reese's body. In the hot, wet cave made just for him. He forced himself to move. He swung his legs over the side of the bed and held out a hand for Reese. She put hers in his and stood, blushing slightly.

She stood naked in front of him, and it took every ounce of Spike's restraint not to shove her right back onto the bed. He hugged her tightly, then kissed her. "Go talk to Isabella. I'll make us something we can eat when you're done. You can have the bathroom. I'll take the guest one."

"We could share," she suggested shyly.

"Nope. If we do, with our luck, Isabella will wander up here wanting to know what's taking so long and if you're okay. Besides, you're sore, you need some time to recover."

His eyes wandered over her body once more, and he grinned when he saw a trail of come leaking down her inner thigh. "Does it always do that?" he asked, nodding toward her leg.

She sighed. "No clue. No one's ever come inside me before."

Her words had Spike hardening, and once again the caveman inside started pounding his chest.

"And I'm guessing with your size, you probably come more than a lot of guys. So yeah, with us, I'm thinking it will always do that. So that means no quickies anywhere outside the cabin. I don't want to be leaking at the lodge, God forbid."

That wasn't something Spike could promise. He had a feeling a quickie with this woman would be better than most normal sex between other people. "I'll be sure to clean you up afterward," he muttered, watching the trickle of come inch down her leg.

Reese pushed him gently and headed for the en suite.

"Reese?"

She stopped and looked back at him from the doorway of the bathroom.

"Thank you."

"For what?"

"For being you."

She gave him a small smile, nodded, and shut the door behind her.

Spike stood in his room as naked as the day he was born with a smile on his face for a long moment. Then he looked at his bed. The covers were completely fucked, he could see a small wet spot on the sheets, and a few blonde hairs on one of the pillows. He freaking loved seeing the evidence of his woman and what they'd done in a place where he'd slept alone for the last four years.

Feeling lighter than he had in ages, Spike went to his dresser. He grabbed a change of clothes and headed for the guest bathroom as he mentally reviewed what he had in the fridge and what he was going to make for dinner.

CHAPTER SIXTEEN

Reese admired Gus as water tumbled over his shoulders, down his six-pack abs, over his cock—which was rock hard and bobbing toward her. They were in the shower together. Finally. It had been three days since they'd made love for the first time.

Three days of pure bliss.

She didn't think she'd ever been happier. She started her new job in a week, her brother was getting married in a few hours, and she'd never had a boyfriend like Gus. He was considerate and attentive and generous and sexy. For the first time in her dating life, she truly felt as if someone liked her exactly how she was. In the past, other men had told her they loved her body, didn't mind that she was overweight, that her curves were a turn-on, but their actions hadn't matched their words.

With Gus, she had no doubt that he liked her body. He couldn't keep his hands off her. He was constantly putting his hand on the small of her back, resting his palm on her thigh when they were sitting together, rubbing his thumb

over her skin absently when they held hands, kissing her...
The list went on and on.

After that first time they'd made love, and she'd returned from helping Isabella, she'd been too sore to have sex again, so he'd gone down on her and showed her what the fuss was all about in regard to oral sex.

Last night, he'd taken her again, but he'd kept his movements easy and slow no matter how much she'd begged him to go faster, promising that she was no longer sore.

This morning when her alarm went off, he'd gotten up and gone to start the shower so the water would be warm by the time she was ready to get in. To her surprise, he'd stepped in with her. And seeing him now, so virile, so damn gorgeous, Reese moved without thinking. She eased down to her knees in front of him and looked up as she reached for his cock.

But Gus caught her wrist before she could touch him. "You don't have to," he said gently. She'd admitted to him that she was nervous about this, giving head. She'd never done it before. She fell in love with him a little more at that moment.

"I know. I want to. But will you..." Her voice trailed off.

"Yes." His response was firm and unhesitating.

"You don't know what I was going to ask," she protested with a small laugh.

"Doesn't matter. You want or need something, I'll do what I can to give it to you."

Reese closed her eyes for a moment and sank back on her heels, giving her knees a short rest from the hard tiles. This man was killing her. She was so far gone for him, it wasn't even funny.

"What do you need from me, Reese?" he asked.

"Will you tell me how to pleasure you? I want to make you feel as good as you made me feel the other night, but I don't know how."

"Yes, but not here. It'll hurt your knees," Gus said. He held out a hand and helped her stand. Then he shifted positions so that her back was to the water and reached for the shampoo.

Reese had never had a shower as sensual as that one. Gus washed her hair, then carefully rinsed it out. He put conditioner on, then used a shower pouf—with his soap—and washed every inch of her body, rubbing against her every chance he got. He then rinsed her hair and let her return the favor. By the time they stepped out of the shower she felt like a wet noodle…a very turned-on wet noodle.

After they'd dried off, he took her hand and led her into the bedroom.

"We don't have a lot of time. You're supposed to be up at the lodge to help Isabella in an hour."

Reese frowned. "Maybe we should wait and—"

"No," Gus said with a shake of his head. "If I've learned anything lately, it's that I need to love you when I have the chance because there's a high probability that we're going to be interrupted."

Reese smirked. He wasn't wrong.

He picked up a pillow from the bed and threw it on the floor. Then he nodded to it. "Kneel, sweetheart."

She wasn't used to following orders, but she had to admit that she liked this side of him. Besides, she'd asked him to teach her. She lowered herself onto the pillow and looked up at him with anticipation.

"Open your mouth," he said in a low, gruff voice.

Reese shuffled closer to him and rested her hands on his muscular thighs. She tilted her head back and opened for him.

"Damn, sweetheart. I'm gonna come just looking at you," he muttered. Then he reached down and took one of her hands and wrapped it around the base of his cock. "Just do what feels good," he said gently. "I guarantee whatever you do, I'll love."

Reese wasn't so sure about that, but since she was eager to give him as much pleasure as he'd given her, she didn't hesitate to lean forward. She took him into her mouth and looked up at him as she did.

"Fuck. Those wide, innocent eyes. Your lips around me...it's so much better than my fantasies. Lick me, Reese. Suck on me. Touch my balls as you're working my cock. Yeah, just like that."

Reese lowered her gaze and got to work. She ran her tongue around the bulbus head of his cock, loving the contradiction of his soft skin and the hardness beneath her hand and tongue. She probed the hole in the tip and felt him jerk against her. Then she lifted his cock and licked up the underside, and he shuddered.

Suddenly she understood why women enjoyed this. The power it gave her was addictive. Having Gus at her mercy, feeling him shudder in pleasure, knowing she was doing that to him, was heady.

She tightened her fist around the base of his cock and used her other hand to caress his balls as she began to bob up and down on his length. He groaned, and she felt his hand tangle into her wet hair. The scent of him wafted to her nose. His soap, and a musky scent that she associated only with Gus.

"That's it, just like that. Shit, woman, are you sure

you've never done this before? Because you're a damn pro. Seriously...*fuck*, I'm not going to be able to take this for long," he warned.

Reese tightened her grip on him. She wasn't ready to stop yet. Her nipples were hard and she could feel herself getting wet. A spurt of fluid left his cock as she sucked hard, surprising her. She pulled her head back and examined him. A small bead of creamy come blossomed on the tip as she watched. Leaning forward, Reese dipped the tip of her tongue into the slit and was rewarded by more of his salty, musky pleasure.

Without warning, Gus reached down and yanked her to her feet.

Reese let out a small squeak before she found herself practically thrown onto the bed. She looked up at Gus as he climbed on top of her. He fisted his cock in his hand and took a deep breath as he used his knees to separate her legs.

"I need you. Now. Are you ready for me?"

"Yes."

Without saying another word, Gus slowly pushed inside her.

They both moaned with pleasure.

"You. Are. The. Best. Thing. That's. Ever. Happened. To. Me!" Gus said, his words staccato and coming with every thrust.

"You didn't let me finish," Reese pouted.

"As good as your mouth and tongue feel on me, this is so much better," he told her. "I want to come inside you. Fill you up. *Mark* you from the inside out."

His words made her belly clench.

"Touch yourself," he ordered between clenched teeth.

"Make yourself come. I want to feel it before I lose control."

She obviously didn't move quickly enough for him, because he raised himself until he could reach her clit and he stroked it hard and fast.

"Gus!" Reese shouted as she tried to wiggle away from him.

"Take it," he said firmly. "Take what I give you. I need you as crazed as I am right now."

If he wanted crazed, he was getting it. His touch both hurt and felt so amazingly good. She wasn't sure if she wanted him to continue or stop. But it didn't matter as he didn't give her a choice. Her orgasm approached without warning, sending her flying over the edge without mercy.

She clung to Gus as he grunted his approval and slammed himself into her over and over, Reese shaking with the force of her release. He buried his cock to the hilt and jerked against her as he came.

They were both panting hard, and Reese looked up into his eyes. The words she felt deep in her heart tumbled out before she could think about what she was saying. "I love you."

She was mortified for a moment, afraid she'd fucked everything up. Afraid he was going to pull out and tell her she was moving too fast. That he wasn't ready for anything as serious as love.

But instead, he smiled widely and said, "I love you too, sweetheart."

Her heart was beating so hard she was sure he could see it, and a relief so great swept through her, every muscle in her body relaxing.

Gus rolled until she was on top, and Reese lifted up to look down at him. He was still buried deep within her, and as usual, she felt their combined juices beginning to leak out of her body.

"I've never met anyone like you. I think I fell in love with you when I saw you drive that truck down in Colombia," he said with a grin.

She chuckled and shook her head. "That's all it took? A little fancy driving?"

"No, that's not all. It's everything about you. Sit up," he said.

Frowning, Reese shifted until she was straddling his lap.

"Look," he said, gesturing between her legs with his head.

She turned her gaze downward and saw where he was still deeply buried in her body. His pubic hair and hers were meshed together, and her pink pussy lips were stretched around his cock.

"We're beautiful together," he said almost breathlessly, as if mesmerized. "We fit perfectly. And not just physically. You can't cook, and I can. You have patience, and I don't. You're friendly and outgoing, and I'm kind of a hermit. But we both would do whatever it takes to help a friend in need. We're determined, and apparently both know a good thing when we see it. I love you, Reese. I've never said those words to another woman in my life, and I don't plan on *ever* saying them to anyone other than you."

"Gus," she whispered.

"I love seeing you like this. On top of me, your nipples hard, your pussy weeping for me. Lean back."

Reese didn't hesitate, although she did remind him, "Gus, I need to get to the lodge."

"I know. I'll be quick. Brace yourself on my thighs."

The position put her at his mercy, but Reese didn't care much at the moment.

His fingers went between her legs and once again he touched her clit. She jumped.

"Easy, love. I've got you."

Instead of the rough, hard touch he'd used to force her to orgasm, this time his fingers were gentle. Almost too gentle. Reese shifted, wanting more. Needing more.

"One more, Reese. Let me feel you come around me again. You have no idea how wonderful it feels on my dick. It's like you're hugging me from the inside out. Knowing I've done that, that I've made you feel that way, it's fucking amazing and not something I'm gonna get sick of anytime soon."

Reese couldn't speak. She'd dreamed about being with a man like Gus her whole life...and dreamed about being with *Gus* like this for years. She still had a hard time believing she was here with him.

This time her orgasm wasn't explosive. It wasn't overwhelming. It was intimate. And she could feel the love pouring off Gus as he kept his eyes glued between her legs as he took her higher and higher.

He was hard again by the time she came around him, and when he smiled at her and took her hips in his hands as if he was going to pull her off his body, Reese brushed his hands aside and leaned in, resting her hands on his chest. "Your turn," she told him as she began to lift her hips up and down.

"Reese, you don't have to...the lodge..." he said, before he groaned as she rocked against him.

"I know I don't have to. I want to. Let me take care of you," she pleaded.

Gus nodded and stared up at her face as she began to ride him hard.

Nerve endings tingled as she lifted up until his cock almost fell out of her body, then slammed herself back down.

"Yes, just like that!" he moaned.

Pretty soon, Reese was riding him like she imagined a cowgirl would ride a bucking bronco. He held onto her hips and dug his fingers into her flesh as he got closer to exploding. His jaw tensed, and Reese knew he was seconds away from coming, when he surprised her by pushing her to her back and jerking his cock out of her body. He leaned over her and began to stroke himself hard and fast.

"Gus," Reese got out before ropes of come were squirting out of the tip of his dick, all over her pussy and stomach.

It was the most erotic thing she'd ever seen. They hadn't been having sex all that long yet, but every time he'd orgasmed, he'd done so inside her.

"Fuck, that's so beautiful," he muttered when he was finally done. Then he shocked her by reaching down and rubbing his come into her skin. Over her labia, her pubic hair, her belly, even onto her breasts.

"Gus." She laughed. "We just showered."

"I know. I'm sorry," he said, not sounding sorry at all. "But I didn't think you'd want to have wet undies all day from my come leaking out of you."

He had a good point. "I think that ship's already sailed," she said dryly, thinking about how minutes ago, he'd come inside her.

Gus looked a little sheepish. "All right, I admit it. I've been dreaming about doing this for a while now…couldn't help myself."

Reese rolled her eyes but couldn't stop smiling.

"Come on, back into the shower you go," he said, scooting off the bed and holding out a hand.

Reese let him help her sit up. He kept her hand in his as he walked them back to the bathroom. "We're never going to get out of here if we both get in that shower again," she warned.

"I'm going to go make you something to eat before you head up to the lodge," he told her tenderly.

"Robert and Luna have been cooking nonstop. There's gonna be a ton of food up there," she told him.

Gus shrugged. "Yeah, but you like the way I make my eggs. And I bought you some of those cinnamon rolls you love so much."

Reese closed her eyes as Gus once again turned on the shower.

"Reese? Are you all right? If you really want to eat up at the lodge, it's okay."

"No!" she exclaimed as her eyes popped open. "I just...I love you so much."

"I love you too," he said gently. His gaze roamed down her naked body, pausing at seeing his come drying on her skin, before he seemed to shake himself. "Breakfast," he muttered before leaning forward and kissing her. It wasn't a short kiss either. It was the kind of kiss that made Reese want to say to hell with any plans she had and take him right back to bed.

"Can't wait to see you in your dress, sweetheart," Gus said. "And to take it off you after the reception." He winked at her, then turned and left the bathroom, his ass muscles clenching as he walked away.

It took Reese a moment before she could work up the energy to move. Before she stepped into the shower to rinse off, she looked in the mirror. She'd never really liked seeing herself naked. But considering how Gus worshipped her body, she wasn't as critical about herself as she usually was.

She lifted a hand and brushed it over her breast, feeling Gus's come on her skin. She smiled, then turned to the water. Time was ticking, and she really did need to hurry.

CHAPTER SEVENTEEN

"Do you, Isabella, take Jack Woodall as your lawfully wedded husband, to have and to hold, for richer or poorer, till death do you part?"

Every eye was on the couple exchanging vows under the arch Hudson had made, but Spike couldn't take his gaze from Reese.

She was standing next to her brother, while Angelo stood next to his sister during the ceremony. Reese had tears in her eyes as she watched her brother marry the woman he loved. Her light blue dress was blowing slightly in the breeze, and Spike had never seen anyone as beautiful in his life.

Yes, Isabella was a glowing bride in her white dress and happy smile, but Spike was completely enamored of Reese and didn't care who knew it.

He jerked when everyone around him started clapping and Woody leaned in to kiss Isabella.

He'd completely missed them being pronounced husband and wife, but he didn't even care. His eyes went to Reese again, and he felt his mood lighten even more at seeing the pure happiness exuding from her.

Looking over at Angelo, Spike took in the small smile on the kid's face. He was glad to see it. The teenager still spent most of his time alone, but in the last week or two, it seemed to Spike that he was actually trying to connect with some of the other people at The Refuge.

It was a relief.

Woody and Isabella walked back down the makeshift aisle toward the lodge. It was a short trip, because there weren't very many chairs creating the aisle in the small clearing where the ceremony took place. All the employees of the lodge were there, Woody and Reese's parents, and a handful of guests who'd jumped at the chance to watch the first-ever wedding ceremony at The Refuge.

A reception had been set up inside, with the cake the ladies had chosen from the bakery in town on prominent display. Robert and Luna had outdone themselves in making enough food to feed twice the number of people in attendance.

"Wasn't that beautiful?" Reese said, coming up next to him.

Spike immediately put his arm around her waist and pulled her into his side. "Beautiful," he agreed, staring at her.

"I don't think I've ever seen my brother so happy," she said with a huge smile, still watching the newly wedded couple walk toward the lodge.

"I loved that so much!" Alaska said exuberantly from beside them.

"It was great," Brick said, wrapping an arm around her. "Although I'm not convinced we should turn The Refuge into a wedding venue. That's not what we started this place for, and I wouldn't want to disturb the guests who are here to relax and try to heal."

Alaska nodded. "As much as I loved Woody and Isabella's wedding, it *is* a lot of work. And I understand what you're saying about the guests."

"But maybe we could make one more exception," Brick said with a small smile.

To Spike's surprise, his friend went down on one knee in front of Alaska. He pulled a small box out of his pocket and opened it before holding it up. "I told you I had a ring, and that I would ask you to marry me someday. That day is today. I love you, Al. I missed what was right in front of my face for way too long, and I'm done waiting to make you mine officially. Will you marry me? Here at The Refuge?"

Alaska stared at Brick with wide eyes, then she smiled and started to cry at the same time. "Yes! Of course I'll marry you, Drake!"

Then they were in each other's embrace, and Brick was twirling her around and around.

Spike looked at Reese and wasn't surprised to see tears in her eyes.

"Did you *see* that?" she asked.

Spike resisted the urge to tease her and say of course he did, he was standing right there next to her. Instead, he simply replied, "I saw, sweetheart."

Tonka, Henley, and Jasna had been walking back to the lodge, but at the commotion, they turned around. Reese was pulled away from Spike and into a group hug with the other women around Alaska.

"That was epic," Spike told Brick.

His friend grinned sheepishly. "I know it's kind of a dick thing to propose on someone else's wedding day, but I talked to Woody and Isabella and they both insisted they didn't care. I'd planned on waiting until later. Maybe when we were dancing or something. But she gave me such a perfect opening, I couldn't resist. What about you, Tonka? When are you and Henley tying the knot?"

Tonka smiled. "We've been talking about maybe doing a Christmas thing. Jasna's already got it all planned out. How Melba will walk down the aisle with the rings around her neck, Wally and Beauty will be our attendants, and we'll do it in the barn so all the animals can watch and feel like they're a part of it."

Spike choked back a laugh, but Brick didn't have any such reticence. "Good Lord, man, I hope you're putting the kibosh on that."

Tonka shrugged. "Don't really care how it happens, just that it does. But Henley's definitely putting her foot down. In fact, I think she's leaning toward us going into town and having a civil ceremony."

"You okay with that?" Spike asked.

"Honestly? Yes. I've come a long way, and Henley's helped me feel more comfortable around people, but being the center of attention? Having everyone's eyes on me? Not sure I'd like it too much."

"I can understand that," Spike said. And he could. After hearing Tonka's story, about how his service dog had been tortured and killed in front of him while he was helpless to save him, he didn't blame him for wanting to stick to himself and the animals he cared for on The Refuge.

"Happy for you," Brick said seriously. "Henley is amazing, and I think I'm jealous that you'll be getting a ready-made family when you marry her."

"Jas is a handful, but she's a good kid," Tonka said with a nod.

"She's been a good addition to The Refuge," Spike agreed.

"What about you?" Tonka asked Spike.

"What *about* me?"

"Don't think we haven't missed the way you can't keep your eyes—or hands—off Reese. I take it that it's official and she's not going back to Missouri with her brother?"

"No. She's staying. She got that job at the laboratory."

"Really? I hadn't heard," Tonka said.

"That's because you spend most of your time down at the barn," Brick teased.

"Hey, I've been better. I've been up at the lodge every day for lunch."

"Because Henley eats there," Brick countered.

Tonka shrugged. "You think I want to come up and eat with your ugly mug every day?" he asked.

The men shoved at each other good naturedly, then Brick turned to Spike. "Seriously, though. She it for you?"

"Yes," Spike said without any hesitation whatsoever.

To his friends' credit, they didn't warn him that they hadn't been together very long. Or that maybe it wasn't too smart to move a woman in that he'd just connected with. Hell, it wasn't as if they could protest too hard, considering how things had gone between them and their women.

"Maybe Alaska will have a few more weddings to plan after all," Brick mused.

Before Spike could respond, he felt an arm wrap around his back and Reese was snuggling against his side. "We should go to the lodge so we don't miss anything."

"What's to miss?" Brick asked, hugging Alaska as she approached. "We're gonna sit, eat, have cake, then Woody and Isabella are gonna go back to their cabin and have married-couple sex."

"Drake!" Alaska scolded, smacking his arm. "That's rude."

"How is it rude if that's what they're going to do?" Brick asked.

Alaska rolled her eyes. "Whatever. Come on, let's go."

Spike held Reese back when she went to follow the others.

"Something wrong?" she asked, her brow furrowing.

"Not at all. I just wanted a moment with you to let you know how beautiful you look in that dress. I didn't get a chance to tell you before the ceremony started."

"You look pretty darn handsome yourself," she said with a small smile.

Spike stared at her for a long moment without a word.

"What? Do I have something on my face?" she asked self-consciously.

"No. I'm just memorizing this moment. Standing on land I own with my friends, celebrating a wedding of one of my former teammates, feeling content for the first time in a very long time. I'm grateful."

Her expression gentled. "You deserve this. You've worked hard to make this place as incredible as it is. And you're an excellent friend, business owner, and boyfriend."

"You forgot lover," Spike teased.

Reese rolled her eyes. "Right, sorry. That too."

"I'm happy," Spike whispered. "And it scares the hell out of me."

"Why?"

"Because every time I thought I'd been happy in the past, something's happened to fuck it up."

Reese put her hand on his cheek. "Nothing's going to happen."

"I love you, Reese Woodall. I'll do whatever it takes to make you happy too. To ensure you never want to leave me. If I screw up, tell me and I'll fix it. I'll bend over backward to make sure you know how much you're appreciated and loved."

"I just need you to be yourself," she told him. "I don't want you to change. Be who you are, because I love that man. Even when he gets bossy and dominant. Even when he won't let me buy twelve boxes of Girl Scout Cookies because they aren't good for me. Because the other stuff... giving those same Girl Scouts a fifty-dollar bill just to support them, making me a carb-filled dinner and not saying a word about how a salad would be healthier, and loving me exactly how I am...makes me want to spend the rest of my life with you."

"We're getting married," he blurted.

She chuckled. "You already told me that," she teased.

"Soon. I'm not waiting until Christmas like Tonka and Henley. I'm not sure I have it in me to be romantic and give you a proposal that you deserve, but just know that I want to be with you and only you for the rest of my life. I want to have babies. A large, noisy family that will drive us crazy, but who we wouldn't have any other way."

Tears shone in Reese's eyes. "That *was* pretty damn romantic, Gus."

"It was? All right then. When?"

"When what?"

"When can we plan our wedding? I heard what Brick said, and I agree with him that The Refuge shouldn't become wedding central, but I want it here. Where we live, where your brother got married."

Reese looked stunned.

Spike frowned. Shit, he'd moved too fast.

"Are you serious?"

"Yes."

"Then...I'll talk to Alaska. Tomorrow. See which dates might work in the schedule."

Spike smiled. Huge. "Yeah?"

"Yeah."

"I love you, Reese. So much."

"I think that's my line."

Spike kissed her then. He would've gone on kissing her, possibly stealing her away to his—no, *their* cabin, but a loud whistle pierced the air from the direction of the lodge.

He lifted his head and sighed dramatically.

Reese giggled. "I'm guessing they want us to get up there."

"Yeah. That was Tiny. I'd recognize his irritated whistle anywhere," Spike said. He licked his lips and tasted Reese. "What kind of ring do you want?" he asked as they started walking toward the lodge.

"Um...I don't know."

"Yes, you do," Spike countered. "You like what you like, and I want to get you something that you'll want to wear every day and never take off. And if I get something you hate, you won't want to do that."

"Nothing expensive," she said quickly.

Spike snorted. That wasn't happening. "What else?"

"I think something nontraditional. Not a solitaire that sticks way up. It would snag on stuff and I wouldn't want to have to take it off while I was working."

Spike made a mental note. "Diamonds?"

"Yeah."

"Gold or Platinum?"

"Doesn't matter."

"What size?"

"Seven and a half."

He nodded. "Got it."

"Gus?"

"Yeah, sweetheart?"

"This is crazy...but it feels right, you know?"

He *did* know. "Yeah, I know."

She squeezed his hand. "I can't stop smiling. I'm happy for Woody and Isabella. For Alaska. For us. About my job. About getting my stuff moved up here. All of it."

Spike made a mental vow to do whatever it took to keep her that way. He loved seeing her happiness shining in her face for everyone to see. Loved how carefree and relaxed she seemed at that moment. Of course life would throw curve balls their way, but he'd always be there to keep them from hitting her head-on. He'd gladly stand in the way of *anything* life tried to throw at them, just to see her smile for the rest of their days.

* * *

Angelo couldn't wait until the day was over. He'd done his best to act like he was enjoying himself. That he was thrilled to be there. But the truth was, he was miserable. He was antsy, ready to go back home, but there'd been no word from Pablo for a few days. He could admit that there were worse places to wait...that The Refuge was in a beautiful location...but he was a city boy. Didn't like the quiet here. Didn't enjoy the sound of the wind in the trees. He wanted to get back to the energy of busy streets. To the excitement of being in the cartel. To women.

It wasn't that Angelo wasn't pleased for his sister. He was. She'd worked her ass off her entire life, and seeing her with Woody today, relaxed and so happy, finally drove home how stressed she'd always been in Colombia.

He hadn't thought he'd been a difficult kid to raise, but apparently he'd been more work than he knew. He hated to think that he'd been a heavy burden to her.

All the more reason to go back to Colombia. So his sister could live her life here in America, without him hanging on her coattails.

She'd told him all about Missouri and how great it was going to be, but Angelo knew better. He nodded and agreed with her anytime she went on and on about their new lives, all the while waiting impatiently for a text from Pablo telling him that the money was wired to the Western Union place in Los Alamos. He'd given him the address over a week ago, and every time he reached out, the other man told him to be patient...when he bothered to reply at all.

As he sat at a table by himself, wishing the stupid reception would be over so he could go back to the cabin —Isabella and Woody were staying in one of the other cabins that was empty for the night, which was fine with Angelo; he didn't want to be a third wheel on their wedding night—his phone vibrated with an incoming text.

Looking down, Angelo's heart began beating faster.

PABLO

It's done. The money should be there tomorrow. Let me know when you plan to go pick it up, just in case something goes wrong.

Angelo's fingers flew over the keyboard. He'd never been more excited in all his life. He was finally going home!

ANGELO

Thank you! I will let you know when I can find a ride.

"You look like you are in a good mood."

Angelo's gaze shot up to see his sister standing next to the table. He quickly clicked off the display on his phone and shoved it into his pocket. The last thing he wanted was her reading over his shoulder and seeing his conversations with a cartel member. She didn't know Pablo, but if she asked too many questions, learned who he was...she'd yell at him, tell him he was ruining his life, and refuse to let him leave.

But he wasn't a kid anymore, and she wasn't in charge of him. She couldn't tell him who to be friends with and he could go where he wanted. He was going back to Colombia, no matter what his sister said.

"I'm happy for you," he said in Spanish. It was crazy how much he missed hearing his native language being spoken. Yes, he and Isabella talked every day, but he missed hearing it in the streets as he walked around. On the TV and radio.

"Thank you. I'm happy too." Isabella pulled out a chair and sat next to her brother. "But I am worried about you, Angelo."

"Don't be," he said immediately. "I'm fine."

"All of this has been very hard on you."

"It's not your fault."

"I know, but I can't help but feel sorry anyway. We never talked about it...what happened to you when we were being held captive?"

Angelo didn't want to talk about this. Not now, not ever. Didn't want to admit to his sister that he wasn't actually being held against his will. That he'd been fed well. He'd explained why he hadn't delivered the drugs on time and apologized profusely. He'd sworn his loyalty to the cartel. Yes, his room was locked, but the small crew at the house had let him out frequently.

He would *never* tell Isabella that he'd lied about wanting to come to the States. That he didn't *need* to be rescued...because he was working with the men who'd taken them to that house.

"Nothing," he finally said in response.

"Come on, it's me. Your sister. You can talk to me. You used to tell me everything," Isabella cajoled.

"Nothing happened. They locked me in that room and the next thing I knew, you were there and we were leaving," Angelo told her.

Isabella sighed. "Okay. But if you ever need someone to talk to, if you ever get overwhelmed, we'll deal with it together."

Angelo nodded.

"Thank you for being here with me today. It means so much. There's no one I would've rather had at my side than you," she told him. "We've been through a lot together, and I don't know how I would've kept going if you weren't there, giving me a purpose."

"You have your husband now," he told her. "You don't need me."

"I'll always need you, Angelo," Isabella said with a shake of her head. "And no matter how old you get, you'll always be my little brother. I'll always worry about you."

He didn't like that. At all.

He was slowly, begrudgingly beginning to accept the idea that perhaps the American could take good care of his sister. She needed to move on with her life in Missouri. He knew that once he got in deep with the cartel...well, deeper...that they'd expect his loyalty and focus to be entirely on the organization. Not on any family. Not on any friends. He'd have to live and breathe the cartel. And it was what he wanted.

For Isabella, he wanted freedom. Freedom to live her life. To have babies with her American husband.

"I can take care of myself," he said. "You need to let me go, Isabella."

She sighed. "I know. You're an adult now. I love you, Angelo."

"I love you too."

She leaned over and kissed his cheek. Isabella smiled at him once more, then stood to go and find her husband. Woody was watching from the other side of the room, giving her space but still making sure she was all right.

Angelo sighed. Maybe the American wasn't such a bad man. He treated his sister with care and it was obvious how much he loved her. He didn't understand that kind of love, but he was still glad Isabella had it.

When he was alone, Angelo pulled out his phone once more. Pablo had sent another text while he'd been talking to his sister.

PABLO

> We will be waiting. We look forward to you proving you are worth the trouble.

Angelo frowned. He'd told Pablo over and over that he would do whatever it took to pay back the money he was sending. And that he'd do what the cartel wanted, no questions asked. He quickly sent one last text.

ANGELO

> I am worth it. The cartel is my family now.

Three dots indicated Pablo was writing back.

PABLO

> We will see.

Angelo's frown deepened. He didn't like the ominous sound of those three simple words, but he'd prove himself. As soon as he got back to Colombia, he'd show Pablo and the others that he was more than a kid. That he was someone they could rely on. Not only to deliver drugs when they needed him to, but to provide security as well. Being an enforcer was one of the most highly sought-after positions in the cartel. Those men were respected and feared. Angelo wanted that for himself. And he'd do whatever it took to earn it.

CHAPTER EIGHTEEN

Reese sighed in contentment as she stretched lazily. Gus had brought her home after the reception and made love to her for hours. He'd worshipped every inch of her body. Had brought her to orgasm with his mouth, then his hand, then he'd taken her in half a dozen different ways...on her knees, with her on top again, with him standing and her face down over the side of the bed, against the wall, and finally—her favorite—missionary style, his gaze boring into hers as they both went over the edge. He was rough, then tender, then out of control, then loving.

She'd never get enough of him and his lovemaking.

The bed next to her was now empty, but Reese wasn't concerned. Gus had left a while ago, but not before kissing her awake and letting her know he was headed out to clean up the main walking trails with Pipe, Stone, and Brick, removing fallen branches and other debris from the storm that had hit two nights ago.

He'd told her once that doing work around The Refuge helped keep him in shape. That he was glad he didn't have to run for miles and miles and work out as hard as he had while he was in the Army, but that he still enjoyed being physical and getting his exercise doing something useful at the same time.

Deciding she'd been lazy long enough, Reese rolled out of bed and padded to the bathroom. She was sore again today, but in a delicious way that simply made her remember how amazing Gus had been the night before.

She showered and wandered into the kitchen, smiling when she saw a note on the counter that said Gus had already made her coffee, although it was chilled this morning instead of hot. Opening the fridge, Reese saw a cup in there with a sticky note with her name on it...and a cinnamon roll with another note that told her to heat it in the microwave for sixty seconds.

She didn't know if Gus would always be this sweet and thoughtful in the future, but she had a feeling he would. He was rough around the edges in a lot of ways, but to her, he was perfect.

Reese didn't have a lot planned for the day, except for meeting her parents, Woody, and Isabella for dinner in town. She ate her breakfast with a smile on her face and was about to wander up to the lodge to find Alaska and talk to her about wedding dates, when a knock sounded at her door.

Furrowing her brow and wondering who the heck was there, she blinked in surprise when she opened the door to find Angelo on the other side.

"Hi. *Hola*," she said with a smile.

He said something to her in Spanish that Reese didn't understand. She held up a finger, hoping he understood that she wanted him to wait, as she dashed back inside to grab her phone, which was still sitting on the table next to where she'd eaten. She scrolled to the translation app and went back to the door. She held it up and nodded at him.

He spoke again.

When he was done, Reese hit a button on the app and it translated what he'd said.

"Will you take me to town?"

Reese was surprised yet again. But then, she supposed it wasn't unusual for him to ask her. Woody and Isabella were probably still enjoying their first morning as husband and wife, and she'd done her fair share of attempting to befriend and talk to Angelo in the past. Plus, she'd given him a ride to town before.

She had no idea what he needed from Los Alamos, but it had to be hard not to be as independent as he'd been back in Colombia. She nodded, spoke into the app, then played it back in Spanish. "I'd be happy to. Give me a moment to write a note to Gus. Want to meet me at my car?"

With a nod, Angelo thanked her then turned and headed back down the path.

Reese wished she could talk to the young man easier. She spun and went back inside to write a note to Gus, letting him know where she was in case he got back before she did. She also decided to change into a pair of cargo pants and her hiking boots. When she got back, maybe she'd head out on the trails to find Gus and the others and see what she could do to help. It was a nice day, and she didn't want to spend it inside, especially since another storm was supposed to move in tonight and last for a few days. She wanted to get out in the sun as much as she could until winter settled in on the mountain.

When she was ready, she locked the cabin and headed down to her car. Angelo was standing next to it, looking down at his phone. She spoke into her phone then played back the words in Spanish. It was a little slow, speaking to each other through the translation app, but Reese was ultimately pleased with how well it worked.

"Where are we going?"

"I don't know the name of the place, but I have the address."

"Okay. How long are you going to be? I can run to the grocery store while you're doing your thing and come back to get you after I'm done."

"You can just drop me off."

Reese frowned and wondered if the app had translated his words wrong.

"How will you get back to The Refuge?" she asked.

"I will figure it out. I do not want to be a bother."

She wanted to protest, tell him that she could wait, that whatever he had to do couldn't really take that long. But he was an adult, technically, and she didn't want to do anything that might annoy Angelo, and make him not want to talk to her anymore. She felt as if she'd made great strides in their relationship. They weren't exactly friends, but he did actually talk to her now and then...through the app, of course.

Deciding she'd track down Isabella when she returned so she could maybe go and find her brother, she simply gave him a nod and opened the driver's side door.

They both got in the car, and Reese noticed that Angelo had a backpack with him. He put it on the floor at his feet. She wondered if maybe he was going to do some shopping, and the bag was for carrying his purchases back to The Refuge. Maybe he was planning on buying his sister a wedding present, which would be a nice thing to do.

Feeling a jolt of relief at her deduction, and feeling

happy that Angelo seemed to finally be moving forward with his life here in the States, she started her SUV and headed toward town.

But ten short minutes later, Reese was back to frowning. The address Angelo had given her was for a Western Union. She had no idea why in the world he'd want to go there.

He turned to her when she parked, said, "*Gracias*," then climbed out of her car and closed the door behind him, not giving her a chance to reply.

Reese was well aware he wanted her to leave him in town, but she couldn't do that in good conscience. She watched through the window of the business as he went up to the counter. For several minutes, there seemed to be a lot of hand gestures and intense conversation before Angelo finally turned to leave.

She hadn't moved from her spot in the parking lot while he was inside, and when he pushed open the door, she got out of her car and stood, waiting for him to look her way.

Then two things happened at once.

A man walked up to Angelo—and someone grabbed Reese's upper arm in a grip so tight, her knees immediately went weak. He said something to her in Spanish, but of course she didn't understand a word of it.

She tried to pull her arm out of his grasp, but he merely tightened his hold, making tears spring to her eyes. He propelled her away from the car, and it was then Reese realized there was a third man. He was on the other side of her SUV, staring at her with eyes so black, so dead, she shivered in fear.

The back door of her car was opened and she was shoved inside. Just as she went to scramble over the seat to the other side and run like hell, the door opened and the man with the dead eyes was getting in beside her.

The man who'd taken hold of her arm snatched her phone right out of her grasp, and Reese's stomach dropped. Shit! She needed that phone. Needed to call Gus. The Refuge. The police. *Someone.*

There was movement outside of the car, and Reese saw Angelo open the door of the passenger seat that he'd vacated not even five minutes ago.

"Angelo!" Reese barked. "Run!"

But either he didn't understand, or he chose to ignore her.

The guy with Angelo reached in, grabbed her purse, took her phone from the other man, then shoved both items at Angelo as he said something.

Angelo backed away from the car—and for a moment, their gazes met. Reese didn't understand what was happening. He didn't look worried or freaked out in the least. There was some mild confusion in his eyes, but that was it. He didn't speak, just turned his head to break their eye contact, taking her purse and phone.

Reese watched as he walked calmly to the far side of the strip mall parking lot, stashed the phone inside her purse, then threw it into a dumpster. He dropped something else onto the ground and stomped on it several times. Then he picked up the pieces of whatever it was and tossed them into the trash can as well.

He came back to the car, got in, and stared straight ahead.

She was sandwiched in the backseat between two men, while Angelo and the guy who'd approached him outside the Western Union were in the front. The vehicle started and they pulled out of the parking lot.

Reese suddenly realized how screwed she was. She knew better than to let anyone take her away in a vehicle, because if an abductor got her away from civilization, she was as good as dead.

She began to fight. Fight for her life.

She didn't want to die. She wanted to marry Gus! Have his babies. Start her new job. Live at The Refuge with Gus and all her other new friends.

The man on her left grabbed hold of her flailing limbs, and the other pushed hard on the back of her neck until she was folded in half and staring at the floor of her car. They said something, but of course Reese couldn't understand. She was breathing way too fast and felt lightheaded. Being bent over made it hard to breathe, and the way the man was holding her arms behind her back, it felt as if he was going to wrench them out of their sockets.

Terror hit her. This was happening. She was being carjacked. Kidnapped. Something.

And Angelo was in on it.

If he didn't know this was going to happen before they arrived, he was certainly going along with it now.

She could hear the four men talking above her head. They weren't arguing, but the man driving was speaking in a very intense tone, as if he was in charge, commanding the others.

Tears begin to fall from Reese's eyes. She couldn't help it. She was outnumbered and at the mercy of whatever the men wanted to do with her.

"Please, let me go. *Por favor*," she begged.

But she was ignored. The hand on her neck kept pressing down and her arms were still held behind her back in an iron-tight grip. All she could do was sit there, stare at the carpet under her feet, and pray someone had seen something. Heard something. That they'd called the police and even now a rescue mission was being organized to come after her.

Because if it wasn't? She was in big trouble.

* * *

Spike wiped his brow with his arm and arched his back. The work that morning had been tough, but it was extremely satisfying to see the trail now clear of debris and branches from the storm the other day.

"It looks good," Pipe said, the pride easy to hear in his voice.

"It does," Stone agreed.

"Not sayin' I love clearing trails, but it needed to be done. If we waited for the incoming storm to blow through, clearing things out would've been even harder," Brick added.

Living in the mountains, it was a fact of life, and a part of having their business here, that they needed to do regular maintenance of this particular trail. It was the easiest and therefore the most popular with their guests. So keeping it clear of downed trees and other debris was important.

"Any word on a wedding date?" Pipe asked Brick.

The satisfied smile on his friend's face made Spike think about Reese, and how they'd spent their previous evening.

"As a matter of fact, yes. Three weeks from now."

"Holy shit!"

"That soon? Awesome!"

"Wow!"

"It seems Al is impatient to get a ring on my finger," Brick said with a grin.

"As if you aren't just as eager to publicly claim her," Stone said with an eye roll.

"I am. But here's the thing, she's mine, just as I'm hers. I don't *need* to marry her, but I *want* to. I feel as if I missed out on so much by not realizing for so many years that we were meant to be with each other. I should've known when I found so much inspiration and comfort from that cross-stitch she made me as a high school graduation present. If I hadn't been so focused on my job, maybe I would've seen what was right in front of my face. I'm done waiting for the perfect time. No time will ever be perfect. We're going to be busy around here for the foreseeable future, so we decided last night to just go ahead and slip our ceremony in between all the other stuff going on."

"Smart man. Tie her down before she realizes she could do better and changes her mind," Pipe joked.

Everyone laughed, except for Spike. Pipe had just verbalized his greatest fear when it came to Reese. He still had no idea why she was with him. Why she loved him. She could be with a literal rocket scientist or nuclear engineer. All he had was a small cabin in the woods, a brain that saw trouble where there wasn't any, and a possessive, protective streak that an independent woman like her probably thought was nice now, but would eventually turn stifling.

"Uh-oh, Spike's thinking too hard over there," Stone quipped. They were almost back at The Refuge now, and Spike opened his mouth to tell his friend to fuck off because he wasn't nearly ready to talk about his insecurities when it came to Reese, but he was interrupted by the ringing of his phone.

And just like that, his mood lifted. It had to be Reese, because he very rarely received calls, especially when three of the six other people who might contact him by phone were with him at that moment.

But it wasn't Reese. It was Woody.

Thinking it was odd that the man was calling him the morning after he'd gotten married, Spike unconsciously braced as he answered.

"Spike here. What's up, Woody?"

"Have you seen Reese?"

Spike stopped walking, and his three friends all did the same, instantly staring at him with varying degrees of curiosity and concern in their expressions. "This morning when I left, she was still sleeping. Why?"

"I can't get a hold of her."

Spike relaxed a little. "I think I saw her phone on the kitchen counter this morning, so she probably just isn't hearing it ring from the bedroom."

"Angelo isn't answering his phone either. Isabella's worried, because it's not as if he really goes anywhere. I called Reese to see if she'd go check on him, since I was enjoying spending the first morning with my wife. But she didn't answer...and I've got a bad feeling."

Spike tried to relax. Woody didn't *know* something was wrong, he was just being cautious and trying to appease his new wife. But he knew damn well that when he or Woody or any of their teammates got bad feelings while on missions, no one ever dismissed them.

"I'm headed over to Tiny's cabin to check on Angelo now," Woody said. "But, Spike, it's not like Reese not to answer when I call. I know what you said, that her phone isn't in the room with her, but it's late. She's a morning person. Even if she slept in, she should be up and about by now."

"She could've forgotten her phone when she went up to the lodge," Spike suggested, not believing his own words.

"Something's wrong," Woody said in a low tone.

"I'm headed to my cabin now. I'll check on Reese and call you back when I find her. Pipe, Stone, and Brick are with me. I'll send them to meet you at Tiny's cabin," Spike said, even as he started walking again.

"Thanks."

"You don't have to thank me," Spike told his friend. "I'm marrying her. She means everything to me."

"So we'll be brothers for real...I couldn't ask for a better man for my sister," Woody told him.

His pleasure felt good, but Spike was having a hard time thinking about anything other than getting back to his cabin and setting eyes on Reese. "I'll talk to you soon."

"Thanks."

They both clicked off the connection and Spike quickly explained the situation to the others.

"I'll go with you to find Reese," Pipe said.

"And Stone and I will meet Woody. I'm sure Angelo is here somewhere. The kid doesn't usually leave the property," Brick said.

They branched off when they got closer to The Refuge, with Spike and Pipe headed in one direction and their friends going another.

The second Spike unlocked the door to his cabin, he knew Reese wasn't there. It felt...empty. He jogged to the bedroom anyway and looked inside. The covers on the bed were mussed, but she wasn't there. The bathroom door was standing open so she wasn't in the shower either. He went back to the kitchen and opened the refrigerator door. The iced coffee and cinnamon roll he'd prepared for her were gone.

"She's not here," Spike said.

"She didn't leave in a huge hurry though, since she took the time to lock the door behind her," Pipe observed.

Spike nodded and looked around. "Her purse and phone aren't here either. Which means she probably didn't just go to the lodge. She usually doesn't take her purse to go visit Alaska or to eat."

Both men went back to the door. They were walking a little faster now, eager to check the lodge to see if Reese was there. Spike's heart was beating too fast and he felt a little shaky. He hadn't felt this kind of fear in a long time, but this time it was different, not like the fear he felt while on a mission.

This was about *Reese*. The woman he'd made long, slow love to last night. Who'd smiled up at him with a look so tender, he could hardly believe it was aimed at *him*. She was the woman he was going to marry. The future mother of his children. The thought of something happening to her, of her being hurt, made him almost physically sick.

"Easy, Spike, don't borrow trouble," Pipe said, reading his mind.

Spike wanted to bite his head off. Tell him he had no idea how he felt right now. How could he? He didn't have a woman who loved him.

For the first time, Spike felt a little sorry for his single friends. He didn't even know what he'd been missing until Reese came into his life. She made him a better person. A better man.

They burst into the lodge, scaring the shit out of Alaska, who was sitting behind the desk typing on the computer.

"Holy crap, you startled me!" she exclaimed. "What's wrong?"

"Is Reese here?" Spike barked.

"Reese? I haven't seen her this morning. Why?"

But Spike didn't pause to explain. If Alaska hadn't seen her, she wasn't here. And if she'd been at the lodge earlier, Alaska would've known and told him.

He spun and went back outside and turned toward the barn. He stopped halfway there, staring at the area where most of them parked their cars.

Reese's Escape wasn't there.

"Shit," he said.

"Her car's gone," Pipe said unnecessarily.

"You guys find Reese?" Brick asked as he approached with Stone. "Angelo wasn't at the cabin. Woody's looking around the property for him."

"Reese's car isn't here," Pipe said, gesturing to the parking lot.

"What's going on?" Tonka asked, coming toward them from the barn.

Hearing footsteps behind them, Spike turned to see Alaska, Robert, Ryan, and Jess coming in their direction from the lodge. Word was getting around that something was wrong.

"We can't find Reese or Angelo," Brick told Tonka in answer to his question.

"I saw them get into her Escape and head out," Tonka told the assembled group.

"When? How long ago?" Spike asked urgently.

"About an hour and a half ago, maybe?"

"Shit."

"Pipe, you go with Spike. Tonka, Stone, and I will go in my Jeep. We'll search Los Alamos. They couldn't have gone far. They're probably at the store or something," Brick said.

"They aren't answering their phones," Spike reminded his friend.

Brick's lips pressed together. That fact hadn't escaped his attention, but he obviously hadn't wanted to mention it.

"We'll hold down the fort here," Alaska said. "I'll get a hold of Owl and Tiny and let them know they're in charge of the guests."

Without further discussion, the five men headed for the parking lot.

Spike could hardly think. Where would Reese have gone with Angelo? He turned to Tonka as they walked. "Did she look like she was in distress?"

"No. If she had, I wouldn't have let her leave," Tonka said. "She and Angelo had a brief discussion, it looked like she was using that app she has to talk to him, then they got in and she drove away normally."

"Fuck. We need to trace her phone," Spike said.

"I'm calling Tex," Brick said as he brought his phone up to his ear.

Spike relaxed a fraction. A very small fraction. If anyone could find Reese, it would be Tex. He'd heard the stories over the years of all the women he'd been able to locate. He had to believe he'd be able to find his Reese too. The alternative was unacceptable.

"I'm driving," Pipe said firmly as they approached the lot.

Spike wasn't about to argue with him. Pipe's Dodge Challenger was a hell of a lot more powerful than his beat-up old sedan.

The men got into the vehicles and peeled out of the

parking lot as they headed toward town. For the first time in forever, Spike had no plan in mind. He didn't even try to think about coordinating with his friends. All he could think about was Reese. Where was she? Was she scared? Hurt? Did she even realize she'd worry everyone by not leaving a note? Hopefully they'd find her SUV in the parking lot at the grocery store. She'd be mortified that she'd caused everyone so much worry.

But deep down, Spike agreed with Woody that something was wrong. Reese was too considerate to not answer her phone. He had no idea what was happening, but it wasn't good. He felt it down to the marrow of his bones.

As they drove toward town, his life passed in front of his eyes. Their wedding, his unborn children, growing old with Reese, all of it. It felt like his hopes and dreams were disappearing in a puff of smoke—and there was nothing he could do to stop it.

Then he straightened. No. He'd just found Reese, he wasn't losing her now. He'd fight the devil himself to get her back safe and sound. He just needed a clue as to where she was and what enemy he needed to fight. Just one. He'd take it from there.

CHAPTER NINETEEN

They were headed south. They'd passed Santa Fe and were headed into the outskirts of Albuquerque now. The men next to her had eventually allowed her to sit up, and Reese stared out of the front windshield, staying as still as possible.

She had no idea what these men wanted with her. They talked amongst themselves in Spanish and it was extremely frustrating not to know what they were saying. They could be talking about what they were going to do with her and she was sitting there clueless.

For the first time, she understood exactly what Angelo must have been feeling this whole time. She vowed if she got out of this alive, she was going to study and learn Spanish. It was an insane thought, all things considered, but thinking about literally anything besides her potential death was preferable at the moment.

Angelo hadn't said a whole lot, but every now and then he'd respond to something one of the other men asked. Reese thought about Isabella, how worried she'd be about her brother. How brokenhearted she'd be to learn that he had something to do with what was happening.

Reese didn't know if he'd meant to involve her or not. He *had* told her she didn't need to stay once she dropped him off. And she remembered the look on his face when the driver had approached him outside the Western Union. He'd been confused, surprised to see him. From what she could guess, he'd gone there expecting to pick up money someone had wired him. What other reason did anyone go to Western Union? She further assumed he was going to get a bus ticket or something and try to go home, back to Colombia. She didn't know for sure, of course, but that was the only thing that made sense.

But instead of money waiting for him, it was these men. Did he know them? It didn't seem as if he was anxious to get away from them. But why take *her*? Why not just steal her car and go? It made no sense to kidnap her too.

No matter how hard she thought about it, Reese couldn't think of a reason why they'd take her...except for the most obvious and horrifying ones.

The thought of anyone touching her, violating her against her will, made her want to cry. Or throw up. Or both. If that was the case, she wouldn't make it easy on them. Even though there were four of them, she'd fight like hell. She'd get their DNA under her fingernails. She'd mark them so if they were caught, the police would know they were lying when they said they didn't know anything about her.

The thought of them raping and killing her and leaving her body somewhere in the New Mexican wilderness to rot made tears fill her eyes. She refused to let them fall though. She willed them back. She wouldn't let them see how scared she was.

Her thoughts turned to Gus. Did he know she wasn't at The Refuge by now? She'd left him a note, so if he'd gone back to the cabin after cleaning the trails, he would've seen it. But how would he know where she was? They'd thrown her phone into the trash, and she'd seen enough crime shows to know the cops used phones to track people.

Despair hit her. If she was going to live through whatever was happening, she'd have to do it on her own. It was obvious Angelo wasn't going to help, he hadn't so much as looked at her since they'd gotten on the road. He was practically pretending she wasn't there. That they weren't related by marriage now.

The fear she'd felt since she'd been forced into the backseat began to morph into something new. Anger.

She and Gus had discussed their future children just last night. He'd come inside her and asked how many kids she wanted. They'd talked about the pros and cons of big families versus small and had decided together that three kids would be perfect.

She'd even told him she would stop taking her birth control pills, and they'd let nature take its course. She'd been so happy. Almost overwhelmed by the fact that the man she'd had a massive crush on was discussing how many children he wanted with her.

She wanted that. Wanted a future with him. Wanted to see him holding their babies, rocking them to sleep. If they had girls, they'd have him wrapped around their little fingers, and their sons would be miniature Guses. The pain in her heart at knowing their future might be ripped away before it had even started hurt so bad, she wanted to curl into a ball and sob.

But she couldn't fall apart. She needed to be alert to the slightest window of opportunity she might have to escape. They couldn't drive forever, eventually they'd have to stop for gas. There would be people around, she could scream, make a scene. Or tell her captors she needed to pee, write a note while she was in there. Or better yet, run like hell. Anything to get away. She'd figure out how to get back to The Refuge once she was safely away from these assholes.

Feeling better now that she had some sort of plan in mind, even though it was vague, Reese took a deep breath. She studied the driver, memorizing every single thing she could about him so she could describe him to the police. His hair, the shape of his nose, the mole under his ear. She'd do the same with the men sitting on either side of her when she had the chance. She wasn't going to be a victim. No way in hell.

* * *

"Anything?" Spike asked Tonka.

It had been thirty minutes since they'd left The Refuge and they'd searched every inch of Los Alamos for Reese's car...with no luck. Tonka had called a moment ago to check in.

"Nothing. We need to stop driving around in circles and meet to plan our next steps."

Spike didn't want to stop. He kept hoping the next street they pulled down, the next parking lot they drove through, they'd find Reese. But there had been no sign of her car. It was as if she'd disappeared into thin air. "Where?" he asked.

Tonka had a quick conversation with the others in his car, then came back and said, "East Park off of the main road."

Spike knew where that was. It was on the east side of town and had a trail, a playground, and a dog park. "We'll be there in three minutes."

"Ten-four."

Spike told Pipe where to go and stared straight ahead as they drove, trying his hardest not to let worst-case scenarios overwhelm him.

Brick and the others arrived around the same time as Spike and Pipe, and behind them was Woody.

They all got out of their cars and gathered in a circle.

"Brick called me ten minutes ago," Woody said, clearly agitated. "Any sign of either Angelo or Reese?" he asked.

Everyone shook their heads.

"I talked to Tex," Brick said.

Spike braced himself for the news.

"He traced Reese's phone to the Western Union in town. When we went there, I was hoping to find her, but there wasn't any sign of her whatsoever."

"And her phone?"

Brick gave him a dire look. "Her purse was in the dumpster in the parking lot. With her phone inside."

"Damn it!" Spike swore, turning and viciously kicking the tire of Brick's Jeep. It didn't make him feel better, only made his foot hurt. He turned back to Brick. "What else?"

"The phone Angelo had was in there too."

"So someone stole them and dumped them?" Pipe deduced.

"Not exactly," Brick said solemnly. "Tex also sent me a

security video." He fumbled with his phone and clicked a few buttons. "I just sent it to you all."

Spike took out his phone and impatiently pulled up the video Brick had sent. It was grainy and taken from the opposite end of the parking lot, but he saw Reese's Escape pull in. Angelo got out and went into the Western Union, leaving the shop not too long after. He was approached by a man. Reese got out of her car and was immediately grabbed by another man, who put her in the backseat of her own vehicle, a third man quickly sliding in beside her. Angelo and the man who'd approached him both walked to the car—and a minute passed before Angelo walked calmly toward the dumpster and threw Reese's purse inside. The video skipped at that moment, and the next thing they saw was Angelo getting back into the car before it drove off.

"What the actual *fuck*? Angelo's involved in this?" Woody exclaimed.

Spike's jaw was clenched so tight, he couldn't speak.

"Isabella's going to be devastated."

It was all Spike could do not to beat the shit out of his friend right then and there. *Isabella* would be devastated? Her brother had just fucking kidnapped Reese! He didn't give a shit what anyone else was feeling right now, only what *Reese* was going through.

He took a deep breath. Then another. Now wasn't the time to get into a fight with his old teammate. His only concern was Reese.

Brick's phone rang, and Spike tensed, praying it was Tex calling to tell them he had a lead on where the men had taken Reese.

"Brick...yeah...no, he won't be mad... You did? What'd

it say? Right, okay...we figured that much out...good job, Al. We will...I need to go...love you too."

Spike's shoulders slumped. It was obviously Alaska on the other end of the phone.

"That was Alaska," Brick said unnecessarily. "She's worried about Reese, and she went to your cabin, Spike, and used the spare key to get in. She thought maybe, just maybe, she'd gone on a walk and had come back after everyone left."

Spike sighed. Reese wasn't in the cabin. He knew that without a doubt.

"Anyway, she found a note Reese had left for you."

"She wrote me a note? I didn't see it."

"Alaska said it was on the floor under your kitchen table. It must've blown off when she left or something. Anyway, it was brief, just said that she was taking Angelo to town and she'd be back soon," Brick said.

"She probably thought she'd be back before you were," Woody said.

Spike felt a little better knowing she'd left him a note, but it didn't help them now. And if he'd found the note, it was possible he would've talked himself out of heading out to look for her immediately. And they'd be even more behind the eight ball than they were already.

Thinking about not finding out she'd been kidnapped for another two hours made a shudder rack his frame. It was bad enough they were an hour and a half behind her... four hours would've felt insurmountable.

"Now what?" Stone asked. "Where were they going? What did those men want?"

"I don't know. Without their phones, Tex can't track them. He's working on the traffic cameras in Santa Fe and down in Albuquerque, but he admitted that with a car as common as Reese's, and with as many cameras as there are, it might take a while," Brick said.

"She doesn't have time," Spike seethed. "If they dump her somewhere in the wilderness, we'll never find her."

"We're going to find her," Tonka said.

"How?" Spike couldn't help but ask. He felt helpless. Worse than helpless. The woman he loved more than he ever thought he could love another human being needed him, and he couldn't do anything to help her because they had no clue where she'd been taken.

The men all stared at each other. No one spoke. No one had any ideas. Whoever her abductors were, they had a huge head start. And once they hit Albuquerque, they could go east, west, or even south toward Mexico.

Then something occurred to Spike. "We have Angelo's phone, right? Can we see if Tex can hack it? Find out if there are any texts or messages on it that will help us?"

"That'd be a great idea," Tonka said, "if it wasn't smashed to pieces. Apparently, someone didn't want us doing exactly that."

"Shit!" Spike swore.

"I can call Owl," Stone said after a long moment. "See if he can get his hands on a chopper. He can search from the air."

"Owl hasn't flown since the mission where you both ended up POWs," Brick said quietly.

"I know, neither have I, but we've both kept our licenses current, and I have no doubt he'd do whatever he had to in order to find Reese."

Spike closed his eyes. This was a nightmare, and he didn't know how to snap out of it. The thought of never seeing Reese again, never hearing her laugh, never touching her, was so abhorrent it made him double over in pain. Leaning over with his hands on his thighs, Spike's mouth watered with nausea. He spit onto the ground at his feet and tried not to lose his breakfast right then and there.

A notification on Pipe's phone sounded loud in the silence surrounding the men.

"What the fuck?" he exclaimed.

Spike straightened. "What?"

"I just got a text. Four words and a map with a red dot, moving south," Pipe said, the confusion easy to hear in his tone.

"From Tex?" Brick asked.

"No, an unknown number."

"It's him," Tonka said.

"Him who?" Stone asked in confusion.

"The guy who found Jasna. Who put her in that bunker."

"We don't know that," Brick started, but Spike ignored him and snatched Pipe's phone out of his hand.

UNKNOWN

I'm tracking her tile.

That was all the text said. It wouldn't have made sense to most people, but Spike had seen Reese's keyring enough to know what it meant. She'd told him that she was constantly misplacing her keys, so she'd bought one of those tile things, that connected to an app on her phone that tracked her keyring.

"Holy fuck. It's Reese," he said, watching as the red dot made its way south out of Albuquerque on Interstate 25.

He heard Brick speaking to someone on his phone, and heard him say Tex's name, but all his attention was on that red dot.

"I'm calling Owl," Stone said firmly.

Spike was all for his friends using their helicopter piloting skills to find Reese, but in the meantime, he wasn't going to sit around and wait for them to find a chopper, get the authorization to take it up, then find her. He had to get to her *now*.

"Get in," Pipe said, reading his mind. "We're going after her."

Spike nodded and turned to go to his friend's hotrod.

"Wait!" Tonka said.

Spike turned to tell him that he wasn't waiting another second, but Tonka was already heading for Brick's Jeep. He returned seconds later with a backpack. "We can't go unarmed," he said grimly.

"Tex's trying to tap into that same feed," Brick called out.

At the moment, Spike didn't care. He also didn't care who was responsible for the text. All he cared about was that they had a way to track Reese. Her kidnappers had done their best to get rid of anything that might leave a trail, but they hadn't even considered the keychain. Hell, neither had Spike.

Whoever had discovered they could track Reese by the innocent gadget attached to her keys was a fucking genius.

Within moments, with Pipe behind the wheel, Tonka in the backseat making sure the weapons he had were loaded and ready to go, and Spike watching the screen of the phone, they peeled out and were racing south.

* * *

As it turned out, Reese didn't have a chance to do a damn thing when they stopped for gas. The men next to her didn't budge when they stopped. Even when she pleaded with them, telling them she was going to pee all over the seats if they didn't let her out to use the bathroom, they barely glanced her way.

Worse, the gas station they'd stopped at was literally in the middle of nowhere. Once beyond the outskirts of Albuquerque, the towns and houses were few and far between. Tumbleweeds blew across the road and even if she'd been able to run, there wasn't anywhere to go.

They were the only people at the gas pumps and the driver didn't waste any time filling up the tank before getting back into the SUV and getting back on the road.

At one point, she heard the men talking about El Paso and assumed that was their destination. It was around a four-hour trip to El Paso from Albuquerque, and Reese dreaded what would happen once they arrived in the city. Her anxiety was through the roof and she felt light-headed with dread as each mile passed.

As the city approached, the men began to talk amongst themselves a bit more, and it sounded like they were arguing. If they were fighting about something, Reese thought maybe she could use that to her advantage. Not to mention, a city meant people. And if even one person heard her scream and got concerned and called the police, she could be saved.

But once again, she was disappointed when they didn't stop and instead switched interstates and started heading east on I-10. Reese's ass hurt from sitting for so long and her muscles ached with tension. She wanted to get out and walk around, stretch, but the likelihood of that happening was slim to none. Her captors had a destination in mind, and she had a feeling they weren't stopping until they reached it.

They'd been driving for most of the day at this point, and another gas stop was just as disappointing as the first. The men had allowed her to use the bathroom, but the experience was humiliating. The man who'd grabbed her the first time had gone with her to the unisex bathroom and watched as she'd peed. She wasn't even allowed to wash her hands before he was hauling her back to her car.

It was stupid to be upset about not having clean hands when she was in the middle of a kidnapping, but Reese wasn't thinking straight anymore. Terror, hunger, and the nonstop adrenaline rush had made it hard to keep her wits about her. All she could do was envision one awful scenario after another waiting for her at the end of their journey.

When the vehicle turned off the interstate and headed south, passing a sign for the tiny town of Marfa, she almost laughed, thinking about the famous "Marfa lights." She actually hoped an alien was watching them, ready to suck up her car and save her from whatever was going to happen when they stopped.

And Reese knew *something* was coming. The men around her were getting antsy, as if they knew something was imminent. She prayed that they weren't excited about finally having their shot with her after the long drive.

Determination welled once more inside Reese. They wouldn't touch her. She didn't want her last moments, her last thoughts, to be of strange men violating her. She wanted to remember only Gus inside her. Only Gus's touch. She longed to be back at The Refuge. In their bed.

Laughing as he tickled her when he ran his hands over her body.

She saw a sign for the Big Bend National Park, and shortly after they pulled off onto a dirt road. It was dark now, the only light for miles coming from the headlights of her car.

The men had started talking again, in low tones, as if the darkness had spooked them somehow. Once again, she braced for whatever was coming. She was almost looking forward to any change at this point. She needed out of this car. Needed to fight—and she couldn't do that while surrounded by the three men.

No. Four. Reese had long since included Angelo amongst her kidnappers. At no time in the last several hours had he made any attempt to help her or even look at her. It hurt. A lot. She'd done her best to befriend him, and this was how he repaid her?

Well, fuck him. Fuck *all* of them. She'd get away, hide out until they left, then somehow make her way back home. To Gus.

* * *

Angelo stared straight ahead. He was scared. This wasn't how things were supposed to go. When he'd gotten to the Western Union place, he'd been surprised when the lady said she didn't have any money under his name. He'd left in disgust—and then Pablo had shown up.

"We've come to take you home," the man said.

Angelo had been happy...until he'd seen the other two men. He knew they were enforcers but didn't know their names. When they'd shoved Reese into the backseat of her car, he was even more confused.

"Take her purse and phone and throw them away," Pablo ordered after he'd gotten into Reese's car. "Then smash yours to pieces and toss it as well. We don't want anyone to track us."

Angelo had done as ordered almost robotically, still trying to figure out what was happening. Why Pablo and the other men had come. Did they not trust him? He decided that must be it. They didn't want to give him money because they didn't trust him.

When he got back in the car, he'd asked Pablo, "Why do we need her?"

"Why not?" Pablo said with a grin. "It's a long trip, we could use some fun before we get home."

In that moment, his blood ran cold.

Angelo didn't mind selling drugs. That was business. He didn't even mind using violence to make sure the money they earned wasn't stolen from them. But hurting women? He wasn't cool with that. And Reese had been nice to him. She wasn't his friend, but she was always smiling, and she made his sister happy.

When Pablo left the parking lot and headed out of town, it was too late to change anything about the situation.

Angelo didn't dare look into the backseat. He could practically feel Reese's eyes on him. Pleading. Asking why. The truth was, he had no answer. He hadn't planned this.

He also hadn't wanted anyone to know where he was going, and why. He'd written Isabella a long letter and had given it to the clerk at the Western Union place to mail later, expecting to be across the Mexican border by the time she received it. He didn't want his sister to worry about him. He would be fine. He belonged back in Colombia and not in the US.

Throughout the drive, his mood darkened more and more. He and Reese were related now by marriage. He didn't want to see her hurt, but he also didn't want the responsibility of looking after her. He needed to be a man now, tough. And he couldn't do that, couldn't prove to Pablo that he was willing to do anything for the cartel, if he looked weak in regard to Reese.

So he sat in his seat and stared straight ahead, pretending she wasn't there. That everything was fine.

When they'd arrived in El Paso, Angelo had thought they'd stop and spend the night in a hotel before meeting up with whoever was going to help them get across the border. But instead, Pablo kept driving. He wanted to ask where they were going and how they were going to get home to Colombia, but he kept his mouth shut.

Eventually, Pablo began to explain the plan. How they couldn't cross the border from New Mexico because of the wall that had been built there. The area was too open, too risky, and monitored too heavily. But the land in Texas, around the Big Bend National Park, wasn't monitored at all. They'd have to cross the Rio Grande, but after that, they were home free. They'd be met by cartel members, mules who regularly ferried their people and drugs illegally across the border. From there, they'd travel through Mexico to South America and back to Colombia.

"What about the girl?" Andres asked. He was the man who'd grabbed Reese and forced her into the backseat.

"She comes with us across the river. Once we're in Mexico, we'll stop and rest for the night..." Pablo grinned. "And we can all have some fun with her. We'll leave her body for the desert to claim and head home."

"I want first dibs," Diego declared.

Angelo swallowed hard. He didn't know the two men

Pablo had brought with him, but they were big. And mean. And he'd seen the lust in their eyes. He supposed their heartless demeanor made them good enforcers, but he didn't want to think about what they'd do to Reese.

"I think Angelo should get that privilege," Pablo said with a smirk. "You've had pussy before, right, boy?"

He didn't like being called a *boy*. And he definitely didn't like Pablo insinuating he was a virgin. Yeah, he'd only been with one girl before, but he wasn't an idiot.

"Yes," he said simply.

"Right, then it's decided. Angelo will have first go at the American pussy. Then me. Then you can go, Diego. And, Andres, you can finish her off."

"Sounds good to me," Andres said, pleasure in his voice.

"I want her ass then," Diego demanded. "I don't want sloppy seconds."

"Whatever."

Angelo swallowed hard. They were talking about raping Reese as if she wasn't a living, breathing person. As if she didn't have a brother who loved her. The thought of Isabella being in Reese's position right now made him want to throw up. He'd known getting involved with the cartel would change him, that he'd have to do things he might not like...but not this. Not hurting a woman he *knew*.

"You have a problem with the plan?" Pablo asked sharply, any pretend friendliness gone from his tone.

"No."

"Because I didn't want to come pick up your stupid ass. But there was no way we were sending you money, not after you fucked up. The cartel *owns* you, and we'll make an example of you." When Angelo glanced at him, Pablo smirked. "Don't worry, we aren't going to kill you. But we'll make damn sure others know that when they're given a task to perform, we expect them to do it. Understand?"

Angelo took a deep breath and nodded. He couldn't protest. He *had* fucked up. If he'd delivered the drugs like he was supposed to, he wouldn't be here right now.

Then again, Isabella wouldn't be married and safe in the US either. Whatever he had to go through would be worth it if his sister was free and happy.

As they continued through the darkness toward the border, Angelo made a vow to do what he could to help Reese. She didn't deserve to be here. It was his fault that she'd been kidnapped...and if the chance came for him to help her get away, he'd take it.

CHAPTER TWENTY

"Drive faster," Spike begged Pipe.

He was being unreasonable, as Pipe was already driving way faster than was safe. It was seriously only a matter of time before a police officer clocked them and tried to pull them over, but they'd worry about that if it happened.

Spike had watched the little red dot on the screen go through El Paso and head east. Nausea swam in his belly. He'd thought they'd stop in the big city, maybe for the night, letting him, Pipe, and Tonka catch up, but they'd simply kept moving east.

Until they'd turned south, heading toward Big Bend.

The Texas park was literally in the middle of nowhere. There were no towns around it, just miles and miles of wilderness. And it was a different kind of wilderness than was around The Refuge. Instead of woods and trees, Big Bend was smack dab in the middle of the desert. There were some rolling hills...some would even call them small mountains...but there wasn't a lot of shade or grass.

More importantly, and the reason Spike assumed they

were headed there, the only thing separating the United States from Mexico in the area was the Rio Grande.

A bolt of lightning lit up the sky, and Spike winced.

"My weather app shows a huge storm moving up from Mexico," Tonka said from the backseat. The last thing they needed was a storm hindering their search for Reese. Spike had a feeling that if those men got her across the border, it would be next to impossible to find her.

Pipe had made up some good time with how fast he was driving, but it wasn't enough. They were still at least an hour out from where the red dot was blinking on Pipe's cell phone. While the kidnappers were driving the speed limit so as not to draw any attention to themselves, Pipe had been pushing his sports car hard.

Tonka's phone rang from the backseat, scaring the shit out of Spike.

"Tonka...okay...yeah, we're on the east side of Texas moving fast...Big Bend, yes...All right, but the weather here doesn't look good...neither of them would want you to crash...I know...okay, yeah. Later."

Tonka didn't make Spike or Pipe wait to hear who he was talking to. "That was Brick. Stone and Owl, with Tex's assistance, are on their way with a chopper."

"Holy shit, seriously?" Pipe asked.

"That's what Brick said," Tonka replied.

Spike closed his eyes. He thought he knew what friendship was. Thought he was actually a pretty good friend himself. But this...this went above and beyond anything he could've ever expected, anything he could ever repay.

Stone and Owl were two of the best chopper pilots the Army had ever seen. They were legendary Night Stalker pilots. They'd been on a mission in the Middle East when they'd been hit by an RPG. Their helicopter went down, and somehow Owl had been able to keep it from crashing into a million pieces, but both he and Stone had been wounded in the crash. They'd managed to get out of the wrecked pile of metal, but hadn't been able to evade capture by the militants who'd shot them down.

They'd been held hostage for two weeks. Fourteen days of torture and hell, broadcast to the world, before a team of Delta Force Operatives had been able to rescue them. Neither man had flown since.

For them to go back up into the air, in this fucking weather, for Reese, made Spike want to cry with gratitude.

"No one takes one of our own and gets away with it," Pipe said sternly as he stared at the interstate in front of them.

"Damn straight," Tonka echoed.

Spike wanted to agree, but he couldn't speak. He was too worried, too nauseous, too overcome with gratitude that he had such an amazing group of men at his back. All he could do was pray they wouldn't be too late. That Reese was all right. That the men who took her weren't hurting her. Until he saw her with his own two eyes, until he was able to get his hands on her to make sure she was alive and well, he wouldn't relax.

* * *

It was fully dark now, and with the darkness, Reese's fear increased tenfold. Somehow in the daylight, things didn't seem so bad. But now that she couldn't see more than ten feet in front of her SUV, fear settled onto her shoulders like a heavy blanket.

The dark brought evil. Brought out the worst in

people. And the last place she wanted to be was with these men. Angelo still hadn't looked at her. Not even once, so she knew she couldn't rely on him to help her in any way. She still couldn't decide if he'd known what was going to happen when he asked her to drive him into Los Alamos, but if not, he still hadn't done anything to reassure her since this whole nightmare had begun.

She was on her own. There was no way Gus and the others would know where she was. She was sure they knew something had happened by now, but there was nothing they could do.

Rain pelted the SUV and the wind made her small Ford Escape sway with each gust as the guy driving resolutely kept moving forward. Wherever they were going, he seemed to be intent on getting there, not sitting out the storm somewhere.

He turned the car down another path in the desert, this one no more than two ruts in the dirt. The undercarriage of her car scraped on a rock, and Reese winced. They traveled for another fifteen minutes or so before the driver finally stopped and said something to his friends.

The rain pelted against the roof, the car rocking in the gusty wind. The three strangers had some sort of argument as they sat there, and Reese pressed her lips together worriedly. She didn't like the anger that she could hear in their tones. So far, everyone had been fairly calm, which had helped Reese avoid completely freaking out.

But now the driver seemed to be egging Angelo on somehow, while the man to her left protested vehemently.

For the first time since Reese had known him, Angelo raised his voice. He yelled something—and the other men fell silent for a moment. Then the driver laughed. He sneered at Angelo, saying something that made Isabella's brother reach for the handle of the door and storm away from the vehicle.

In shock that Angelo had left the safety of the car in the middle of such a hellacious storm, Reese jerked when the guy to her left grabbed the back of her neck and squeezed, hard.

She gasped in pain and tried to pull away, but with the man on her right sitting so close, she had nowhere to go. She tried to reach up to pry the guy's fingers off her neck, but he ignored her weak attempts and grabbed her chest. He squeezed one of her breasts, saying something that made the other two men laugh.

Fear had Reese shaking violently. Was this it? Was she going to be raped by these men? Terror threatened to freeze her limbs—but then she began to fight. Her adrenaline spiked. She wasn't going down so easily. She'd been calm and docile all day, but she was *done*.

She spun toward the man to her left and raked her fingernails down his face, trying to use her digits to gouge his eyeballs out.

He yelped in surprise and let go of her neck as he threw a hand up to defend himself. The man on her right wrapped an arm around her chest, rendering her hands useless by pinning her arms, but she could still use her feet —and she did.

Glad she'd decided to put on her hiking boots before going into town, Reese brought her knees up and kicked at the man who'd touched her chest with all her might. The three men were all yelling now, but she tuned them out. She couldn't understand them anyway. She screamed at the top of her lungs, swearing at them, telling them she wasn't going to make anything they did to her easy.

She fought as if her life depended on it, and it probably

did. Reese had no illusions that she could defeat three men all by herself, but she was damn well going to try.

The man she was kicking fumbled for the door handle and practically fell out of the car when it opened. Rain and wind immediately soaked the seat where he'd been sitting.

Reese had a single moment to feel proud that she'd beaten at least one of the men, before her heart sank as the guy leaned back into the car and grabbed her ankles. She was caught between the two men, and no matter how much she writhed and fought to get free, it was no use.

The driver turned in his seat. Reese's gaze flew to him, and she saw that he was laughing. *Laughing* at her. He said something, and the man holding her arms began to scoot toward the open door. His friend helped by pulling her legs.

The rain hurt when it pelted her face, but Reese barely noticed. She was being carried away from her SUV. She had no idea what was about to happen, but she knew down to her bones it wasn't going to be good.

* * *

Angelo ignored the storm raging around him. He felt sick. When they'd stopped, Pablo told him that he'd changed his mind. They were going to have their fun with the American before they crossed into Mexico. They had time, and it wasn't as if anyone could find them in the storm. He'd told him to go to the cargo area of the SUV, that Diego and Andres would lower the back seats and hold her down while he took his turn first.

Diego had once again argued to be first, but Pablo had told him to shut the fuck up or he wouldn't get a turn at all. That had turned into a shouting match, and Angelo had frantically tried to think of a way out of this. He didn't want to hurt Reese. And he didn't want the others to hurt her either.

But he had no idea how to help her. How to stop this. He felt sick that she was in this situation. In the last nine hours, he'd had more than enough time to think as they drove south. Angelo knew that he'd fucked up—again. He'd led the cartel right to his sister. If it had been Isabella with him instead of Reese, they could've hurt *her*. Taken *her*. Maybe they'd even expected Isabella to be with him. For all he knew, because he'd told them the name of The Refuge, they would send someone else to retrieve her.

And in the meantime, he'd put Reese's life in danger.

"It's decided," Pablo said firmly. "Angelo, me, Diego, then Andres. Diego, I already said you can have her ass since you're being such a dick about going third." Then Pablo turned to Angelo. "Get in the back. My cock's been hard for hours, let's get this done so we can go home."

"What happens after?" Angelo asked.

"I've decided to take her with us. It's a long trip to Colombia...we'll need something to do along the way."

The man Angelo used to look up to, used to want to emulate, licked his lips and stared into the backseat with lust in his gaze, and it made Angelo's blood run cold. He was scared. He didn't like the feeling.

"No," he blurted.

"No what?" Pablo asked in a hard, cold voice. "I know you're not telling me what to do, because that wouldn't be smart...not after I came all this way to bring you home like you asked, no, *begged* me to do."

"I don't want her!" Angelo shouted, scared out of his mind. He'd never been afraid of Pablo before, but seeing the look in his eyes now made him regret ever taking up with the cartel.

Isabella had been right. These men were evil.

But that realization was coming far too late.

"Fine. Get out. The three of us will have our fun then we'll get the hell out of this fucking country."

Angelo didn't know what else to do, other than what he was ordered. He exited the vehicle into the heart of the storm, like the coward he was, and walked away, not wanting to see or hear what was about to happen.

The guilt made it hard to breathe. Made his chest hurt. This was his fault. The woman who'd always been so nice to him, no matter how badly he treated her, was about to be brutalized.

He heard her screams, and tears ran down Angelo's cheeks, mixing with the rain. If he lived to be a hundred, which he knew he wouldn't, he'd never forget the anguish, pain, and fear in that scream.

He couldn't stop himself from glancing back at the car —and to his surprise, Diego's door flew open and the large man stumbled out, holding a hand to his face as he cried out in pain. Then his upper body disappeared back into the car.

The next thing Angelo knew, Diego and Andres were carrying a squirming and fighting Reese out of the backseat. Pablo got out of the driver's seat and exclaimed, "Don't let go of her! Bring her over there, under that tree by the river!"

Looking to where Pablo was pointing, Angelo realized for the first time how close they were to the Rio Grande. It was so dark, he hadn't seen it. But now he couldn't take his eyes off the racing water. Was *this* where Pablo expected them to cross into Mexico? The water was frothy and angry. It looked more like the ocean during a tropical storm than a river.

Angelo heard Reese scream again and turned in time to see Diego and Andres drop her onto the ground, right on her ass. He winced, knowing it had to hurt. But if it did, she didn't let it show. She immediately rolled, got her knees under her, and tried to stand.

Diego tackled her, and she landed face down on the muddy riverbank.

"Hold her, Diego!" Andres shouted, sounding excited.

"Grab her arms," Pablo told Andres, taking a knife out of the sheath on his belt. He held it up and smiled. "Gotta get those pants off. If she doesn't hold still, she's gonna get cut."

Angelo swallowed the bile that rose in his throat. Was he really going to stand there and watch this happen?

What choice did he have? He couldn't overpower Diego, Andres, *and* Pablo. They'd kill him, then still do whatever they wanted to Reese.

Diego was straddling Reese now, holding her down as Pablo knelt next to her with his knife at the ready. Reese was still struggling, fighting with everything she had, even as Pablo made his first cut.

Angelo turned his back on the horrifying scene, unable to watch...

And heard something else over the wind and rain and Reese's frantic screams.

An engine.

He spun around and realized the others had heard it too. All three men were looking around, trying to discover where the sound was coming from.

To everyone's shock, a helicopter appeared out of

nowhere, coming straight at them down the river, a spot-light bobbing from an open door on the side.

It landed on Diego and the others—and everyone froze.

The bright light allowed Angelo to see what the darkness had hidden. Reese's tearstained face as she lifted her head. Her shirt lying next to her, cut off by Pablo's sharp knife. The blood welling from where the knife had sliced her arm and shoulders. Andres had a hand on the back of her neck, the other clutching both of her wrists. Diego was astride her thighs, one hand fisted on the waistband of her pants. It was obvious he'd been in the process of pulling them off of Reese.

And Pablo had already shoved his jeans down, one hand on his knife, the other around his cock, preparing to rape the woman struggling in the mud.

"*Fuck!*" Pablo growled viciously as he quickly stuffed his dick inside his pants. "To the river! If we're in Mexico, border patrol can't touch us!"

Angelo had a feeling whoever was in that helicopter wasn't border patrol. He didn't think anyone would be crazy enough to fly in this weather...except for one person.

Spike.

Isabella had told him about Woody and Spike, how they used to work for the US Army and were special forces soldiers. She'd been so excited when it became obvious Reese and Spike were dating.

Angelo had seen the way Spike looked at Reese. It was the same way Woody looked at his sister. With a love so strong, they'd face down the devil himself if it meant keeping them safe.

And right now, Pablo was the devil.

Hell...*Angelo* was too.

The last thing he wanted to do was go into that raging river, but he didn't have a choice. He'd burned his bridges here in the States. Even if he wanted to stay, that wasn't a possibility any longer. Not after he'd been responsible for Reese's kidnapping. He'd made his bed. Now he had to man up and deal with the consequences of his actions.

Pablo ran several yards down river and grabbed a rope that Angelo hadn't noticed before. It was obviously placed there to help people get across the river. This wasn't a random stopping place. The cartel likely used this location to ferry people across the river all the time.

Pablo started across the water without waiting to see if the others followed, without even a glance behind him, intent on saving his own ass.

Angelo's hopes rose. This was Reese's chance. Surely she'd be left behind in the rush to get to Mexico.

His hopes were instantly dashed when Diego grabbed hold of Reese's arm and hauled her to her feet. Then he cocked his fist back and punched her once. Twice. Before wrenching her arm behind her back so hard, Angelo was afraid he'd broken it.

"If you don't come willingly, I'll make you regret it," he growled in her face.

Of course, Reese had no idea what he was saying, but she was so dazed from being hit, she didn't even fight as Diego dragged her toward the river.

Angelo hurried behind them, not surprised when Andres pushed ahead of Diego and started across without offering to help with Reese.

"You—kid," Diego growled. "Watch her. If she doesn't make it to the other side, I'll fuck *you* instead. I'm getting a piece of ass one way or the other—understand?"

Angelo stared at the huge man in horror.

Diego shoved Reese toward him and grabbed hold of the rope, stepping into the rushing waters.

Angelo had no idea how the hell he was supposed to cross the river and hold onto Reese at the same time. He was big, but he wasn't sure he was strong enough to hold them both upright in the fast current.

The chopper was circling above them now, and every few seconds, the spotlight from the door lit up the area.

Reese said something to him, and Angelo looked down at her. Her face was bloody from Diego's fist, and she looked terrified. But then she did something that Angelo would never forget, whether he continued to live for many years or mere minutes.

She patted his arm soothingly.

She was comforting *him*.

She'd been kidnapped and beaten, almost raped, and he'd ignored her all day, hadn't done a single thing to help her...and she was reassuring Angelo.

Regret beat down on him fiercely. He had to fix this. But he had no idea how.

"Move, Angelo! *Now!* Or I'll fucking shoot you myself!"

He didn't know who yelled the words, had barely heard them over all the noise, but he could hear the truth in the man's words. Pushing Reese forward, he reached for the rope. He brought her hand up and carefully curled her fingers around it.

"We have to cross," he said, knowing she wouldn't understand him, but saying the words anyway.

But Reese seemed to comprehend him as she took a wobbly step toward the water and grabbed the rope with her other hand, her knuckles white in the spotlight as she held on as tightly as she could.

Ahead of him, he could see the water almost up to

Diego's hips as he passed the middle of the river. Angelo was surprised the water was as shallow as it was, but the cartel and other people going into and out of the US obviously knew this was the ideal place to cross the notoriously dangerous river. It might be relatively low where they were crossing, but he had a feeling it quickly deepened as the water rolled downstream. And if his feet were swept from beneath him, if the current grabbed hold, he'd surely drown either way, shallow or not, since he couldn't swim.

He swallowed hard as he started across the river, holding the rope with a desperate grip.

The storm made the undertow especially strong, and Angelo immediately struggled to stay upright. He had one hand on Reese's belt loop, holding onto her as well as the rope as they struggled to make their way across to the other side.

When they were halfway across, the chopper lowered until it was only about three meters above the rolling waves of the river. The pilot was fucking crazy, but he had skills Angelo had only seen in the movies. He turned the helicopter parallel to the river, and Angelo could see two men standing in the open doorway. One held a rifle pointed directly at him, and the other held the spotlight.

Angelo had made a lot of decisions in his life. A lot of them bad. He'd been a shitty brother, thinking only of himself, and only recently coming to understand all of the sacrifices Isabella had made for him. He'd taken her for granted, hadn't appreciated how hard she worked to keep them both fed and safe.

And he'd made the worst decision yet when he'd asked Pablo to help him return to the cartel.

It was time to make the right decision for once in his life.

He leaned forward, keeping his gaze locked on the man with the rifle in the helicopter, and yelled into Reese's ear, "I am sorry! Tell Isabella I love her."

Then he let go of Reese's pants, swung his arm up and brought the edge of his hand down on Reese's wrist. Hard.

When she lost her grip on the rope, he shoved her shoulder...

And she fell into the river, where she was immediately swept downstream.

Relief swam through Angelo's veins. She was free.

The helicopter banked to the left and the light that had been on him disappeared—a split second before a large tree that had been washed into the river somewhere upstream slammed into Angelo's legs, knocking him off his feet and sending him tumbling into the water after Reese.

CHAPTER TWENTY-ONE

Stone had called Spike when they were turning onto the desolate road leading to Big Bend, informing them that he and Owl were five minutes out from their location and wanting to know if Spike wanted to be picked up.

It was a no-brainer.

It was insane to be in a helicopter in this weather, but if he could get to Reese faster, Spike didn't even have to think twice.

Tonka had jumped into the chopper as well, leaving Pipe to follow in his Challenger.

Spike had left his phone with Pipe, as his friend was still using his own cell to follow the red dot. Keeping Stone on the line, Pipe had notified them when the dot stopped moving. And it hadn't started again—making Spike's stomach roll with the implications.

The car was no longer moving, which could mean any number of things.

Tonka put together one of the rifles he had in his bag as Spike held a high-powered spotlight out the door, searching for Reese's car and the assholes who'd taken her.

The chopper weaved and swayed in the wind, and Spike held onto the doorway with an iron grip. He hadn't ever flown with Owl and Stone before, but he trusted them with his life. Hell, he trusted them with *Reese's* life.

When the river came into view, and as he shone the light downward, Spike could only stare in awe. The river was...angry. That was the only word he could come up with at the moment. There were whitecaps where the rapids crashed against rocks and as a large tree was pushed downstream, he could see just how fast the water was moving.

Only an insane person would risk crossing it. But he had a feeling the men they were after—probably the same ones they'd escaped from down in Colombia, the ones who'd kidnapped Woody and Isabella—wouldn't even think twice about risking it if it meant getting into Mexico. They likely assumed Spike wouldn't follow them into the other country.

They were wrong. He'd break any law, incite an international incident, do whatever it took to get Reese back safely.

They flew down river, and when Spike finally spotted movement near the bank, he aimed the powerful spotlight —and nearly lost his goddamn mind. He could make out his Reese...down on the ground, surrounded by three men...one of them holding his dick as he looked down at her.

He'd wanted to shoot them all right then and there, but after freezing for a split second in the blinding light, the men scrambled like rats, quickly fleeing toward the river.

When he followed their progress, it looked like a man had grabbed some sort of cable or rope, assisting him to cross. The water was up to his thighs, which wasn't as deep as Spike expected. Right behind him came another man.

Switching his attention back to the three people still on the riverbank, he watched one of the figures hit another. Twice.

It took a moment for his brain to comprehend what he was seeing. That the person being hit was much smaller than the other.

Reese.

His brain's first instinct was to flood his body with a measure of relief. She was alive! But the fact that she was being punched made a red haze fall over his vision just as swiftly.

The man who'd hit her began to traverse the river, and the one left behind lifted Reese's hand to the rope. Slowly, they began to cross.

"I'm going in closer!" Owl yelled. "Don't let him get her across!"

"I'm on it!" Tonka shouted back, aiming the rifle toward the man right behind Reese.

Fear hit Spike, hard and fast. "Do *not* fire until you have a clear shot!" he warned his friend.

"Ten-four," Tonka told him, not looking up from the scope of the rifle. The chance of Tonka hitting his mark was slim to none. With the way the chopper was being buffeted in the wind, there was no way anyone could get a firm bead on the man with Reese.

It was frustrating as hell that all Spike could do was point a light at the pair and watch as they inched their way across the raging river. Owl hovered just downstream from Reese and her captor, and even though all of Spike's attention was on the woman he loved more than life itself, he was still aware of the skill it was taking to keep them airborne.

Suddenly, the man and Reese stopped almost in the middle of the river. The water was hitting them hard and doing everything in its power to knock them off their feet. The man looked up, and Spike realized for the first time that it was Angelo. For a tense moment, they stared at each other—then Angelo swung his arm up, bringing it back down and striking Reese.

Suddenly she was falling into the water, immediately disappearing under the surface.

Spike roared in frustration, anger, and fear. "*No! Reese!*"

"Hold on!" Owl yelled before banking hard to the left.

Spike lost sight of where Reese had fallen into the river for a moment before the river appeared below him once more.

"Go lower. I'm going in!" Spike yelled at Owl.

"No! It's suicide!" Stone told him.

"Do it!" Spike roared.

To his relief, the chopper got even closer to the water. He could practically see it lapping at the skids. Not thinking twice about what he was doing, only thinking about getting to Reese, Spike jumped.

The cold water closed over his head, and Spike was immediately tossed head over heels as if he was in a washing machine. His head popped out of the rapids for a moment, and he took a deep breath before slamming into a boulder under the water and going under once more.

When he came up again, Spike looked around frantically. He didn't see Reese anywhere. Panic almost got the better of him, but he clamped down on the feeling. If he lost it, Reese would die. He knew that down to the marrow of his bones. The water tried to suck him under once more, but using all his strength, Spike kept his head above the waves.

There!

Something caught his eye to the left. He swam toward it as hard as he could. It was Reese! She was still conscious, and fighting like hell to keep her head above water.

"Hold on!" he yelled, but there was no way she could hear him over the roar of the river.

Just as he was almost close enough to grab her, Spike's foot got caught in debris under the water. He struggled to free himself as he watched Reese get farther and farther away. He grunted in frustration and tore his foot out of the obstruction, ignoring the bolt of pain that shot up his leg.

He swam faster than he ever had before when he heard something that made his blood run cold. It wasn't the normal sound of the river and the wind. It was worse. Rapids. By the sound alone, he knew they were more dangerous than the ones they'd already gone through. He had to get to Reese before they reached them.

He saw her attempting to get to the shore on the left side of the river. She got close before being swept downstream once more.

Spike caught up to her just as they reached the rapids.

He grabbed hold of her hand—and she screamed in fear.

"It's me! I've got you!" he yelled.

The look of disbelief and relief on her face would stick with him forever. Spike put one arm around her waist—immediately realizing she was topless in the cold river—and shouted, "Keep your feet forward, no matter what! Head up, ass down, feet forward, Reese!"

She nodded—and then they were in the rapids. The water moved faster, sweeping them along like they were nothing but bathtub toys. Spike refused to let go of her. He wouldn't lose her. No fucking way.

Water crashed over their heads, into their faces, branches hit them, their bodies bounced off rocks...but they made it through the rapids. The water wasn't calm by any stretch, but Spike knew he could get them to the shore now that the water had slowed somewhat and there weren't any huge boulders looming, threatening to bash their heads in.

Using all his strength, Spike stroked with one arm to propel them to the riverbank. She was attempting to help, but Spike could tell that she was weak. If he hadn't arrived, there was a good chance she ultimately wouldn't have been able to get herself to safety.

"Almost there!" he told her.

When his feet touched ground, Spike could've cried. He struggled to get out of the water, which was still doing its best to pull him and Reese under. She lay limp in his arms as he dragged her onto the muddy bank. Rain still fell, and the wind howled around them, but Spike barely noticed.

He stared down at Reese, breathing as hard as if he'd just run a four-minute mile.

"Reese?" he shouted frantically.

"You found me," she wheezed.

"I wasn't going to stop until I did," he swore, putting a hand on her cheek. When she winced, he frowned and removed it.

"I'm okay," she reassured him.

She wasn't, but she was alive. For the moment, Spike would take it.

"He saved me," Reese told him.

"Who?"

"Angelo. He pushed me into the river."

"That doesn't sound much like saving you," Spike growled.

But Reese shook her head. "They were going to rape me, the three of them. Then your helicopter showed up. I'm pretty sure one of the men told Angelo to get me across or he'd kill him. The others ran like cowards. Angelo had his hand on me, holding me steady. We would've made it," she said, her brow furrowing. "But he stopped, looked up, then knocked my hand off the rope."

"Asshole," Spike spat out.

"No, you don't understand," Reese said, shaking her head weakly.

Spike put his hands on either side of her, stilling her. "Don't move, baby. You're going to hurt yourself even more than you already are."

Her hands came up and gripped his wrists. "We would've made it across," she insisted. "Pushing me into the water was the *only* thing he could do to save me."

Spike took a deep breath. He wasn't ready to think charitable thoughts about Angelo. But he'd seen what Reese was describing with his own eyes. "Where are you hurt? Did they—" His words cut off as his throat closed. He didn't even want to think about what could've happened to her, let alone say the words out loud.

"No. They didn't get a chance. They were trying to get my pants off when the helicopter showed up."

"Thank fuck!" Spike breathed.

"My face hurts. One of the guys hit me. There are some cuts that sting. But I'm alive. I can deal with bumps and bruises. Are *you* okay?"

"I'm fine." He shifted next to her—and blinding pain shot up his leg.

"You aren't fine!" Reese said, trying to sit up. "What's wrong?"

Spike helped her into a sitting position before he looked down at his leg, pulling up his pants to check his ankle. It was already swollen to twice its normal size, and he winced as he tried to move it. "It got caught in branches or something in the river. I must've tweaked it when I yanked it out."

"Crap. Between the two of us and the storm, how are we going to get out of here? Do we even know where we are?"

"The guys'll find us," he told her as he reached for her.

Even though they were sitting in the mud, rain pounding down, the wind howling, and the river raging... with both of them in pain...Spike felt better than he had all day. He had Reese in his arms. She hadn't been hurt in a way that he wouldn't be able to fix, and he knew his team —yes, he thought of the other men who owned The Refuge as a team, rather than just friends—would find them.

He pulled her into his lap. She straddled him and burrowed against his chest as she lay her head on his shoulder and wrapped her arms around him so tightly, it almost hurt.

"Okay," she mumbled in his ear.

Her faith in him and in their friends, her resiliency, the fact that she was alive...it all hit him at once. Tears rolled down Spike's face, mixing with the rain. They were both extremely lucky, and he knew it.

CHAPTER TWENTY-TWO

Reese sat on one of the leather couches inside the lodge surrounded by...well...everyone. All the guys, Woody, Isabella, Alaska, Henley, Jasna, Luna, Robert, Ryan, Jess, Carly, Hudson, her parents, and even Savannah, The Refuge's accountant. No one had slept since finding out she'd been carjacked, and even though she'd lived through it herself, Reese was still having difficulty wrapping her mind around the events of the previous day.

It was hard to believe just yesterday morning, she'd woken sated and replete after another amazing night with Gus, only to find herself kidnapped in her own vehicle hours later.

Her and Gus's rescue had been surreal. They'd been huddled by the side of the river, soaking wet, shivering with adrenaline and cold, when Owl and Stone had flown by, Tonka spotting them with the extremely bright light. To her amazement, Owl had landed the helicopter in a small—*very small*—clearing not too far from where she and Gus were sitting.

Within minutes, she and Gus were safely inside. Tonka

had rappelled out of the chopper near her car, where he'd met up with Pipe and they'd driven back to The Refuge.

Owl and Stone had flown her and Gus back up north, to a small airfield where Brick, Woody, and Tiny had met them. After Reese's very tearful reunion with her brother and the others, Gus had insisted she go to the medical clinic in Los Alamos to get checked out. She agreed to go only if he'd have his ankle checked. While waiting to be seen, Reese explained to the men what had happened. She didn't have a lot of information, unfortunately, since her captors had spoken in Spanish.

Then Gus took her home, undressed her lovingly, and pulled her gently against his side in their bed, holding her tightly all night long.

They'd slept in until around lunchtime, when Gus woke her and told her they were headed up to the lodge. Reese hadn't wanted to go. She wasn't sure she could face Isabella. Didn't want people to see the awful bruising on her face. But Gus had insisted, and she didn't have the energy to deny him.

So here she was...and she was so thankful Gus hadn't let her hole up inside the cabin. She needed this. Needed the support and concern from her friends. She'd been terrified the entire time she'd been held, especially at the end, when she was seconds away from being violated. Yet amazingly, here she was.

But, as she'd feared, the reunion with Isabella had been...difficult. Long before Reese and the others made it back to the resort, someone had broken the news to Isabella that her brother was involved in the kidnapping, and from what Reese understood, she hadn't taken it well.

Now, her sister-in-law was sitting on one of the other couches with Woody glued to her side. Her face was puffy and her eyes were red, despite everyone reassuring her as best they could. No one blamed her at all for anything that happened.

"I wish you guys could've seen Owl and Stone," Reese said seriously. "I thought I was a goner, that those men would take me into Mexico and no one would ever see me again. And then through the storm came this helicopter out of nowhere. The wind was buffeting it around but Owl kept it completely steady."

She looked at Owl, then Stone. "Thank you," she whispered. "I doubt it was safe for you to even be up in that weather, and I'm thinking you probably broke at least ten aviation rules being there but...without you..."

Reese shuddered, and Gus's arm tightened around her shoulders, pulling her more snuggly against his side.

"And you," she said, pulling away a fraction and glaring at Gus. "What the heck were you thinking? I can't believe you jumped into the river after me. Are you crazy?"

Gus stared at her with such love and devotion, Reese's breath caught in her throat. "Haven't you figured it out yet? Without you, I'm nothing. I have no purpose in life. I would've rather died with you than gone on living without you."

"Don't say that," she breathed. "I mean...don't *say* that!"

"It's true," he said with a small shrug.

Tears formed in Reese's eyes as she stared at the man she loved more than she ever knew it was possible to love someone. The crush she'd had on him seemed so silly and superficial now that she'd gotten to know him.

A phone rang, breaking the intense moment, and Reese turned to look at her friends. Woody brought his cell up to his ear. She couldn't tell what the person on the other end was saying, but from her brother's facial expression, it wasn't good. He thanked the person for calling, then clicked off the connection. He turned to Isabella.

Reese braced, dreading what he had to say.

"That was the Texas Ranger in charge of the case," he told his wife gently. "They found Angelo. God...I'm so sorry, honey. His body washed up another mile down river from where Spike and Reese crawled out of the water...he's gone."

Isabella collapsed into her new husband's arms, and Reese closed her eyes in sorrow.

"That wasn't him," Isabella sobbed desolately. "I don't know what happened, but he couldn't do this! I raised him better, I swear!"

"I know, honey. I know. It's okay," Woody soothed as he ran his hand over her dark hair, trying to console her.

Reese felt horrible for her sister-in-law. She should be on cloud nine, celebrating her marriage and new husband. "For what it's worth, Isabella," she said gently, "I think he just got in over his head. He was unhappy the entire time we were in the car."

Everyone was silent, listening to her, but Reese's concentration was solely on Isabella. She stood, and she felt Gus's hand steadying her until she got her balance. She walked over to Isabella and sat on her other side, taking her hands in her own.

"He didn't harm me. When the others tried to...hurt me...he refused. I don't understand what was said, but it was clear he disagreed with them. I think he simply wanted to go home, back to Colombia. He didn't expect those men to be at the Western Union. I saw the surprise on his face. He even told me to go back to The Refuge after dropping him off, but I didn't want to leave him there all alone."

"We reviewed the security tapes," Brick said quietly. "The men didn't drive there, they simply appeared in the frame on foot. Our best guess is that they came into town on a bus."

Reese nodded and looked back at Isabella. "The main guy, the one who seemed to be in charge, was so worried about getting away from the helicopter that he left the rest of us behind without a second glance. All he cared about was himself. One of the other men ordered Angelo to get me across. The river was raging, it was difficult to cross with just yourself to worry about, but Angelo made sure I had a strong grip on that rope and he held onto my belt loop so I wasn't washed away."

"But you *were* washed away," Isabella said in confusion, tears still falling down her face.

"No. I wasn't. We stopped in the middle of the river," Reese told her. "I was confused. Wasn't sure why we'd stopped. I looked up and saw Gus hanging out the side of the chopper...and the next thing I knew, your brother shouted that he was sorry, and asked me to tell you that he loved you."

"He said that? In English?" Isabella asked in surprise.

Reese gave her a tender smile. "No. But I know what *lo siento* means, and I've heard you and Woody saying you love each other enough times to understand that too. I just had to look up the word I didn't know. 'Tell.' He loved you, Isabella. So much. I think he regretted what happened, and he did the only thing he *could* do to make amends."

"What did he do?" she whispered.

"He made me let go of the rope, then pushed me into the water."

"*Madre de Dios*," Isabella whispered.

"It was the only way," Reese insisted. "If I made it across the river, those men would've finished what they'd started. They would've abused me so badly, I'm not sure I would've lived through it. Angelo did the only thing he could think of to save me."

"But the river...you could've..." Isabella's voice trailed off and she cried harder.

"I didn't. Gus got to me in time, and we both made it out."

"There was a tree rushing downstream. It hit Angelo hard right after he pushed Reese," Stone said. "I saw it from the cockpit of the chopper. It swept him off his feet, there wasn't anything he could've done to prevent it... except maybe not have stopped in the middle of the river in the first place. But even if he did make it to the other side...I don't think he would've survived."

"Why not? What'd you see?" Woody asked.

"All three of the other men were waiting on the other side of the river with knives in their hands. I think they might've killed him the second he stepped foot on dry land."

Everyone was quiet for a moment.

"I'm proud of Angelo," Reese said, breaking the silence. "He made a mistake by contacting his friends and asking for their help in getting back to Colombia, but in the end, he did what he could to save me. To make amends."

"I'm so sorry!" Isabella said, yet more fresh tears fell down her cheeks.

"No, *I'm* sorry," Reese countered.

"I thought you'd hate me," Isabella admitted.

"And I thought you'd hate *me*," Reese countered.

The two women fell into each other's arms, hugging hard.

Reese felt someone at her back, and she instantly knew it was Gus. Being there for her, just in case she needed him.

She eased back from Isabella and gave her a sad smile.

The mood was subdued, the previous day extracting a heavy toll, but Reese had never been more grateful for The Refuge employees than she was right then.

As the next couple of hours passed, everyone approached one at a time and told her how relieved they were that she was all right and back home. They all ordered her to relax and not work too hard. Robert threatened that if he saw her doing too much, he was going to tie her to a chair in the kitchen so he could keep his eye on her.

They were equally kind to Isabella, offering quiet words and condolences.

Carly and Luna both cried when they studied Reese's bruised face, but Jess got mad. *Really* mad. It was obvious she wanted the people who'd hurt her to pay, but since that wasn't possible—they were somewhere in Mexico at the moment, or maybe even back in Bogotá for all they knew—she left to take out her frustration on the laundry that needed to be done. She stormed out of the lodge after telling Reese how relieved she was that she was back.

Ryan followed her, but before she left as well, she gave Reese a long, heartfelt hug. It seemed as if she wanted to say something, but in the end, she merely smiled and headed out after Jess.

Reese loved being around her friends, but even though

she'd slept in very late, by dinnertime, she was exhausted and could barely keep her eyes open anymore.

Gus noticed, of course, and told the others that he was taking Reese back to the cabin.

Everyone hugged her—carefully, since she was still extremely sore. When it came time for Woody to say his goodbye, he held onto her for an extraordinarily long time. Then he pulled back and tenderly caressed her sore cheek. "Love you, Reesie."

"Love you too. But don't call me that," she teased.

He smiled sadly. "I'm gonna miss you back in Missouri. I don't know if I can even leave you here, especially now."

"You don't have a choice, big brother. Besides, I don't think Gus is gonna let me out of his sight for quite a while. I'm safe with him."

Woody nodded. "Yeah, you are. He was always the guy we counted on when things went south on missions. Glad to know that hasn't changed. He's good for you, sis."

"I love him. So much," Reese whispered.

"I know. It's the only reason I'm leaving without you."

"But not for a few more days, right?" she asked, suddenly not wanting him to leave just yet. "Isabella is devastated about losing Angelo, and I'd hate for her to have to deal with moving to a new city and having no friends while trying to grieve."

"We'll stay for a while longer. I want Isabella to spend some time with Henley," her brother reassured her. His gaze lifted to someone behind her, then met hers once more. "Besides, I think we might have another reason to stay..."

Reese frowned. "What does that mean?"

But Woody simply smiled, leaned forward, and kissed

her forehead, before turning to head back to where Isabella was talking to Jasna and Henley.

An arm came around her chest, and Reese leaned back into Gus grateful. "What was that about?" she asked.

"Come on, let's get you home and off your feet."

"You're the one who should be off his feet. I know your ankle has to hurt. But, Gus? What aren't you telling me?"

"Home, sweetheart. Then we'll talk."

There was no budging Gus when he got stubborn like this. And she didn't really mind his protectiveness. "Fine," she said with a small huff.

But her fake annoyance didn't even faze her man. He steered her around the furniture, keeping a firm grip around her waist as they headed for the door.

They were waylaid by her parents, who were still overwhelmed with emotion that their baby girl was all right. Eventually, Gus extricated her from them, and they were once again on their way to the cabin.

Before she knew it, Reese was on the couch, covered by a blanket, while Gus got busy warming up dinner. She'd protested, saying he was the one with a hurt ankle, but he ignored her and insisted on getting them something to eat. Chicken soup, of all things. He told her that he used to eat it all the time when he was sick, and that it had a miraculous ability to "cure what ails ya."

How could she argue with that? She couldn't. The fact was, she wasn't the only one hurting right now. Gus had taken his fair share of knocks while they'd been in the river. No, he hadn't been punched in the face right before going swimming, but still.

She reluctantly allowed him to pamper her because in doing so, he was pampering himself. They ate their soup in a companiable silence. Reese didn't feel the need to fill the quiet with chatter. She was safe, warm, and Gus was by her side.

All the shit she used to worry about seemed stupid now. She'd never take her loved ones for granted again. Wouldn't worry about dirty dishes or an unmade bed or mud on the floor. It was inconsequential compared to what had almost happened to her.

When they were finished eating, Gus took their bowls back to the kitchen and returned immediately. He moved her until she was practically on his lap, but Reese didn't mind. She snuggled against him, resting her head against his chest, hearing the *thump thump thump* of his heart under her cheek.

"So...I was thinking..." Gus said.

When he didn't continue, Reese lifted her head and looked at him. "Yeah?"

"What do you think about getting married tomorrow?"

Reese blinked and stared at him in shock. "What?"

"If yesterday taught me anything, it's not to take life for granted. I love you, and I want you to be my wife. Why wait? Your brother and Isabella are here, as well as your parents. There's no waiting period; as soon as we get our license, we can have the ceremony. I can call and arrange to have a civil ceremony right after we get the license tomorrow."

"Are you being serious right now?"

"Yes."

Reese bit her lip. "But my face...the bruises..."

Gus took her head in his hands and kissed her gently. His lips didn't lift off of her, and with every word he spoke, his lips brushed against hers. "Those bruises on your face hurt my heart every time I see them. But they also make me so damn thankful that you're still here. With me. In

330

my arms. You can ask Alaska and Henley to help you with your makeup to hide them if you want, but don't do it for me. We can wait until you've healed to get pictures taken, if that will make you feel better. All I want is for you to be mine, and to belong to you in return. Forever. What do you think? If you truly want to wait, we will, but everything in me is pushing to get this done. To get my ring on your finger."

He pulled back so he could see her face, but didn't let go of her.

Reese grabbed hold of his wrists as she studied him. "What if this is a knee-jerk reaction to what happened? If you regret it later?"

"It's not, and I won't."

"I don't have a ring for you," she said with a frown.

"We can stop and get one on the way to the courthouse tomorrow. I haven't gotten your diamond yet, but we can pick out our wedding bands together."

"You're totally serious."

Gus nodded.

And for the first time, she saw the uncertainty in her man's eyes. In everything else, he was confident and had a take-charge attitude. But this...he was actually worried.

"Yes," she whispered.

"Yes?" he asked as if he hadn't heard her right.

Reese nodded. "Yes, let's do it. We'll get married tomorrow, then have a party later when we have time to plan it. With pictures, cake, fancy clothes—a celebration of life. For now...we'll do this for us."

"I love you," Gus told her, his lip quivering.

"I love you too," Reese returned with a big smile. For the first time in over twenty-four hours, she didn't feel like crying. She threw her arms around Gus and hugged him tightly, wincing as the wrist Angelo had hit throbbed a bit.

But she ignored it. Nothing could dim her happiness right now. She was going to be Mrs. Reese Fowler. Tomorrow. It was literally a dream come true.

EPILOGUE

"How much farther?" Reese asked, sounding impatient as hell.

Spike grinned. "You've been here before," he reminded her.

"I know, but that was different. I didn't know where we were going and what was waiting for me. And," she added with a gleam in her eye, "I didn't know what was going to happen when we got there."

"You might not be quite as excited about this when we *do* get there," Spike warned.

"Making love to you in 'our' cave, with your ring on my finger, and mine on yours? Not a chance," she informed him.

The last month had been full of ups and downs. Their wedding was everything Spike could've asked for and more. Woody and Alaska had been their official witnesses, but the room was full of their friends. Her parents cried, and were thrilled that both their children were now married.

Reese had started her new job at the Los Alamos

National Laboratory and absolutely loved it. Business at The Refuge was as strong as ever.

The not-so-good thing had been Reese's nightmares. She'd been surprised by the first one, telling Spike that she honestly didn't know why she'd had it because, all in all, what happened to her hadn't been that bad. He'd insisted she talk with Henley, and while that helped, she still occasionally woke up fighting and screaming.

There was also the matter of the cartel members having disappeared into Mexico. They knew where Reese lived, and that hadn't sat well with Spike or the rest of The Refuge owners. While they were confident in the security measures they'd implemented, they couldn't keep their eyes on their women at all times, and they weren't willing to confine them to The Refuge's property.

Brick and Alaska had decided to put off their own wedding until things had calmed down a bit, and they were sure the cartel wouldn't be coming back for any reason. Spike knew Reese hated that her friend had to wait, but Alaska reassured her that being married or not changed nothing about her and Brick's relationship. They'd waited this long to get married, they could wait a little longer.

Spike and the guys had also had a conversation with Tex about whoever it was who'd tracked the tile on Reese's keychain, and he was no closer to finding out who'd helped them than he'd been when Tonka had received the text about Jasna being safe and sound in one of the bunkers on the property.

Whoever it was, they were extremely knowledgeable about covering their tracks, which Tex admitted was frustrating not only on a personal level—he prided himself on his own skills—but also because abilities like that often came about because someone had a very good reason to want to stay untraceable.

But Spike *had* received some good news today, and he wanted to share it with Reese.

He'd hiked out to the cave the day before while Reese was at work, to prepare it for them. He'd definitely found the woman of his dreams when instead of wrinkling her nose and telling him he was crazy to want to actually spend the night in a cold, dark cave, she was over-the-moon excited.

He walked hand-in-hand with her, and even though it was chilly now that winter was approaching the mountains, he didn't feel the cold at all.

"I never would've thought this is where I'd end up when I made that decision to go down to Bogotá to find Woody," Reese said quietly.

"Me either," Spike agreed as he lifted their clasped hands and kissed her fingers wrapped around his own.

As they got nearer to the cave, Spike began to get nervous. He hoped she liked what he'd done to prepare for their arrival. He wasn't sure it was enough to make it special. This was essentially their honeymoon. They'd been busy since their civil ceremony. Hell, he hadn't even wanted to chance making love with her until she was fully healed.

Reese, though, had other ideas. She'd only tolerated his holding back for a few days after the ceremony before she'd told him in no uncertain terms that if he didn't make love to his wife right that second, there was going to be hell to pay.

He'd been cautious with her for the last few weeks, wanting her sore muscles to heal and her bruises to fade, but tonight they were both more than ready to let their passion fly.

Taking a deep breath as they reached the cave, Spike let go of her hand and nudged her forward. "Go on. See what you think," he urged.

With a huge smile, Reese didn't hesitate. She jogged ahead and entered the cave. Spike followed to find her standing just inside the entrance with her mouth hanging open.

The day before, he'd brought a blow-up mattress, a few blankets, two pillows, flowers, and a dozen candles. He brushed past her and put down his backpack, which had food, clothes, and an extra blanket just in case, and pulled out a lighter. He lit all the candles he'd strategically placed around the space and stood back.

The light dancing on the walls highlighted the petroglyphs, almost making them come alive.

"This is...Oh, Gus...it's amazing!"

Smiling, and feeling a sense of relief wash over him, Spike turned and pulled his wife into his embrace. "I love you, Mrs. Fowler."

"Love you back, Mr. Fowler," she said with a small grin as she stared at him.

"I once told you that I'd bring you back here to honor the men and women who were here before us. Who maybe lay in this exact spot, although not on a blow-up mattress with pillows and blankets, and made love to the person they couldn't imagine being without."

"You did," she agreed. "I think this is the most romantic thing anyone's ever done for me. No, I *know* it is."

"Good. I want you to be happy, Reese."

"I am."

He smiled at her. There was nothing more he wanted than to lay her down, strip all her clothes off, and make love to her right then and there, but he needed to tell her something first. The news he'd found out that morning.

"Sit, sweetheart," he urged, leading her to the bed.

She frowned. "What's wrong?"

"Nothing. But I need to have a talk with you about something before we eat."

She sat. "What is it? Spit it out because I can see it's bothering you."

"Actually, it's something good. I talked to Tex this morning."

Reese frowned. "Your hacker friend?"

"Yeah, him. I mentioned he was a Navy SEAL, and he's dedicated his life to helping others. He has a friend who lives in Hawaii. Another SEAL. His name is Baker."

"Baker. Is that his last name?" Reese asked.

"No, his first."

"It's unique. I like it."

Spike chuckled. "Right. Anyway, Baker has connections. Not like Tex, but connections all the same. He knows people who know people. People who aren't necessarily on the right side of the law. What I'm trying to say, and doing a shit job of it, is that you, *we*, don't have to worry about the cartel showing up one day, wanting revenge or to get their hands on you."

"Why not?" Reese whispered.

"This guy, Baker? He called in some markers. Made it clear to certain people in power that The Refuge and everyone associated with it is off limits."

"And that's all it took? They just agreed?" Reese asked skeptically.

"Well...no. Baker knows people."

Reese frowned, looking frustrated. "I don't understand."

"You don't need to," Spike said. "Just be reassured that it's over. Pablo and his men won't be returning. They were made examples of to the rest of the cartel. It's been made very clear that if *anyone* decides to step foot back in New Mexico, the entire cartel as they know it will implode from the inside out."

"This Baker guy is *that* influential?" Reese asked.

"Yes." Spike held his breath, not wanting to explain any more. The less she knew, the better off she'd be. She didn't need to know how the dark side of the world worked. He hated that she'd been touched as much as she had by the lust, money, and power that certain industries could inspire. And that was what the cartel was. In the simplest sense of the word, it was a business. And money was their ultimate goal. Baker obviously had pull with those who could bring down the cartel like a house of cards.

"Okay," Reese said after studying his face for a moment.

"Okay?" he asked.

"Yes. If you say we're safe, I'll believe you. I trust you, Gus. With my life. With the life of everyone at The Refuge. Our friends."

Spike closed his eyes in relief. He loved this woman. So damn much. His eyes opened and he pushed Reese back until she was lying on the mattress. "How hungry are you?"

"Are we talking about food or something else?" she asked with a gleam in her eye as her hands slipped under the hem of his shirt and caressed his lower back.

His cock hardened immediately, eager for her touch. For her mouth. He didn't need to clarify his question; he'd received his answer. He stood abruptly, his hands going to the belt around his waist. "Clothes. Off," he grunted.

But he didn't have to bother. She was already rushing to disrobe while keeping her gaze glued to his.

This was going to be fun. Making love with Reese always was.

* * *

"I can't believe Alaska talked us into this," Pipe grumbled as he straightened his bow tie. He felt as if it was strangling him. It had been a very long time since he'd worn a tuxedo, and he wasn't exactly thrilled to be in one now.

"Right?" Owl said with a grimace. "I would think if anyone should be here, it's Brick. Or even Tiny. They're the pretty ones."

Pipe nodded. The long sleeves covered up most of his tattoos, but the ones on his hands and fingers were still visible above the cuffs of the jacket. He stood out like a sore thumb in the room of bigwigs and cleaned-up men and women. His hair was too long, his beard too bushy, his accent out of place.

Basically, he was the last person who should be at this fundraiser.

When Alaska had first broached the topic of raising money for veterans, he was all for it. Said he'd be glad to do whatever was necessary. That was, until he'd learned that it was not only all the way across the country in Washington, DC...but it involved a bachelor auction.

By that time, it was too late. Alaska, Henley, little Jasna, and even Reese were already rolling with it and super-excited.

So, here he was, along with Owl.

"How long do we have to stay again?" Owl asked.

Pipe sighed. "You? You're a spectator, you can go at any time. Though I appreciate you hauling ass all this way to have my back. Me? I'm third to last to be auctioned. Then I have to play nice with whoever bought me before I can get the hell out of here."

Owl chuckled. "That sounds so wrong."

Pipe's lips turned down. It did. The whole idea of bachelor auctions, of "buying" anyone, for any reason, was ridiculous and outdated to his mind.

His phone vibrated with a text, and he pulled it out, praying it was Brick texting with some emergency that would necessitate him and Owl immediately flying back to New Mexico to The Refuge to deal with it.

He wasn't so lucky.

ALASKA

> Thank you for doing this. You're gonna raise so much money, I know it!

Pipe sighed. The only person who could've gotten him here, dressed up in this tux, parading in front of a bunch of women who scared the crap out of him because they were so out of his league, was Alaska. Or one of the other women who now lived at The Refuge with his friends.

PIPE

> You owe me.

Alaska sent a bunch of emojis in response and Pipe put his phone back into his pocket.

"Alaska or Henley?" Owl asked.

"Alaska."

His friend nodded and ran a finger under his collar. "You have to admit, the women aren't hard on the eyes," Owl observed as they looked around the crowded ballroom.

The event had around three hundred people in attendance. Pipe was supposed to be mingling with the guests, chatting with the women, and maybe men, who might bid on him later. It was supposed to be a chance to get to know people, and let them get to know him, to hopefully raise the bids in the auction.

But Pipe had never been good at small talk. He was too rough around the edges. So he stayed on the side of the room, leaning against the wall, praying the night went by quickly.

There were twenty men who would be auctioned tonight. Whoever won them would get a one-on-one dinner with their date. That was all that was promised, but Pipe had the feeling some of the women circling the room, looking like hyenas hunting for their next meal, were hoping for more.

They wouldn't get it from him. Dinner was all Pipe had signed up for. He didn't want or need a woman. Nope, he was perfectly happy being single.

After getting out of the SAS, the British special forces, he'd been lost. He'd seen and done too much to go back to a "normal" life. He saw bad guys around every corner. He'd started getting tattoos the day he left the military, and didn't care that many people looked down on him because of his ink. Definitely didn't mind that people shied away from him because they were leery. He preferred it, actually.

Being invited to be a part of The Refuge had been a lifeline for Pipe. He'd gone to America, to New Mexico, without a second thought. He loved what he and his friends had built. It truly was a refuge. Not only for them, but for the men and women who came to escape their lives for a short while.

And because he truly believed in the mission of The Refuge, to help those who suffered from PTSD, no matter if they were military or not, he was here. To raise money to help even more people.

"What time is it?" Pipe asked Owl.

His friend chuckled. "Two minutes after you last asked."

"Bloody hell," Pipe swore.

"Come on. Let's walk around. Maybe if you keep that scowl on your face, you'll scare all the ladies away and no one will bid on you."

"Oh, that would be awesome," Pipe breathed. Taking a deep breath, he pushed off the wall. He could do this. He'd promised Alaska.

* * *

Cora Rooney took a deep breath. She didn't want to be here. Didn't fit in. She knew it, and everyone she met knew it. She'd spent a lot of money she couldn't afford to waste on the ticket to the gala, just for the chance to win a date with Bryson "Pipe" Clark. She'd read everything she could find on the man, and The Refuge. She knew all about his time in the service, as well as the backgrounds of

342

the other men who owned the retreat. They were all former special forces of one sort or another.

And she needed them.

She'd sent several emails begging for a chance to talk to one of them, but they'd all gone unanswered. She'd even called a couple of times, but no one had ever called her back. Cora supposed she could understand that they wouldn't be interested in talking to someone who needed the kind of help only they could offer. But it was still extremely frustrating.

The last three months had been nothing but one disappointment after another, and she was desperate. Which was why she was here. Her clothes weren't designer, her makeup amateur at best, her hair not in a fancy updo like most of the other women's. She had no diamonds around her throat or wrists.

Cora had sold as many of her belongings as she could to get the money she thought she'd need to succeed tonight. She'd scrimped and saved and done everything in her power to come up with more cash. It was pure luck that she'd seen the flyer announcing the bachelor auction tonight. Money was being raised to help veterans, and when Cora had seen that one of the men from the now well-known and successful Refuge was going to be there, she'd been determined to do whatever it took to attend.

And here she was.

She was nervous as hell. Social gatherings weren't her forte, but if she was going to succeed, she needed to suck it up...and play nice. Which was another thing that wasn't a strong point for her. She was too blunt. Too impatient. And she didn't trust anyone in this room. She'd learned that the hard way. She only trusted one person in her life... and that woman was the reason she was here tonight.

Taking a deep breath, Cora scanned the room. She hadn't seen Pipe or anyone else from The Refuge yet, and she hoped he hadn't backed out. Just when she was beginning to think all her planning was for naught, she caught sight of a bearded man across the room.

And her breath caught in her throat.

Bryson Clark was an amazingly handsome man, even with the current scowl on his face. Maybe because of it. He wasn't smiling and kowtowing to the simpering women in the room. He looked as if he'd rather be anywhere but here.

For some reason, that drew Cora to him even more. Maybe she could talk to him before the auction. Plead her case. And she wouldn't have to spend any of the money she'd saved to purchase a date with him.

She took a step toward him—but it was too late. A man's voice came over the loudspeaker, telling all the bachelors who would be participating in the auction to meet behind the small stage that had been set up at one end of the room.

Cora cursed her bad luck. The train she'd taken to the venue had mechanical issues and she'd been way late arriving. Too late to try to talk to Pipe or anyone else who might've come with him from The Refuge.

Determination rose within her. She had to win that date. She'd spend every dollar she had if she needed to. Getting a chance to speak to Pipe one-on-one, to explain why she needed him and his friends, was literally a matter of life and death. He had to help her...if he didn't, she had no idea what to do next. She'd gone to the police, the FBI, and the media, and no one believed her.

She had one more chance to get someone to listen, to *believe* her.

Closing her eyes for a moment, Cora whispered, "This has to work. Please, it *has* to work." Then she opened her eyes, threw her shoulders back, and headed toward the stage, along with everyone else in the room.

*

Bachelor auction, missing best friend, and a Hero who wants to be anywhere other than he is...what could possibly go wrong? Find out in *Deserving Cora*.

Want to talk to other Susan Stoker fans? Join my reader group, Susan Stoker's Stalkers, on Facebook!

Scan the QR code below for signed books, swag, T-shirts and more!

Also by Susan Stoker

The Refuge Series
Deserving Alaska
Deserving Henley
Deserving Reese
Deserving Cora (Nov)
Deserving Lara (Feb 2024)
Deserving Maisy (TBA)
Deserving Ryleigh (TBA)

SEAL Team Hawaii Series
Finding Elodie
Finding Lexie
Finding Kenna
Finding Monica
Finding Carly
Finding Ashlyn
Finding Jodelle (July)

Eagle Point Search & Rescue
Searching for Lilly
Searching for Elsie
Searching for Bristol
Searching for Caryn
Searching for Finley (Sept)
Searching for Heather (Jan 2024)
Searching for Khloe (TBA)

Game of Chance Series
The Protector
The Royal (Aug)

The Hero (TBA)
The Lumberjack (TBA)

SEAL of Protection: Legacy Series
Securing Caite
Securing Brenae (novella)
Securing Sidney
Securing Piper
Securing Zoey
Securing Avery
Securing Kalee
Securing Jane

Delta Force Heroes Series
Rescuing Rayne
Rescuing Aimee (novella)
Rescuing Emily
Rescuing Harley
Marrying Emily (novella)
Rescuing Kassie
Rescuing Bryn
Rescuing Casey
Rescuing Sadie (novella)
Rescuing Wendy
Rescuing Mary
Rescuing Macie (novella)
Rescuing Annie

SEAL of Protection Series
Protecting Caroline
Protecting Alabama
Protecting Fiona
Marrying Caroline (novella)

Protecting Summer
Protecting Cheyenne
Protecting Jessyka
Protecting Julie (novella)
Protecting Melody
Protecting the Future
Protecting Kiera (novella)
Protecting Alabama's Kids (novella)
Protecting Dakota

Delta Team Two Series
Shielding Gillian
Shielding Kinley
Shielding Aspen
Shielding Jayme (novella)
Shielding Riley
Shielding Devyn
Shielding Ember
Shielding Sierra

Badge of Honor: Texas Heroes Series
Justice for Mackenzie
Justice for Mickie
Justice for Corrie
Justice for Laine (novella)
Shelter for Elizabeth
Justice for Boone
Shelter for Adeline
Shelter for Sophie
Justice for Erin
Justice for Milena
Shelter for Blythe
Justice for Hope

Shelter for Quinn
Shelter for Koren
Shelter for Penelope

Ace Security Series
Claiming Grace
Claiming Alexis
Claiming Bailey
Claiming Felicity
Claiming Sarah

Mountain Mercenaries Series
Defending Allye
Defending Chloe
Defending Morgan
Defending Harlow
Defending Everly
Defending Zara
Defending Raven

Silverstone Series
Trusting Skylar
Trusting Taylor
Trusting Molly
Trusting Cassidy

Stand Alone
Falling for the Delta
The Guardian Mist
Nature's Rift
A Princess for Cale
A Moment in Time- A Collection of Short Stories
Another Moment in Time- A Collection of Short Stories

ABOUT THE AUTHOR

New York Times, *USA Today* and *Wall Street Journal* Bestselling Author Susan Stoker has a heart as big as the state of Tennessee where she lives, but this all American girl has also spent the last fourteen years living in Missouri, California, Colorado, Indiana, and Texas. She's married to a retired Army man who now gets to follow *her* around the country.

She debuted her first series in 2014 and quickly followed that up with the SEAL of Protection Series, which solidified her love of writing and creating stories readers can get lost in.

If you enjoyed this book, or any book, please consider leaving a review. It's appreciated by authors more than you'll know.

www.stokeraces.com
www.AcesPress.com
susan@stokeraces.com

facebook.com/authorsusanstoker
twitter.com/Susan_Stoker
instagram.com/authorsusanstoker
goodreads.com/SusanStoker
bookbub.com/authors/susan-stoker
amazon.com/author/susanstoker